Myriad Mysteries

The First Year

Claire Logan

Published by Red Dog Press, LLC
Printed in the USA

Praise for the Myriad Mysteries

"Claire Logan spins a tale that keeps you interested and wanting to read more."

— SHERRY LEGAN

"All the characters are well developed, and the story is delightful."

— BARONESS BOOK TROVE

"I recommend this to cozy mystery readers that enjoy the look and feel and flavor of Prohibition Chicago."

— KAREN SIDDALL

"I absolutely love the colourful characters that range from a dowager duchess to mobsters to a wide variety of working-class people to a couple in hiding ... A fun take on the 1920s I thoroughly enjoyed."

— INFOSLEUTH

"It is a gentle tale, well-told, with characters of depth and an unusual relationship."

— JOHN R. SHEEHAN

Discover more about the Myriad Mysteries at
AuthorClaireLogan.com

To the mystery lovers throughout time.

Preface

This is not historical fiction. It's cozy mystery! No actual historical figures will appear in this story. Certain details known to the early 1920s in Chicago (radio call signs, business names, etc.) have been altered, and are not typographical errors.

Also, cozy mysteries should be fun! Just as regular people would never be involved with homicide investigations in real life, I do realize that my dear couple are living an idyllic life, unlikely to be seen in real 1920s Chicago.

So if you're looking for historical realities, gentle reader, please look elsewhere.

Table of Contents

Ring-A-Ding Dead!

The Myriad Mysteries #1

To those of you taking second chances.

1

When they first arrived in Chicago, the couple took a leisurely breakfast at a posh little cafe in the station, then spent an hour or so shopping for new, stylish clothes, suitable for their new city. While they were out, they had their hair cut and colored in the fashion of the day.

At first, the lady balked at displaying her ankles in public, not to mention bobbing her long hair. But afterward, she showed her new self to her new husband. "Mr. Jackson, how do I look?"

"Perfectly charming, my dear, as always."

As his tight-coiled hair was pressed and her thick curls dyed, she said, "We must decide what to do. Where shall we stay? What shall we do for a living? Shall we rent rooms? Or perhaps purchase an office?"

"Nonsense, my dear," Mr. Jackson said. "Everything has changed. After all that has happened, we deserve nothing but the very best."

When the hairdressers finished their work, the couple strolled out to the street, a porter carrying their purchases. Cars bustled past as the work day began.

Mr. Jackson flagged down a cab. "Myriad Hotel."

"Right away, sir." And off they went.

Mr. Jackson marveled at how quickly things could change. Yesterday he was a bachelor; just hours later, a husband.

As they rode, he watched his new wife. How fortunate he'd been to follow his instincts and offer her this marriage. How grateful he was that she'd accepted!

Mrs. Jackson peered out of the window, astonishment on her face. "The architecture is magnificent!"

Mr. Jackson felt surprised. "I didn't know you cared for such things."

"Oh, yes. I love it! Many of the buildings remind me of my home." She paused, eyes distant. "I wonder if they had the same architects." She leaned back on the cushioned seat. "What a wonderful place this is!"

The cabbie glanced quickly back. "First time here, then?"

"I've been here many a time," Mr. Jackson said. "But it's her first."

"What brings you here?"

"We're on our honeymoon," Mr. Jackson said.

The cabbie seemed touched. "Well, fine congrats to you both." He glanced at the lady. "You're gonna love it. Nice place, though it does get chilly in the winter. You arrived at the perfect time. And the nicest people you'll ever meet anywheres."

6

The exterior of Myriad Hotel was sumptuous: gray-white marble, trimmed in rosewood and brass. Yet no one greeted them out front, or stood to hold the door, as Mrs. Jackson had seen done at other hotels.

So the cab driver held the door for them, for which he got a good tip.

"Odd," Mr. Jackson said. "This hotel normally has such fine service."

Mrs. Jackson gaped at the lobby of Myriad Hotel: marble floors, rosewood paneling, Art Deco murals, and brass trimmings. In the center of the magnificent hall, an exquisitely carved fountain twice her height shot water past the second floor railings towards a glittering chandelier high on the vaulted ceiling. She turned to Mr. Jackson. "Oh, this is lovely!"

He beamed. "I so hoped you'd like it."

Yet for all its splendor, the lobby was empty.

The couple went across the wide hall to the front desk, a gleaming paneled affair, and rang the fine silvered bell.

No one answered.

So they stood there, waiting.

After a time, Mrs. Jackson called out. "Hello! Is anyone there?"

They waited a while more, but there was no answer.

"This is quite odd," Mr. Jackson said. "The last time I came here, the place was full at all hours of the day and night! Where could everyone be?" Mr. Jackson took her arm. "Come, my dear, let's sit."

Gratefully, she followed him to brass chairs cushioned in black velvet to rest herself, while Mr. Jackson (carrying their many packages) sat to her left.

Weariness washed over her. With everything that had happened over the past twenty-four hours, she hadn't slept — she couldn't.

A clock chimed ten. Good smells came from across the way, and from far off behind frosted doors of beveled glass, the sound of a dining room's chatter. But other than that, the place seemed deserted.

Mr. Jackson gestured at her right arm, which was in a sling. "How do you feel? Shall I find someone to help us?"

She patted his hand. "I've survived worse." She smiled at him. "Someone will be along soon. Let's just rest a while."

So they waited.

After a few moments, a stout woman with dark curls walked past. She wore a standard maid's uniform, black with a white apron and hat, and a white tag ringed in brass with dark lettering which read: Maria. "Have you been helped, sir?"

"Why, no," Mr. Jackson said. "We rang some time ago, but no one's answered."

The woman frowned towards the front desk. "That clerk has left his post again!"

She stormed over to a side door, then appeared at a doorway behind the counter. She looked down, then recoiled, eyes wide, letting out a startled scream.

Leaving their packages, the couple rushed to the desk, peering far over the counter.

Under the counter, a man lay there — dead.

2

At once, the lobby filled with people rushing around: maids, bellhops, busboys, and door men. The couple retreated to their seats to view the commotion.

Yet Mrs. Jackson felt disturbed. The man had been lying there, dead, the entire time!

After a while, police and coroner's men entered the lobby. These men, carrying black leather cases, strode towards the crowd milling around the front desk.

One, a stern older man in a cheap brown suit, focused on the couple. "You found the body?"

"The maid saw him first," Mr. Jackson said, "but we sat here for at least twenty minutes before that. We wanted to check in, but no one answered the bell."

The man gestured to a uniformed officer, who stationed himself at the end of the row of chairs. "Stay here until you're called." The man went to the door beside the front desk, disappearing behind it. Beyond that, the dining room's doors opened, confused guests pouring out. They stared at the scene, curiosity on their faces, before being waved past by uniformed men.

Mrs. Jackson had never seen anything like this in a hotel before. She turned to Mr. Jackson. "What do you think?"

"The man seemed quite uncommonly pale."

She had to agree: his face was much too pale, even for a dead man. And there was a familiar smell, one she couldn't quite place. Grief came from, it seemed, nowhere. She didn't even know the man! "The timing of this is distressing."

Mr. Jackson took her good hand in both of his. "My poor dear. I never wanted this to greet you on our arrival."

She clung to him, trying to put past memories of death behind her. There seemed to be nothing they could do but wait.

Men photographed the body, dusted for prints. Others marked and cordoned off the whole lobby this side of the magnificent marble fountain as the couple watched. Far past them, near the entrance, patrons milled about. Some stood in front of the gift shop staring across the lobby in their direction. A crowd peered through the beveled glass front windows behind them.

Mrs. Jackson felt exhausted. Her injured arm ached, tingled. She wanted nothing more than to lie down.

But first the police wanted to speak to them.

The stern-looking man brought the couple to a side room. A polished wooden table with four chairs sat in the center. "Never did see such goings-on here before," he snapped.

The man sounded annoyed with the whole affair!

He made a quick, dismissive gesture towards the chairs, so they sat. Then he sat across from them, opened a notepad, and frowned at them. "Sergeant Benjamin Nestor, Chicago Police. And you are?"

Mrs. Jackson didn't know whether to laugh at or be angry with his tone. But she stayed still, curious as to what bothered the man so.

Mr. Jackson extended his hand. "Hector and Pamela Jackson."

Sergeant Nestor ignored Mr. Jackson's hand, instead making notes on his pad with a jerking motion. "Your occupation?"

Mr. Jackson appeared unruffled by the man's sharp tone and angry demeanor. "I have lands and investments throughout the country. Well, to be honest, I have a small property overseas as well." He spoke of this wealth as if it were quite modest. He relaxed, leaning back. "I live off the income, and travel whenever the need arises."

Sergeant Nestor's jaw tightened, and he scratched on his notepad. "Your business here?"

"We've only just arrived," Mr. Jackson said, as if having embarked upon a grand adventure. "We're on our honeymoon."

The sergeant's face turned sour, cynical. "Congratulations." Then he frowned. "Tell me what you saw."

They recounted the little they did see: an extremely pale, dark-haired man lying dead, a bone-dry teacup and saucer on the floor beside him. "It did seem odd," Mrs. Jackson said (when asked), "that the door-men were absent."

"That is odd." Sergeant Nestor seemed to honestly consider the matter.

Mrs. Jackson had the sergeant pegged: uncomfortable with those above his station. A perennial chip on a pugnacious shoulder. A man who preferred being in control.

He probably hated being called to such an opulent hotel.

The sergeant frowned at her sling as if it offended him. "What happened there?"

She decided simple candor was the best option. "I had surgery."

"Before your wedding?"

"It was somewhat of an emergency." She shrugged, unsure how much more to say. "It couldn't be helped."

He scowled at this, but apparently could find nothing more to ask.

Mr. Jackson gave her a quick glance. "We both have experience as private investigators. If you —"

"Both?" The officer seemed dubious.

"Why certainly," Mr. Jackson said. "I've only ever been an amateur. But my wife was a professional investigator for some time. Before our marriage, of course." He turned to her with a fond smile, and she nodded. "You might say that's how we came to know each other."

Mrs. Jackson felt amused, both by Mr. Jackson's words and the sergeant's expression. "Do you not have woman detectives here?"

"Well, uh ... of course!" Sergeant Nestor glanced between the couple as if at a loss. Then he frowned, straightening. "Certainly."

Mr. Jackson said, "I'm sure you have your own people for such things, but if we can be of any assistance —"

A hint of sarcasm laced the man's tone. "I'll be sure to ask." The sergeant rose, handed Mr. Jackson his card. "If you remember anything else, call."

After the sergeant left, a young uniformed officer poked his head in. "Wait here." He pulled the door shut.

The couple glanced at each other and shrugged.

Mrs. Jackson said, "Call?"

"This place is a marvel. It has telephones in every room!"

"Telephones in every room?" She shook her head, astonished. "A far cry from home, I must say."

"Indeed it is."

***

14

Mr. Jackson surveyed his wife. She looked pale, with dark circles under her eyes. He needed to get her to their rooms.

He wasn't used to this. All his life, he went where he pleased, when he wanted, and it'd been rare that another person was dependent upon him.

But the situation was out of his control. These police would take anything which caused a break from their protocol as suspicious, and the last thing they needed right now was to fall under suspicion.

A few moments later, the manager came in. He offered credit to their account for a full week's stay, which seemed quite generous. "Do you need anything else? Anything at all."

"Your best two-bedroom suite," Mr. Jackson said. "Money is no object. And my wife needs a lady's maid. Preferably one with experience in caring for wounds."

The manager glanced at her arm in its sling. "I'll send for one right away."

"You're too kind," Mr. Jackson said.

"And will you be needing a valet, sir? To assist you in dressing."

This was the first time staying in Chicago that he'd been offered one. "Why, if one is available, of course."

"Most certainly, sir. Never fear, we only use the finest procurement services. You may hire by the day, hour, or week."

15

"We'll be here at least a week," Mr. Jackson said, amused. "But I'll meet the fellow first."

"Of course, sir." the manager said, and began to rise. "Now, if you'll —"

To Mr. Jackson's surprise, his wife said, "A question, if you please, sir."

The manager blinked. "Why, of course."

"Was your clerk scheduled to work today?"

"No," the manager said, and he also seemed surprised. "Certainly not. I'll have to look into it, but it seems another fellow switched with him for this morning without notifying me. He'll get a stern talking-to."

"The poor man," Mr. Jackson said. "To help a fellow out, then die? A pity."

"Indeed it was," the manager said, but he didn't sound sincere. "Now, if you'll return to the lobby, I'll have someone show you to your rooms shortly."

By the time the couple stepped into the hallway, the body of the young man had been carried away.

Yet the lobby was full of commotion. A dark wooden rectangular folding table laden with many paper bags and one pale yellow folder had been set up off to one side. Sergeant Nestor stood behind the table, conversing with a man in a similar suit.

Uniformed men moved back and forth between the table and the front desk. Some carried baskets filled with sealed brown paper sacks, which they placed on the table. Others carried documents, which they placed in the folder. Still other men stood, clipboards in hand, making notes and flipping pages.

Shades had been pulled over the windows against the late morning sun, which streamed in through the glass front entryway.

To Mr. Jackson's relief, reporters were being kept outside by uniformed police. He moved his wife and their packages to a seat well away from the doors.

They hadn't slept the entire trip, and his wife must be weary. She'd made no complaint about her injury, but it worried him just the same. He put his arm around her. "Rest your head on my shoulder." To his surprise, she did so without protest, but her eyes stayed open.

The trip to their suite was a noisy affair. Maids and bellhops followed them with questions all the way to the elevator.

Mr. Jackson turned to face them. "My dear people. We've had a long, tiring journey. Might we discuss this another time?"

"Of course, sir," they mumbled, moving away.

The bellhop pushing the cart with their packages clearly wanted to ask more but fortunately stayed quiet. For that, Mr. Jackson gave the man a good tip.

Their suite was on the thirty-second floor, and the rooms were even finer than he remembered. Two bedrooms, freshly painted, with new bed-covers. They had separate baths and a generous parlor with its own door to the hallway. The rooms held fruit, flowers, a stunning view of the lake, and every amenity one might hope for.

Once the door closed, his wife sagged onto a bed. "At last."

He sat, wrapped his arms around her, lay her head on his shoulder. Kissed her forehead with a tenderness which surprised himself. "We'll be safe here. We can finally rest."

3

At first, all Mrs. Jackson wanted was to sleep. But alas, it was not to be: the lady's maid, a Mrs. Octavia Knight, arrived soon after. Mr. Jackson had retired to the other bedroom with his packages, leaving her to deal with the woman.

However, when she stood, she found that she felt refreshed. So she interviewed the woman, who was perhaps forty, at a small table of polished rosewood which lay near the window. "How long have you been a lady's maid?"

Mrs. Knight smiled to herself. "A little over a year. But before that I was nurse to one of the great families. Been taking care of injury all my life. Don't suppose you'd know any of them, being from out of town as you are."

Mrs. Jackson felt a bit embarrassed. "Is it that obvious?"

"Your accent." Mrs. Knight stopped, face puzzled, then continued. "But their children are grown and gone. The older ones are down at the heels, so I was let go." She let out a regretful sigh. "It caused some trouble with the finances at first as my husband's ill. I'm busy enough now with this temporary work. I've come to meet many a fine family this way."

Mrs. Jackson felt impressed. "It sounds quite an adventure."

"It has been, ma'am."

"Will your husband's illness cause problems with your schedule?"

"Oh, no, ma'am. He was injured in the war, then he had that horrible flu, then pneumonia after. He still doesn't breathe well. He can't work much, but he can take care of himself just fine."

This woman seemed competent enough. "I'll need you to help with my bath, and dress me for breakfast and dinner," Mrs. Jackson pointed to the sling, "so long as I have this on."

"Yes, ma'am. And I'll put away your packages. Would you like a bath? The manager said you'd just arrived."

"That would be wonderful."

The bathing room was large, decorated in black and white tile with brass trimmings. The tub was white porcelain, legs and all. The fittings for the sink and tub were brass, and the tub had three black ceramic handles.

Mrs. Knight took off Mrs. Jackson's sling and put it to soak in the sink. The maid tsk'd and shook her head at the large, newly sutured wound in the bend of Mrs. Jackson's right elbow. But she never asked about it, for which Mrs. Jackson felt most grateful.

Mrs. Knight said, "What good fortune that you've chosen this place!" She pointed at the center tap. "The Myriad has mineral spring water piped in — just lovely for healing wounds and all sorts of sickness."

"Is that so?"

"Yes! People come from all over the world just to bathe downstairs at the spa!"

Could this be the reason that Mr. Jackson chose this hotel? If so, it was certainly quick thinking! And it showed a care for her welfare that she found touching.

If I only would have known, she thought, remembering their bitter battles in the past.

She felt an instant's hesitation to be undressed by a stranger. And in all the commotion, she'd completely forgotten about the gun in its holster just below her right knee until the maid saw it, eyes wide.

Mrs. Jackson felt amused at Mrs. Knight's expression. "There's no need to touch the gun. Unbuckle the holster from my leg, if you will, and place it on the dresser."

To her surprise and relief, the maid never asked why she had it.

It felt wonderful to soak in the hot water while her sling was being washed and dried. But the injection the surgeon had given her was wearing off, and her arm began to hurt in earnest.

Mrs. Knight gently patted the wound dry and applied an ointment, wrapping it with the bandages she'd brought with her. "Changing this once or twice daily should do just fine." She slipped a cotton day dress over Mrs. Jackson's head, then measured out a dose of pain medication. "That sling will be a while drying. Do you need help putting it on?"

"Mr. Jackson can do that if needed."

"Very good, ma'am." She glanced around, then took a wide-toothed comb from her bag. "Come into the other room and I'll comb out your hair."

While the maid dried and combed her hair, Mrs. Jackson surveyed her bound arm. She'd had little experience in such things, but the bandaging seemed at least as professionally done as when applied by the surgeon's nurse the night before. "I'm glad to have you, Mrs. Knight — you've done fine work."

The maid curtsied. "Thank you." She began to collect her things. "I'll be back at seven to dress you for dinner."

Whether from the medication or the bath, Mrs. Jackson felt quite sleepy. "No need: we'll be staying in. Perhaps tomorrow morning at nine?"

"Yes, ma'am. I'll see you then. Rest well."

Once the maid left, Mrs. Jackson put her holster and gun in the top drawer of the dresser, placed a shawl atop it, then lay in bed with her day dress still on.

***

While Mrs. Jackson was being attended to, Mr. Jackson went to his room on the far side of the parlor and set down his packages by the wall.

Collapsing into a chair, he surveyed the room. Everything had changed since the last time he'd been here. And the last twelve hours had gone differently than he could have possibly imagined.

A few moments later, his manservant arrived, a Mr. Norman Vienna. Brown hair and eyes, pale skin. A well-cut black silk suit.

Quite the looker, indeed.

"Good morning, sir," Mr. Vienna said. "May I enter?"

Mr. Jackson felt a bit flustered, and berated himself. None of that here, not now. "Yes, please, do come in." He gestured towards the room, and the man came past. "I presume you're sent by the management?"

"Yes, sir, I work for the Howell-Green procurement agency, contracted by the hotel. You pay the hotel for my services once I send them the bill."

He seemed quite young. "How long have you done this work, if I may ask?"

"Several years now, sir. I began as valet to a young man who died of malaria while on vacation." His gaze fell. "He was much loved. His death broke the family, sad to say. I was let go when the property was sold."

"How dreadful!"

Mr. Vienna shook his head, not meeting Mr. Jackson's eye. "It was, sir. The young master was only seventeen. He never would have wanted things to end so." Then he straightened. "After that, I served as valet to a medical officer in the war. I have excellent references, sir, and will do you well for as long as you stay here."

Mr. Jackson felt touched by the man's tale. "I don't have much here." He pointed at the packages along the wall. "But I'll require you before breakfast and dinner, for a dress and a shave. And perhaps a trim here and there."

At the last, the man raised an eyebrow. "How long do you plan to stay, then, sir?"

"Our plans are open at present." He gave a quick glance at the closed door leading to his wife's bedroom.

"How many are in your party, sir? If I may ask."

"Just my wife and I. She's speaking with her maid now."

"Very good, sir. I'll put away your things then, if we're done here."

Mr. Jackson sat watching the young man work with a sense of loss. So much death.

Why did the clerk downstairs die? Could it have been natural for such a young man to fall dead on the job?

Something about it felt wrong.

After Mr. Vienna left, Mr. Jackson knocked softly at his wife's door. Hearing no answer, he peeked in.

She lay upon her bed, eyes closed, black curls spread across her pillow.

He pulled the covers over her shoulder, feeling a surprising fondness for her. He kissed her forehead, then returned to his rooms to lie down, falling asleep at once.

A small noise woke him.

His wife peered in through the door to her room. "I'm sorry to bother you." She looked abashed. "But I need your help."

It took him a moment to remember where he was. "I'll be in momentarily." He pulled on his trousers and a shirt, then went into his wife's room.

She stood in the middle of the room fumbling with her sling. The late afternoon sun streamed golden onto the floor. "I can't seem to manage the straps."

For a moment, he sat on the back of a chair, trying to make sense of the task at hand. Adjusting the straps, he fit the sling to her arm.

Their eyes met, and she turned away. "Thanks." She took an apple from the bowl on the dresser. "Did your manservant arrive yet?"

"He did! Ever so congenial fellow. Not that I have a great many things with me, but it'll be nice to have someone else fuss over them."

"And they call them valets here."

"Indeed. And the men who bring the cars, too, although you must never confuse them." He laughed at the thought. "To ask a personal manservant to fetch your car would be most offensive, and vice versa."

"I suppose never leaving my town makes me quite unaware of the world beyond." She sat at the table by the window.

25

He remembered the first time he'd traveled. This place must be quite different than what she was used to.

"Do you think we might be able to travel more? Once I'm well, of course."

He slumped into the chair across from her. "We can go anywhere you wish."

"How long do you think we should stay here?"

He shrugged. "We have a week's credit. But we can stay as long as you like."

Fear touched her eyes. "It's just ... I don't like all the police about."

"Let's stay in our rooms tonight. I'll call room service for dinner." He'd more than half expected to find her gone when he woke. A change, but a fortunate one. "We've given our statements, so they should have no further use for us." He grinned. "Just the way I like it."

She smiled to herself at that last bit. "You made it sound that you were a busy man. Do you not have a schedule?"

He stretched back, hands behind his head. "I'm on my honeymoon, don't you know?" He gave her a wink and a smile. "Unless some disaster occurs, I don't need to be anywhere." He chuckled. "Perhaps not even then. I have men in every city, capable of handling most situations." Which was fortunate, as none of them knew where he was at present.

"I never realized." She sounded both awed and impressed. "Perhaps someday I'll have a retinue of my own." She raised her injured arm with a wry smile. "If I survive this."

A knock came at the parlor door.

Mr. Jackson struggled to his feet. "Whoever could that be?" He turned to his wife. "I'll take care of this."

He left his wife's room, closing the door behind him, then tucked in his shirt and answered.

To his surprise, the manager stood there. "May I come in?"

"Is something wrong?"

"Why, no — not at all. I'm ever so sorry to intrude. But I need to speak with you most urgently."

What could this possibly be about? He opened the door wide. "Of course. Come in."

Their parlor had a long sofa by the windows, with a coffee table and overstuffed chairs. But there was also a large round rosewood table off to the side with several straight-backed chairs around it. Mr. Jackson gestured to one. "Please, sit down."

They went to the table, sat.

"I hope you're both well," the manager said.

"We are. Thank you." This situation was unlike anything he'd experienced here before. "How may I help?"

The manager, who had been looking out of the window, hesitated.

Mr. Jackson felt weary. "You said the matter was urgent?"

"Well —" the manager seemed embarrassed. "I listened at the door when you spoke with the police." Then he leaned forward. "You said you'd been private investigators ..."

Mr. Jackson peered at him, trying to understand. "Are you offering us a **job**?"

"I know you're on your honeymoon. I get it." He shifted, glanced around. "But the man who owns this hotel wants answers, and —" his face paled. "Let's just say he's not the sort of man you want to make angry."

Mr. Jackson nodded sagely. "We do have some small experience with that sort."

"Anything you can learn — anything at all — we'd be grateful. Most grateful."

Interesting, Mr. Jackson thought. If this owner was the sort of man he sounded like, this might be an opportunity. "I have permission to speak with your staff, then?"

Relief crossed the manager's face. "Of course! Any time. Whatever you need is yours."

After the manager left, Mr. Jackson went back to his wife's room. "You're not going to believe this."

"What did he want?"

"He wants us to poke around, talk with the staff — by order of the hotel's owner. Who apparently isn't someone you make unhappy."

His wife's face turned amused. "Ah. So things are not so different here after all."

4

No one knew where the couple had come from. They didn't order lunch. Which was understandable, given that they had just witnessed death. But they didn't order tea or supper either. The waitstaff fidgeted: were the couple well?

"Good grief," the manager said, clearly annoyed at the crew. "They're on their honeymoon. What do you imagine they're doing? Go on, now, get to work!"

But many in the staff let out a sigh of relief when the couple ordered a late dinner in their rooms.

When the bellhop returned from serving them, the others clamored around him. Surely there was something, anything they could learn about the couple who found the body of their co-worker. Something that might tell them how or why he died.

But the bellhop had little to tell. "The gent answered: said the missus was a-sleeping. Tipped well, he did."

So after a while the staff returned to their duties, wary, disturbed, and some, afraid.

***

Mr. Jackson lay in his room late at night, his door to the parlor open, the lamp on, gazing at the ceiling, not really thinking of anything. And yet he heard a soft weeping.

He crept to his wife's door, opened it softly. His wife lay curled on her left side, facing him, her face awash with tears.

"I'm sorry," she sobbed.

"No," he said. "Don't be. Is it your arm?"

She shook her head and wept harder.

He knelt before her, moving wet curls from her face. He kissed her forehead gently, marveling that she of all people felt safe to cry near him. "It feels unbearable."

She nodded. Her body shook with sobbing, yet after a time, she seemed more at peace, her eyes far away. "How did you bear it?"

He let himself collapse upon the floor to gaze upon her face, and spoke in utter honesty. "I don't know. I suppose you just do."

Her hand came from under the sheets to grasp his. "Don't leave me."

It broke his heart. He climbed into bed beside her, lying on top of the covers, and held her as if she were a small girl. He had a sharp, poignant memory of his little sister climbing into his bed late at night, back in the days of childhood.

His sister was now prosperous, grown and married, with children of her own, who were very likely crawling into bed beside her now. That thought made him smile.

But he missed her. And under the circumstances, it was doubtful he'd ever see her again. "I'll never leave you." He held his wife close, listening to the quiet sounds of the room. "I promise. I'll never leave you, no matter what."

***

The pair did come down for breakfast the next day, and the staff all agreed that they looked impressive. The gentleman — for clearly he was a gentleman, by his manners and dress — was all a fine gentleman should be. Tall, past thirty, quite dark-skinned, and very handsome.

The lady was a few years younger. Slender, with light brown skin and blue eyes, she was fashionably yet modestly dressed, as befitted a respectable woman of means, a cute little cloche hat atop thick black curls. Her right arm was in a sling, and she didn't speak much. Perhaps her injury pained her.

The vast dining room was filled with large round tables, which the guests sat around.

A waiter approached. Young, slender, brown hair and eyes. His face, an even tan. The tag on his shirt read: George. He said to Mr. Jackson, "What can I get you, sir?"

"Coffee, heavy cream, no sugar," Mr. Jackson said. "Make it about your color."

"Right away, sir."

The Myriad Hotel's most illustrious guest, the dowager Duchess Cordelia Stayman, had come to breakfast with her husband Albert in a silk morning dress, with a beaded hat and robe. "Horrid business," she said, as the waiter served her. "Imagine, such a young man simply dropping dead!"

Mrs. Jackson went pale, her eyes red.

"Now, Cordelia," Albert said. "You'll spoil breakfast."

Mr. Jackson turned to his wife. "Are you well?"

She dabbed her eyes. "I agree. It's horrid."

Mr. Jackson put a glass of water into his wife's left hand. "Here. Drink something. You'll feel better."

So she did, but it seemed an effort for her to smile.

"I'm sorry, my dear," the dowager said. "My old mouth runs away with me." She turned towards the large frosted-glass doors. Past them, the clear light of a sunny late morning streamed onto the lobby floor. "What a lovely day it is."

Having served drinks, the staff began to serve the breakfasts.

"It is lovely," Mrs. Jackson said after a moment. She turned to her husband. "Perhaps after breakfast, we might take a stroll?"

"That would be splendid," Mr. Jackson said. "And we must see all the sights."

"Oh, yes," the dowager said. "There's so much to do here! There's a park right nearby. And the weather is lovely this time of year. Is this your first visit?"

"Her first," Mr. Jackson said.

"How long are you here for?"

Mr. Jackson said, "Our plans are open as yet."

"Marvelous." She turned to Mrs. Jackson. "We must plan out your stay here, so you don't miss a thing!"

"Cordelia," Albert said. "Surely these people can plan out their own stay."

She laughed, but her cheeks colored. "I'm sorry — I just get so excited to show everything. It isn't often you get the opportunity to share such a fine city."

A pretty young blonde woman came by carrying a tray. Her name-tag read: Agnes. "Cigars? Cigarettes?"

"I'll take some," Mrs. Jackson said. "And matches, if you have them."

"No, thank you," Mr. Jackson said at the same time. He turned to the dowager. "What brings you to Chicago?"

"Oh, we've lived here at the hotel these three years," Albert said. "Quite economical. Everything you need, and no servants or lands to manage." He turned to his wife. "Remember how much bother we had?"

The dowager, in the midst of drinking her tea, stopped with a grimace, then nodded. "Terrible expense."

Mrs. Jackson put the cigarettes and matches in her pocket and said, "Living at a hotel? I'd never considered such a thing!"

"It's ever so fashionable," the lady sitting to Mrs. Jackson's left said. She was perhaps twenty, with straight brown hair topped by a beaded headband which went straight across her forehead. "My husband and I are off to visit my parents in the countryside. We arrived last night." She became animated. "But if we ever did want to stay downtown, this is where we'd be! Why, the nightlife, the scenery, the shopping ... this lies at the center of it all."

Several heads nodded around the table, and the waitstaff smiled at each other.

Mrs. Jackson said, "I had no idea."

"Well, my dear, if you're going to stay in Chicago any length of time, you should definitely stay here," the dowager Duchess proclaimed. "This is the place to be!"

***

And yet, Mrs. Jackson mused, they'd likely just been witness to a murder.

5

The garrulous old dowager annoyed her. Not only that, she was dangerous. They couldn't dodge too many questions about themselves before rousing suspicion.

So Mrs. Jackson fired a return salvo. "My Lady, what sights should we see first?"

This set the dowager into a stream of recommendations, each with its own set of observations, quips, and amusing stories. It was left for Mrs. Jackson to simply nod, smile, and exclaim from time to time.

As the woman spoke, Mrs. Jackson glanced around the table. Most were dressed in casual finery, ready for venturing forth into the street. The dowager's husband Albert had on a red felt vest which looked handmade, decorated with small wooden beads.

Her interest caught his eye and he glanced down, then grinned, pulling at the bottom of his vest. "You like it? Got this on our travels."

"Oh," the dowager said, "let me tell you about that trip." And so she set off again, to Mrs. Jackson's great amusement.

The Duchess herself wore a simple necklace of golden-brown beads, which as it turned out, were seeds hand-drilled by her husband. "Oh, he just loves making things," she gushed.

Her husband beamed.

"Would take a steady hand, that," Mr. Jackson said.

This sent the dowager's husband into an explanation of the tools he used, with exclamations and witty stories from the dowager along every step of the way.

Once they'd finished eating, Mr. Jackson rose, shaking hands all round. "We're so pleased to meet you! Have a wonderful day." Then to her relief, he took her arm and moved off towards the lobby before anyone could insert themselves into their day.

She giggled at that thought. "You're a master at handling people."

"You didn't do so poorly yourself." The dining room door attendants opened the beveled glass doors for them. "Do you still fancy a stroll?"

"No." Her arm had begun to ache, and the exertion of fending off the dowager fell upon her. She felt suddenly gray, transparent. "Let's go back upstairs." She looked up at him. "I hope you weren't looking forward to it. Going out, I mean."

Mr. Jackson put his arm around her waist, then took her left hand in his, steering her towards the elevators. Which she felt grateful for, as the effort of making the decision seemed beyond her right then. "Not at all, my dear. I'm here for whatever you need."

She hated feeling so weak, hated needing someone to bring her places like some invalid.

"Is she well?" The concerned face of a bellhop swam before her.

"Is a wheeled chair available?"

"Wait here, sir, I'll get one right away."

Her vision cleared. They stood before the array of elevators.

"Here," the bellhop said, and something pressed upon the back of her legs. She sat, placing her hands on the armrests.

"Thanks," Mr. Jackson said, and a rustle of cash followed.

"Thank you, sir!" The bellhop sounded quite pleased.

A group had gathered, yet moved aside when the elevator door opened to let them pass in.

"Let's get you to your bed," Mr. Jackson said. "We've had enough excitement for today."

***

Mr. Jackson felt helpless when his wife sagged in his grasp out by the elevators, utterly grateful for the bellhop's assistance with the chair. He should never have taken her down to breakfast so soon after surgery.

He'd seen sickness and injury many a time, yet it'd always been someone else who handled the details. He'd had to ask his wife how much medication she took, and somehow, he felt he should know.

But he could help his wife into bed, keep watch over her. He could hold her hand, listen to her soft breathing.

It reminded him too much of another bedside, another hand. That scene had ended in death, right in front of him, and he felt a brief instant of terror that she might die as well.

His wife woke well after tea. "Welcome back," he said.

She stretched lazily. "Have you sat there this entire time?"

He shrugged. "The view is lovely whichever way you turn."

"Since when have you become a flatterer?"

"Never. I prefer to speak the truth, when I can."

She smiled at that. "And what will you do now?"

"Read the afternoon paper. Order dinner in our rooms. Converse with my wife. Go to bed early." He stretched. "I am on vacation, after all."

"Do you really travel all over, visiting your properties, as you said?"

"When the need arises."

She smiled, falling quiet for some time. To his surprise, she said, "Do you remember when you captured me?"

He chuckled at that, rubbing the ugly old scar on his upper left arm. "One hardly forgets getting shot."

Her voice seemed playful, but a sharpness lay beneath her words. "You brought that on yourself. If you hadn't tricked me, none of that would have happened."

He felt humbled at the memory. "I suppose I did. Why do you ask?"

She sat quietly for a while. "Who took care of you?"

"Why, my sister, of course. And two of my retainers."

"Those must have been trusted retainers. Everyone thought you were dead!"

He nodded. "They were." He still wasn't sure what she wanted. "Why do you ask?"

"Oh, I don't know — I want to know you better, that's all. I feel like my entire life has been spent trying to kill you." She let out an ironic chuckle. "Yet today I've wakened alive, with you guarding me."

His eyes stung. But he smiled, picking up her hand and kissing it. "I'll be here always, dear girl. For as long as you need me."

***

To Mrs. Jackson's surprise, a knock came at the parlor door.

Mr. Jackson went to answer it. A few minutes later, he returned, closing the door behind him. "Duchess Cordelia is here to see you. Should I send her away?"

Mrs. Jackson considered the matter. She felt well, and was still in her day dress. "How does my hair look?"

Mr. Jackson smoothed her hair down on both sides, tucked the back part behind her head, then drew back to survey her. "Perfect."

"Then I feel fit to receive visitors."

Mr. Jackson left, returning a bit later with the dowager Duchess, who rushed to sit beside her. "Oh, my dear, I've been so very worried for you! I heard you'd fell ill after breakfast, and they called for a wheeled chair!" She pressed her hands to the sides of her face, eyes wide. Then she dropped her hands to her lap. "I do hope you're improved?"

Mrs. Jackson felt amused. "I am, thank you."

Mr. Jackson retreated, closing the door behind him.

An awkward silence fell, so Mrs. Jackson said, "I hope you and your husband are well?"

"Oh, Albert's fine — he's off on a walk." The old dowager surveyed her. "I do hope I'm not intruding."

"Not at all. What can I do for you?"

Duchess Cordelia drew back, nose reddening. "My dear girl. I'm here to visit you!" She reached over and took Mrs. Jackson's hand in hers. "My poor dear. You're not used to such things."

Mrs. Jackson shrugged.

"Well, where I come from, friends have a duty to help each other, or at least offer support. And although we've just met, I wish to act as a friend."

"That's very kind of you," Mrs. Jackson said, and meant it. "I'm flattered."

The old woman's eyebrows rose, and her mouth dropped open.

Mrs. Jackson said, "A Duchess here, at my bedside, wishing to befriend me?"

The dowager chuckled. "Oh, that. I've never been much for putting on airs. My Duke is dead, the estates sold." She shrugged. "Hardly seems worth all the fuss."

Mrs. Jackson smiled at her. The woman seemed sincere, but she had to be cautious about revealing too much. "I'm honored to have your company."

The old woman's cheeks reddened. "Can I do something for you? Get you anything?"

"Might you ask Mr. Jackson to come in?"

"Of course, my dear." She went to the door to the parlor, returning with him.

"Sir," Mrs. Jackson said, "would you call my lady's maid? The number's on the stand beside the telephone. I was thinking we might take dinner here in our rooms."

From the expression on his face, she knew he was amused at her formality. "My dear, I am ever at your service." He picked up the slip of paper beside the phone, disappearing into the parlor.

From the expression on the dowager's face, Mrs. Jackson knew she'd made a mistake: she'd aroused the old woman's curiosity. "Have the two of you known each other long?"

This question actually surprised her, threw her suddenly back to the night they met. "Why, yes, many years now. Why do you ask?"

Duchess Cordelia appeared flustered. "Uh, well, I don't mean to intrude. Just making small talk."

Perfect! Small talk it would be, then. "How did you come to marry a Duke? That seems so grand."

The Duchess chuckled. "Well, I suppose it was. My family was a very good one, but nowhere near as grand as all that. It was all arranged: both myself and my Duke were the last heirs to survive to that day, and our fathers felt it the best way to preserve our fortunes."

The last to survive? "Oh, I'm so very sorry."

She shrugged. "I was, strangely enough, an only child. My Duke's family suffered quite a bit of tragedy, though." This seemed to dishearten her. But then she brightened. "It turned out well, when you consider everything. It was a good match, and we made the most of it."

Mrs. Jackson smiled at the old woman. "I'm glad for you." But then she felt at a loss as to how to proceed. She didn't want the dowager to begin asking questions again. "Do you have any advice?"

The Duchess beamed, her eyes growing moist. "Oh, if I only had such a sweet nature at your age, to ask for advice!" She grasped Mrs. Jackson's hand in both of hers. "Right now, all you need to do is to rest and get well." She grinned. "Let your young man care for you.

Once you're stronger, we can talk all you want." The clock struck seven. "I must dress for dinner. Please take care of yourself."

"I will."

After she left, Mr. Jackson came in. "What did she want?"

"It seems simply to be my friend."

He let out a breath, slumping into the chair Duchess Cordelia had used. "That's a relief."

Her stomach rumbled. "Let's order dinner now, shall we?"

"Ah, yes, my poor dear, you slept through tea. You must be starving!"

She giggled at that, then sat forward, tucking her feet under her knees tailor-fashion. "But I feel stronger somehow. You want to explore that park tomorrow?"

He grinned. "Only if you feel well enough." His tone turned playful. "I will be sincerely vexed at another fainting spell on my watch!"

***

After dinner, Mr. Jackson opened the afternoon news, which had the desk clerk's death on page 8:

CLERK FOUND DEAD AT POSH HOTEL
Police Ruling: "Suspicious"

A desk clerk was found dead at his post yesterday morning at the Myriad Hotel on Lake Shore Drive.

At this time, police have not released the name of the victim nor the cause of death, yet a spokesman for the police department stated the death is considered suspicious.

The hotel manager released this statement: "Our deepest sympathies go to the family and friends of the deceased. The Myriad Hotel offers its full cooperation into the investigation."

The Myriad Hotel, established in 1897, is one of the premier hotels in Chicago, visited by notable and prominent people from around the world. The Hotel anticipates no alterations in service due to this unfortunate event.

Mr. Jackson showed his wife the article. "They ruled it suspicious."

"It certainly seemed that way to me. I hope they find whoever did it soon."

He closed the paper, leaned back, stretched his legs out. Hopefully, the police would have no further interest in them. Once his wife was well, they could speak to the staff as the manager requested.

The manager barging into their rooms the day before like he had still annoyed Mr. Jackson to no end. It was unnecessary. The matter certainly wasn't urgent, and the police seemed well-equipped to pursue the culprit.

His wife looked pale, and while the dark circles around her eyes had improved, he didn't like seeing them there. "How's your arm?"

"I might need some medicine soon."

He rose to fetch the bottle. "Same amount?"

She considered the matter. "Yes, I think so. It makes me much too sleepy, but it's time for bed in any case." She grinned up at him. "A good night's sleep should help."

***

The next morning was a fine one: a blue sky, children playing in the sun, trees fluttering in a light breeze. Cars chugged past, steam spouting from tail pipes. A bird flew by.

The couple sat arm in arm on a park bench. Mrs. Jackson took a deep breath, savoring the clean, crisp air. So different from home, with its perpetual gloom.

She felt much more rested today, clearer-minded. And she was reminded of the manager's request.

At first, it seemed odd that the owner would ask two strangers for help in a police matter. Yet on further consideration, she'd decided that if the owner's priority was to keep things quiet, the fewer people who knew about the matter, the better.

"Last night, you said the police ruled the matter suspicious," Mrs. Jackson said. "But you never offered your opinion."

"I suppose it could have been natural," Mr. Jackson said. "But the man was so young. And his face so pale. I agree with the ruling: this feels like foul play."

The man's face was certainly an unnatural shade. If only she'd had a chance to examine the body more closely.

Mr. Jackson said, "The teacup on the floor was quite evocative. Poison, perhaps?"

She squeezed his arm, a sudden wave of fondness passing over her. "If nothing, you are sharp of mind. I hesitated to take tea with breakfast for that very reason."

"As did I. But poisoning suggests the offender knew the person, or at the very least, his habits. Unless, of course, he wished to kill us all."

Mrs. Jackson smiled at him as they rose, moved along the sunny path. "Yet everyone made it from the table alive. Point well-taken, sir."

For her, the conversation was merely chitchat, a way to pass the time. The man was dead: surely the police would care for the situation.

It felt good to stroll in this park for a moment, to smell the breeze, watch the clouds pass. Forget everything which had led up to this day. Never in a thousand years could she have anticipated being in this city, strolling in this park today, arm in arm with this man — much less being married to him. How things had changed!

Mr. Jackson tipped his fedora at a passing couple, then said, "Yet who would wish to kill a desk clerk?"

She smiled to herself. "I'm sure the police ponder the very same question." She let go of his arm, pulled out her cigarettes, the matches with them. "Light one for me?"

His eyes narrowed. "Very well." He handed a cigarette to her, lit it. "But I won't have this in our rooms."

"Fair enough."

They continued to walk side by side as she smoked. "What do you think is happening back there right now?"

"At the hotel? I have no idea."

"No, back home."

He chuckled. "I imagine quite a lot." He stopped then, faced her. "My dear, you must forget it all. Consider yourself reborn. None of that," he made a wild, sweeping gesture, "will bring anything other than grief and trouble." He began to walk, and she followed. "For us, today is all that matters."

She dropped the cigarette, stepped upon it, then held onto his arm. Could it be possible to make a clean break with the past? In some things, perhaps. But not others. "Is there a pharmacy nearby?"

"I can ask if it's important. Is there something you need today?"

Mrs. Jackson considered this. "A day or so probably won't hurt."

"If you're sure."

"I'm sure." He truly seemed concerned for her welfare. "If you'd like to find the address, we can visit the pharmacy the next time we venture out."

***

Mr. Jackson strolled back towards the hotel with his wife. To his relief, her cheeks had good color, and the dark circles were almost gone from around her eyes. Rest had been all she needed.

The streets were busy, and so was the hotel lobby. Tourists gazed at the murals above the rosewood paneling, families stood around planning their day.

Leading his wife by the hand, Mr. Jackson made his way through the throng towards the front desk to fetch their room key. An older woman scrubbed the wooden floor in the hall beyond: a dark stain lay there.

The new desk clerk was an eager young man with blond hair, just bloomed into adulthood. As he handed over the key, he said, "Anything else you need, sir?"

Suddenly, a list of things they needed appeared in Mr. Jackson's mind. He chose the one with highest priority. "Where is the nearest pharmacy?"

The clerk wrote on a pad, then handed over a slip of paper. "There's the address." He pointed past Mr. Jackson's left shoulder. "Three blocks that way, just past the gun shop. It's open until nine tonight."

"Excellent," Mr. Jackson said, slipping the paper into his jacket pocket. On to number two. "I wonder if we might speak with the manager."

The young man seemed uneasy. "I hope all is well?"

"It is. Very well indeed. We just need to speak with him on a private matter."

Relief crossed the man's face. "Very good, sir. You'll find him in his office," he pointed behind him, "down the hall. The door is on your left."

The couple edged past the scrubbing maid and moved down the hall.

"Mr. Flannery Davis, Manager" lay marked upon the door. Before they reached the open doorway, the manager's voice came forth in a shout: "By thunder!"

Mr. Jackson peered inside. "Is all well, sir?"

The manager glanced up, an open lunch-pail marked with his name in front of him. "Someone's been at my lunch again! I'd always blamed that poor foolish clerk, but —"

Mr. Jackson stared at the man, horrified. "Where do the staff take luncheon?"

"Continue down the hall and turn right. The lunchroom is downstairs. Why do you —?"

"Don't touch a thing!"

Mr. Jackson raced down the hall, but as he got to the corner, screams emerged from below. He turned to his wife, who remained standing in the doorway, mouth open. "I'm afraid we're too late."

49

6

Sergeant Nestor stood observing the lunchroom turned crime scene. He'd deliberately placed himself near the couple, who'd inexplicably been witness to two murders in three days.

A clump of uniformed officers stood around the contorted body of a blonde girl. Agnes Odds, age eighteen, worked at the Hotel these past three years. Rented a room in the basement. No one knew of any family.

The rest of his men were busy. They gathered evidence, took samples, photographed the body, spoke with witnesses.

Across the lunchroom, the manager paced up and down, wringing his hands. "I shall be ruined! If this gets out, no one will stay here. We'll all lose our jobs!"

The staff gaped at him.

The manager stopped, turned to them. "Not one word of this to anyone, not one. You hear?"

Fearful nods all round, then the room filled with discussion.

Sergeant Nestor thought the man was likely right. The rich men who owned places like this tossed their employees away like day-old trash at a moment's notice. But the manager's order would now make it much more difficult to get any of these people to talk.

One of the officers stood near a distraught middle-aged woman with black hair. "She just came in, started eating, and got the most horrible look on her face! Oh, I'll never forget it!" The woman began sobbing, her friends around her.

Mrs. Jackson seemed notably unaffected by the sight. "I suspect strychnine."

Her husband nodded, uneasy.

The sergeant said, "The manager told us you knew this might happen."

"We went there to see him," Mr. Jackson said. "The manager mentioned his lunch had been tampered with in the past. He'd suspected the clerk who died yesterday of being the culprit. It occurred to me that if this clerk had been pilfering lunches, then perhaps he wasn't the true target."

The sergeant nodded. "And this young woman was?"

Mrs. Jackson shrugged. "Perhaps. Although the manager claimed his lunch had been tampered with today as well."

This didn't seem like something a killer would want known. The sergeant turned to an officer beside him. "Bring every lunch to the lab, including the manager's.

Search them all for poison. And put a round-the-clock guard on the food pails until the killer's found."

"That does seem wise," Mr. Jackson said.

The couple weren't acting like killers. And they'd been upstairs with the manager at the time of death.

Mrs. Jackson said, "Is there anything we might do to help?"

She sounded too eager. And he didn't believe for one minute she was a professional investigator. "I don't want you involved." He pointed at them. "I don't want you two to do any nosing about whatsoever. Stay out of it. You understand?"

Mr. Jackson chuckled. "Very well."

Sergeant Nestor regretted his harshness. He didn't want to discourage people from coming forward. "But if you do hear something —"

"We'll inform you at once," Mrs. Jackson said, with a smile which made the sergeant more than a bit envious of her husband. She took her husband's arm. "Let's see to the manager before he has a coronary."

As the couple strolled away, Sergeant Nestor watched her go. How did that fellow get a woman like her?

He walked over to the group of police standing around the dead woman. One of his officers glanced past him towards the couple. "You suspect those two?"

"I suspect everyone." A couple of people claiming to be private investigators — one a woman! — appearing right as a rash of deaths began. And then offering help — on their honeymoon?

They found the body. And now they wanted to be part of the investigation. "Something tells me they're going to be trouble."

***

Mr. Jackson and his wife walked over to the manager, who was most distressed indeed. "Let me assure you, sir, that we have NEVER had such goings-on here before. I want to —"

Mr. Jackson raised his hand. "We're quite confident in your hotel. I've stayed here many a time. But there is a matter in which you might aid us."

The manager's shoulders slumped. "How much do you want to keep quiet?"

Mr. Jackson felt amused. "Nothing so crass. We're both gentlemen here!"

Relief crossed the manager's face. "How then may I help?"

"Might you recommend a discreet private surgeon? For my wife. We were told to contact one in a few days."

The manager glanced at Mrs. Jackson's sling. "We have one on retainer. No charge to you whatsoever."

"Very good," Mr. Jackson said. "You may call him in whenever it's convenient." He gestured to the group still milling about. "I'll let you get back to your staff."

"Thank you, sir," the manager said. "And please, not a word to the other guests?"

"Of course not," Mrs. Jackson said. "I dislike even to think on it." She glanced at the contorted body and shuddered. "How horrid!"

"I'm most grateful. If you need anything — anything at all, you have only to ask."

***

Mrs. Jackson considered the pretty little blonde who'd sold her the pack of cigarettes a day earlier lying crumpled on the floor.

Whatever the girl might have done, killing her this way was wrong.

Once the manager left, Mr. Jackson said quietly, "My ... wife. I feel astonished. I never thought such words would ever come from my mouth."

Mrs. Jackson chuckled, taking his arm, and the couple moved towards the lobby. "And yet here we are."

They strolled through the lobby, past the grand fountain, towards the elevators. Then Mr. Jackson spoke. "It surprised me that you mentioned strychnine."

"Oh?"

"And offering to help a second time. I'm not sure either was wise. I'm certain the sergeant suspects us."

She felt amused. "He's the sort to suspect everyone." She smiled up at Mr. Jackson, and to her surprise, he blushed.

"Well," Mrs. Jackson said. "Our stay has become much more interesting than I would have ever thought."

7

The couple ate lunch in her room. Then Mrs. Jackson took her pain medication and lay in bed reading the paper. "Tell me about Chicago," she said, "since you've been here before."

Mr. Jackson downed his coffee, then shrugged. "It's a place, much like any other. The police here are competent; the criminals, somewhat less so. Only alcohol is forbidden. But of course, because alcohol's forbidden, everyone wants it. There are speakeasies on every corner, if you know where to find them. But many of the police will look the other way, especially if you hand them a fiver."

Mrs. Jackson nodded.

"And there's every amusement one might possibly imagine." At that, his face brightened. "Oh, my dear, we must see the talkies."

"Whatever are talkies?"

"Pictures which talk and move! And they often have the most wonderful music. Like a play, only characters are projected upon the screen using light. They're all the rage!"

Mrs. Jackson folded the paper, astonished at the idea. She felt positively sheltered! What else in the world went on that she knew nothing about? "That does sound interesting."

"Then we shall go, just as soon as you feel well enough."

Her wound did hurt quite a bit, especially when she moved her arm. And she hadn't quite gotten the dose right on the medication: it still made her sleepy. "Perhaps in a few days."

"Anything you desire is yours, my dear; you have only to ask."

She recalled his blush. Which, although attractive and sweet, conflicted with what he'd said just before they arrived. "May I ask something personal?"

"You may ask anything at all."

"Why are you being so kind to me? The truth."

He leaned his elbows on the table, rested his chin on his closed hands. "Because, strange as it sounds even to me, I like you. I find you fascinating. I'd like to spend more time with you." He leaned back, crossed his arms. "And I always try to speak the truth, as much as I can." He relaxed, just a bit. "I'll understand if you need to be alone, after everything that's happened, but if you do need me, even to talk with, I won't feel it a burden."

She felt abashed. "I don't mean to be ungrateful. And I'm sorry for not trusting you. It's just —"

Mr. Jackson put his elbows back on the table, his face in his hands. Then he raised his head and smiled at her. "Things certainly could have gone better."

In spite of how awful she felt right then, she chuckled, wiping her nose on her handkerchief. "It certainly could have." She took a deep breath and let it out, feeling better. "So what do you think of these murders?"

"Ever the investigator, are we? Well, it's possible that someone had it in for the young lady, badly enough to try again when failing the first time. The real question is why? Once we know why, well, then who is never far behind."

This threw Mrs. Jackson into some thought. Why would someone poison a girl's lunch? And with strychnine, of all things. "If they simply wanted to kill her, they could have killed her down in the basement. Or used some more peaceful solution. Or some longer acting agent which would kill many hours later to hide their involvement."

But they didn't. "Is it possible this killer meant to send a message to another member of the staff?"

Mr. Jackson smiled. "There you have it."

"But why kill a young woman? She had her whole life ahead of her." She shook her head, eyes stinging. "This is wrong."

***

Mr. Jackson surveyed his wife. Her eyes were drooping. She'd be asleep soon. But the young woman's death had affected her. He knew his wife well enough: if he didn't persuade her to remain still, she'd begin searching for the girl's killer despite her injury.

"I can't just lie here — a girl is dead! And to kill her in this way?" She shook her head, face turned away. "There must be something I can do."

"What you can do is rest. You've just had surgery."

She slid down in the bed, eyes sleepy. "But to do nothing seems wrong."

He shrugged. "The sergeant strictly forbade our involvement. He already suspects us as it is."

"Yet the manager asked us to speak with the staff. They need us."

What should he do? "How about this: once you're asleep, I'll walk through the hotel, take a look around. It's likely someone will speak with me."

She beamed. "If you should find a clue to these murders, I suppose the time I have to spend asleep won't have been entirely wasted."

He laughed. "If you think my amateur questioning adequate."

"Don't be silly." She gave him a sleepy smile. "I can't wait to see what you discover."

"Shh, dear girl. Rest now." He moved his chair beside her bed, rested his hand upon her forehead. "Sleep. You must get strong. Then we can find this killer."

She smiled, eyes closed.

He sat, stroking her thick black curls for a long while as he watched the clouds play over the sky.

As soon as his wife seemed firmly asleep, Mr. Jackson slipped out, locking the door behind him with the "Do Not Disturb" sign on.

He stood in the hall, hesitant. Normally, he wouldn't leave someone so recently injured unattended.

But in her eyes, this girl's murder had changed everything. She'd never truly rest until the matter was resolved.

So he set off.

The halls were quiet, as was the elevator. But the lobby bustled with people. Bellhops brought gleaming brass carts filled with luggage to and fro. Valets brought keys, escorted men to their cars. Families strolled the walkways on the upper levels, guarded by wrought iron, gazing and pointing at the sights.

Beside the busy front desk, the dining room doors stood open, its tables full of people reading, drinking coffee, and talking. Waiters and maids moved to and fro. A handsome young man with dark hair played the grand piano in the center of the room.

While Mr. Jackson had stayed at this hotel before, he'd been a guest for the night, simply using it as a place to sleep while conducting business. Downstairs, he'd only visited the dining room and lobby. If they were to stay at the Myriad Hotel until his wife recovered, he wanted to see what it had to offer them. And perhaps he'd learn something.

He moved back across the wide marble-tiled lobby, past the glorious fountain and the grand curving stair. As he passed the foot of the staircase, a large grandfather clock upon the first landing struck two.

Just past the stair was a wide expanse. Down a hallway to his left, people waited for the elevators. On the wall straight ahead was a soda bar. Ahead and to his right (near the front of the hotel) lay the gift shop. Between the two, a hallway marked "Library" stood before him.

The soda bar's counter stretched eight feet in and twenty long, made of polished rosewood trimmed in brass. Brass barstools with cushions of black leather stood at intervals. Golden light came from decorative bulb fixtures in the ceiling.

Six small tables nestled in the room. The one in the far back right held a couple sipping drinks through paper straws.

The soda jerk — a boy of perhaps sixteen — glanced up from wiping the bar. "Care for a glass, sir?"

"What do you have?"

The boy gaped at Mr. Jackson, eyes wide. "We have over two hundred flavors — more if you combine them!" He gestured at the bottles lined floor to ceiling along the wall, each labeled with their syrup's flavor.

"That's quite impressive." He peered at the array. "How about lemon and ginger?"

"Right away, sir."

Mr. Jackson sat on a bar stool, watching the boy work. "I don't recall this place being here the last time I stayed."

"How long ago was this?"

"Several years now."

"Well, sir, they put this in before I come to work here."

A large stuffed owl stood perched at the corner ceiling in an alcove above the many bottles. A rosewood door with a brass knob had been set diagonally into the corner directly underneath, which seemed an unusual arrangement for any building.

"That's a fine specimen," Mr. Jackson said, pointing at the owl.

The boy smiled to himself, his cheeks coloring.

"Your work?"

The boy twitched, focusing on the counter. "No, sir. Been here as long as I remember." He handed over a glass of soda. "Two bits."

"Would you put it on my tab? Hector Jackson, 3205."

"Of course, sir."

The soda was quite good — not too sweet.

A light fell upon the owl, and its eyes began blinking. Mr. Jackson laughed, pointing at it. "Would you look at that!"

The boy glanced over his shoulder. "It does that sometimes." His tone became falsely bright. "Would you like anything else, sir?"

This was interesting. Out of curiosity, Mr. Jackson asked, "What else do you serve?"

The boy hesitated. "Ice cream sodas, with real imported vanilla. Best in town."

Mr. Jackson leaned back, surveying the lad. "My wife might like that!" He extended a hand, which the boy shook. "A pleasure to meet you," he peered at the boy's name-tag, "Thomas. I'm sure I'll be seeing you again. Oh, and when you submit that, give yourself a nickel tip."

The boy's face brightened. "Yes, sir! Thank you, sir."

Very interesting indeed.

Mr. Jackson walked a pace or two into the lobby then to his right, just out of the boy's view. He surveyed the room, watching people go up and down the wide stair to the second floor. The lobby was just as full as it had been a few moments before. Yet at that moment, not one of any of the people in the huge room were workers.

He'd wondered more than once about the lack of staff when they'd arrived. Now he thought he'd stumbled upon the answer.

8

As he continued on past the crowd waiting for the elevators, Mr. Jackson considered the mystery of the owl. Its blinking clearly was a sign, but to whom?

He whirled, returning to the place he'd stood. The valet stand outside was clearly visible. An older, olive-skinned man now stood there, dressed in a valet's uniform. The man returned his gaze with a set face and a slight nod.

A chill ran down his back.

Clearly something untoward went on here in the hotel. Would it be something worth killing for?

Mr. Jackson moved back towards the elevators. Whatever was going on, they certainly wouldn't tell him of it.

Past the elevators, he came upon the striped pole of a barbershop. The barber swept the floor, glancing up as Mr. Jackson arrived. "Can I help you, sir?"

Mr. Jackson had his personal manservant Mr. Vienna, who normally took care of such things. Yet he felt he might learn more were he to visit here. "Just taking a look-round, but now I know you're here, I'll return."

The man smiled. "Very good, sir."

The man hadn't been downstairs with the others. "Are you employed here, or do you rent the booth?"

"Oh, I rent. Not interested in being employed by others, sir. Keeps my options open."

Mr. Jackson smiled. "Good man. That's the spirit."

"Let me know if you'd care for a freshening up before dinner," the barber said. "I get several in starting a bit after tea."

"You know," Mr. Jackson said, "I may just take you up on that." His manservant had been hired for breakfast and dinner, but he wouldn't be round until seven. And if many men would be here, this might be a perfect opportunity to learn more.

"Very good, sir. I look forward to seeing you."

A ladies' hairdresser appeared next, a glassed-in affair with a fine beveled-glass door. Past that, a wide hall went to his right, marked with a sign:

Dog Grooming & Veterinary Services

A smartly dressed woman with golden blonde hair said, "Excuse me."

He moved aside while she and three dogs with hair matching hers pranced past and down the side hall to another beveled-glass door.

"Astonishing," Mr. Jackson murmured.

Through windows to his left, a courtyard appeared, with an extensive, luxurious garden. He glimpsed moving water past foliage. A conservatory? Perhaps his wife might like to visit there.

When he reached the end of the hall, a small tree at the back corner caught his eye: glossy green leaves of a sort he'd never seen before. Instead of one vein down its center, these leaves had three, equally spaced.

"Extraordinary," Mr. Jackson said to himself.

The main hall went to the left, and so did he, the view of the courtyard soon lost. To his right, he passed three offices, then a wide hall transected his. The sign on the left pointed to the kitchens; to the right, the hall ended at an open door.

A brown-haired man dressed in brown khaki work clothes stood past the door on a metal balcony. He turned as Mr. Jackson approached, taking a lit cigarette from his mouth as he leaned on the black metal railing. His name-tag said: Eugene. "Need help, sir?"

"Just taking a stroll. I was curious as to what was out here."

Eugene smiled to himself, taking another drag from his cigarette.

Stairs led down both sides to a ramp wide enough to hold several trucks. A few parked there, while a rather large truck backed in, guided by a man wearing blue denim overalls. On the side, it said:

Carlo Brothers Imported Olive Oil

The Best of Italy

"What do you do here?"

Eugene shrugged. "Me? Maintenance."

"I thought they had maids for that."

Eugene snorted in derision. "I don't scrub floors. I fix what needs fixing."

"Ah, forgive me. I see. Like the trucks?"

"More like the drains." He sucked at his cigarette, blew out smoke. "But whatever. Yesterday I fixed a hand rail. Sometimes I go round to check for rats."

"Do you get many here?"

"Rats?" He let out a short laugh. "Not if I can help it. Wouldn't be in business too long if it got out we had rats, now would we?"

Mr. Jackson chuckled at that. "What all do you use for them? Traps?"

"Naw," Eugene said. "Manager doesn't like that. He's got me setting out poison." He shook his head with a slight frown. "Just makes my job harder."

"In what way?"

"That stuff's dangerous. A dog or cat gets hold of it — it's not pretty." He shrugged. "Means I have to put the bait back where the bigger animals can't find it."

"Does seem like more trouble than it's worth."

The truck had disappeared, and the sounds of men unloading came from below.

"I know you," Eugene said. "You're the bloke that found the body. You were in the lunch room, too."

"I was indeed," Mr. Jackson said. "I'm very sorry for your loss."

Eugene shrugged. "Everyone thought the new guy was stealing people's lunches. But Agnes? A sweet little tomato, that. Don't know why anyone'd bother hurting her."

"Not too bright, then, I take it?"

He chuckled. "A few cards shy of a deck, if you get my meaning. She'd do whatever you asked, but you had to tell her exactly what." A hard look crossed his face for an instant. "That fellow that got killed — not even here a week, and he had her pinned in a corner." He shook his head grimly. "I set him straight, all right."

"How chivalrous of you."

Eugene gave Mr. Jackson a startled glance. "I didn't kill the man. Just pulled him off her. Poor little gal had the shakes after." He let out a breath. "If he hadn't got killed first, I'd have put it on him."

Interesting. Mr. Jackson leaned a hand on the railing. "Did they know each other? Before that?"

"Not that I know of."

"How was she after that? Before she died, of course."

Eugene shrugged. "She seemed fine. Always smiling. Always with a good word for others." He lapsed into a morose silence, staring out over the loading area.

"It's strange," Mr. Jackson said after a bit. "The manager said someone was at his lunch today."

Eugene's eyebrows raised. "Well, now that makes me glad they put a guard on them. If you can't eat in peace, what else is there?"

67

Mr. Jackson turned at a clanking noise. The doors to a large elevator — which he hadn't noticed — opened. A maid rolled a covered cart out and towards the kitchen.

"I'll leave you to your smoke," Mr. Jackson said. "A pleasure meeting you."

Eugene nodded. "Likewise."

Mr. Jackson went to the main hallway and stood listening to the noises of the kitchen.

Was it just a coincidence that the major component of rat poison here was strychnine?

He shook his head, unsure what to make of it, before continuing to the right. More offices appeared, and in the corner, another wide hallway went to the right, this time marked "Laundry."

He turned left to follow the main hall once more, which was marked:

Ladies' Spa
Indoor Pool
Gentlemen's Sauna and Baths
Lobby

All was as marked, and he came back round to the lobby once more.

"May I help you, sir?" The blond young man still stood behind the front desk.

Perhaps this was his chance to learn something. "How are you faring?"

"Sir?"

"Everything that's happened must be terrifying."

68

The man hesitated.

"I know, you aren't supposed to speak of it. But my wife and I found your coworker. The man who was here. We know everything that's happened — well, I suppose as much as anyone else does." He held out his hand. "Hector Jackson."

The clerk shook his hand. "Lee Francis."

Mr. Jackson grinned. "Used to be an investigator, once upon a time." At that, he shrugged. "Just offering an ear. Your manager seemed to think it would help." He glanced around; no one stood waiting. "I won't bother you any —"

"Not at all, sir," Lee said. "It would help, sir. To talk. I didn't know the other clerk; he'd just been hired. But I did know Miss Agnes." His face fell. "It's been hard."

Mr. Jackson nodded. "To stand at your post even so ... that's bravery."

Lee straightened. "I don't feel brave, sir. I don't want to be fired. Lots are talking about getting other jobs. But there aren't many these days. And if they hear you're looking, they cut your hours to nothing and hire someone else." This seemed to dishearten him. "My wife's with child. We need the money."

"Why would someone do such a thing?"

The young man rested his hand on the edge of the counter. "That's what I've been trying to understand. I don't know anyone'd want to hurt either of them."

"Has Agnes had trouble with anyone here?"

Lee shook his head. "If she had, I'd not have known it, sir. One of the maids might've; she was friendly with them all." Suddenly his face changed. "Jackson, right? I almost forgot; you have a message." He handed over a folded slip of paper.

Mr. Jackson took it and nodded: the surgeon would be by to see his wife later today. "Thanks. Never you fret: I'm sure the police'll have it sorted soon." Mr. Jackson glanced around; a woman waited with a pile of luggage. "I should let you return to your work. But any time you want to talk, just look me up."

"Yes, sir. Thank you, sir."

Mr. Jackson went to the dining room and took a seat at an empty table. People had been asking questions of him since he'd arrived; perhaps if he sat here long enough, someone would answer a few of his own.

9

Instead of making assumptions or forming suspicions, Hector Jackson preferred to approach things — as much as a grown man might — with the open mind of a child. What had he observed? What did he observe now?

George, the young waiter from breakfast the other day, came to his table. "How may I help, sir?"

"Coffee, heavy cream, no sugar," Mr. Jackson said. "And the paper, if you please." George had been in the sun recently. Too much sun, if the skin behind his neck spoke true.

The staff in the dining room moved like people free from care and worry. Their voices were cheery and warm.

Yet the occasional flinch, the sideways glance when passing, all spoke volumes: is this the one who may murder me next?

Not the most comfortable of working environments.

And not the most congenial place to stay, either. They had a week's credit here at the hotel. But should he move his wife somewhere else? Or would it put too much strain upon her?

"Your coffee and paper, sir." The waiter's left sleeve rose, revealing a recent rope burn.

"A boating man, I see," Mr. Jackson said.

George appeared astonished. "However did you know?"

Mr. Jackson smiled up at him. It seemed obvious. But he liked this fellow, so he said, "You've been in the sun recently. The sun at your back, I'd say. Many prefer to sail so, and it looks as if the wind kicked up." He pointed to the man's arm. "I've had many such in my day."

George stood speechless.

"What size is your boat?" And how a waiter afforded one was a question Mr. Jackson wished to ask, yet refrained, feeling it perhaps too intrusive.

At that, George relaxed. "It's my pa's, sir. We went out for the week end. Well, rightly, it's my grandpa's, but he rarely sails anymore."

A matron across the room had a hand raised, trying to get George's attention. Mr. Jackson gestured towards the woman with his chin. "I'll let you attend to your work. But I'd love to talk boats, any time."

George beamed. "Right, sir. Any time!" He gave a small bow and hurried off.

Mr. Jackson didn't feel any more enlightened than he had, but he'd made a friend. Perhaps one who might know more of the place than he. With a close family and an elderly yet well-to-do grandfather.

Who worked as a waiter?

The news had nothing as yet about the most recent death, which didn't surprise him — the afternoon paper wouldn't be out for another few hours. But he was surprised to see nothing more about the first one. A man dying at a place like this drew reporters like flies to honey.

Which made him consider: who would be harmed by such unwanted attention?

The manager and staff first came to mind. Then he recalled the owner, the "man you wouldn't want to make angry".

Were these deaths part of a feud among the staff, with these two caught in the middle? Or could these deaths be a strike against the hotel? A way to "encourage" the customers and staff to abandon it, perhaps instigated by some rival chain?

Chicago was a city known for its rivalries. Low-class gangsters and uncouth men of all sorts struggled for power here, only partially kept in check by the cops. Was the Myriad Hotel's esteemed owner one of them? Or had he gotten himself on the wrong side of their battles?

He sipped his coffee, which was excellent.

"Might we join you?"

Mr. Jackson looked up from the news. The old couple from breakfast the day before stood there. He rose to greet them. "Please. I insist."

The three sat.

The dowager Duchess glanced at the paper. "What news?"

Mr. Jackson folded the paper and passed it to her.

"Cordelia," her husband Albert said, "where are your manners?" Then to Mr. Jackson, he said, "Forgive her, sir. She's been too long among the common folk."

Mr. Jackson smiled to reassure them. "Not at all, sir: I had finished with it. I hope you both are well?"

"Quite well," she said, her lined cheeks coloring, "and yourself?"

"Splendid."

"And your wife?"

Now that was amusing. "She's resting at present. But much improved."

"Ah, yes," the old man said, "her injury. Very good."

It was obvious they wished to ask all the juicy details. So he said, "You mentioned the last time we met that you stay here at the hotel."

"Oh, yes," the dowager Duchess said. "Three years now. Wouldn't have it any other way."

"So you must know the staff quite well."

"Most," Albert said. "The young man who died —" at this, he seemed genuinely sorrowful, "no, he'd just been hired. Most distressing."

"And all the hotel's various amusements as well."

"Ah," he said, as if he'd finally understood something.

George came up then, speaking to Albert. "Would you like to order anything, sir?"

Albert glanced at his wife. "Tea for us both, with lemon. Steep it well." Then he turned to Mr. Jackson. "Yes, this place is a marvel! Did you know that there's a glassed-over courtyard with a simply wonderful garden? They let you help tend it."

That must have been what he saw earlier. "Is that so?"

"Yes! I so love trimming the flower bushes. That's the one thing I missed from the estate, tending the garden."

Mr. Jackson said, "What made you decide to move here? If it's not too intimate a question."

"Oh, no, not at all," Albert said. "I —"

"Well, Bertie —" the dowager said, clearly uncomfortable.

"Now, Cordelia, never you fret," her husband said. "I was only going to tell Mr. Jackson that the estate was yours," he turned to Mr. Jackson, "you see, we married late in life, after the death of her husband. Old money, that. But times are changing. No children to inherit, and the house just got too big for us." He patted his wife's hand. "We're much happier here."

It could have been the lighting, or perhaps Mr. Jackson's imagination, but the dowager Duchess didn't look quite so pleased to be here as her husband seemed. "Do you also like tending the garden?"

She gave a one-shoulder shrug. "I'm content to watch him work, although I am very fond of flowers."

Albert beamed at her. "I make sure she's well-supplied."

Mr. Jackson couldn't say why, but he felt something more was at work here. "What other amusements catch your fancy, my Lady?"

Her face brightened. "I do so love reading. The library here is a delight! And if there is some item not in stock, why, the Main Library is just a short trip away."

"What sorts of books do you favor?"

"Oh, she loves any sort of book imaginable," Albert said. "She was ever so bright as a child. Much more so than I."

"My word," Mr. Jackson said. "So you've known each other quite some time."

"Indeed we have." The old man glanced at his wife fondly, his cheeks coloring. "Indeed we have."

"Perhaps one day you might show my wife and I around," Mr. Jackson said.

"I would love to."

Cordelia leaned forward. "How is your wife, really?"

Mr. Jackson shrugged, not sure how much to reveal. "Rest is what she needs right now. Her medicine makes her sleep, which is for the best."

"Poor dear," Cordelia said. "Well, you be sure to give her my regards."

***

No one else approached, and to his dismay, the dowager and her husband never left. After his coffee, Mr. Jackson returned to his suite, leaving the old couple chattering about a book on flowers.

His wife stood on the balcony, a lovely picture in shadow framed by the sunny lake beyond. The breeze fluttered her gown and hair.

He put his hands beside hers on the wrought-iron railing. "How do you feel?"

She shrugged. "I'm not sure how to feel, to be honest." She smiled to herself. "What did you discover?

He hesitated, taking a deep breath. "They're hiding something. An underground speakeasy, I'll wager."

"Oh?"

No restaurant, no matter how grand, needed that much olive oil. "And I wonder: were these killings meant to discredit the hotel? If so, then the real question is why?"

Mrs. Jackson considered this. "Are the deaths related?"

He shrugged. "Our young clerk was no paragon of virtue. A dockworker told me the man tried to force himself upon the young lady who next perished."

"Really."

"Yes. The whole matter angered him greatly."

"Do you suspect him?"

"I suspect everyone. And the staff is afraid. There's talk of leaving."

She nodded soberly. "So if we are to help our host, it would be best done quickly."

He let out a laugh. "You are relentless! I'm glad to have you on my side this time." He surveyed her archly. "Quite formidable."

At that, she gave him an amused smile, holding up her injured arm. "Imagine once I'm well!"

The surgeon arrived at half past four. He was a man in his middle fifties with a solid, competent air to him.

Mr. Jackson stood watching as the man examined Mrs. Jackson's arm, asking her to move it, testing its sensation. "The wound looks to be without infection," the doctor said. "How is the pain?"

"Improved," she said. "I cut the dose the surgeon gave me to half, as it makes me much too sleepy otherwise."

"That's a good sign," the doctor said. "I'll return next week to remove the stitches. In the meantime, you may move the arm, as long as there's no pain when you do so." He smiled at her, as one might to a young girl. "Yet be gentle with yourself. It'll take a while to fully heal, and you'll need rest for your body to do so."

Later, the doctor took Mr. Jackson aside. "I've never seen such a botch job in my life."

Mr. Jackson felt alarmed. "Is she in danger?"

"Danger?" The doctor shook his head. "It seems to be healing well enough. But this is going to leave a terrible scar. How did it happen?"

Mr. Jackson hesitated, unsure how much to relate. "A ... tragedy occurred just prior to our marriage. Family members were murdered. She was injured, and ... I wasn't consulted on the matter until after the surgery."

The doctor stood there, mouth open. "I had no idea, sir. My deepest condolences."

Mr. Jackson nodded, pensive.

"The manager said you were on your honeymoon. I hope —"

Mr. Jackson stared at the man, horrified. She'd just had surgery. How could anyone be so cruel? Yet he understood where the question came from: other men might have taken advantage. He smiled to himself. "I've been kind to her."

The doctor patted Mr. Jackson's arm. "Good man. I've been married thirty years now. Kindness is a sure investment."

"Her arm. What can be done?"

The doctor retrieved a notepad and fountain pen from the breast pocket of his tweed jacket. "I'll give you the name of a specialist. A bit of a journey, but he's the best at this sort of thing. A real artist. He'll have her fixed up in no time."

"We're most grateful."

The man handed the paper over. "You should wait until the wound's fully healed to contact him. Scars often improve over time."

Mr. Jackson reached into his pocket for a tip.

But the man waved him off. "Not necessary, sir, it's all paid for." He took on a jolly demeanor. "One of the perks of fine hotel living."

It was then Mr. Jackson remembered. "You're on retainer."

"Indeed I am," the doctor said. "So if you need anything at all, don't hesitate to summon me."

When Mr. Jackson told his wife what the doctor had said about her wound, she snorted. "Figures."

He laughed at her tone. "Well, at least we have a few weeks before we need to make a decision."

"Perhaps in that time, we can find our poisoner."

Mr. Jackson chuckled, shaking his head. "You're like a bloodhound in your persistence." He smiled at her fondly. "If much more attractive."

Her cheeks colored as she glanced away. But a shy smile touched her lips, quickly fading. "You don't understand: I need to be useful, especially now."

He sat beside her, rested his hand on hers. "Usefulness is overrated. What you need is to recover." A wave of grief and fear for her washed over him. "I won't lose you too."

She hesitated, then her shoulders slumped. "Oh, very well. You and the doctor have persuaded me, for now." She stretched upon the bed with a smile. "The beds are so beautifully soft. That's some compensation for my enforced idleness." Her smile turned into a wicked grin.

"Will I be served in bed from your hand? Perhaps strawberries and whipped cream would do."

This made him laugh out loud. "My dear, you may have any pleasure your heart desires." He rose. "In fact, I'll call for it now."

She sat up. "I was only teasing."

"Very well." He sat beside her and put his arm round her shoulders. "Do you want to take tea here, or downstairs?"

"Downstairs, I think. I've had enough of being in here for now."

10

By the time the couple descended for tea, the dining room was packed — every table full, every seat in the lobby taken.

The cook, a forty-year-old brown-haired woman, glanced at Mrs. Jackson's arm and smiled at the couple as she passed by. "Afternoon tea, or early supper?"

"We're here for tea," Mrs. Jackson said.

"Very good," the cook said. "I'll have a girl get you set up, sir, ma'am."

"Much obliged," Mr. Jackson said.

Mrs. Jackson watched as a young maid arranged teacups, saucers, a pot of tea, and a large plate of small sandwiches from the buffet area onto a tray. Then she and Mr. Jackson followed the woman to an empty table in the soda shop.

A young man behind the bar waved to Mr. Jackson when they entered.

He seemed to make friends everywhere he went. However did he do it?

Mrs. Jackson was intrigued by the owl, especially after Mr. Jackson told her — in whispers, once the maid left — about the blinking. And the tremendous array of bottled flavors!

She'd never had an "ice cream soda" before, so they resolved to return for one after dinner. "This is the most marvelous hotel," she said. "By all accounts, one might never have to leave!"

"That seems to be the aim," Mr. Jackson said with a grin. "More profits for them!"

"Indeed," Mrs. Jackson said. "And I must say, well done!"

They feasted upon the sandwiches — egg, but like nothing Mrs. Jackson had seen before. These were made with whole quail's eggs, hard-boiled and sliced thin upon a spicy creamed spread. She wiped her mouth. "Delicious!" She took a sip of her tea. "I never imagined such a dish."

Mr. Jackson nodded. "The chefs in Chicago are superb." He drained his teacup and poured another. "There are dozens of restaurants in the downtown area alone." He took a sip, then became animated. "We must visit them all!"

She enjoyed his enthusiasm, yet ... "Do you think it wise to stay here that long?" She leaned forward to speak more softly. "Perhaps once we find this killer, we should be on our way."

Mr. Jackson's face sobered, and he put down his cup, leaning over to cover her hand with his. "I would never do anything to put you into harm." He leaned back, gazing off to one side. "No one in all the wide world is looking for Hector and Pamela Jackson. And even if they were, the chance of finding us here is astronomical. So relax, my dear. Enjoy yourself!" He gave her a fond smile. "Life's much too short to do otherwise." He sipped his tea. "I propose we stay until you're completely well, then we'll decide."

She felt relieved that they might not have to rush away. That they might truly be safe here.

Just then, the old man from breakfast the other day walked by, and spying them, hurried inside. "My dear Mr. Jackson! I was just going to check on the garden." He turned to Mrs. Jackson. "Your husband expressed an interest in touring the gardens." The man glanced back and forth between them. "Would you care to join me?"

The couple exchanged a glance, and she nodded. Gardens seemed a pleasant enough diversion.

"Why, of course," Mr. Jackson said. "Just as soon as we're done here."

"By all means, take your time."

***

Just then, the manager strode in, coming to their table. "There you are!"

Mr. Jackson felt amused. Not wanting to force his wife to rise, he remained in his chair, just as he had when Albert arrived. "Indeed we are, sir. How may I help you?"

"Well, I told the owner about the situation here, and he's come to tour the facility today and talk with the staff. Stay the night. It'll settle their worries, I think. He'll probably take dinner in his room, but he wants to meet with you both sometime after."

Mr. Jackson felt surprised. "I'd be honored." He glanced at his wife. "If my wife is well enough, of course."

"Certainly. Mr. Carlo knows the situation — you being on your honeymoon and all — but he did so want to at least meet you."

"It's settled then," Mr. Jackson said.

Albert had watched the exchange without a word, arms crossed.

The manager glanced at him, then back at Mr. Jackson. "I'll let you get back to your tea, then."

Mr. Jackson said, "Would you like to join us?"

"No," Albert said, "My wife needs me to have something sent up from the gift shop. I'll meet you back here afterward."

Mrs. Jackson beamed at Albert. "We're looking forward to your tour."

At that, Albert smiled, but it seemed forced. "Be right back."

Mr. Jackson pondered the exchange. "I don't think Albert Stayman likes the manager very much."

His wife nodded, eyes far away, seemingly lost in thought. But then she said, "I imagine living in such proximity, anyone would have a spat from time to time."

He chuckled at that.

She put her cup down. "I'm ready to go, as soon as your friend returns."

As they waited for Albert, the cook came by their table. "How did you enjoy your tea?"

"Lovely," Mrs. Jackson said. "I particularly liked the sandwiches."

The woman blushed. "I'm so happy you liked them!"

Mr. Jackson said, "How kind of you to stop by!"

"I try to meet everyone while they're here," she said. "It helps me to know how to improve."

This seemed quite admirable. Mr. Jackson held out his hand. "Hector and Pamela Jackson."

She took his hand and curtsied. "Miss Goldie Jean Dab, sir."

Mrs. Jackson said, "Have you worked here long?"

"Ten years in May, and a nicer place to work you'd never find."

Albert walked up, and the couple rose.

"Just leave everything here," Miss Dab said. "I'll get a girl to take these for you. I hope you have a wonderful stay."

Mr. Jackson and his wife followed Albert across the lobby. To his surprise, a wide hallway with a sign marked "Gardens" lay behind the stair. Down the hall, a beveled glass door appeared.

The door opened into a vast courtyard. Trees both large and small dotted the area, with flower bushes around them. A path of grayish-brown brick wound past these. The air was warm, humid, and fragrant.

During the chill of winter, Mr. Jackson thought he and his wife might enjoy this as much as walking the park.

Some trees held fruit! Mr. Jackson turned to Albert in astonishment.

"This is really a conservatory," the old man said. "It gets so cold here in the winter, thus the glass roofing."

Mr. Jackson nodded. The buildings stretched high above them, white clouds in the deep blue sky. The roof itself reminded him of some giant crystal, inlaid with pipes of brass. "Do you get much snow?"

"Yes, but it melts straightaway. Heated, you see."

As they continued on, a pond appeared to the left. Lily pads, brightly colored fish, and smooth oval rocks lay in the clear water. Further on, a short waterfall dropped from a small brook as the path wound slightly upwards to another garden area.

"This is lovely," Mrs. Jackson said.

The old man beamed.

They went on for some time. Off in one corner, the small tree he'd seen before appeared upon a raised area in the corner by the window, far from the path with no other plants in its bed. Mr. Jackson said, "What is that tree? I glimpsed it from the hallway."

The old man smiled broadly. "Ah, the snake-wood tree! Fascinating. I picked up seeds while traveling, the summer before we came here. The tree which used to be in that spot died, so I took it out for them and planted this here."

Mr. Jackson thought it a remarkable plant. "I've never seen leaves like that before."

"It's a most singular tree," the old man said, yet he seemed uneasy. "It'll produce these pale greenish flower bursts, and fruit of a sort once it's old enough — in about fifteen or twenty years." He let out a laugh. "I might even still be around to see them." At that, he sobered. "Nothing you'd want to eat, mind you. I imagine it tastes terrible. But quite pretty." He gestured towards the path. "Want to see more?"

Mr. and Mrs. Jackson moved along as directed. "You seem to enjoy plants quite a bit," Mrs. Jackson said.

"I do! Much more reliable than people." He laughed softly to himself.

Mr. Jackson said, "You mentioned you've known your wife since childhood. Did you live there at the estate?"

"Oh, yes. I was the groundsman's son. It was my father gave me the love of growing things. I did up all the flower beds, planted most of the trees there ..." His face turned wistful. "It was a beautiful time."

"And she was an only child," Mrs. Jackson said. "I recall her saying so."

Albert said, "Yes, she was."

Mr. Jackson smiled. "And so the groundsman's son became the groundsman. And the little girl, a woman."

The old man smiled to himself. "Indeed."

Mr. Jackson said, "Were you in love with her even then?"

Albert gave Mr. Jackson a startled glance. "Yes, I suppose I was. Of course, then, she was too far above me to even consider it. She married, they split the time between their properties. I saw her less, to be sure, but it seemed we had a bond even then. It was all very proper, though. I never dared speak until her husband's death."

Mrs. Jackson said, "What happened?"

"It was his heart."

"I meant, how did you end up marrying? Her being so far above you and all."

The old man glanced away, his cheeks coloring. "I suppose it just happened. She needed a great deal of help after her husband's death. I provided all the flowers for the funeral. A grand thing, it was, befitting the Duke. But it cost more than the estate could bear."

Mr. Jackson said, "And now you've been married these past three years."

"Close to four, now. Three of them here. We traveled the world at first." He paused for a moment, then said, "I don't much care where I live. So long as I can be close to her, that's good enough for me."

Mr. Jackson found that touching. "Thank you for taking us round." His wife's face looked relaxed and happy for the first time in a long while. So when he next spoke, it was with sincerity. "We love this garden."

"So you might stay, then?"

Mr. Jackson said, "We haven't decided as yet. But we'll most certainly enjoy it while we're here."

"I'm so glad." Albert seemed relieved. "I've always felt a certain pride in my gardens, a responsibility to the things I grow. Like a parent who brings children to the world — to tend and care for them."

Mr. Jackson nodded, fascinated by the man's assertions. "I never considered it that way. But then, I've never been a gardener."

"Well, any time you want to come with me, you're more than welcome. I usually come out early, before breakfast. Not so many people then."

"I'll keep that in mind." They approached the door, and his wife took his arm as they returned to the lobby. "Thanks again for the tour," Mr. Jackson said.

"Don't mention it." Albert pointed to their left. "Have you seen the library?"

"Not yet," said Mr. Jackson.

At the same time, Mrs. Jackson gasped. "You have a library?"

"Did your husband not tell you? Come this way. Cordelia is there now." He moved ahead, and they followed.

Mrs. Jackson whispered, "You never said anything about a library!"

Mr. Jackson replied, "I never knew you enjoyed them!"

"I do," she said. "Very much so."

They reached the long hall to the library. "Then it seems you could just as well recover here as anywhere else."

His wife beamed. "Perhaps I shall like staying here after all!"

The library was rather large, stretching (it seemed) clear the length of the building's front on that side. Narrow windows of beveled glass let in the dim light of an early evening. The room was decorated in the same dark rosewood and brass which graced the rest of the building. The lampshades were finely-made panels of cobalt glass, and the chairs were upholstered in black velvet.

The dowager sat upon a chair, a pile of books on the round table before her. She rose once she saw them. "How lovely to see you!"

Several people looked up.

"Oh, silly me," she said, half as loudly, "come, let me show you around." She and her husband moved ahead.

"This is her garden," Mrs. Jackson whispered.

Mr. Jackson thought the idea quite amusing.

Bookshelves eight feet high ran around the walls of the entire room, and many more lined up within.

Mrs. Jackson's eyes were wide with wonder. "I love it!"

"I'm so glad you like it, my dear," the dowager said. "I'm here almost every day. I would most enjoy your company." She turned to the rows. "Here, walk with me and look around."

So they did, moving well to the back to browse the collection there.

The dowager whispered, "I never asked. What brings you to the city?"

Wishing he had a dollar for every time he'd been asked this, Mr. Jackson whispered, "We're on our honeymoon!"

"My congratulations to you both," the dowager said, and her husband nodded.

Mrs. Jackson smiled at her. "Thank you!"

The old woman smiled to herself. "I do so love a good romance tale." She focused on Mr. Jackson. "When did you know she was the one?"

He felt himself blush; why, he wasn't sure. "Well. It's perhaps awkward."

"Oh, come now," the old woman said with a quiet laugh. "I can't imagine you doing anything remotely improper."

He grinned. "You'd be surprised." He hesitated, casting a glance at his wife. "It's a rather long, somewhat embarrassing story. Yet I had chance to see her legs, and —"

Mrs. Jackson went crimson, and Albert glanced away.

"Oh, this is a good tale," the dowager whispered.

" — and I have to say I was smitten." For an instant, he felt foolish. But he collected himself, meeting his wife's eyes. "For quite some time I could think of little else."

Mrs. Jackson stood gaping at him.

"Well," the dowager said with quiet glee, "this is fascinating! One day you must tell me the entire story."

A woman's voice came from above: "Dinner will be served at eight. Hotel guests have a standing reservation. Others should come to the concierge desk at once to make reservations if they wish to dine."

A grandfather clock stood at the back end of the room: five minutes to seven. "We should dress for dinner," Mr. Jackson said to no one in particular. "It was good to see you," he said to the old couple. "And thank you for the tours."

They went out into the lobby. Mrs. Jackson said, "So — all this time?"

Heat rushed to his face. "Yes."

She didn't reply.

As they waited for the elevator, he said, "I wonder — when you return to the library — if you would mind learning what you can about the snake-wood tree."

"Oh?"

"It very much interests me."

She bristled. "Well, the library stands ready. Tomorrow you're welcome to go look for it."

"I'm sorry. I didn't mean to imply —"

The elevator opened, and people went in and out, but they stood off to one side, facing each other.

"I'm no servant," Mrs. Jackson said. "I never have been, and I never will be. I didn't ask you here; I allowed you to come with me. I even married you, at your advice, even though now it seems you've lied about the reasons. But if we are to be married, then let us see each other as equal. And speak true to each other in all things, as you claimed you prefer. Or we can part ways."

He felt abashed. "Forgive me. I meant no harm." Then he felt dismayed. He'd taken a vow, long ago, to protect this woman. One he could never break. Had he driven her away? "I — I've never done this before."

She surveyed him for a long moment, then rose on tiptoe to kiss his cheek. "All is forgiven." She took his arm. "I suppose we shouldn't leave Mrs. Knight and Mr. Vienna waiting for us."

As his wife had suspected, the maid and valet stood waiting in the hall to dress them for dinner. Mr. Jackson introduced them to each other. "Would the two of you be so kind as to purchase nightclothes for us? We seem to have forgotten to pack ours."

Mrs. Knight and Mr. Vienna exchanged a quick, amused glance. "They'll be in your rooms after dinner, sir," Mr. Vienna said.

The couple went down to dinner shortly thereafter. This time, they were seated with newcomers, and ate in silence as talk swirled around them.

Mr. Jackson felt a certain agitation. Why did he share that story? He should have known it would upset her.

But there was no help for it. He considered what might be best to say. Finally, he ventured, "I hope you're well."

Mrs. Jackson smiled then. "I am, so far as that goes. I was simply pondering a matter best left out of dinner conversation."

"Ah." She must mean the murders, all accomplished by food. At least so far. "Indeed."

"Yet I did wonder when the next event might occur."

"Oh?"

She put down her fork, and turning towards him, spoke for his ears alone. "Unless you believe the young woman to be the true target."

It was a good question. From all accounts, the young lady hardly had the capacity to poison someone on her own. And it seemed doubtful she'd have knowingly poisoned herself. At least, not in a room full of her friends.

So the poisoner was still in the hotel with them.

Would someone poison their own coworkers? Yet who had access to the lunch room, other than employees?

"How are you enjoying your meal?" George, the young boating man turned waiter, stood across the table holding a tray full of dishes.

Mr. Jackson glanced at his plate: much of the food remained. "Forgive me; I'd become distracted. It's very good."

"I'd be happy to get you something else if you prefer."

"Not at all." Mr. Jackson looked round the table. Some of the guests were sampling desserts, others had left. His wife's empty plate held the remains of a lemon-cake. "Would you care to try a soda?"

She nodded, and he turned to the waiter. "Would you get us —"

George's body jerked violently, and he dropped his tray with a crash.

11

Mr. Jackson, shocked speechless, stared at the empty space George had just occupied.

Mrs. Jackson leapt to her feet. "Doctor!"

Her shout jarred him from his immobility. Heart pounding, Mr. Jackson followed his wife to George, whose face twisted in agony.

"I'm a doctor," an elderly man said.

Mrs. Jackson, who now knelt beside the young man, looked up at the old doctor. "It's strychnine."

"Good gracious," the doctor said.

"There's a veterinary around the corner there," Mr. Jackson said. "Might they have something which could help?"

The doctor stared blankly back. "They might." He hobbled out.

Meanwhile, George's back arched, his eyes frightened, pleading. Mr. Jackson stood helpless, hands shaking, not knowing what to do.

"Peace, good sir," Mrs. Jackson said, brushing hair from George's forehead. "We'll stay with you." Then she called out, "We need an ambulance!"

The room scattered as people ran about. The doctor returned, out of breath. "I have activated charcoal and tannic acid," he panted, "and a mouth syringe."

"Do what you must, sir," Mr. Jackson said, feeling relieved.

The doctor fumbled with the containers, his hands shaking, as everyone watched. But finally he got a solution down George's throat in between the young man's spasms.

Mr. Jackson said, "How long will this take to work?"

"It depends on how much he ingested and how long ago." He bent over the man, trying to get his attention. "Did you eat or drink anything?"

George's face was red with the strain. "Lemon-cake," he groaned.

A woman began screaming, "AAAAA! AAAAAAA! I had lemon-cake!" People began running towards her in agitation.

Then another screamed, "I did too!"

Mrs. Jackson stood. "SHUT UP!"

The first woman seemed shocked, then offended. "Well, I never!"

"If you'd been poisoned, you'd be dead by now," Mrs. Jackson snapped. "So take your hysteria elsewhere."

Mr. Jackson had never respected anyone more than he did his wife right then.

She returned to kneel by the man's side. George seemed to be less agitated, then a spasm twisted his face once more.

Mr. Jackson looked to the doctor, who shrugged. "Never treated this before. Only read about it. But I'll try a bit more of the charcoal. A glass of water, sir, if you please."

Mr. Jackson fetched his own, and the doctor gave the young man a slurry of the activated charcoal by mouth. After George swallowed it, the ambulance arrived, along with the police.

As the ambulance men carried the young man off, the sergeant said, "You two again."

"They saved me, sir," George moaned. He looked at Mrs. Jackson. "Thank you."

The dining room was in an uproar. Everyone had questions, concerns, expressions of outrage. Mr. and Mrs. Jackson retired to their original seats at the table to await the inevitable visit from the sergeant's men.

"Quick thinking, that," Mr. Jackson said to his wife, hoping his voice wasn't shaking as much as it sounded. "Well done." He took a deep breath, trying to calm himself. "I'd hate to see such a fine young man succumb to this poisoner."

She nodded, face pensive. "This person — whoever it is — becomes more bold."

"Surely this is being done by a man," Mr. Jackson said, "is it not?"

The sergeant, who'd been standing across the table where the young man once lay, looked over. "Poisoners are generally women. Or shall I say, women who kill are usually poisoners." He shook his head wearily. "Every woman in this building is now a suspect."

***

Once the young man was carried off, Mrs. Jackson felt weak, shaky, and her arm ached. The sergeant questioned them, then said they could go, warning them not to leave the building.

So the couple went across the lobby to have their ice cream sodas.

"This is quite good," she said. "And I love how it fizzes so. It's a unique flavor!"

Mr. Jackson didn't reply.

She peered at him. He still seemed shaken by the night's events. "Are you well, sir?"

"I don't rightly know," he said, staring at the table. "I feel as if something of great moment has happened —"

A laugh burst from her. "A man almost dying would qualify!"

He glanced up at her, and the look in his face made her feel chagrined. "Forgive me." Then what was happening dawned on her. She leaned forward, eyes stinging. He'd given up a great deal for her, perhaps more than he should. "Truly. I should not have laughed. It was wrong for me to do so. I'm sorry."

At that, he sighed, shoulders slumping.

"Listen to me," she said. "Everyone reacts to sudden events in different ways. You must not berate yourself, or feel shamed at how you did so." She reached across with her good hand to take his. "The doctors here are excellent. All will be well."

A bit of a smile touched his lips. "I'm supposed to be comforting you."

She shrugged. "We're married, are we not? I believe it goes both ways."

Once they'd finished their sodas, they returned to their rooms. "Another eventful day," Mrs. Jackson said, sagging into a chair.

"The reporters couldn't fail to feature this," Mr. Jackson said, an edge to his tone. "I feel certain whoever is doing this targets the management."

"But why? Why not kill whoever the person has it in for?"

"Maybe he — or she — has it in for all these people. Perhaps the deaths are related. But what does a new, unprincipled desk clerk, a young woman who by all accounts wouldn't hurt a fly, and a waiter from a good family have in common?"

"The hotel," Mrs. Jackson said. "They all work the day shift. Might this waiter have been sampling lunches as well?"

"You don't kill someone for stealing your lunch," Mr. Jackson said, sounding annoyed. "Not unless you're mentally deranged. Besides, the dinner pails are under guard as well."

"The lemon-cake." Mrs. Jackson kicked her shoes off, put her feet up on the side of her bed. "Individual cakes. Easy to poison one without harming others. And I imagine easier to hide a strong taste in a lemon-cake than in some other food."

"Indeed."

"So your young waiter swipes a lemon-cake —"

"Wait," Mr. Jackson said. "George served me earlier today. After luncheon."

"So he was on an extra shift, perhaps," said Mrs. Jackson.

"Yes."

She leaned forward. "So maybe the poisoner doesn't know this. Maybe this order was to go to someone in particular, but the young man —"

"Swipes the lemon-cake," Mr. Jackson said, then chuckled. "Apt way of putting it."

Mrs. Jackson smiled at him. "And almost pays dearly for it." Her heart sank. "How will we know who the cake was to go to? That's our next target, I'd wager."

Mr. Jackson rose. "Stay here. I'll relay this to the sergeant. Surely they have someone searching the kitchens by now."

She held out her hand, feeling suddenly afraid. "Be careful."

"Oh, dear." He gave her a soft smile, taking her hand in his. "First, apologies, now this? Who are you, and what have you done with my wife? I'd almost think you were concerned for me."

She ignored his levity: he had to understand. "If this poisoner thinks you pursue him — or her, they might become desperate. Take care."

He leaned over to kiss her forehead, something he'd never done before. "I will."

She really needed her pain medication by this time, but she didn't dare sleep until he returned. So she took a part dose, struggled into her new nightgown, and — more than a little frightened — sat up in bed to wait for his return.

***

Locking the doors to their suite, Mr. Jackson hurried down to the lobby.

A huge crowd milled about. Reporters and high-class men demanded answers which the young officers guarding the doors to the dining hall couldn't give. Off by the chairs, a few richly-dressed ladies were being fanned and fawned over by their retainers.

Mr. Jackson felt a deep gratitude that he traveled with a sensible woman. She'd saved George with her quick action.

Pushing through the crowd, he approached the dining hall doors. A familiar-looking officer glanced at him and said, "Ah, yes — the sergeant asked me to let you through."

Exclamations of outrage followed him inside — some quite rude — and he felt glad when the door shut behind him.

The dining hall swarmed with police. The far area was filled with people being questioned. Off to one side, Albert Stayman paced as the dowager Duchess sat speaking with an officer. The area where George had fallen was being measured and photographed, much as the area around the front desk had been.

The sergeant walked over to meet him. "I hope you and your wife are well."

"She's resting," Mr. Jackson said. "The pain medication makes her sleep." He smiled to himself fondly, imagining her face peaceful.

"Very good," the sergeant said. He seemed to relax a bit. "First marriage?"

"My first," Mr. Jackson admitted. "My wife was widowed."

"I'm sorry to hear that. I did wonder at such a lovely young woman marrying so late in life."

Mr. Jackson felt amused. "Thank you." He realized then what was happening. "This isn't a social call."

Sergeant Nestor snorted.

"Very well," Mr. Jackson said, feeling weary. "What do you want to know?"

"You were speaking to the young man when he collapsed."

"He stood across the table." He struggled to recall the scene. "I don't remember what we spoke about. But then he fell."

The sergeant nodded. "And your wife came to his aid."

"Yes, and I'm grateful for it. I happened to speak with him this afternoon. Most congenial young man."

"Oh?"

"We both like boating."

"Certainly fortunate that she did. And that a doctor was present who knew the remedy. And that the veterinary was still open."

"It was indeed," Mr. Jackson said. But something in the sergeant's tone disturbed him. "You aren't suggesting she had something to do with this?"

"You've been seen about quite a lot for a man on his honeymoon."

Mr. Jackson felt confused. "I don't understand."

Sergeant Nestor frowned, his tone sarcastic. "I knew your kind the moment I lay eyes upon you. You speak with a young, handsome waiter — thrice — then he falls, your wife the one to 'save' him. That's one way to win back your attentions."

Mr. Jackson felt dismayed. "You have the situation mistaken." A chair stood nearby, and he leaned upon it. "My wife is just days from having had surgery. The hotel surgeon instructed her to complete rest, but —" he took a breath to stop his voice from shaking, "my wife is, if nothing else, headstrong. Enforced idleness chafes at her." He felt then as if rambling, and collected himself. "Our relationship is none of your concern. But if you think she would harm someone out of petty jealousy, then you know nothing about her!"

Normally, he was a calm man, but at this, Mr. Jackson felt angry. "And do you really think I would betray a woman I **married**? I made **vows**, sir, ones I would not break even on pain of death. I came to offer help, but I will not stand by as my wife and I are slandered."

The sergeant gave him a soft smile. "I had to ask these things." He hesitated a second, then held out a hand. "I would be glad for your help."

Mr. Jackson hesitated, still feeling annoyed. But then he shook the man's hand. "Very well. What do you want?"

"What most here want. To find our murderer."

Mr. Jackson felt unsettled. "May we sit?"

"Of course."

He sat, heart pounding. Had he been so transparent? Worse yet, should he have stayed beside his wife, not left her up there alone? He'd thought collecting information would help her feel as if something were being done.

The sergeant let out a breath, "Don't berate yourself. You're in a difficult situation — I'm sure you've done your best." His tone turned businesslike. "I need you to focus on the matter at hand. I know you've spoken with the staff. What did you learn?"

"Learn?" He had actual proof of very little. "The staff are — naturally — disturbed by these events. There's talk of leaving for new employment." He didn't want to mention his suspicions of an underground speakeasy just yet, so he shrugged. "That's all."

Then he remembered. "I did hear something of interest. A dockworker — Eugene, I believe his name was — told me that the desk clerk who first died had tried a few days earlier to force himself upon the young lady who died next. This dockworker is also the rat-man. I don't know if it matters, but —"

The sergeant's face didn't change. "We'll speak with him."

"Do you know yet how the clerk died? After seeing what the waiter endured, it doesn't seem like strychnine to me."

"The coroner is still investigating," the sergeant said. "It may take days to learn the truth."

"Well, then," Mr. Jackson said. "How may I help? Do you wish us to investigate?"

"Absolutely not," the sergeant said. "Stay out of it. I'll let you know if I have any further questions."

"But my wife and I believe —"

Voices raised above the crowd from behind, and Mr. Jackson turned towards them. The beveled glass doors were open; two men walked in.

Sergeant Nestor went to meet them. Fine clothing both, yet one had stiff, dark hair, deep-set dark eyes, and an imperious manner. The other, who resembled the young waiter, although much older, looked worried, and after getting some information from the sergeant, hurried away.

That must be the father, Mr. Jackson thought.

The remaining man seemed to be lecturing the sergeant, who appeared to be giving as good as he got. When the doors opened yet again, the manager rushed over to the two with a cringing, subservient mien.

Mr. Jackson rose, walked over, and held out his hand. "You must be the owner of this establishment. Hector Jackson at your service, sir. A pleasure to finally —"

The man's jaw dropped. "However did you —"

"— meet you," Mr. Jackson continued, speaking over him.

The owner seemed flustered, yet shook hands. "And you, sir." He glanced around. "I take it you discovered the first body?"

"I did."

"Davis here has kept me informed."

Mr. Jackson felt relieved at him not mentioning the arrangement he had with the manager, at least not in front of the sergeant.

The owner turned to the sergeant. "This has gone on long enough. No more arguments. You know what to do."

12

The next morning, the front page of the paper read:

MURDER AT THE MYRIAD
Cook arrested for poison

Mrs. Jackson put down the paper, dismayed. "Surely the cook isn't to blame for this! That's much too simple an answer."

Mr. Jackson nodded. "The owner insisted they arrest someone."

"This is bad," she said. "Two murders — and one attempted — in four days? And by the look of it, missing the real target each time. I fear another death will come soon."

He nodded. "After our servants are through with us, shall we spend the day in the city? I don't fancy staying around the hotel today."

There came a knock at the door. Mr. Jackson rose. "They're here early, it seems!"

But it was the dowager Duchess come to call. Mrs. Jackson wasn't sure whether to be amused or annoyed that without so much as asking, the dowager pushed past Mr. Jackson and into the room.

Mrs. Jackson did, however, feel very glad that Mrs. Knight had found her a proper nightgown!

"I'm sorry to disturb you so early," the dowager said, glancing at them both. "But my Albert is in a state of agitation! I've called the doctor, who's with him now. In all my years, I've never seen him like this!"

"Come in, sit down." Mr. Jackson sat on the bed. "Whatever has distressed him so?"

The dowager Duchess said, "That's just it, he won't say. I think it was the unpleasantness last night. It's entirely unnerved him!" She looked to Mr. Jackson. "He learned last night of the young lady's death — Agnes, I believe it was. She used to run errands for us. He was very fond of her and of the young man who fell ill last night. Poor dear, he hasn't slept a wink. I thought for certain you might be able to help — he's quite taken with you."

"Why, certainly," Mr. Jackson said. "What room are you in?"

"Thirty-two twelve," she said, rising, "just down the hall and around."

Mr. Jackson stood, tightening the belt on his striped robe (courtesy of the hotel). "Well, then," he said, "let's see what this is about."

***

Mr. Jackson followed Duchess Cordelia down the hall and around the corner to Albert's rooms.

On the walls hung artifacts and souvenirs from around the world. Books sat on every surface possible. In the parlor, a small hand drill with a wooden handle sat upon a bookcase full of books on plants, along with a dark blue mortar and pestle. A row of three satiny gray buttons a bit larger than a nickel hung down a strip of red cloth the size of a bookmark pinned to the wall behind them.

On going into the bedroom, they found the old man weeping on the bed. But when he glanced up, he began to berate his wife. "How dare you bring him here!"

"But Bertie," she said, "you're so upset! I thought he might be able to help."

The doctor who'd seen Mrs. Jackson the day earlier stood by. "Merely overwrought — I've given him a sedative. He should feel better once he wakes."

"Thank you, doctor," the dowager said. She turned to her husband. "Don't be angry, dear — we're just concerned for you."

"I don't want your help. The situation is catastrophic! Intolerable!" He put his face in his hands. "Ohhh," he moaned. "Why has Fate cursed us so?"

"Well, if you do need anything, sir," Mr. Jackson said, "I'll be right around the corner for the next hour. But we planned to go sightseeing. Should we delay?"

Albert's face took on a sudden chagrin. "No, you go. I'm sorry for being such a bother."

"Not at all, sir," Mr. Jackson said. "I hope you feel better." He turned to the dowager. "Poor fellow. Overwrought indeed. I'd stay with him if I were you."

"As I intended. Where did you plan to go today?"

"We might visit the young man in the hospital. But after that, I thought to take my wife to the Main Library. She does so love books."

"Splendid! Well, you just have a marvelous time."

***

The couple went out for breakfast at a little pastry shop nearby, and Mrs. Jackson treated herself to a jelly donut with whipped cream.

"You know," Mr. Jackson said, "when we do visit the specialist surgeon, we must send mail."

"Of course." That would be the perfect opportunity. Anyone investigating where the mail came from would have a jolly time searching in the wrong city. That thought made her smile.

"Where would you like to go afterward? You'll need somewhere quiet to recuperate. I have a lovely little property in Tuscany."

She gasped at the idea of traveling overseas. It was what she'd always dreamed of. "That sounds wonderful!"

Mr. Jackson gave her a fond smile. "I'm so glad you think so."

A man wearing a brown work uniform walked in, going to the counter. The woman behind the counter lit up when she saw him.

Mr. Jackson turned behind to follow her gaze, and smiled at them.

"Someone you know?"

"A man I met at the docks."

The man and woman stood flirting for a few minutes, then the woman handed over a bag. He paid and left without noticing them at all.

The woman came over to their table. Her name-tag read: Helen. "Did you need something?"

Mr. Jackson smiled up at her. "Just saw someone I know, that's all."

Her eyes grew wide. "You know Eugene?"

"Just met the once," he said. "We're staying at the hotel."

"How wonderful! Then I suppose you know the dowager Duchess. She knows everyone."

Mrs. Jackson felt surprised at this. "You know Duchess Cordelia?"

She giggled. "Of course. Me and Eugene play dominoes with her and Mr. Stayman in the evenings sometimes."

Mrs. Jackson said, "I don't believe I've ever played that!"

"Well, next time you'll have to join us," Helen said.

"We wouldn't want to impose," Mrs. Jackson said.

"No! Not at all," Helen said. "Whoever wants to come is welcome. The maids come play with us too from time to time." She smiled at Mrs. Jackson warmly. "We'd love to have you."

Mr. Jackson said, "How are you and Eugene acquainted?"

"We're to be married," she said, showing a cute little engagement ring.

Mrs. Jackson took Helen's hand, admiring the ring. "It's lovely! Congratulations."

The woman beamed. "Thank you."

Mrs. Jackson said, "What does your fiancé do there?"

"Maintenance," she said. "Clearing drains, mostly. They're giving him the dirty work still, but he hopes to move up soon."

"That sounds good," Mr. Jackson said. "Does he like it there?"

Helen shrugged. "All but the manager. Constantly in everyone's business. 'Just let me do my job,' Gene says, about every time he comes home."

Mrs. Jackson felt surprised. "Really."

"Yes!" Helen dropped her voice to a whisper, leaning over to speak privately. "Everyone hates the man. Wouldn't surprise me at all if the next bit of poison went to him!"

13

After the couple ate, Mr. Jackson flagged down a taxi to take them to the hospital. There they found the young waiter abed, his parents beside him.

When George saw them, he smiled, reaching his hand out. "Here they are! My benefactors."

His parents stood, turning to the couple. Going past them, Mr. Jackson took the young man's hand and shook it. "I hope you're improved."

Their eyes met, and to Mr. Jackson's surprise, George's cheeks reddened. "Much."

"We're much obliged to you, sir," George's father said. "The hotel doctor told us your quick thinking saved him."

"It was entirely my wife," Mr. Jackson said, looking into George's eyes. "I must admit the suddenness of his malady took me so aback, I hardly knew what to do."

The older man turned to Mrs. Jackson then, taking her hand in both of his. "Then I am forever in your debt. He's my only son." He stopped for a moment, head turned away.

Mrs. Jackson smiled at him. "You're most welcome."

There were other chairs in the room, on the other side of the bed, so Mr. Jackson said, "May we join you?"

"We insist."

The couple sat then, Mr. Jackson towards the head of the bed. "What happened? It was all so sudden."

"It was," George said. "I broke a lace, so I'd gone in to take a break. There was a long row of room service trays to go up, and the kitchen girls were busy putting lemon-cakes on them. I sat down off to the side to thread a new lace in. I couldn't see the trays from where I sat, but all the girls went past me to get back to their work. I got done threading my lace, and I got up to go. The trays to go out were still there. Right then, Miss Goldie Jean went down the row and said one of the cakes had a bubble — did I want it? She was a-swapping it out and other than the bubble, it looked fine. Well, of course I said yes!" At that, he faltered. "Is it true? Did she poison me? I've never done her a wrong, ever."

"I don't believe so," Mrs. Jackson said.

The older man's face darkened. "Young lady, why don't we let the courts determine such things? She gave him the cake, and now he lies here."

Before she might speak, Mr. Jackson put his hand upon hers. "My wife means no disrespect, sir." He clasped her hand and rose. "We'll let your son rest now."

Once they were outside, Mrs. Jackson said, "I hope I'm wrong."

"I do too," Mr. Jackson said. "But I don't think you are."

Mr. Jackson took his wife to the pharmacy there at the hospital to fill her prescription. The pharmacist puzzled over the paper Mrs. Jackson presented him. "Too much of a dose to fit into a pill."

"Oh, I just take it with water," his wife said.

The pharmacist, an attractive older man with brown hair, grimaced. "This must be so bitter!"

"It is," Mrs. Jackson said. "But it's always been. Is that unusual?"

The man blinked in confusion. "No, I suppose not." He peered at the script. "It's essence of tea! Among other things, of course." He mumbled as he went down the list. "And you're to steep this how long? My word! The tannic acid alone would pucker you for sure." He chuckled. "Well, if this is what you're prescribed —" He glanced up at her. "And you feel well?"

"Entirely, other than this," she said, holding up her arm. "And the surgeon just checked me yesterday."

The pharmacist chuckled. "I presume you're supplied with medication for that."

"Oh, yes," she said. "I have plenty."

"Very well. Have a seat, and I'll get this for you."

As they waited, Mr. Jackson felt sure his wife was right. "Not only is the cook innocent, but more deaths are sure to follow."

117

Mrs. Jackson said, "The poor woman! Slandered, led off in chains to sit in some cell. How will she ever find employment again?"

"We'll help her, my dear," Mr. Jackson said. "If we can prove she didn't do this, they'll have to reinstate her."

"Unless they plan to make her an example." Mrs. Jackson sounded bitter. "It's unjust."

Mr. Jackson put his hand on hers. "It is. But let's put that aside for now and try to enjoy the day."

"I'll try. But we must prove her innocent," his wife said. "I won't be able to rest until we do."

After some time, they were presented with a paper sack full of smaller sacks, along with an instruction page. Then they took a taxi to the Main Library.

His wife seemed enthralled with the sheer number of books in the building, and for a long moment stood staring in joyful astonishment. The look on her face held Mr. Jackson's gaze so that for a while he forgot all else.

Then she met his eye and gave him a real smile, the first since they'd come here. "Let's look around."

They passed row upon row of novels, then factual books on every subject imaginable. They came to the books on plants. There were so many!

His wife stood peering over them. "This is what you wanted, is it not?"

"It was," he said, "but we may look at any you wish. We have no schedule to keep."

A red-haired man stood behind a cluttered counter perhaps ten yards off. A sign hung from the counter's front, labeled "Natural History."

Mrs. Jackson approached the man. Curious, Mr. Jackson followed.

"Thank you," his wife said as he approached. Then she turned to him. "I'll return shortly."

The librarian said, "Your wife?"

Mr. Jackson watched her as she went. "Indeed."

"Lovely lady, I may say."

Mr. Jackson chuckled. "Thanks."

The man poured himself coffee. The cup still had sugar in the bottom, yet he put in more.

"You must like sugar," Mr. Jackson said.

The librarian grinned. "I guess I do."

Then Mr. Jackson recalled what he came here for. "Do you have any books on the snake-wood tree?"

"Let me look." He went to an array of small drawers behind him and pulled one out. Inside were dozens of cards, which he began to page through. "We do have one, but it's been checked out. But we have more general ones on trees which may be helpful." He took the card out of the drawer. "This way."

Mr. Jackson followed the man down a row of books. The man stopped, peered at the numbers on the spines, squatted to retrieve a thick one on the second shelf from the bottom. He presented the book, which read "Trees of the World."

119

"Thank you, sir," Mr. Jackson said.

"Put it on any of the carts when you're done." The man returned to his desk, putting another spoonful of sugar into his cup before drinking his coffee.

Mr. Jackson found a table in view of the desk and sat to read.

"There you are."

Mr. Jackson looked up as his wife set a volume on the table across from him. Glancing at the book, he exclaimed, "I didn't know you'd read Emerson. I once knew a man who was a great admirer." The memory left him melancholy, so he focused again upon his page. "Did you know there are three trees at least called snake-wood? But one of them is where strychnine comes from."

Shock crossed his wife's face. "Really?"

"The seeds, apparently." He picked up another book he'd found called "Poisons from Plants," which unfortunately had no drawings or descriptions of the tree itself. "And they're devilishly hard seeds — very difficult to get the poison from." He considered the matter. "But that little thing planted in the hotel conservatory won't make seeds for twenty years, if what Albert Stayman says is true."

"Albert Stayman?"

"The husband of the dowager Duchess."

"Oh, yes," Mrs. Jackson said. "Now I remember. Does your book say anything else?"

Mr. Jackson shook his head. "Just a few lines. The book about the poisonous tree has been checked out." He sighed. "I suppose we'll have to wait until it's returned."

"That's quite a coincidence, isn't it?"

"That Mr. Stayman planted a snake-wood tree?" Mr. Jackson shrugged. "I'm not even sure the tree at the hotel is the poisonous kind." He thought about poisons for a moment. "But you can get strychnine at any grocery in the city. Sounds as if it'd be quicker just to go to the store and buy rat poison." He got up, went to the desk. "When will the book I wanted be returned?"

The man checked the file again. "Next week."

"Thanks, I'll come back then."

"Or I can get your number and call when it's here."

"Splendid!" Mr. Jackson gave him the number for the hotel. "Thanks ever so much."

His wife checked out the book she'd picked up and the couple went out to lunch. Afterward, they returned to the hotel for her pain medicine.

"I'll just take a drop," she said. "That way I won't sleep the rest of the day away."

A knock at the door, and Mr. Jackson went to answer it. A busboy stood there. "Good day, sir. The Myriad Hotel's owner, Mr. Montgomery Carlo, requests you and your wife dine with him at his residence this evening. A car will come for you at eight."

"Excellent! Please tell him we accept. Oh, and send up luncheon, if you will."

"Anything particular?"

"Whatever's good."

The busboy shrugged. "Hard to say, sir, now Cook's gone. They got a new lady in charge. I don't think she's nearly as good, but I'll do my best."

"Good man." Mr. Jackson gave him a tip and sent him on his way.

His wife fell asleep briefly, but woke when the food arrived a half hour later. The busboy was right: the food was merely adequate.

"I fear this hotel's reputation will suffer if they don't replace their cook with someone of equal caliber," Mr. Jackson said.

Mrs. Jackson snorted. "I wouldn't come back if they paid me, after having my name plastered in the papers so rudely."

"I hope for the Hotel's sake Miss Goldie Jean Dab has a more forgiving nature. Once we clear her name, that is."

"We must, if we're to stay here." She put down her fork. "I don't know if I want to stay somewhere with a poisoner in it for very long."

Mr. Jackson shook his head. "This feels too personal. I don't think we're in any danger. If it makes you feel better, I'll taste every dish before you eat it!"

She laughed at that. Then her face sobered. "I must sound like some anxious old woman."

"Surely not. You've had a difficult time." He pondered this a moment; when he glanced next at her, her eyes were red. He spoke gently, wondering what had upset her so. "But you're correct: we must find this killer, or we can't stay here for long." At that, he recalled George's reaction at the hospital, the way he'd suffered, and he leaned across the table to take her hand. "You wish to clear the cook's name, and to find whoever killed that young woman. I very much wish to stay here, and to find that poisoner for my own reasons. Shall we put aside our doubts and suspicions of the past and work together?"

14

His wife's eyes filled with tears, and she squeezed his hand tightly. "I'm sorry for how I've doubted you, so wrongly, over the years."

A pang of remorse. "Much of the fault was mine." He leaned over to kiss her hand. "I'm truly sorry for my part in it."

She rested her forehead on their hands, still joined. "How I wish I would have just spoken with you. So much hurt could have been avoided."

He smiled at her black curls, kissed them. "Don't berate yourself for the past. It's gone now."

She raised her head, dampness on her cheeks. "To answer your question: I can only promise to try."

Feeling a new energy, Mr. Jackson sat back. "There we have it!" He chuckled at the irony of the situation. "Now all we need to do is form some idea of how we might solve this."

"The killer is among us," Mrs. Jackson said, face pensive. "Right here, still, in the hotel. She holds such anger!"

"Yes," Mr. Jackson said, "and about something which likely happened long ago." He considered this. "Could the poisoner wish to frame the cook for some past slight?"

His wife shook her head. "For what, I have no idea." She let out a short laugh. "From your theory, we must know why first. But I disagree. We may never know why this woman does this, if it is indeed a woman at all. Knowing the facts of the matter will bring you to the answer."

He found this amusing. "Very well, Madam Investigator. What are the facts?"

His wife peered at him sideways. Then she chuckled. "I did sound rather imperious there." She began to tick off points on the fingers of her left hand. "There appear to be two kinds of death here. First is the young man, whose cause of death is still unknown. The second is two poisonings by strychnine." She paused, frowning. "Two murderers?"

"If the first was indeed murder."

"Yes," she said. "We still don't know if the deaths were related." She rubbed her left temple. "There's so much we don't yet know."

"There are still areas of the hotel yet unexplored, people yet to speak with." He considered this. "Every evening after tea, men gather in the barbershop downstairs. Perhaps one of them has seen something which may help."

Mrs. Jackson nodded. "The second point: so far as we know, all the poisonings have targeted the staff."

"And whoever should have gotten the lemon-cake with the bubble. Remember what George said? The cook noticed the bubble and switched the cakes."

His wife's eyes went wide. "I'd forgotten! Was there anyone of note in the list of room service calls that night?"

A shock ran through him. "The owner," Mr. Jackson said. "He was here last night, in his room. Remember? We were supposed to meet with him after dinner."

Mrs. Jackson's eyes narrowed. "You suspected earlier that these poisonings were meant to discredit the hotel. What if this person actually targets the owner?"

"You mean that —"

"When the deaths didn't get the attention the poisoner wished, they decided to poison the owner directly."

Mr. Jackson leaned back. "Surely she didn't believe a few days' scandal would be sufficient to ruin a hotel of such magnificence? If so, this woman has clearly not thought the matter through."

His wife nodded. "A third point, then: the woman in question holds a quick and impulsive nature."

"But to plan this out, then change their tactics so suddenly?"

"Perhaps the poisoner doubted themselves." She paused, her eyes far away. "It's easy to plan someone's death. The reality is often very different."

Mr. Jackson shuddered, remembering a scene of his own in which this was true. The memory left him feeling vaguely ill. "The swarm of police may have shaken the poisoner's resolve as well."

"Yes. To come so close to success ... then to see the police?" She shook her head. "It would take a will of steel to stand firm when your ultimate goal is endangered. It seems our killer is not such a person."

Mr. Jackson considered this for a moment and came up with exactly nothing. "I still have no idea what to do to find this woman. We need more information."

***

Mrs. Jackson put her sling on. "I shall go mad cooped up here much longer." The luncheon dishes lay upon their table waiting for the maids to return.

"Let's go for a stroll," Mr. Jackson said. Then he chuckled. "We shall have no madness here!"

She thought this quite amusing.

They left with the door sign turned to "Please clean room now" and descended to the lobby. As always, people bustled about in groups, gazed at the fine chandelier and the lovely fountain, chatted with friends.

The couple strolled through the vast lobby towards the front doors.

A middle-aged uniformed man at the valet stand turned his head towards them, frowning as he gazed downward.

A doorman opened the way for them, then also glanced down, moving his foot out. "Keep out, you!"

Mrs. Jackson looked down as well. A pair of liquid brown eyes encased in a mat of charcoal fur gazed hopefully up at her, its tail wagging a similar mat like a small flag. "What's this?"

"Just a stray, ma'am," the doorman said. "Been hanging about the past day or two."

Mrs. Jackson moved out of the doorway and knelt before the dog, whose feet and tail never stopped moving in its excitement. "Look how sweet its nature. This is someone's pet."

The dog hadn't stopped bounding up and down on its little legs, licking her hands, her face. She felt a collar under the thick mat. Twigs and leaves lay buried in the dog's fur.

People continued to pass in and out of the front doors, casting curious glances at her and the dog as they went.

Mr. Jackson knelt beside them. "They have a groomer here. Perhaps we —"

The man at the valet booth came over, frowning, and said to the doorman, "Is there a problem?"

To Mrs. Jackson's surprise, Mr. Jackson picked up the dog and rose. "Not at all." He grinned at her. "Let's see what's under all this nonsense, shall we?"

The groomer looked just as surprised when they brought the dog to him. "Looks like a sausage with legs!"

But after some dog food, a bowl of water, and an hour of clipping and coaxing, a rather thin toy poodle emerged. There was a ragged collar, sure enough, but any name-tag was long gone. Her skin was raw in spots, and the groomer gave them a salve to use for the next few days.

Mrs. Jackson looked into the little dog's eyes. "Where are your people?" She turned to Mr. Jackson and the groomer, "Someone is missing her dearly. How would we find her owner?"

The groomer shrugged. "She must have been on her own for a while, for all this to have grown and matted so. Maybe as long as a month."

Mr. Jackson said, "Do you have leashes for sale?"

"Why, yes," the groomer said. "There's a display case on the way in."

Moving out to the front area, they selected a fine black leather leash and a collar to match. Mr. Jackson said, "Would you bill our room?"

"Certainly, sir." The groomer handed over a slip of paper, which Mr. Jackson signed. "And if you need someone to walk her, just return here, or call down. My sons are available day and night, and we book appointments by the hour."

"Excellent!" Mr. Jackson put the dog down and handed her the leash. "Now, let's see where this little one takes us."

Freed from the constraints of matted fur, the little dog leaped and bounded back and forth, yet once out of the lobby, went right, then kept moving in a direct line.

"Go home," Mrs. Jackson said firmly. "Take us to your people."

The little dog began to pull on her leash with a purpose, and the couple followed several blocks before the dog pulled them to the right, across the busy street and down a tree-lined row of houses. A uniformed policeman stood outside one house, and the dog rushed up the steps towards him.

"Whoa," the policeman said to the trio. "You can't come in here. This is a crime scene."

Just then, Sergeant Nestor emerged, and which of them were the most surprised would be difficult to say.

The sergeant said, "Why are you here?"

Mrs. Jackson felt amused. "The dog brought us."

The sergeant's mouth dropped open, then he followed Mrs. Jackson's pointing hand to the dog and focused upon it for a good second. He put his hand to his forehead. "How did you find it?"

So they told the story of how the dog — more or less — found them. "We asked it to go home," Mr. Jackson said, "and here we are, it seems."

The dog pulled on its leash towards the open doorway. Mrs. Jackson, feeling compassion for the poor thing, picked it up. "Hush, there, little one." She felt sure the story the sergeant had to tell was an unhappy one. "We're here now."

Whether the dog understood Mrs. Jackson's words or not, it settled and became quiet.

The sergeant escorted them to the street. "The old lady was found dead inside. A few weeks is my guess. We saw the empty bowls yet no one knew where the dog went."

Mrs. Jackson felt shocked. "And the woman was just found now?"

"Last night," Sergeant Nestor said, wrinkling his nose. Then he focused on the dog. "You found it like this?"

Mr. Jackson said, "The poor thing was hungry, encased in a mat of fur." He shook his head in distaste. "Had been nosing about the front of the hotel a day or two, perhaps looking for food, I don't know."

Mrs. Jackson said, "The poor little dear." Feeling a surge of compassion, she kissed the little dog's forehead. "So now what?"

The sergeant shrugged. "If you don't want the dog, we can —"

"I want it," Mrs. Jackson said. She glanced over at Mr. Jackson, who had a bemused smile on his lips. But he nodded, so she said, "We want it."

The sergeant chuckled. "I thought you might. Very well. If we need to ask anything —"

"You know where to find us," Mr. Jackson said. He tipped his fedora. "Good day, sergeant."

They returned to the hotel. Standing out on the sidewalk, Mrs. Jackson took the small dog in her hands, peering into its eyes. "This is home now." At that, she felt amused. "At least for now." She set the dog down; it went to the gutter to relieve itself.

Mrs. Jackson felt impressed. "You have good manners, at any rate."

Mr. Jackson stood watching. "What shall we call her?"

This brought back a fond memory: a small child on a large farm with a black cow. "Let's call her Bessie."

As she knew he would, Mr. Jackson laughed. "Bessie it is then!"

"Come on, Bessie," Mrs. Jackson said, and the little dog barked. "Let's show you your new home."

15

Bessie had great interest in sniffing every corner of the elevator, the hall, and most especially, their rooms.

"I hope the servants won't be too put out with her here," Mrs. Jackson said.

Mr. Jackson shrugged. "It's none of their affair. We'll keep her in the bathroom overnight, though, until we learn each others' ways."

Mrs. Jackson thought that a good plan. "We'll need food and water bowls. And a little bed."

Mr. Jackson chuckled. "I never knew you fancied animals so."

She'd never considered the matter before. "I suppose I do. I've always had animals of one kind or another." Looking at Bessie, she patted her knee. Bessie leaped onto her lap to snuggle there. For an instant, she was reminded of her little son, gone forever, and grief washed over her. "How cruel the world can be!"

"Yes," Mr. Jackson said, "but think of what might have happened had we come down a few moments later, and not been there to take her in."

At that, Mrs. Jackson hugged the little dog, grateful. Bessie was no replacement for the husband and son she'd lost forever, but with a dog's pure love, she was there.

***

The couple took tea in their rooms, just to let Bessie get used to them and her new surroundings.

They had some discussion about whether to bring Bessie with them to Mr. Carlo's home for dinner. Since Bessie had not been invited, they decided to leave her with the groomer's sons. The boys — ranging from ten to sixteen — instantly took to the little dog, with much fun being had on all sides.

The car which picked Mr. and Mrs. Jackson up from the hotel was a marvel: expensive, with fine leather seats and gleaming brass fixtures. The driver, a middle-aged man with an impressive mustache, wore a black uniform with brass buttons, much as the door-men did.

Mrs. Jackson felt excited to finally meet the owner, yet had some trepidation. Why would this important man wish to meet them? She leaned over to speak in Mr. Jackson's ear. "What can you tell me about this man?"

Mr. Jackson shrugged. "Our meeting was quite brief. Perhaps I ought not cloud your perceptions with my own as yet."

Mrs. Jackson sighed, then nodded. She really wished to have some secure knowledge of what they walked into, yet his idea had merit. She settled in to view the scenery.

It appeared that Mr. Carlo lived in the countryside. The buildings and shops grew shorter, farther apart, and homes appeared. Trees lined the streets, and the lights came on. Finally, the car passed beside a tall fence of wrought iron to the right, and a grand mansion came into view, lit from above and below. They turned right. Men stood guard beside large gates, which opened, and the car drove down the fifty-yard drive past wide fields. Sheep grazed in the half-darkness.

White columns framed a wide overhang. The auto entered a circle and drove round to stop at the front door, which was painted red.

Men opened the doors for the couple, then escorted them up the steps and inside.

The owner, a stern-appearing man of middle age, came forward to greet them. A brown-haired woman — perhaps half his age — came up beside them.

Mrs. Jackson expected this to be his daughter, yet she was introduced as his wife Maisy.

"A pleasure to meet you both," Mr. Jackson said.

The brown-haired woman who'd sat next to Mrs. Jackson at breakfast at the hotel that first time was also there: Mr. Carlo's daughter Margaret. All around came the refrain: "What a surprise to see you!"

The dinner was excellent: a salad with walnuts and apples, roasted pheasant, creamed potatoes with rosemary, with a sweet rice pudding and biscotti.

After dinner, the group moved to the parlor. Mr. Carlo and his family drank as if it were not forbidden to them by law, which amused Mrs. Jackson no end. Finally, the younger couple took their leave for bed. "We have an early start tomorrow."

Mr. and Mrs. Jackson also rose.

"Oh, don't leave on our account," Margaret said. "Visit with my parents as long as you like."

"Please stay," said Maisy, and her husband agreed, so they did.

Mrs. Jackson still wasn't sure why they'd been invited. "To what do we owe the honor of your invitation?"

Maisy Carlo smiled. "We've so wanted to meet you, but especially after you rescued George."

Mrs. Jackson felt perplexed.

"The waiter you saved from the poison," Mr. Carlo said. "My wife's cousin."

"Ah," Mr. Jackson said. "A fine young man."

"He is," Mr. Carlo said. "I admire his desire to make his own way, rather than live idly on his family's money." The man nodded. "Good spirit, that."

"Thank you so much for visiting him," Maisy said. "We all appreciate your kindness." She seemed sweet and gentle enough, but a glint of steel lay in her eyes.

"Truly we mean to have this poisoner pay for her outrage."

"This is something I meant to speak about, if it wouldn't offend," Mr. Jackson said.

Mr. Carlo leaned back, and became very still, his gaze hooded. "The sergeant told me of your assessment."

Maisy looked back and forth between them. "What?"

Mr. Carlo said, "It's nothing, my dear."

"Mrs. Carlo," Mrs. Jackson said, "we believe the cook to be innocent of these crimes."

Maisy Carlo turned to her husband. "Monty, what's going on?"

Mr. Carlo didn't look happy. "Madam, I'd rather you hadn't told her that."

"Why? She's a grown woman. She deserves the truth. I said as much to your cousin's father, and he dismissed it out of hand. But I tell you," she pointed at Mr. Carlo, "there's sure to be more murders. And I believe whoever it is targets you."

The man raised an eyebrow. "Me? Whatever for?"

"I have no idea," Mr. Jackson said. "But last night's poisoned lemon-cake may have been meant for you."

Maisy Carlo gasped. "Well, then, you must find this killer!"

Mr. Jackson's shoulders slumped. "The police have forbidden us to do any real investigation. I've spoken with some of the staff, at your manager's request, but —"

"Continue to do so," Mr. Carlo said. He stood, went to a set of cabinets, where he took a pad and wrote upon it. He folded the paper in half and handed it to Mr. Jackson. "Call me if you need anything."

It seemed then — just like that — the visit was over.

***

The couple had never used their parlor as yet, but it had the largest table. Once they returned to their suite, Mr. Jackson went to walk Bessie. On his return, he found that his wife had collected stationery, note pads, and fountain pens from every room. Lists were placed at intervals along the table, with the pens standing in a water glass in the center.

Dismayed, Mr. Jackson watched her write another list. "Doesn't all that writing hurt your arm?"

She shrugged. "If it gets too painful, I'll take my medication and go to bed."

"But the doctor said you needed rest."

She set the pen down. "I fail to see how that's your concern."

"All I care about is your welfare." Mr. Jackson said. "What if you re-injured it? For all you know, you may be prolonging the process."

She gave him a piercing glance, full of doubt, hope.

She still doesn't trust me.

"This is what we know about the first death," she muttered. Her black and brass pen flashed reflections from the lamp as the pad jostled it. "He lay facing

138

towards us, cup in hand. Yet the cup had not one drop in it."

Across the room, Mr. Jackson leaned back in his overstuffed chair, seeing nothing but his own remorse at how he'd hurt her. "Perhaps he'd just washed it, and liked to keep it at his post." He pictured the scene. "Perhaps he sensed he was dying, and tried to get help, without even time to lay the cup aside."

His wife's eyes turned red, and he instantly regretted speaking. "Forgive me."

She let out a soft snort, smiling to herself. "For inspiring me to compassion?" She sat staring at the table.

He didn't know how to reply. She'd said nothing of what happened the night before they wed. He knew the outcome, of course, but not how or why. Until now, he'd thought it best to let her speak of it when she was ready.

"For all my life, I've been a hard woman. Focused, driven. And everyone around me has paid for my pursuit." She raised her eyes to his. "It's likely that more compassion is what I need."

He leaned forward, feeling uneasy. "First have compassion on yourself! What's likely is that the police will find this killer, or if not, perhaps I will. In any case, you're allowed to rest, to enjoy safety. To let yourself heal." He let out a bitter laugh. "You don't need to save everyone."

Her gaze dropped. "I remember telling my husband that once." She shook her head, her eyes reddening once more.

He moved to sit on her left side. "I know I can never replace him. Or your son." He felt lost. "I don't even know where to start."

"You don't have to." She grasped his hand tightly. "Don't give up on me."

A laugh burst from him. "All I ask is the same." He enveloped her in an embrace, kissed her hair. "How did we — of all people — end up here?"

Her arm moved warm around his waist, and when she spoke, he heard the smile. "You know as much as anyone."

16

After his wife left for her bed, Mr. Jackson lay upon his, feeling drained yet unable to sleep. How was he to find this murderess?

It seemed all he could do to protect his wife and keep her from harm.

He'd told the sergeant he'd been a private investigator, but amateur was too strong a word for it.

I don't know what I'm doing.

He didn't know what he was doing, in either this investigation or this marriage. Yet in the past he'd always had friends, family to rely on. To ask for advice and help.

Albert Stayman and the dowager Duchess seemed happy in their marriage. While they'd be no help with investigating a murder, perhaps they might be able to give advice on other matters.

***

Early the next morning, Mr. Jackson left his wife sleeping, a note on the table as to where he'd gone, and went to the gardens.

He found Albert Stayman slowly sweeping the stone walkway beside the pond.

"My gracious me!" Albert seemed astonished. "How grand to see you here!"

"I did say I might visit," Mr. Jackson said. "And I thought you might be here now. I'm glad you're feeling improved."

The old man gazed over the water. "My favorite time of day."

He followed Albert's gaze. Toads croaked, small birds chirped, and the water gurgled along. "It's quite peaceful."

Albert smiled to himself, scooping up his pile of leaves, which he deposited off of the path with trembling hands. "First spat?"

"What? No, I mean, not the first. But how did you know?"

"Cordelia saw your lights on late when she got in. Couple on their honeymoon wouldn't have reason for lights that late unless they were set to discussion." He winked. "Then here you are." He rubbed the back of his neck. "Only been married the once, and not yet four years at that." He shrugged. "But I'm glad you came by."

What could he say which wouldn't reveal too much? "Well, my wife's a widow, and —"

Albert nodded. "I see." He let out a breath. "I remember how Cordelia cried, after he passed. About broke my heart." He bit his upper lip, nose reddening.

"It's a difficult matter, coming after a marriage, even when she loves you. As she said it, nothing's the same. For a while it seems she'll never be happy again. And you love her, so you'll do anything to make it right. But you don't know what, or how."

Mr. Jackson felt unsure right then which of them Albert referred to.

Albert glanced up and sniffled. He got out his handkerchief. "I'll have Cordelia talk to your wife, see what she can do."

"I'd be much obliged, sir."

Albert laughed. "Don't 'sir' me. Makes me sound old and much more important than I am. Please, call me Albert."

"All right, Albert. And I'm —" It'd been years since he'd said it, but all of a sudden he came too close to giving his real name. "Hector."

Albert gave him an amused smile. "Pleasure's all mine. Come on, let's find some flowers for our young ladies."

***

Mrs. Jackson woke at a knock on the door. She struggled into a robe and answered it: Mrs. Knight stood there.

The lady's maid bustled in. "Good morning to you! Did you sleep well?"

"I did. What time is it?"

"Nine, ma'am."

"Oh! Well," at this, she laughed at herself. "I suppose we best get started."

Her arm ached from her writing exertions the night prior, and as she soaked in the hot water, she considered what Mr. Jackson had said. *You don't need to save everyone.*

"It's twenty to ten," Mrs. Knight said.

She felt amused by this. "Up I go then." She rose, took the towel the maid held up for her. On the side of the maid's right thumb lay a pale patch of skin, which reminded Mrs. Jackson of the young dead man's face. "What's happened there?"

The maid let out a short laugh. "My daughter's got this new cream for clearing the skin. Asked me to put it on her. I used gloves, but it must have soaked through there."

"My word," Mrs. Jackson said. "What sort of cream is it?"

"For blemishes," the maid said. "I might have it in my purse here." She left for the other room, returning with a small metal tube, which read, "Doctor Smith's Facial Brightening Cream." She handed it to Mrs. Jackson, saying, "My daughter says it's all the rage these days. You know how kids are. They constantly say, 'All the young people are doing it,' as if that means it's safe. I didn't want her to use it until I'd investigated, but apparently it's true. Makes your skin ghastly pale for a day, then it peels, and your skin is ever so much clearer."

She chuckled. "Only problem is you look ghastly pale for a day, then your face peels. Most people take a few days off work."

Mrs. Jackson turned it over, where it read, "Contains Phenol". She let out a laugh. "So that's what I smelled!"

"Smelled, ma'am?"

She recalled a sick room, long ago. "Oh, nothing. Just talking to myself." She felt happy to have solved this particular mystery!

***

Mr. Jackson hurried upstairs to ready himself for the day, a bouquet of azalea blossoms in hand. His valet stood waiting. As he was being dressed, Mr. Vienna said, "There's not time to shave you before breakfast, sir. I have another appointment across town at half past ten."

He shrugged. "No matter. One day shouldn't make a difference."

Mr. Vienna helped him into his jacket. "Sir, I did want to speak with you briefly on a private matter."

Mr. Jackson felt surprised. "How may I help?"

Mr. Vienna seemed hesitant. "Well, sir, I've asked my sweetheart to marry me."

"Congratulations! Will you need time off so soon?"

Relief passed over the man's face. "It's just — I mean — I thought you might be angry, sir."

Mr. Jackson chuckled to himself. "Not at all. You're a fine young man, and I wish you the best."

"Thank you, sir."

"What will you do once you're married?"

"Oh, I'll continue with the agency."

"Splendid! We should be here at least a week longer, I'd think, then we might take a trip abroad. But when we return, I'll ask for you."

A soft knock. Mr. Vienna extended his hand with a real smile. "Thank you very much, sir." He went to the parlor door, opened it.

Mrs. Jackson stood there. "Sorry to intrude."

"No, not at all," Mr. Jackson said. He took up the bouquet. "For you."

"How lovely!" His wife rushed out with the flowers.

"I'll be leaving now, sir," Mr. Vienna said.

"And I'll see you this evening?"

"Of course, sir."

Mr. Jackson went into the parlor, where the flowers stood, his wife having pressed a water carafe into use as a vase. "Where would you like to have breakfast today?"

"Let's go down to the dining room," his wife said. "Perhaps this new cook is better at breakfast than luncheon."

So the couple went down to eat. The dining room was only half as full as it had been the first day they arrived, and very few new faces lay among those there. As Mr. Jackson sat with his wife to wait for their meals, he considered of the conversation he'd just had with his valet. How long had the young man worried over what he might say? Did he fear being given a bad report, or even fired?

How difficult the life of a servant must be, he thought.

But Mr. Jackson felt quite pleased when his wife gave him the news about the facial cream. "So that's why the man's face was so pale. How extraordinary! But how appalling! Your face **peels**? And people actually **use** this?"

"They do. Apparently it's quite well known."

He shook his head. "What people will do for appearances."

She let out an ironic laugh, and he grinned at her.

The stout little maid, Maria, who'd found the first man's body when they arrived, came to the table. "Care for something to drink?"

"Just water, thanks," Mrs. Jackson said.

"Coffee with heavy cream, no sugar," said Mr. Jackson.

"Right away," Maria said, disappearing into the crowd.

Just then, the doors opened and the clerk he'd met earlier came in. "A message for you, sir," he said, handing over a slip of paper.

Mr. Jackson took the slip from him, got out a tip. "Mr. Francis, is it not?"

The man beamed. "It is, sir, thank you."

"Give my regards to your wife."

"Yes, sir. I will, sir." The man hurried off.

Mr. Jackson unfolded the note: the librarian reported that the book had been returned early, and could be picked up at his convenience. "Wonderful!"

Mrs. Jackson said, "A new clue to report?"

"Not particularly." He handed over the slip for her to read. "But it just occurred to me that the back entry to the kitchens has no door."

"Is that so?"

"Indeed. Anyone could simply walk in." He considered this for a moment. "In fact, they wouldn't even have to enter the building through the front door. The exit to the dock lies not ten yards away."

"That's disturbing. I wonder if the good sergeant has put a guard there."

"Hmm," Mr. Jackson said. "It's likely he did. But I'll take a look later on."

"Good thinking. No need to stir that hornet's Nest-or —"

At that, he laughed.

"- unless need be."

"You are incorrigible," he said, quite amused at the comparison.

The dowager Duchess and her husband came to the table. "It's so good to see you smiling," Cordelia said.

Mr. Jackson stood. "Please join us!"

Mrs. Jackson said, "Why smiling?"

Cordelia sat beside her. "My dear, dear girl. Your Mr. Jackson told my Albert about your predicament —"

Mrs. Jackson turned to Mr. Jackson, face alarmed.

"Now, now," the dowager said. She lowered her voice. "He merely told him you'd been widowed. As I was widowed myself, I completely sympathize."

From the set of her jaw, Mr. Jackson felt certain his wife would have words with him later on. "It's true," she said. "But —"

The dowager patted Mrs. Jackson's hand. "Nothing more need be said." Her tone turned bright. "After breakfast, would you like to sit with me here in the library? We can find a nice corner where no one will be bothered by our clucking."

Mr. Jackson tried very hard not to laugh at the look which crossed his wife's face. Being compared to a chicken did not amuse her in the slightest. "Very well," she said. "I did want to spend time there. Reading."

"Well, my dear, we can do whatever you prefer," the dowager said. "I don't want to be a bother. I just know how hard it is to lose a husband."

Mrs. Jackson nodded, eyes on the tablecloth.

"Well, that's perfect," Mr. Jackson said. "You'll be entertained while I'm off to the Main Library." He brandished the slip, then turned to Cordelia. "A book I very much wanted to read has come in."

"Your drinks," the maid Maria said, placing them.

Albert said, "Which book?"

"You might like it as well," he said. "It's the only one they have on the snake-wood tree. Want me to check it out and bring it by once I'm done reading?"

"That won't be necessary," Albert said. "I've read it before."

Maria turned to Albert and Cordelia. "What would you like?"

"Tea with lemon for us both," Albert said. "Steep it well."

"Yes, sir, I remember," she said in reply, but as if she'd said so a dozen times already.

"We're ready for our meals," Mr. Jackson said.

"Right away, sir."

It seemed Maria was the only one taking care of the huge room, and it was some time before their meals arrived. "So sorry for the wait. We're short on staff today."

Mr. Jackson said, "I hope no one's ill."

"No, sir. Today's the funeral for the two who passed away. Miss Agnes and ... that new man. I've forgotten his name."

Dismay crossed Albert's face. "That's today? Right now?"

"At noon, sir. Trips Cemetery."

Mr. Jackson said, "Does the girl have family?"

Maria shook her head. "Just us at the hotel." She glanced towards the room. "Enjoy your meal."

She moved off, but Albert rose. "Wait!"

150

"Now, Bertie," Cordelia said. "Let the woman get to her work!"

The maid returned. "Is something wrong?"

"Who's taking care of the expenses?"

"The owner —"

Albert flinched, and his jaw tightened.

"He's offered a back room for lunch afterward." She glanced behind her. "Please excuse me."

Mr. Jackson recalled what the dowager had said about Albert employing the young woman for errands. "Did you know her well?"

Albert said, "What? No. Not really."

They ate in silence. A woman shouted from far off, and pots clattered.

All the while, Albert picked at his food.

Mr. Jackson said, "Is something amiss, sir?"

Albert said, "What? No."

Why was Albert so cross all of a sudden? "It seems kind of the owner to foot the bill for his employees' funerals."

Albert scowled.

Cordelia patted Albert's hand. "Monty's a good man, once you get to know him."

"Oh," Mr. Jackson said, "you know Mr. Carlo well, then?"

"He's her former brother-in-law," Albert said sourly. "Husband's sister's husband. That is, until he ran off with that girl. Not much older than his daughter!"

"Bertie!" Cordelia looked horrified. "I know you two don't get along, but you shouldn't speak of such things in public." She turned to Mrs. Jackson. "They were so unhappy — it doesn't surprise me that —"

Albert drained his teacup and rose, leaving his plate half full. "I have errands to run."

Cordelia blinked. "You do?"

"I'll be back shortly." He turned to Mr. Jackson. "Enjoy your book."

Cordelia frowned as he went off. Then she sighed. "He was ever so fond of Agnes. I bet he's gone to cut flowers for her grave."

"Perhaps so," Mr. Jackson said. Yet he felt something more was going on.

"I'm going up to get my shawl," Cordelia said to Mrs. Jackson. "Would you like to meet in the library?"

"That would be fine, thank you." Once she'd left, Mrs. Jackson said, "Why did you tell her I was a widow?"

He looked at her, feeling sad.

Her eyes reddened. "I know I am. A widow. But this is the second time you've told them things about me. You didn't even ask! I know you like them, but can we trust them? The woman's mouth runs on about anything. If she tells the wrong person something —"

He put his hand on hers. "What might she tell? That you're a widow? That I saw your legs once?"

At that, she went crimson.

"Look at me."

152

She turned to meet his gaze, chin held high, defiant tears in her eyes.

"All will be well." He felt compassion, and resolve. "Don't be afraid. What I told you on the way here, I meant. Literally. I would give my life before I let anyone harm you."

Her shoulders slumped, then she glanced at Albert's plate. "The meal wasn't so bad as all that."

Perhaps it wasn't acceptance, but it was enough. "Something troubles him, that's clear. I suppose he'll tell us when he's ready." He leaned over to kiss her cheek. "Let me collect this book, then I'll look behind the kitchens."

He could tell she'd forgotten by the way her face changed. "Oh! Yes. I'm glad you remembered!" She chuckled, wiped her eyes with her napkin. "Hopefully everything will be in order."

"I do hope so, for all our sakes."

***

Mr. Jackson caught a cab to the Main Library. As it was well after eleven, the streets were busy. The day was breezy and bright, perfect for an outing.

He still didn't know how they were going to find this killer, but for a moment, it didn't matter. The police were ever so busily on the case, and his wife would be in the hotel's library with the dowager Duchess, as safe as she might be anywhere. Surely a short detour to read a book for pleasure's sake wouldn't hurt anything.

As Mr. Jackson climbed the steps to the Library, he thought: Albert was right. What Mrs. Jackson needed was a kindly, sympathetic ear, which Duchess Cordelia Stayman could certainly provide.

Mr. Jackson felt glad they'd found friends here. The dowager Duchess was a bit nosy and at times lacked tact, but he enjoyed being with Albert. The old couple could show them around the city once his wife was well enough.

And he hoped once young waiter George was well, they could go boating together — with his wife, of course. It wouldn't be quite proper otherwise, under the circumstances.

But did she like boats? He didn't even know.

It'd been a while since he'd sailed the river in his yacht back home. Of course, his men were caring for the boat, but it was unlikely he'd ever sail it again. Perhaps his sister might like it.

Yes, he decided. He'd give it to her, the next time he wrote.

He went through the enormous main hall and up a small flight of wide steps to the non-fiction section. A crowd of people milled around up ahead near the Natural History desk, and as he approached, he saw the uniforms of police. Men carried away a body covered in linen.

Mr. Jackson hurried to the desk, alarmed. "What happened?"

Sergeant Nestor turned to face him, then frowned. "You again." He gestured at the body with his chin. "The librarian's dead."

17

Mr. Jackson leaned on the desk, feeling unsteady. "Dead? How?"

"The same as the rest, sir. Poison."

For a moment, Mr. Jackson was too astonished to speak. "This is incredible."

The sergeant peered at him. "What are you doing here?"

He felt as if in a fog. The man had just been alive! "I — I got a message from him. The librarian. My book was ready."

Sergeant Nestor grabbed his arm. "Let's sit down."

Mr. Jackson was led to the very table where he'd sat during his last visit. "It doesn't seem possible. How could this be? Who would kill a librarian?"

The sergeant's eyes narrowed. "Who knew you were coming here?"

"Um ... the desk clerk. What was —? Oh, yes. Lee Francis was his name. He took the message. Then, let's see. The dowager Duchess and her husband were having breakfast with me and my wife." He glanced at the sergeant. "I mentioned it to them. I don't know who else." His head felt all a mush, and he rubbed his temples. "A maid waited on us — Maria — the same one who found the first body!" Could she have done this? "Perhaps she overheard us, I don't recall." He tried to focus. "I'm sorry. I can't think of who else might have known."

"What book were you here for?"

"A book about the snake-wood tree."

The sergeant laughed. "A whole book about a tree?"

Mr. Jackson shrugged. "One's growing in the Hotel gardens. A tree, not a book." He felt flustered, tried to collect himself. "I think it's the same one. Same tree, I mean. The book would have told me for sure. The book's about the tree that makes strychnine."

That got the sergeant's attention. "Is it now?"

"Well, not that little tree — I guess it takes twenty years or so to get the seeds. If it's the same tree. That's where the poison is."

"Didn't that strike you as odd, though?"

"I suppose. But I read that the seeds are incredibly hard and tough, so it takes a great deal of effort to grind them. It seemed to me that it would be easier to just buy some strychnine at the grocery. If you wanted to kill someone, that is."

"And did you want to kill someone?"

Mr. Jackson stared at the sergeant, shocked. "Of course not! What kind of man do you take me for?"

Sergeant Nestor let out a sigh. "The common factor in three murders and one attempted murder has been you. I don't know if you're doing it, or if it's possible someone's trying to frame you. But you have to admit it's disturbing."

A laugh burst from him at the absurdity. Then he sobered. "Well, yes, you're right — it's quite disturbing." Especially the idea that someone might be doing all this to frame him. No one of any real importance knew he was even here. "Who'd want to frame me for murder?"

"You got me on that one." Then his eyes narrowed. "I still don't know who you even are."

Mr. Jackson raised an eyebrow. "I recall telling you all about myself."

"You're on your honeymoon, you're rich, and you arrived the morning of the first murder. But from where?"

"You never asked! Do you want my ticket stubs? My itinerary? I've been to a dozen cities in the past month. As I told you, my business takes me all over the country."

"I want you to level with me."

"I have. I've answered all of your questions. My property holdings here in Chicago are public record. I'm not sure what else you want me to say." He felt more than a bit annoyed at this man. "Am I under arrest?"

"No."

"Then I'll get my book and go."

But when they searched for the book, and the card on file listing who had it before this, both were gone.

***

When Mr. Jackson returned to the hotel, reporters were everywhere. Yet his wife and the dowager Duchess weren't in the library.

He went to the front desk, where Mr. Lee Francis still stood. "Have you by any chance seen my wife?"

"I imagine she's up with the Duchess, sir."

"In her rooms?"

"Yes." He shook his head. "Terrible thing to happen."

Alarmed, Mr. Jackson said, "What happened?"

"Someone's attacked the Duchess!"

Mr. Jackson stared at the young man, horrified, then dashed for the elevators.

The wait seemed interminable, and he pushed his way in. "Thirty-two, please."

The elevator seemed to take forever to climb, and every time it stopped his dread mounted.

Who would attack Cordelia Stayman? Was this related, or was it a coincidence? Had his wife been with the Duchess during the attack, and if so, had she been harmed? If a Duchess wasn't safe, were they safe here?

Finally, the elevator opened, and he ran to Albert and Cordelia's suite. Uniformed police stood in the hall, yet let him pass without so much as a glance.

Duchess Cordelia lay upon a sofa in her parlor, a pack of ice on her right temple. Albert sat beside her, holding her hand, while Mrs. Jackson stood pacing the room.

When Mr. Jackson entered, out of breath, his wife rushed to him. "You're here at last!"

He held her in his arms. "I came as soon as I heard." He squeezed her tightly, heart pounding, eyes stinging. Then he let go, grasped her arms. "How could such a thing happen?"

His wife shook her head. "I went to the library and she wasn't there. I waited quite some time, then came up here. Mr. Stayman had found her on the floor," she pointed to a spot by the coffee table.

She lowered her voice to a whisper. "Poor man was so upset he couldn't think straight. He didn't want any scandal, and she kept insisting she was fine. But a woman of her age suffering a blow to the head? A robber in the hotel? I called for the police and a doctor straightaway."

"You did exactly right." He turned towards Cordelia, trying to consider what best to say. He finally settled on, "How are you?"

The dowager chuckled. "As well as can be expected. And before you ask, a man was in my suite. I didn't see him — he pushed past from behind and knocked me down." She considered this. "I must have hit my head on the table; the next thing I remember is Bertie putting me on the sofa." She rubbed her husband's hand with her thumb and smiled up at him.

Albert's face was set in stone, wet with tears. "I almost lost you through my foolishness!"

"Oh, Bertie," she said, "flowers for a grave is never foolishness. Besides, nothing like this has ever happened before! How could you have expected it?" She pressed his hand to her cheek. "You mustn't blame yourself."

Mr. Jackson turned to his wife. "And the doctor?"

"Come and gone. He said we must keep watch over her, but he'll be back in an hour or so."

It was then Mr. Jackson noticed an empty spot on the bookcase. "Was anything taken?"

Albert looked dazed. "I don't believe so." He turned back to Cordelia. "Perhaps she surprised him before he might make off with anything."

"We don't have much worth taking," Cordelia said. "Everything was sold with the estate when my first husband died." A hint of sadness crossed her face. "Most of the jewels. What I have might fetch a few hundred dollars, that's all."

Mr. Jackson said, "What do the police say?"

He heard Sergeant Nestor's tread before the man spoke. "I say, Mr. Jackson, that you do get around."

18

Mrs. Jackson felt horrified. "What's this about?"

Mr. Jackson turned to her. "This man," he said, pointing at the sergeant, "believes I am the — how did you put it? The 'common factor' in three murders and one attempted. And, I suppose now, this assault?"

"That's absurd," Albert said. "Why would anyone blame him for this? He wasn't even here when it happened."

Mrs. Jackson felt confused. "Three murders?"

That was how she learned of the librarian's death.

It frightened her. Could someone know they were here and be trying to bring their presence to the attention of the law without the two of them knowing? They were doing a fine job of it. She turned to the sergeant. "Is that really what you think? Or is this some play to see what we'll do?"

Sergeant Nestor's face hardened. "I need to solve these cases! And as yet, we have no real idea who's doing them."

Mrs. Jackson felt bitter. "And yet you hold an innocent woman behind bars."

Albert flinched.

"That said," Sergeant Nestor replied, "we have no proof she didn't do the poisonings in the hotel, and a great deal of evidence she did." He glanced at Mr. Jackson, then back at her. "Since the two of you feel compelled to insert yourselves into this investigation, I'll tell you. Lunches are provided as an employee benefit. They're set up each day by the Hotel under the direction of the cook. Each lunch-box is labeled with the employee's name, so someone wishing to kill a particular person had the exact means to do so. On the day the young woman died, one person's lunch had an icing on the dessert that the others did not. Can you guess what was in that icing?"

Mrs. Jackson gasped in horror.

Albert pressed his face into the cushions beside Cordelia.

Mr. Jackson said, "So the target was the young woman." He turned away, shaking his head. "I suppose that unless we catch this killer, we'll never know how she offended him. Or her."

Mrs. Jackson blurted out, "Who would want to kill a young woman? This is monstrous!"

Without turning from the cushions, Albert snapped, "Would you take this discussion elsewhere? My wife needs her rest!"

Sergeant Nestor said, "Of course, sir, you're absolutely right. My apologies."

The three of them went into the hall.

Mrs. Jackson leaned against the wall, eyes closed. How could they possibly find this killer? They had so little information to go on. Yet it would be wrong to sit idly by while people died around them.

She felt weary, and her arm ached. She'd need her medication soon.

A hand rested on her shoulder; on opening her eyes, she saw it belonged to Mr. Jackson. His dark eyes looked concerned, and she smiled at him. "I'm just tired."

Sergeant Nestor stood peering at them both. "Perhaps we might go to your suite, sir. Then we can continue this discussion while your wife rests."

The relief on Mr. Jackson's face touched her, and she clasped his hand, feeling a surge of emotion. He cared about her, more than just any promises he'd made. Why, she didn't know, the story of her legs notwithstanding, but that didn't matter. More than anything, she wanted to be safe, with someone she could trust, at least until she got well.

And he wanted to take care of her.

Perhaps she'd made the right decision to let this man into her life.

***

As they walked to their suite, Mr. Jackson considered what the sergeant had told them. Not only that, how he'd told them, in front of the old couple.

Once he got his wife settled in her room, he went back to the parlor, where Sergeant Nestor still stood. "What aren't you telling us?"

The sergeant gave him a quick glance. "You're good, I'll grant you that. Sit down."

So he sat, wondering what could have possibly happened that the sergeant couldn't just come out and say. Bessie trotted over, curled up at his feet.

Sergeant Nestor settled himself upon the sofa. "The first rule — well, a first rule — of homicide is that the prime suspects come from those who 'find' the body. So of course, I suspected you two at once."

Mr. Jackson nodded. That seemed fair.

"Especially when you inserted yourselves into the investigation." He glanced aside, then back. "But you've never acted like suspects. You've volunteered information which killers wouldn't want known. You've shown concern for the victims. It's become clear to me that you're trying to solve these cases," he let out a short laugh, "whatever your reasons, rather than perpetrate them."

This surprised Mr. Jackson. "I'm glad of that."

The sergeant peered at him. "Besides, it's unlikely you managed to appear in two places at once."

"Sir?"

"The interesting thing about strychnine is that while it acts quickly, it doesn't act instantly. The body must take it in first. So we have a fairly precise time of action for each poisoning. You were in a taxi at the time of the first death, seen walking the park with your wife at the time of the second. You and your wife were at dinner when the waiter was poisoned. You and your wife were seen at breakfast by numerous people when the librarian was poisoned. And you were with me when Duchess Stayman was attacked."

Mr. Jackson chuckled. "There is that." He remembered something. "Do you have the back way into the kitchens guarded?"

"Of course."

"Good." Mr. Jackson felt relieved. Then he felt startled. "The first death, you say. Have you learned the cause of it?"

The sergeant shook his head. "Only that it wasn't strychnine. The man's stomach was completely empty, and no signs of poison were in his body."

This was an entire surprise. "So what caused it?"

Sergeant Nestor shrugged. "The coroner is as puzzled as anyone. He's doing another, more detailed autopsy. But the rest surely are related." He hesitated, just an instant. "You asked several very good questions back in the dowager's suite. What you don't know is that the young lady's lunch wasn't poisoned."

Mr. Jackson peered at the sergeant, trying to understand. "It wasn't?"

"Nope," the sergeant said. "The one being poisoned — who you saved, by the way — was the manager."

***

Sergeant Nestor watched as Mr. Jackson's face went from confusion to astonishment. Unless he was a better actor than any other, it was unlikely this man had anything to do with the poisonings.

The coroner was convinced the poisonings were related — the man had tried to explain the science of it to him, but Sergeant Nestor didn't really understand. What mattered was that someone was poisoning people in his precinct, and he wasn't going to stand for it. He no longer believed this Jackson fellow was involved. Yet somehow, the man kept coming to the center of it all.

But how much to reveal? Sergeant Nestor honestly had no idea who was perpetrating these crimes — if they were indeed related. And he couldn't keep the cook in jail forever. Her family had hired a lawyer, and were threatening to go to the papers if they didn't either release her or show proof of her guilt.

Sergeant Nestor had never accepted unqualified civilians onto an investigation. Not only did it put them at risk, it made it near impossible to convict later on. He'd heard horror tales of rules broken, evidence damaged, chain of custody ruined.

But these people seemed determined to assist, and if he didn't at least let them think they were, they were likely to ruin things. "I'll allow you to help. But it's going to be done my way. And you're going to — right now — tell me everything you know about these murders."

While he was speaking the last sentence, something changed in the man's face. He knew something, but not about the murders. Something else was going on that he hesitated to share. "Look, I'm not interested in your personal life, or whatever nonsense is going on in the hotel, unless it has to do with these murders! But let me be the judge of that."

The man gave him an odd glance — deciding whether to talk, perhaps — then he relaxed. "Very well, then."

In truth, it was a sad story. Mr. Jackson's closest friend (but not lover — the man was horrified at the idea) was in love with a woman not his.

On his deathbed, the friend made Mr. Jackson take a vow to care for the woman he loved. When the woman became a widow, Mr. Jackson found that the only way to keep his vow was to marry her himself. They arrived here, found the body. The rest seemed a curious chain of events, the two blundering into one crime scene after another.

It explained much. "What do you think of this latest death?"

For an instant, Mr. Jackson seemed confused. Then he said, "The librarian."

"Yes."

"If it's not related, it seems a terrible coincidence." A knock at the door, and Mr. Jackson went to open it. "Yes, he's here. I'll give it to him."

Sergeant Nestor took the slip of paper from Mr. Jackson's hand and read it. "I don't believe in coincidence." He held up the paper. "The old lady we found dead, the one this dog belonged to? We've finally identified a next of kin. Not that it'll help much."

"What do you mean?"

"She was our dead maid's grandmother."

***

Mr. Jackson looked down at his wife's dog, who now nestled in his lap. "Today is full of revelations."

"Indeed," Sergeant Nestor said. Then he rose. "May I use your phone?"

Mr. Jackson gestured towards where it sat on its stand. "I insist."

While the sergeant got connected to whoever he called, Mr. Jackson pondered the news. How was this old woman's death related? It happened weeks ago.

"Yeah, get them both up here," Sergeant Nestor said. "3205, parlor door. And bring a portrait of the old lady with you." He put down the phone.

The dog began to whine, and Mr. Jackson called down for someone to walk her.

Soon after little Bessie trotted off with the groomer's boy, the others arrived: an officer with the old woman's portrait, the stern head valet, and the manager.

"Yeah, I remember her," the valet said. "Walked down here almost every day for a while. I wondered why the dog seemed familiar."

Mr. Davis, the manager, didn't remember her. "Was it about an application?"

"No," Sergeant Nestor said, "she was the grandmother of the young lady. Miss Agnes."

"Oh! Well, I don't deal with family. Shouldn't have been allowed to visit the girl at work in the first place. If she'd been coming down here, I wouldn't know of it."

So they all went down to see the desk clerk. Mr. Lee Francis was fortunately still at his post, as he'd been here as long as any. "I do remember her. Not right in the head; would tell me the same story every day." He frowned. "She's not been by for weeks now."

When told she'd been found dead, he appeared shocked. Even more so when he learned she was the young lady's grandmother. "But she never asked for Agnes — she'd just come by. Been coming by for years now, every day at the same time like clockwork. How strange."

Sergeant Nestor said, "What story did she tell?"

"About some plant that would kill you. She said even the bark would kill you. 'Stop your heart dead,' she said." He laughed. "It was strange, but every hotel's got a story like that. The things my buddies tell me about!" He stopped then, sobered. "Then one day she quit coming. I didn't think anything of it until a few days later. I asked, but no one knew where she lived."

"Now that is strange," Sergeant Nestor said. "And you're sure she never mentioned Agnes?"

"She never asked for anyone. She'd just come up and start talking. Then when she was done, she'd leave."

A line was forming, presumably people waiting to check into the hotel. "Very well," Sergeant Nestor said. "I'll let you get back to work." So everyone left.

But Mr. Jackson thought this sounded too much the coincidence. So he waited.

Finally, the clerk had a moment. "Did you need something, sir?"

Mr. Jackson smiled. "I wanted to see how your wife was faring."

Mr. Francis shrugged. "Sick in the mornings. The doctor says that's normal."

"And I suppose you're rather busy here."

"About the same, tell you the truth. Some have quit, but we have fewer visitors these days. So I'm not getting any overtime."

"Sorry to hear that."

"Well, sir, I'd rather not anyway. I like the money, but it's better to get home to my wife."

"Good man. Listen, I'm still curious about that old lady. She never had anything to do with anyone here but you?"

His eyes widened. "Not that I recall. Strange, that you put it that way." He seemed to consider this. "Now that you mention it, I do remember once. It was one of the last times I saw her, I guess."

"What happened?"

"Well, she was here, talking like usual, and the dowager Duchess came up and greeted her! They talked like they were old friends. Then the Duchess says to me, 'We'll walk her home.' Then her husband comes up and off they go. Didn't think anything of it. I saw her again the very next day, and at least three or four more after that, too. Same time as always."

"And you never asked the Duchess about her? Where she lived?"

The young man paled. "I never thought to ask, sir."

"Busy as you are, with a wife and a child on the way, it's not surprising it slipped your mind. You mustn't blame yourself."

Lee stared at the desk. "Yes, sir." Then he raised his head. "What does it mean?"

Mr. Jackson thought about this. "It's not likely to mean anything. But I'll give them the sad news." He shook his head. "On top of everything else."

"How is the Duchess, sir?"

"She's as well as can be expected."

"Terrible shock. I hope they catch the man. Who would come into a hotel like this and attack an old woman?"

Mr. Jackson shook his head. "I honestly don't know."

When Mr. Jackson returned to his suite, he was pleased to discover his wife had ordered luncheon. She'd had it set up in her room.

"I thought you might be hungry after all that running about," she said.

While he was gone, Bessie had returned, and was now excitedly running from him to her empty food bowl.

So he filled her bowl, and as the three of them ate, he told his wife about the old woman.

"How strange," she said. "The dowager knew this woman. And where she lived. Yet no one visited her for weeks?"

"Yes," he said. "I haven't told them yet, what with the attack and all. But it's very odd indeed."

"And she spoke of the poison tree. It sounds very much like the one you read about."

It did, and this bothered him, yet he didn't know why. He still had no proof that the tree in the conservatory here was the poison kind. "If this is the same tree, might Albert Stayman have told the old woman about it? The desk clerk said she'd been coming by with the same story for years. That would correspond with the time Albert and the Duchess have lived here."

Mrs. Jackson nodded slowly. "If they'd known each other in the past, perhaps so."

"But why come here every day, with the same story? And why never ask after her granddaughter? Or ask about her friends?"

"Old people do strange things. Perhaps she came here to see the girl, or the Duchess, then forgot. The only thing which impressed itself upon her mind was the tree."

He drank his coffee, not really thinking of anything. Then he rose. "Let me see if the Duchess is able to take visitors. She shouldn't hear of her friend's death from a desk clerk."

19

When he went to their suite, Albert answered the door. "We're eating luncheon at present. Would you care to join us?"

Mr. Jackson stepped inside the room, speaking in a whisper. "How is she?"

Albert nodded. "Come see."

The dowager Duchess sat in their parlor at the table, looking much less pale. A bandage lay on her right temple. "Oh, my dear sir! Please, come join us."

Mr. Jackson went to her and knelt, kissing her hand. "My Lady, I'm pleased to see you improved."

She laughed. "Goodness me! No one's called me 'My Lady' in ages. Sit down! I insist. Have you eaten?"

"Just now." How could he possibly say this? "Unfortunately, I come with sad tidings."

Albert leaned forward. "What's happened?"

So Mr. Jackson told them about the old woman. "No one had any idea you knew her."

"Poor, poor Luella," the dowager said, wiping her eyes. "To end like that! Yes, I've known her since childhood. Her mother was a maid in our household. You might say we all grew up together."

Albert's face soured.

Cordelia glanced over at him. "Now, Bertie, I know the two of you never got along, but —"

He nodded, not meeting anyone's gaze. "So how did you learn of all this?"

Mr. Jackson told them of the dog, and how it brought them to Luella's home. "So I suppose something good has come from this. My wife adores her little Bessie."

Cordelia said, "I remember the dog. She had it when we brought her home that once. She never let us in, which seemed unusual. But she was spry, and alert." She shook her head. "Such a pity."

"And you never went back to visit?"

The dowager's eyes widened. "Goodness, no! Not without an invitation. There are rules for the higher classes, sir." She smiled then. "Which you should well know."

Albert said, "She didn't seem ill at all. Although from what you say, she must have been."

At this, Cordelia rose. "Excuse me, sirs." She went to her room.

Albert said, "May I ask something personal?"

"Of course, sir. Anything."

A brief smile touched the old man's lips. "What did the sergeant mean, when he said you'd inserted yourself into the investigation?"

Why ask this? Mr. Jackson felt uneasy. "We've merely asked questions. The sergeant seems quite prickly when it comes to his case."

"I see. It just sounded odd to me. You're on your honeymoon, right?"

Mr. Jackson chuckled. "Of course we are! And I do say, enjoying ourselves, in spite of the difficulties. My wife's arm is improving, our room is splendid, and we're so happy to have found friends here." He studied Albert for his reaction.

But the man seemed distracted. "What? Oh, yes. Of course." He smiled back, but it never reached his eyes. "I feel honored to have you call me friend."

Cordelia returned, sat down, then peered at him. "Are you planning to grow a beard, Mr. Jackson?"

He laughed. "You're entirely correct, my Lady. I neglected to shave in my enthusiasm to trim trees with your husband this morning." He rose. "Perhaps I should visit the barber."

Cordelia grinned. "I'm only teasing." She held out her hand. "Must you go?"

"I should. Enjoy your luncheon."

He left, going back towards his rooms.

After letting his wife know he planned to visit the barbershop, there he went.

But the scene nagged at him. Something felt off about the whole exchange.

The barbershop had one other man in it, a portly pale fellow who wished his thick curly hair cut. A talkative one; while Mr. Jackson waited with a hot towel on his face, the man went on and on about the scene two nights earlier. "As soon as they called for a doctor, I knew the police would arrive. I knew it."

"Seems reasonable, sir," the barber said.

"Yes! I thought so too. But my wife wouldn't leave! Said it was her duty to stay, but I was sure she just wanted to see the scandal. Well, I said to her, I'm not staying here half the night just to see a scandal! I told her, if we don't go now, we'll be there until close to midnight. The very last thing I wanted was to be questioned by police. So I went out of the back way and to my room. She didn't get upstairs until close to midnight! She's still cross with me for saying it, but I told her so!"

Mr. Jackson held the towel on his face, moving it aside enough to say, "What back way?"

The man glanced over, eyes wide. "You didn't know? There's a back way from the dining hall! It's the same color as the walls, the handle too, so it's not very noticeable. But we got seated nearby the first time I came here. Goes right out to that hallway. You go right and the kitchens are just there! You can just walk right in. Of course, I wouldn't. Full of grease, and busy as all get-out. But you could go right in, if you wanted to. Not even a door!"

"Really," Mr. Jackson said.

"Yes, really! I was astonished the first time I saw it. Right into the kitchens! If you go left, it leads to the docks and all, but you can go round to your right after that and straight to the elevators." He gave a sharp nod, the barber jerking his scissors back in alarm. "You go that way, you don't have to push through the crowds after dinner. It's much faster to get to your room."

"Keep your head still, sir," the barber said, "and this will go quicker."

Mr. Jackson felt impressed. This answered a question he'd had all this time. "Thanks for the tip."

The man beamed. "My pleasure, sir. No trouble at all."

***

While Mr. Jackson was at the barbershop, Mrs. Jackson decided to look in on the dowager Duchess. Bringing Bessie with her, the two found the Duchess and her husband sitting in their parlor over the remains of luncheon.

"Come in, my dear," the dowager said.

The dowager's husband seemed less pleased, but said nothing, so Mrs. Jackson came in and sat at the table with them. "I hope you're well?"

"Oh, I'm just fine," she said. "I do wish they'd bring the old cook back." She pushed her plate away. "This new one's just not up to snuff."

Her husband rose. "Will you be here a while? I have something to do, and the doctor said she must be watched."

"I'd be happy to remain," Mrs. Jackson said with a smile. "You go about your business."

The dowager beamed. "I've ever so wanted to just sit and talk with you."

Mr. Stayman said, "I'll be back soon." He disappeared into his rooms.

When he said this, the dowager was in the midst of drinking her tea. "Yes, dear," she called out. "Hurry home."

The old lady turned to Mrs. Jackson. "How have you been?"

How had she been? "I'm well," she said, yet wasn't sure.

"Such enthusiasm!" The dowager patted Mrs. Jackson's hand, her tone somber. "I recall very well what it was like on our honeymoon. I loved Albert something terrible, I always have. But everything — a word, a kiss — reminded me of my first husband." She shook her head, glancing away, and Mrs. Jackson wondered if it would be the same way for her, four years from now. "You just want to do something, anything, to not remember," the dowager said, "yet, you never want to forget him either. It seems disloyal."

Mrs. Jackson nodded, eyes stinging. "Even being happy seems that way at times."

"Yes! Especially at first." The old dowager took Mrs. Jackson's hand in hers. "But you must focus on today, find a way to become ... I don't know. A new woman." She rubbed Mrs. Jackson's hand, then let go, sitting back. "Oh, it sounds all a foolishness —"

"No," Mrs. Jackson said, feeling hope for the first time and wanting to hear more. "Not at all."

The dowager smiled warmly. "I've been watching your young man. He's a good one."

"It's just ... we married so soon."

The dowager smiled to herself. "I had the same fears as you. Love can come to you in an instant, without warning. How long it stays is entirely up to you."

Mrs. Jackson nodded. It had happened that way before, and ended with so many regrets. "Death follows me wherever I go." She shook her head. "How can I allow this to go on?"

The dowager smiled to herself. "Do you love him?"

Mrs. Jackson peered at her hands. Did she? "It's complex."

The dowager chuckled softly. "As is all of life worth having." She took Mrs. Jackson's hand in hers. "Dear girl, when you find someone who loves you, even for a moment, it's a gift! Seize it." She gave her a knowing smile. "Enjoy it. You don't know how long it'll last."

Could she possibly love this man, in the midst of such crushing grief? "I wish I knew how to proceed!"

"With kindness, my dear. Beginnings are such delicate times. Be kind to yourself and to him both. Teach yourself to trust him. And if you feel more warmly towards him, act on it at once," with this, she ground her fist into the palm of her hand, "crushing any harsh words before they emerge. It's all a matter of self-control."

Mrs. Jackson began to weep. "Oh, my dear husband! He loved me so very much. How I wish I'd been a better woman!" She lay her forehead on her crossed arms, pressing them to her knees as the tears flowed.

She sobbed for a long time, feeling the dowager's hand warm on her back. When the storm subsided, the old Duchess said, "Dear girl. We always wish we'd done better. But you can do better now, can you not? You have a second chance. Take it."

***

After his shave, Mr. Jackson headed to his suite. One of the bellhops stood waiting for the elevator. "I hope the funeral went well."

The young man nodded.

"I'm sorry for your loss," Mr. Jackson said.

"Thank you," the man said.

They stood waiting in silence.

"What sort of flowers did Mr. Stayman bring?"

The young man blinked. "Bring? I have no idea." Then he frowned. "I don't actually recall seeing him there."

Odd. "I heard he planned to attend."

The bellhop shrugged. "I suppose. He did dote on Miss Agnes — had her do all his errands for him. Paid her well, too. She'd always pay for a round when we went down to the —"

His face went pale, and he pressed his gloved hands to his mouth.

Mr. Jackson smiled to himself. "No need to fret. We all deserve a night out once in a while."

The young man's cheeks reddened. "Thank you, sir."

The elevators opened, and Mr. Jackson returned to his suite, where his wife handed him a message. "We're invited for dinner again."

He chuckled. "I suppose we must have made a good enough impression."

"But we were just there last night! I wonder what he wants."

This seemed a fair question. "Perhaps he's gotten some new information he wishes to share with us."

"Oh," Mrs. Jackson said. "A package came for you as well. I had them put it in your room."

"Now what might that be?"

On his dresser sat a large flat rectangular brown paper parcel an inch thick tied with twine. On opening it, he exclaimed, "Would you look at that!"

Mrs. Jackson hurried in. "Are you well?"

He opened the note inside:

Contacted every library in the area. Schaumburg had it. — Nestor

He held the book up. "It's the one! The book I wanted."

Her face grew pale. "The one you went to see the librarian for?"

"Why, yes."

His wife's face turned alarmed. "You must let no one know you have it. This is too much of a coincidence."

Could the librarian have been killed to stop him from reading a book about a tree? It seemed quite unlikely. "Then I shall read it at once."

And so he did. The book was old, with large print and margins. It went into great detail, mostly about the tree's various medicinal and poisonous characteristics. He did, however, find a section on the tree itself. Much of it was how to grow the thing, but then he found an illustration!

"This is it," he murmured, feeling excited. This was the tree in the hotel's garden! He turned the page, which had a drawing of a man's hand holding one of the seeds. The seed was almost the size of a quarter, but thicker. Something about it seemed familiar.

His wife walked in. "Find anything?"

"I don't know," he said.

"Is it the same tree as in the garden downstairs?"

184

"Most definitely," he said. "But there's something else ..."

She sat beside him. "What?"

"I don't know." He shook his head. "It'll come to me." He smiled at her, patted her knee. "It always does." He put the book underneath the bed, up in the springs so no one might stumble across it. "Now, where would you like to go for tea?"

***

As his wife needed her medication, they decided to stay in their rooms for tea, visiting Mr. and Mrs. Carlo for dinner.

After dinner, the couples moved to the parlor. Mr. and Mrs. Carlo had alcohol, Mrs. Jackson had tea, and Mr. Jackson, coffee. For a few minutes they drank silently, then Mr. Carlo rose. "Might I have a word in private, sir?"

Mr. and Mrs. Jackson glanced at each other. "Very well," Mr. Jackson said. He leaned over. "Let me see what this is about," he whispered, then kissed her cheek and followed Mr. Carlo to his study.

The room was paneled in oak, stained a dark golden brown. The fixtures, brass. The lampshades, white frosted glass. Mr. Carlo moved behind his desk, but didn't sit. "How's the investigation coming?"

"Difficult to say. As yet we have much information, yet little idea as to how to proceed."

"We?"

"Well, yes. My wife has been helpful, and I believe the sergeant on the case is becoming amenable to our help as well."

Mr. Carlo gave a tiny snort of amusement. "Then you perhaps may not want him to see this." He pulled out a large sheet of white paper.

Upon it sat the words "Wanted For Questioning."

It also had a photo of Mr. Jackson's wife.

20

Mr. Jackson's mind went utterly blank.

Mr. Carlo said, "My people control Chicago Station. Nothing gets shipped in or out — at least not that way — without going through me. So imagine my surprise when sixty cases of this flier arrived today!"

Mr. Jackson stared at Mr. Carlo in horror.

"A woman wanted for questioning by the Feds in connection with several high-profile murders checks into my hotel, and people begin to die. A coincidence? I don't believe in them." He smiled, but it was unpleasant. "I don't like my hotel being sullied in this manner. So you have a choice. You stop this madwoman — whoever she might be — or my sixty cases of fliers find their way to your sergeant's desk."

Mr. Jackson peered at the man: a most dangerous snake indeed. "What's to stop you from sending them to him anyway?"

Mr. Carlo chuckled. "Nothing so crass. We're gentlemen here!" His lip curled in disdain. "Prolonged blackmail is a most unpleasant business."

Yet short-term blackmail didn't seem to be beneath the man. "You know, I've told the sergeant everything — except about the speakeasy beneath your soda bar."

Mr. Carlo's eyes narrowed. Then burst into laughter. "You think I'm afraid of that? At most, we'd get a week's shutdown and a bit of publicity. But all publicity is good, and that kind is even better!"

For an instant, Mr. Jackson felt dismayed. Then it came to him: his wife had been right. He held out his hand. "You have a deal." The two men shook hands. "And I'll take that flier."

"What could you possibly want that for?"

Mr. Jackson didn't move or speak. Finally, Mr. Carlo handed it over.

Mr. Jackson folded the flier into quarters. "What I want this for is my concern." He slid the flier into his jacket pocket. "I'll find your killer. But I'll also do whatever it takes to protect my interests."

Mr. Carlo gave him an amused smile. "As I will to protect mine."

***

Mrs. Jackson and Maisy Carlo had spent the time Mr. Jackson was gone engaged in small talk. Mrs. Jackson heartily disliked small talk, so when Mr. Jackson returned from his meeting with Mr. Carlo, at first she was glad.

But one look at him told a different story: Mr. Jackson seemed uneasy, quiet. As the couple got into Mr. Carlo's car to return to the hotel, Mrs. Jackson asked, "What was all that about?"

Mr. Jackson's eyes flickered to the driver. "Perhaps we can discuss this another time?"

She nodded. The driver surely reported what was said here to his employer. Yet what might Mr. Carlo have wanted to speak to Mr. Jackson about which she couldn't be party to?

When they got to their suite, Mr. Jackson immediately left for his room, leaving her to stand in the parlor. It sounded as if he was telephoning someone.

The whole situation unnerved her, and the longer she stood there, the more uneasy she became. Whatever was going on?

The door opened and Mr. Jackson emerged. "Come, sit."

"What's going on?"

"Please, my dear, sit down."

So they sat at the big round table.

Mr. Jackson said, "You asked about the meeting I had with Mr. Carlo." He presented a "Wanted" flier with her portrait on it.

She stared at it in terror. "I knew it!" She rushed to her room.

Mr. Jackson followed her. "What are you doing?"

She began taking her clothes from the closet. "We have to get out of here!"

"Nonsense. This is the least of our worries."

She tossed a dress on her bed. "I don't understand. What are we going to do?"

"I'll take care of everything." He rested his hands on her shoulders. "Tomorrow, I'll visit the sergeant, and —"

"And what?"

"Show this to him."

He planned to betray her? She began to cry, throwing his hands off her. "What? No! I **trusted** you!"

Mr. Jackson's voice was filled with compassion. "Come here."

For an instant, she hesitated. Had her worst rival trapped her in this marriage only to betray her? But then, the dowager's words came to her: *he's a good man ... teach yourself to trust him.*

With an effort, she let him take her into his arms, hold her. And her mind began to work once more. He wouldn't betray her: he'd made his vow. He seemed to care about her.

But she couldn't stop crying. When they finally thought they were safe, everything was falling apart. And she had a sudden fear: had she doomed him as well?

"Oh, my dear girl. I'm sorry to frighten you so," he said, smoothing her hair. "But don't you see? Of all the perils we face, Mr. Carlo is the most dangerous. If we don't pull his fangs, he'll hold that flier over us forever."

"But what if we're arrested?"

He kissed her forehead, then drew back, gazing at her, his hands holding her face. "My dear girl. No one's going to arrest us."

"But why?"

He grinned. "I know who the killer is."

Astonishment, and hope. "Oh ..."

"They need us. All will be well, you'll see." He chuckled fondly, smoothed wet curls back from her face. "I will never let anyone harm you. You have my word. Here's what we'll do ..."

21

To Mr. Jackson's delight, the newspaper headline read:

LIBRARIAN MURDERED
Poisoner Strikes Again

He made a short phone call to an old friend, then headed on his way.

When Mr. Jackson arrived at the police station, reporters had camped out in the parking lot. The station itself swarmed with people. He had to push through the crowd to get to the front desk, but was brought into the sergeant's office at once.

Sergeant Nestor put his newspaper down, and took his feet off his open lower desk drawer. "What can I do for you?"

Mr. Jackson tossed his newspaper onto the sergeant's desk.

"Yeah," the sergeant said. "I got a call at 6 A.M. from the Chief of Police." He rubbed his eyes and yawned. "Whoever thought putting telephones in houses was a good idea —"

"How's the investigation going?"

The sergeant shook his head. "I have no leads, and the situation is getting stickier by the minute."

Mr. Jackson leaned a hand on the sergeant's desk. "Now would you like my help?"

"That depends. What sort of help are we talking about?"

"I know who the killer is."

Sergeant Nestor jumped to his feet. "Close the door."

When Mr. Jackson did so, the sergeant said, "How do you know?"

"At this point I have no tangible proof." Mr. Jackson shrugged. "Just a very good hunch. And my observations, of course."

The sergeant let out a breath. "So you don't know." He turned away, sat down. "Okay. Tell me about your hunch."

Mr. Jackson sat. "First, I need your help."

"Sure," the sergeant said. "What's wrong?"

Mr. Jackson took out the flier.

Sergeant Nestor's eyes widened. He glanced up at Mr. Jackson. "Is this real? Is she involved in all this?"

"This came to my attention last night. I thought bringing this to you would be the best course of action, since you wanted to know everything."

"This explains the evasions." The sergeant put his elbows on his desk. "How exactly did this come to your attention?"

That was an item Mr. Jackson hoped could be held back for later. He hesitated, wondering what to reveal.

Sergeant Nestor peered at him. "You're braver than I thought. Who's blackmailing you?"

So he saw right through it. "Carlo," Mr. Jackson said. "He has sixty cases of them." But they still had a play. "If you'll help us, I'll tell you everything."

Sergeant Nestor's eyes narrowed, but his voice was surprisingly kind. "What's going on, son?"

Mr. Jackson took a deep breath, let it out. Perhaps this would work after all. "Neither of us ever wanted to be involved with the Mob," he gestured at the flier, "back home. But we got caught up in it. We're trying to get out. There was an ambush, and my wife was injured. She lost her husband and her son in one night. But she found a surgeon who would treat her. We met up at the station." He smiled to himself. "Got married on the ship," he glanced at the sergeant. "I wanted to make life easier for her."

Sergeant Nestor nodded.

"But they have Feds on their payroll. Don't you see? This," he pointed at the flier, "they're using them to find us."

"So you want protection."

"Yes."

"You want me to impede a Federal investigation."

"Well, if you put it that way, yes."

194

"And in return, you'll help me with this investigation."

"Free of charge. Just keep us out of it."

Sergeant Nestor glanced aside, then back. "Why does this feel like you just played me?"

Mr. Jackson made his face all innocence. "Whatever do you mean?"

"If I turn you in and you're telling the truth, you'll be killed. I'd have that on my conscience forever. But even if this entire story is a fabrication — which I suspect it is — I can't get your help if you're shipped out of the city." He glared at the flier. "The two of you will disappear into Federal custody. If there's a plea agreement having anything to do with this matter, it'll come weeks from now, if ever. Who knows how many will be poisoned in that time?"

"Then it's settled." Mr. Jackson held out his hand. "I'll take that back, if you please."

"Most certainly not!"

"It's not worth anything to you, and my wife would feel ever so much better if she knew I had it."

"Why would I ever give it back?"

"Because if you don't, I walk out of here."

"Not if I arrest you for obstruction."

"Sergeant Nestor, I'm not obstructing anything. I came here voluntarily, to help." He shook his head mournfully, letting his shoulders droop. "Such a pity. You could have been a hero! But even though I came to you with the name of the killer, risking my life to do so, you turned me down. If you arrest me, my lawyers will stand up, right in the middle of the press conference your Chief of Police is planning out front, and share the entire sordid tale. Imagine his reaction to that! He'd have to at least censure you, just from the embarrassment alone."

The sergeant paled. "You wouldn't dare!"

Mr. Jackson chuckled. "I dare quite a lot these days. Makes life exhilarating." He checked his watch. "My lawyers should be here by now. Should I send them off, or invite them in?"

Sergeant Nestor's eyes narrowed. "What's the name?"

"Name, sir?"

"Of your lawyer?"

"Whoever they sent from River, Heater, and Rock."

Sergeant Nestor pressed a button on his desk, and a blast of crowd noise came forth. "Allen?"

Silence, then in the cacophony came: "Yes, sergeant?"

"Is anyone out there from River, Heater, and Rock?"

A silence, then, "Looks like all three of them, sir."

"What color are they?"

"White, sir, all three."

Sergeant Nestor gave a weary sigh. He punched the button. "Send them home."

"Sir?"

"Tell them Mr. Jackson won't be needing their services today." He let go of the button, handed over the

196

flier. "One day, you're going to tell me what that's really about."

Mr. Jackson looked the man straight in the eye. "She didn't kill anyone."

"So you say."

Mr. Jackson smiled. He had him.

"Very well," the sergeant finally said. "But if it gets out that I made this deal with you, the last thing I do before I'm sent to Federal prison is to drag you two there myself."

"I would expect nothing less," Mr. Jackson said. "Now let's discuss how to lure our culprit into the open."

22

The next day, Mr. Montgomery Carlo, the prestigious owner of the recently beleaguered Myriad Hotel, made an announcement. Due to the recent troubles, he proposed "sweeping changes" to the establishment.

To prepare for this, he planned to take a tour of the Hotel the next day, examining every area of it to see what might be eliminated.

The staff was abuzz with the news. What did it mean?

Some hoped it meant their widely disliked manager would be fired. Others worried their own jobs were in danger.

At dinner, Albert Stayman was furious. "Sweeping changes? What does the pompous fool mean by that?"

"Now, Bertie," his wife Cordelia said. "Monty means well."

"I wouldn't put it past him to take out my gardens, just to spite me."

"Well," Mr. Jackson said. "I don't know if you knew, but he and his wife invited us to dinner the other day. He did mention something about the gardens. Just in passing, of course."

Albert's face darkened. "You see?"

Mrs. Jackson said brightly, "Who knows? Perhaps he wants to expand them."

"But where? Would he move them? Some of those plants don't do well with moving."

As if on cue, a desk clerk came up to Albert with a note.

Cordelia said, "What is it, Bertie?"

"He wants to meet with us both tomorrow, by my tree at noon," Albert said. "About 'the future of the gardens'."

"I wonder what that means," Mr. Jackson said.

"I'm sure it'll be fine." Cordelia put her hand on his and said firmly, "I'll make sure no harm comes to your gardens — I promise you that."

Albert abruptly rose. "I need some air." He hurried off, leaving the entire table staring after him.

"Talk of change always upsets him," Cordelia said. "He'll be fine."

Mr. Jackson rose. "Let me see to him."

Following out to the lobby, he glimpsed Albert moving towards the front doors from the direction of the front desk. He hurried across the wide lobby and through the doors. Albert turned left and rushed up the street.

"Mr. Stayman!"

Albert glanced back but didn't stop.

Mr. Jackson ran to catch him. "Mr. Stayman, please."

Albert snapped, "What do you want?"

"What's wrong? What troubles you so?"

"What troubles me, young man, is that the shop I wish to visit closes at nine, and the clock just struck half past eight. So if you'll excuse me?" He hurried off, leaving Mr. Jackson gaping after him.

What could the man possibly need to purchase in such a hurry? The front desk could order anything needed immediately, or he could wait to order it tomorrow.

Shaking his head, Mr. Jackson returned to his dinner, which had gone cold.

***

The next day dawned stormy. Thunder boomed, rain beat against the windows. Mrs. Jackson turned from the balcony, closed the glass doors. "Do you think your plan will work with all this noise?

Mr. Jackson held up the paper. "The storm will pass before breakfast. One thing they say here: Don't like the weather? Wait an hour."

She grinned at him, amused.

Their servants arrived, and Mrs. Jackson went for her bath. "Your arm is looking much better today," Mrs. Knight said. "How does it feel?"

"Improved," Mrs. Jackson said. The pain was improved, true, but the arm didn't wish to entirely straighten.

But she didn't despair. After all, the doctor said that her arm hadn't been sewn correctly — perhaps the specialist would be able to help.

Mr. Jackson had been right: by the time she came out of her bath, the storm had passed. After Mrs. Knight fixed her hair, Mrs. Jackson felt chilly, and went to fetch her shawl. When she lifted the shawl from the dresser drawer, her holster sat empty.

She stared at the empty holster, shocked. Where was her gun?

"Is something wrong, ma'am?"

Her mind raced. Her heart pounded. "Have you spoken to anyone about my gun?"

Mrs. Knight came up beside her. "No, ma'am — oh, good gracious!"

Mrs. Jackson closed the drawer. "This is bad." She looked at the maid, who'd gone pale. "Please call your next client and let them know you'll have to cancel."

"Cancel, ma'am?"

"The police will wish to speak with you."

23

Sergeant Nestor was not happy. "Why did you have a gun here in the first place?"

She'd never noticed how dark the carpet was until now. "It was a gift from a friend. I don't even have bullets for it. I had need of it when I was a private investigator, but now ... I keep it for sentimental reasons."

The sergeant squinted at her for a moment in a frowning sort of way, then pointed to the open drawer. "Yet here sits a well-used calf holster."

She shrugged. "It seemed the best way to carry it."

"Who knew it was here?"

"Mrs. Knight," she frowned, trying to recall. "That's all."

Mr. Jackson stood a few paces away, hand to his chin. "I never knew she had it with her. Although I should have guessed."

The sergeant let out a breath. "If it sat in your drawer, half the maids in the hotel knew it was there." He shook his head. "The hotel has a safe in it for a reason." He turned to Mrs. Knight. "You can go."

Mrs. Knight looked devastated, and Mrs. Jackson felt compassion on her. "I'll see you at seven tonight, then?"

The color returned to the woman's face. "Yes, of course, ma'am."

Once she'd left, Sergeant Nestor said, "When did you last see it?"

"Several days past," Mrs. Jackson said. "The first day we arrived. I put my shawl atop the holster, and I haven't needed either until now."

The sergeant turned to Mr. Jackson. "Now there's a good chance our culprit is armed. Are you sure you want to continue with your plan?"

"I do," he said.

Mrs. Jackson thought it best to say nothing.

The sergeant looked at her, then at Mr. Jackson. "Well, I suppose we best start questioning the staff."

24

At breakfast, the dowager Duchess seemed even less amused than the sergeant. Her husband looked a wreck. Circles lay dark under his eyes, and the old man's hands shook so that he could hardly keep his food upon his fork.

Mrs. Jackson said, "I hope you're well, sir."

The old man gave her a level look. "Thank you. I only wish this day to end. And it will, one way or another."

His wife patted his hand. "All will be well, my dear, never you fret."

Mrs. Jackson said, "All days end, sir. I hope that today yours becomes more pleasant."

To her surprise, the old man's eyes reddened. "Such a sweet girl you are."

"Why, thank you, sir."

***

As they left the dining hall, the lobby was in a commotion. Preparations were being made for the owner's tour, and reporters had begun to arrive.

The couple went for a stroll in the park after breakfast, discussing their plans. As Mr. Jackson had predicted, the day was now sunny, if cool.

Mrs. Jackson said, "Are you certain this will work?"

Mr. Jackson shrugged. "The sergeant seemed to believe so."

"But what if our culprit is armed?"

"It's unlikely the same person took your gun." But although Mr. Jackson intentionally made his words sound convincing, he wasn't so sure. "Even so, do you really think this will end in violence?"

Mrs. Jackson nodded. "It is unlikely."

He hoped for all their sakes that this was true.

The couple returned to the hotel as the clock struck noon.

"I could fancy a stroll in the garden right now," Mr. Jackson said. He turned to his wife. "My dear, let's give the Duchess and her husband some moral support. Albert in particular may have need of us."

The garden was empty but for the fish in the pond, a bird here and there, and at the back by the snake-wood tree, Albert and Cordelia. A freshly-turned patch of dirt lay near the tree, neatly tamped down.

Cordelia sat on a bench. Albert paced, wringing his hands. He stopped to stare at the couple when they moved into view. "What are you doing here?"

"Now, Bertie —" Cordelia said.

"We just fancied a stroll," Mr. Jackson said. "And we wanted to offer our support. I hope you're well?"

Albert let his hands drop to his sides. "How did it ever come to this?"

"Let's sit down," Mr. Jackson said. "We'll wait here with you."

Albert sat beside Cordelia. Mrs. Jackson sat next to her, while Mr. Jackson sat beside Albert.

A slight movement ruffled trees in the distance.

Mr. Jackson said, "You've been upset many a day, sir. As your friend, I'd like to help." He glanced at his wife, who nodded. "We both would. Please, tell us what's wrong."

"How can I?" Albert put his face in his hands.

"Well, then," Mrs. Jackson said. "I suppose we'll have to share what we've observed." She gazed down, hesitant. "But we have a confession to make."

This captured their attention at once. Cordelia said, "Confession, dear?"

"Indeed," Mr. Jackson said. "You were right," he said to Albert. "We are on our honeymoon." He grinned at his wife. "But I wasn't entirely honest with you on another matter."

Albert seemed subdued. "What matter is that?"

Mr. Jackson took a deep breath, let it out. "Before we came here, we've both worked as private investigators —"

"Oh," Cordelia said, impressed.

" — and we've been helping the police find this killer."

"Oh," Albert said, dismayed. "Somehow, I knew it!"

Mrs. Jackson turned to Cordelia. "My dear Lady, I must ask: why did you do it?"

Cordelia blinked. "Do what?"

"Kill all those people."

Albert's face turned outraged. "What?"

Cordelia laughed. "I could never —"

Stern-faced policemen moved out from behind the trees, hands on their holstered guns. Sergeant Nestor was with them.

Cordelia looked horrified. "Why — how?"

"I'm sorry, My Lady," Mr. Jackson said. "I truly am. But if you promise to go quietly, they won't have to use the handcuffs."

Albert said, "No!" His eyes turned red. "You can't be serious. Not Cordelia! She didn't do it!"

Sergeant Nestor said, "Then who did?"

Albert peered at his hands. "It was me."

25

The dowager Duchess looked as shocked as her husband had moments before. "But Bertie, why?"

Sergeant Nestor took out a notepad and pencil. "Sir, let's start from the beginning."

"Very well," Albert said, still peering at his hands. "But you must believe me: I didn't kill the clerk."

"I know," Sergeant Nestor said. "I've just heard from the coroner: it was entirely natural. An aneurysm burst in his brain. Poor fellow died at once."

"I suppose that's a relief," Albert said. "But him dying got me thinking it was a good time to begin."

"Begin?" Sergeant Nestor seemed confused.

"Yes! I hated that fool manager, always sneering at us, calling us 'tenants'. Like my darling Cordelia was a servant! And once he even called me a four-flusher! As if I was only with my wife for her money. The very idea! So I sent Agnes with the sauce for the manager's cake." At that, his face crumpled, his eyes reddening. "But I told her — I **told** her not to **eat** it! She must have tasted it anyway." Tears stood in his eyes. "Oh, the poor girl!"

"Why do you care so much?" The sergeant put his foot up on a rock. "Who's Agnes to you?"

"Oh, Bertie," Cordelia said, horrified realization dawning in her face. "No."

But Albert seemed not to hear her. "Cordelia always tried to match us, me and Luella. She never thought it worked. But we were mad for each other, though we could never stand being in the same room for more than an hour." He shook his head. "It makes no sense, when you say it that way."

Mrs. Jackson said, "What happened?"

He gave out a self-mocking snort. "What usually happens. She came with child and was dismissed. She moved away. It was either that or marry me, I suppose, and we both knew that would have been a disaster."

Sergeant Nestor said, "When did you learn Agnes was here?"

"Soon after we moved here," Albert said. "Her mother — our daughter, I suppose — had passed away. I knew that, but I never knew of Agnes until I saw her. I knew her when I saw her, though: she looked just like Luella did when she was young." He shook his head. "Luella had the poor girl almost a slave. I went to call on her and Agnes was out front, beaten up and scared. I took her out to eat and she told me of it all. I told Agnes come with me, I'll get you some place better."

"So that's how she got the job here," the sergeant said.

Albert nodded. "I never told her who I was, and Luella never saw me. But I think she must have heard Agnes was here, because she showed up a few weeks back."

"Now that's odd," Mr. Jackson said, "because the desk clerk said she came often, and spoke of your tree."

"Oh! I remember," Albert said. "I'd written Luella about the tree when we went to India, before we moved here. She always loved plants; it was the only thing we had in common."

The whole time, Cordelia had been staring at Albert, mouth open. "Agnes was your granddaughter?" The dowager Duchess seemed appalled. "Oh, my poor Bertie." She wrapped her arms around him.

The rustle of the waterfall was all one might hear, at least for a while. Finally, Sergeant Nestor said, "And the waiter?"

"I didn't know Agnes was dead," Albert moaned. "But when the manager didn't die, I thought I'd done something wrong. Not put enough in. I heard the owner would be staying here, and —"

"You put poison in his lemon-cake," Mrs. Jackson said.

Albert nodded.

Mr. Jackson said, "But why kill the librarian? He'd done nothing to you."

"You saw my seeds! And my drill! I couldn't let you get the book, too — once you saw the drawing of the seeds, you'd have known everything."

Sergeant Nestor said, "The seeds and the drill was for —"

"It's how I got the poison," Albert said mournfully.

"Bertie," Cordelia said, horrified. "Was it you that knocked me down?"

"I'm so sorry," Albert moaned. "But I had to get everything out! And I couldn't let you see me in there — you thought I was at her funeral. I didn't mean it." He took her hands. "I'd never do anything to harm you, not on purpose."

"I know," she said.

"So you took advantage of the desk clerk's natural death to kill the manager, and on failing to kill him, you tried to kill the owner," Mr. Jackson said. "And when you thought I might learn the truth, you killed the librarian as well, to keep me from it."

"Yes," Albert said.

Mrs. Jackson said, "But why?"

"Yes," Sergeant Nestor said. "You said the manager sneered at you. But the owner lets you live here free of charge. By all accounts from the staff, you've seemed happy. Why try to kill him?"

"I spent my life tending the Duke's estate. His gardens. Once he died, though, we had to sell the properties to afford a funeral fit for a Duke. I couldn't help her, not really. She was in such a state. And I knew nothing about such matters." Albert's head drooped. "All that — the mansion, the gardens — everything I'd worked for my entire life, gone."

"Surely the new owners enjoy your work," Mr. Jackson said.

"Carlo bought the estate." Albert shook his head. "Claimed all would be cared for. But not ten minutes after my wife signed the papers, he told us he'd changed his mind. He planned to turn it into another of his hotels. My poor plants! He ripped out my entire flower garden to put in," at this, he faltered, "tennis courts!"

The sergeant looked up from his notepad. "Was it then you decided to kill him?"

"Yes, but only with the vaguest of idea as to how, until I saw the seeds in a shop and learned of their properties."

Mr. Jackson said, "But why not just kill him then? Why wait until now?"

"We had nothing." He shook his head, spoke with fierce anger. "We were sent packing like tramps. My wife wept so bitterly when we left that day. And on that day, I made my plan: I wanted Montgomery Carlo ruined, utterly ruined. I wanted him disgraced. I wanted him to fall into scandal and bankruptcy, to lose everything he had, just as she did. I wanted everything taken from him, just as he'd taken everything from her."

The dowager had sat quietly, sadness in her eyes. "Oh, Bertie. That day, I wept for my husband. I wept for the memories there. Not for the house. Not even for the properties or the money or any of it."

He looked appalled at this. "Was I not good enough for you, then?"

"I have always loved you. Yet I also loved him. I still had to grieve."

"But I did it for you!" Tears stood in his ancient eyes. "And when the value of the hotel declined, I had enough saved to buy it for you! So you might have property again. Be respected. Have an income."

She clasped his face in her hands. "Whatever would I do with a hotel, Bertie? How would I manage it? I know nothing of such things." She let her hands fall to his shoulders. "And now we're to be separated yet again, after all we've been through."

"I know," he said. "I'm so sorry."

Sergeant Nestor closed his notebook and went to Albert, who stood. "Albert Stayman, you're under arrest for murder." The sergeant patted Albert down, taking something from the old man's jacket pocket. "Your gun, ma'am," he said to Mrs. Jackson, and handed it over.

Cordelia stared at her husband, appalled.

Mrs. Jackson — much relieved — put the gun in her pocket. "How did you know it was in my room?"

"I overheard the maids talking." He shrugged, head drooping. "I'm sorry I stole it." Albert sounded defeated.

"I think I went a bit mad at the idea of Monty ruining the garden here — I thought I'd kill him at last." He looked around. "He's not coming, is he?"

The sergeant handed Albert off to a couple of uniformed men. "No, he never was."

The policemen brought Albert a few yards away, and his wife followed. Mr. Jackson pointed to the freshly turned patch of dirt by the snake-wood tree. "I believe you'll find all the things Mr. Stayman took from their rooms there."

Albert's face fell.

Sergeant Nestor gestured to his men, who began digging. He turned to Mr. Jackson, and asked quietly. "How did you know he'd talk?"

"He wouldn't, if you questioned him directly. But I knew he'd talk when we accused his wife." Mr. Jackson smiled at the old couple. "He might love her even more than his gardens." He went to Albert, then turned to the officer. "Might I speak with him in private for just a moment?"

The officer glanced at Sergeant Nestor, who nodded. Cordelia and the officer moved a few paces away.

Mr. Jackson said quietly, "Mr. Stayman, there's something which still troubles me."

Albert raised red eyes to him. "What?"

"What really happened to Miss Luella?"

He nodded, glancing away. "After what she did to Agnes, I was convinced she'd gone completely mad. I told Helen I wanted to make a friend cookies, and she let me into the shop one night." At that, he faltered. "I sent Luella cookies made with the crumbled hard bits of one of the seeds." He shook his head. "I thought it'd kill her, and my little Agnes would be free. When I spoke with the desk clerk just now, and he told me how she was ... and I realized what I'd done to her —" Tears filled his eyes. "Three years, she lived that way." His head hung low. "I've made a complete mess of everything. I regret it all, every bit."

Mr. Jackson put his hand on the old man's shoulder. "Thank you for telling me the truth. I think you'll feel much better now." He stepped back, let the officer take hold of Albert's arm again.

Sergeant Nestor came up to him. "What was that about?"

Mr. Jackson said, "The truth. I think he's truly sorry for what he's done."

Sergeant Nestor shrugged. "I just catch 'em. What happens next is in the court's hands."

A cloth bag came free of the dirt below the snake-wood tree. When opened, it held the library book, its record card, the mortar and pestle, the hand drill, and the bookmark-sized strip of red cloth with three poison seeds attached.

Sergeant Nestor stared at the bag, then at Mr. Jackson, blinking in astonishment. "How did you —?"

Mr. Jackson shrugged. "Another hunch. But it seemed reasonable."

Albert turned to Mr. Jackson. "Take care of Cordelia, will you? And make sure she has flowers."

Mr. Jackson smiled at him. "I'd be honored."

They led Albert Stayman off, the dowager Duchess trailing behind.

Mr. Jackson put an arm around his wife's shoulders. "The things we do for love."

26

The couple stayed at the hotel — all expenses paid, of course — until all the questions and searches ended and they were declared free to go. It was nice to be able to relax without the worry of catching a killer.

They went to a posh little cinema near Grant Park to see their talkie, and Mrs. Jackson thought that the sight and sounds of it were just as astonishing as Mr. Jackson had described. Afterward, the two strolled along the boardwalk, a magnificent view of the lake before them, their little dog Bessie running back and forth alongside.

Mr. Jackson said, "Do you find this marriage agreeable so far?"

Mrs. Jackson pondered this a moment, then smiled up at him. "I do!"

He appeared pleased with himself. "And how do you find our accommodations?"

She shrugged. "Beautiful, sumptuous. Nothing a murder here and there can't undo."

At this, Mr. Jackson chuckled. "My dear, I find you most amusing."

"An 'entertaining companion', as you once put it," she said, also amused. Then she considered recent events. "You're quite perceptive. A masterful job discovering the man behind all these murders. And the stolen items!" She felt humbled. "Perhaps a better investigator than I."

"I'm quite honored. Then shall we remain here in Chicago for a while? At this Myriad Hotel?"

"I don't see why not," Mrs. Jackson said.

They continued to stroll along.

Mr. Jackson said, "How do you feel?"

She considered this most seriously. "I feel good. I feel well." She moved her injured arm in its sling. "It doesn't pain me." *You must find a way to become a new woman.* She stopped, took the sling off, then tossed it into the lake, where it floated, sank. "I feel free."

Mr. Jackson chuckled. "You know, you might need that again, after we consult the specialist."

She shrugged. "I'm sure the doctor will have another one if I do."

"Well, now that you're well, I intend to give you a proper honeymoon." He gestured with enthusiasm as he spoke. "We'll dance at the nightclubs, sail the lake —"

Amused by the mention of sailing, she turned to face him, looking into his dark eyes. Then she took his hands, interlacing his dark brown fingers in hers. "Have you ever been with a woman?"

He didn't flinch, nor glance away, but to her surprise, he blushed. "I have not. Men have always been my downfall." He smiled shyly, still gazing into her eyes. "But I'd be willing to make an exception with you."

She smiled. "Ah, yes. For the sight of my legs."

"For the sight of your legs. They ... are ... stunning."

"On one condition."

"I'll do anything you ask."

"Kiss me."

"Here? In public?"

"No one will care." She gave him a wry smile. "Besides, I don't show my legs to just anyone."

"Ever the investigator, are we? Well, then," he said, moving closer, "I —"

Looking into his dark eyes reminded her so poignantly of another kiss, the dark eyes of another man now dead, that her vision blurred. "I —"

"Let me love you," he said softly. "I know it's much too soon to expect your love in return. But can you forget the griefs of the past and your fears for the future, and just for this one instant, be happy?"

It was too much, too close to what that man she'd loved so very much had said the day he died. And she couldn't help herself, couldn't stop herself, couldn't hide from the reality in front of her, not anymore. *You have a second chance. Take it.*

"I can," she said, and kissed her new husband with all her heart.

As it turned out, he was a very good kisser.

Some time later, she took his arm, as seagulls flew high across the lake in the sunshine. "I think it's time we began our proper honeymoon."

Epilogue

Albert Stayman was convicted of the librarian's murder. He was also convicted of the attempted murders of manager Flannery Davis and hotel owner Montgomery Carlo, which led to the negligent poisonings of Agnes Odds and George Neuberg. Mr. Jackson arranged to have Albert transferred to a prison which had a garden.

Mr. Carlo was charged with blackmail, but charges were dropped after Sergeant Nestor watched sixty cases of fliers go into an incinerator.

Duchess Cordelia Stayman continued to live at the Myriad Hotel, and true to Mr. Jackson's word, was kept well-supplied with flowers.

George Neuberg recovered from his poisoning, and returned to being a waiter at the Myriad Hotel. The couple spent many a happy weekend thereafter, sailing the lake with George and his family.

Mr. Lee Francis was promoted to head desk clerk, a title which came with a raise. He and his wife were blessed with a son several months later.

Eugene and Helen were married, and while Eugene still did much of the "dirty work," the hotel hired an outside service to take care of the rats.

After the manager failed to find a Cook who would agree to join the Hotel, the couple recommended a young Chef of their acquaintance — a recent graduate from the Cordon Bleu — who was most happy for the opportunity.

The snake-wood tree was donated to a conservatory specializing in poison plants, where it lived happily thereafter, visitors from around the world marveling at its story.

After an outpouring of sympathy, a settlement from Mr. Carlo, and the encouragement of the couple, Miss Goldie Jean Dab opened a shop of her own. Its sign read:

THE EXONERATED COOK
Dishes To Die For!

It became the most popular bistro in town.

Acknowledgements

Thanks so much to Melissa Williams for beta reading for me, and to Patricia Loofbourrow for the cover design. I appreciate it so much!

About the Author

I've loved reading since I can remember! I love puzzles and mysteries and intrigue, and of all the cities I've been to, Chicago is my favorite. My four years living in Chicago during grad school were wonderful. Plus I love history. And wasn't the 1920's wild? I've always wanted to write a series set in Chicago and now here's my chance.

The Vanishing Valet!

The Myriad Mysteries #2
Claire Logan

For those of you who are starting over.

1

A blue sky over Lake Michigan with just a few wisps of cloud, the buildings on Chicago's Lake Shore Drive clear and glittering in the distance.

The sails on the spacious yacht barely fluttered.

Mrs. Pamela Jackson reclined on a chaise lounge, now in a patch of half-shade cast by a sail, browsing a fashion magazine. She took a drag of her cigarette. Her black toy poodle Bessie nestled beside her, eyes closed.

Mrs. Jackson wore a bathing suit with a skirt which reached to her mid-thigh, covered with a sheer long-sleeved robe, which when she stood up grazed the floor. The whole outfit felt quite daring, but everyone she'd met assured her that here, it was entirely proper.

Her right arm held a four inch wide gauze bandage on the inside of her elbow. She rubbed at the skin beside it, which itched a bit.

Fashion didn't interest her too terribly much. But she'd just found something astonishing.

A full-page article lay before her bearing the photo of a young man with pale skin and straight black hair. He wore the tall white hat and high-collar jacket of a master Chef. The headline:

Prodigy Revitalizes Chicago Cuisine

Mrs. Jackson smiled fondly at the photo. Bringing the magazine closer, she began to read.

Footsteps approached from behind. Bessie sprang up, barking.

Mrs. Jackson petted little Bessie. "Hush, dear."

Although Bessie quieted, a suspicious gleam remained in her eye.

Mr. and Mrs. Neuberg approached: brown hair, slightly tanned, brown eyes. With the exception of Mr. Neuberg's red linen vest and tan deck shoes, the pair were entirely dressed in white. They held drinks, relaxing into the chairs across the table. Mr. Neuberg said, "Can I get you anything?"

Mrs. Jackson lay the magazine on the small, low rectangular wooden table beside her, then gestured to her half-full glass of lemonade, the ice mostly melted. "No need, thank you."

Mrs. Neuberg said, "Where are the boys?"

Mrs. Jackson felt amused. Her Mr. Jackson was over thirty, and even Mrs. Neuberg's son George was in his middle twenties. Hardly boys. "I checked on them an hour ago. Exhausted, poor dears."

Mr. Neuberg chuckled. "Fishing will do that to you. Fresh air, vigorous exertion. The battle for mastery of the beast. It's good for them. Young men need to be out more often, I say. Back in my day we didn't stay indoors all the time like they do now."

A deep voice said, "Is that so?"

Mr. Hector Jackson emerged onto the deck. Tall, very dark-skinned, he wore dark round spectacles he called "sun-glasses" (an affectation certain celebrities had taken up of late), a navy and white striped shirt, and navy Bermuda shorts (with deck shoes to match). He beamed at them all. "I suppose you're right." Mr. Jackson knelt beside her and took her hand, kissing her cheek. "Have you been enjoying yourself?"

"Ever so much." Mrs. Jackson had always enjoyed sailing, and the day was excellent.

Bessie barked, ears up and tail wagging.

Mr. Jackson took the little dog into his arms and stood, ruffling her curly black hair. "And how do you like this lake today? Hmm?"

A chuckle came from below, and George Neuberg emerged onto the deck. Not nearly so tall as Mr. Jackson, George dressed in a white shirt and tan khaki trousers. His face held a pink tinge, perhaps from spending all day in the sun.

A chorus of "George!" came forth.

Mr. Jackson took off his dark spectacles, folded them, and slid them into his shirt pocket.

George's mother went to hug her son. "Did you boys rest well?"

George grinned, his cheeks reddening. "I'd say so." He surveyed the sparkling lake around them. "I feel quite refreshed."

"Come join us," his father said. "We were napping up front and just got here."

Mrs. Jackson held out her hand, feeling a great fondness for the young man. "Dear George."

At that, George took her hand and kissed her cheek as well. Then he knelt beside her, still holding her hand, and spoke earnestly. "My dear Mrs. Jackson. I hope you weren't feeling abandoned."

Mrs. Jackson laughed. "With such a glorious view? Never. And I had Bessie for company the entire time." The little dog seemed to like boats, which was fortunate, given the amount of time they'd spent aboard them over the past few months.

Mr. Neuberg said, "What do you think? About time to start dinner?"

George chuckled. "That means he's hungry."

"Come, Pamela, dear," Mrs. Neuberg said to Mrs. Jackson. "Let's get everything set up."

Mrs. Jackson looked up at Mr. Jackson. "That last fish you caught was splendid." She glanced at Bessie, who still lay in his arms, little ears perking up at the attention. "I'll bet there's a fine slice waiting for you!"

The two women descended to the galley and began gathering the pale green Lusterware dishes and silver flatware onto a tray.

It took Mrs. Neuberg a while to speak. "We're very grateful for your attentions to our son."

Ah. As she'd guessed. "Such a dear friend. He and Mr. Jackson have so very much in common."

"And you?"

"Me? We both like to sail, although I've much to learn." She shrugged. "I think your son's very sweet." She patted the older woman's hand. "He worries he's taking too much of Mr. Jackson's time, us newly married and all. But he forgets we've spent the past few months in close proximity!"

Mrs. Neuberg chuckled. "I do see your point."

Mrs. Jackson smiled to herself. "I'm grateful your son and my Mr. Jackson have become friends."

The yacht was grand: an oiled wooden deck large enough for parties, with several bedrooms and a spacious galley below. But on this day, Mr. Neuberg grilled fish upon a small charcoal stove bolted to the deck. The couple sat under an umbrella, its pole running through the center of a fine table made of white wire.

Mrs. Jackson sat to Mr. Jackson's right; little Bessie lay nestled on the deck between them. After bustling about with salad and sliced fruit, Mrs. Neuberg sat beside Mrs. Jackson.

Mr. Neuberg brought the fish and sat next to his wife, that is to say, directly across from Mr. Jackson.

Mrs. Jackson set a slice of fish on a saucer and tested the temperature before giving Bessie her promised prize.

The little dog danced about, tail wagging, as she set upon her meal.

"Good girl," Mrs. Jackson said, smoothing Bessie's soft black curls. When Mrs. Jackson returned to her plate, it had been filled!

A glimpse at Mr. Jackson's face told the story. "Thank you!"

He leaned over with a smile to kiss her cheek. "Think nothing of it."

As everyone ate, Mrs. Neuberg said, "Mr. Jackson, you're quite the good influence on my George! Beds made, sheets changed and everything!" She sounded astonished, and a bit embarrassed. "I could've done all that for you."

Mr. Jackson laughed, nudging George, who sat to his left. "So you're a slovenly fellow, are you? We'll have to fix that!"

George grimaced, appearing embarrassed.

Mr. Jackson turned to George's mother. "No trouble at all. I believe in being a good guest."

George's mother sounded impressed. "You've been well-taught!"

Mr. Neuberg said, "What are your plans?"

Mr. Jackson let go of her hand, took up his plate, and leaned back, holding his plate at the level of his heart. He gestured with his fork as he spoke. "We don't need to rush off. Unless some disaster occurs, we should be in Chicago for as long as we like."

Mrs. Neuberg leaned forward. "Won't you come to stay with us? It'd be no trouble at all."

Mr. Jackson said, "Certainly not! We've imposed upon your hospitality long enough."

This was the third time Mrs. Neuberg had asked this. Mrs. Jackson said, "We've enjoyed our time here with you ever so much."

Mr. Jackson glanced over at her. "Indeed we have! And we'd love to sail more in the future."

Having said what she wished, Mrs. Jackson decided to completely let go of the discussion. "I would enjoy that." She set her fork down, then gazed over the water, letting the air calm her, and spoke with sincerity. "I truly do love boats."

George said, "Aww, come on, Ma. Stop badgering them. I'm scheduled in for the whole week! And I'm sure they have their own plans."

Mr. Neuberg glanced at his wife, who seemed mollified at her son's words. "Very well. Will you stay at the Myriad, then?"

Mr. Jackson said, "Of course. They have our suite held for us. I called from the station to let them know we were in town."

Mrs. Neuberg said, "I'm surprised you'd go back!"

Mr. Jackson laughed, setting his plate and fork on the table. "It really was a misunderstanding all round."

"I suppose ..." Mrs. Neuberg didn't seem convinced.

"In any case," Mr. Jackson continued, "we simply must visit our friends there as well!" His face changed, as if he'd come into an idea. "Why don't you meet us one night for dinner? I hear this new Chef is excellent."

That, of course, reminded Mrs. Jackson of the article. The thought of seeing her young friend after so many years felt thrilling.

"Oh," Mrs. Neuberg said, "I'd like that. I read about him in the paper."

"Then it's settled," Mr. Jackson said. "Telephone when you decide on a date — we'll make a reservation."

Mrs. Neuberg said, "Why not next Monday? George will be off, and we can spend as long as we like."

George didn't seem entirely pleased with eating dinner on his day off at his own place of employment, but he said nothing.

"I'll make all the arrangements," Mr. Jackson said.

Mr. Neuberg stood. "It's getting late."

Bessie leapt to her feet, barking until Mrs. Jackson took the little dog onto her lap.

George checked his watch, then tapped it. "I think it's stopped."

Mr. Neuberg began to gather the plates. Mrs. Neuberg collected the glasses. "Isn't it past time for a new watch, dear?"

George shrugged. "I like this one." He examined the brown leather band. "Although I suppose it is getting a bit ratty."

Mrs. Neuberg said, "But you've had it fixed three times now."

Then Mr. Neuberg said, "George, take us back to shore, if you will."

"Sure, Dad." George headed for the anchor.

Mrs. Jackson glanced at Bessie, then at Mr. Neuberg's retreating back, then at Mr. Jackson. "Something about him startles her."

Mr. Jackson ruffled the little dog's hair. "But you are an excellent little alarm, though, aren't you?"

Bessie wagged her tail, eyes bright.

This amused Mrs. Jackson no end. "Did you enjoy your weekend?"

Mr. Jackson put an arm around her then gently kissed her cheek. "I most certainly did. And you?"

She considered this. "I did. The weekend has been most pleasant."

Mr. Jackson rested his head on hers, face turned toward the approaching skyline of Chicago. "I wonder what's been going on at our dear old Myriad Hotel."

***

After docking, everyone changed into clothes suitable for the street, then stowed the umbrella and furniture. The Neubergs insisted on driving Mr. Jackson and his wife to the Hotel.

By the time they arrived, darkness had completely fallen. The sidewalks were busy: people going to and fro, in and out of the hotel. Bright electric bulbs lit the underside of the wide overhang which sheltered their guests. Cars lined up in the circle drive in front of the Hotel as people left for their evening entertainments.

Mr. Neuberg parked his car alongside the others. As everyone got out of the car and came round to the sidewalk, Mr. Jackson clipped on Bessie's black leather leash, and set her on the ground. Then he turned to the Neubergs. "Thank you so much for your hospitality."

George's mother hugged them both. George shook hands with Mr. Jackson, kissed Mrs. Jackson on the cheek, then said, "See you tomorrow." Then George and his mother returned to the car.

Mr. Jackson shook hands with Mr. Neuberg. "See you next Monday then?"

Mr. Neuberg grinned. "Wouldn't miss it. You two have a good evening!"

A red-haired valet got into the car in front of them and drove off.

Mr. Neuberg unlocked the car's trunk.

A brown-haired bellhop with round spectacles took the couple's bags. The man's name-tag, white and ringed in brass with dark lettering said: Melvin. "Need someone to park you?"

Mr. Neuberg waved him away. "Just dropping off."

"Very good, sir." Melvin turned to the couple. "Right this way, please."

Mr. Jackson took his wife's arm and started towards the doorway.

Bessie, however, began pulling to the left.

2

Mr. Jackson tugged her back towards them. "Come on, girl."

His wife said, "Is something wrong?"

The bellhop stood at the heavy glass outer door with their bags, waiting.

Grateful he'd put the leash on, Mr. Jackson picked Bessie up, tucking the little dog under his left arm. It would've been a nightmare if she'd gotten loose here in the open street. "I'd wager someone dropped a bit of food." He grinned at Mrs. Jackson, offering her his right arm. "Let's get her settled."

What a chase she'd led them on, that last day aboard the steamer! They'd neglected to apply her leash, thinking Bessie would stay close by, but off she went. He never realized there were so many dogs on that ship until then.

The couple moved past the doormen and into the wide lobby, which was every bit as spectacular as he recalled: a tall fine fountain in the center, surrounded by tan marble floors and rosewood trimmed with brass.

They followed the bellhop through the crowd to the front desk, and this time, the Head Clerk stood there.

Mr. Lee Francis, a blond man in his early twenties, broke into smiles when he saw them. "Welcome back! I'd hoped to see you before I left for the day."

Mr. Jackson shook hands with the man. "So good to see you. I hope you and your family are well?"

"Quite." He fumbled with his wallet, drawing out a small photo of a newborn baby. "My son."

Mrs. Jackson peered at the photo. "He's lovely!"

"Admirable chap," Mr. Jackson said, and meant it. "How old is he now?"

"One month tomorrow," Mr. Francis said, beaming.

"My most sincere congratulations," said Mr. Jackson. "Glad you're here! I quite thought we'd miss seeing you. Working late?"

"One of our men fell sick and went home early." He shook his head with a wry grin. "The bad part about being Head Clerk is you end up filling in."

Mr. Jackson chuckled. "Quite."

Mr. Francis put the photo away. "Let's see to your rooms." He thumbed through a small file. "Here you are! Suite 3205, as requested." He peered at the card, which had yellow paper attached with a clip. "Looks like Effie spilled something: she's still cleaning it." He glanced aside, then back. "Would you wait while I call up?" Mr. Francis moved down the long front desk to the phone.

***

Mrs. Jackson glanced down beside her: their bags sat neatly upon the floor by her feet.

It felt good to be back. To see familiar faces again.

The desk clerk, who her Mr. Jackson seemed to know well, stood a ways off, using the telephone.

As she waited, Mrs. Jackson's eyes strayed over the area behind the front desk. A door, which from previous experience went to a hallway beyond, then a whole array of keys, each in their own wooden square, fobs dangling. On the rosewood counter in front of her and to the right sat a number of brochures for the Hotel.

The front read:

Live In Luxury!

A photograph of the Myriad Hotel had been taken from so far back that its cobblestone alleyways could be seen on either side. She wondered: since the building faced Lake Shore Drive, how did he get this shot? Perhaps a stand of some sort out on the shore? That must have taken some doing.

It truly was a splendid photograph, although the photographer would have had to take the image from a boat to display the Hotel's full height. The day would have to be quite calm, she thought. Or could you take a photograph from an aeroplane?

She shook her head, amused at herself, and opened the brochure.

The fabulous Myriad Hotel has been among the best in fine living and dining in Chicago since its opening in

1897. Whether visiting for a day or a year, the Myriad has everything you'll need.

The desk clerk said, "The room's ready for you now. She was just letting the carpet air out." He handed the suite keys to Mr. Jackson and a small brown paper sack to her. "Some chopped meat from dinner for your dog. I had Effie lay a saucer on your dresser."

Bessie's ears went up. She began struggling in Mr. Jackson's arms, tail wagging, her nose going towards the paper sack.

Mrs. Jackson felt touched at his thoughtfulness. "That's very kind of you!"

The clerk smiled. "Enjoy your stay!"

A different bellhop came up and took their bags. Mrs. Jackson followed him and Mr. Jackson to their suite's parlor, which smelled faintly of soap. Two doors, one on each side, led to the bedrooms, each having its own door to the hallway. The three rooms each had their own balcony. A magnificent view of the lake faced them through plate windows.

Mr. Jackson pointed to the left door. "Those bags go in her room there." Then he pointed to the right door. "Mine go there."

The man hesitated just an instant, then brought everything to where directed.

Once the bellhop left, Mr. Jackson unclipped Bessie's leash and set her on the floor, where she set to smelling the thick black carpeting around her, then everything in the suite. He gestured for the small paper sack. "I'll set that out for her."

Mrs. Jackson handed the sack over and gazed around the parlor. The room was much as it had been when they left it: painted white, furnished in rosewood, with brass trim and cobalt blue cushions.

Mr. Jackson had disappeared into her bedroom; Mrs. Jackson trailed after him.

Her bags had been set neatly at the foot of her large bed, which was made up in black and white. A clink of a saucer being set on tile and the crinkle of a paper bag emerged from the bathroom. Bessie rushed past, all a rattling of little claws on little paws.

Mr. Jackson appeared from her bathroom. He chuckled, glancing behind him. "Guess she's hungry after all."

Mrs. Jackson let out a breath, feeling as if she were home. "I enjoyed sailing, but I'm glad to be here." She smiled at him, and he blushed, giving her a shy smile in return. Going to him, she cradled his face in her hands. "I really am happy you had a good time."

Mr. Jackson wrapped his arms around her waist. "My dear girl, the sight of you in that bathing suit has tormented me all weekend. I'm well glad to be alone with you at last."

3

Mrs. Jackson woke lazily, the sky outside the glass doors to her balcony a clear blue. She smiled at the dear sleeping face of the man she'd come to trust and admire these past months since their marriage.

Half-lit by the morning sun streaming onto his cheek, he reminded her of another man who'd loved her so deeply, yet now lay dead.

None of that will bring anything other than grief and trouble, Mr. Jackson had said once.

But memories weren't so easy to forget.

Perhaps if I focus on today, she thought, I might find some peace. She took a deep breath and let it out, relaxing into her pillow as she gazed about her room.

The door to the parlor stood open, as did the one to Mr. Jackson's room beyond. This amused her: they'd completely forgotten to close them.

A hissing noise came forth.

She sat up. In place of the usual white painted radiator, a metal one — bronze, or perhaps brass — stood there, shaped like golden flames!

Mr. Jackson said sleepily, "Hmm? What is it?"

She pointed. "An addition to our rooms."

Bessie leapt onto the bed, clambering back and forth over them.

Mrs. Jackson smoothed her little dog's hair. "Very well, Miss Bessie, I'll serve your breakfast."

Mr. Jackson chuckled, stretching out on the bed. "Who owns who, I wonder."

Mrs. Jackson retrieved her day bag. They'd bought a package of dog biscuits outside the station on the way into town. Mrs. Jackson put a handful into Bessie's little green ceramic bowl, which Bessie set to with enthusiasm.

A knock came at Mr. Jackson's door.

Mr. Jackson said, "Is it that late already?" He got up, putting on his trousers. "The clerk must have called for Mr. Vienna last night."

Mr. Norman Vienna was Mr. Jackson's hired manservant — or valet, as they called them here. They used the same word as for those men who parked the automobiles, yet their duties were completely different.

Mrs. Jackson found this amusing. "Ah. Then Mrs. Knight won't be far behind." She folded up the package of dog biscuits and put it aside. "You go on. I'll call for someone to walk our Queen Bess."

Chuckling, Mr. Jackson left for his room.

Mrs. Jackson put on a blue and white striped robe (courtesy of the Hotel) and went to the telephone. She'd gotten quite used to having a telephone in her room since she and Mr. Jackson first arrived here. A remarkable and useful tool indeed!

The veterinarian seemed thrilled that they'd returned. "My boys will be so excited. I'll send one up right away."

***

When Mr. Jackson answered the knock at his door, a young man he didn't recognize stood there. Early twenties, brown eyes, pale freckled skin and straight brown hair, he stood a full head shorter. The man wore a tweed cap, white shirt, brown tweed vest, brown trousers, and no gloves. "Good morning," Mr. Jackson said. "May I help you?"

The man doffed his cap, holding out a hand. "Stanley Raymond, sir, at your service. From the Howell-Green Procurement Agency. I'm to be your valet."

Mr. Jackson peered at the man, feeling foggy.

Mr. Raymond drew back a bit, hand still extended. "You did call for a manservant, did you not?"

"Oh," Mr. Jackson's confusion lifted. "Yes, of course!" He shook the man's hand. But then he felt concerned. "Has something happened to Mr. Vienna?"

"Not at all, sir," Mr. Raymond said. "His current assignment has gone longer than planned, that's all. I'm here to fill in."

Then Mr. Jackson remembered his manners and opened the door wide. "By all means, come in!" As the man came past, Mr. Jackson felt chagrined. "Forgive my rudeness: I've only just awakened."

Mr. Raymond glanced at the immaculate bed, the set of still-packed bags neatly placed upon it. "Think nothing of it, sir."

The sound of Bessie's feet came from the other room.

"My wife and I arrived last night," Mr. Jackson said, then felt foolish.

The man grinned. "No need to explain, sir. I'll get your things put away once I've run your bath." He went to the bathroom, and there came forth the sound of running water. "It should be ready in a few minutes, sir." He surveyed the room and Mr. Jackson's face. "Do you have special plans for the day?"

Mr. Jackson shook his head. "We might go walking, I suppose. But no, nothing special."

"Very good." He went to the bathroom and turned off the water. "Come now, sir, let's get you undressed."

"Mr. Vienna always wore gloves. Is there a reason you don't?"

Mr. Raymond grinned, holding out his hands. "I'm an odd size. Large gloves are too big and mediums are too small."

"Not even in winter?"

The new valet chuckled. "Mittens do fine outside. But at work?" He shrugged. "I just wash my hands."

And so he did, before and after each of his duties.

Mr. Jackson didn't know why he felt unsettled. The man seemed perfectly capable. His bath was just the right temperature. His shave was perfect.

This comes from waking so late, Mr. Jackson thought, and being startled awake at that.

As his tie was being straightened, Mr. Jackson noticed the valet's tie clasp: silvery metal with room for three gems. But only two stood there, both a deep murky red. "You're missing a gemstone."

Mr. Raymond looked down, face alarmed. "Oh, no." He began to peer around at the floor.

Mr. Jackson began looking as well. "Is the stone valuable?"

That sent the man into some thought. "I'm not rightly sure. But my grandfather gave me that clip before he died, and I'd hate to lose it."

"This sounds serious," Mr. Jackson said. "I'll leave a note for the maids."

Relief spread over the young valet's face. "Thank you, sir. My sister's the maid for this floor; she'll surely recognize it."

***

While Mr. Jackson spoke with his valet, Mrs. Jackson answered a knock on her door; Bessie followed. A boy of ten stood there.

His face burst into a smile. "Bessie!"

Bessie seemed just as excited to see him.

Amused, Mrs. Jackson knelt to clip Bessie's leash on (with some difficulty for all of Bessie's dancing about) then handed the leash to the boy.

As Bessie dragged the veterinarian's son down the hall, up the hall came Mrs. Octavia Knight.

Mrs. Knight was perhaps forty, a lady's maid for hire. She seemed ever so pleased to see Mrs. Jackson again, especially without her sling. Mrs. Knight helped Mrs. Jackson out of her robe. "How is your arm?"

"Very well," Mrs. Jackson said. "Don't mind the bandage; everything's perfectly healed. It's to protect my arm from the sun, so the scar fades instead of browning."

After undoing the bandage, Mrs. Knight examined the scar. "What a difference! You can hardly tell anything's been done!" She glanced at the pile of bags, which lay in a disorderly mound upon the floor. "Let's get you in your bath, then I'll take care of these."

The mound of bags, the disheveled bed, and all it implied set Mrs. Jackson's cheeks to burning. "Thank you," she finally said. "Choose out the long-sleeved dress, then we won't need the bandage."

"That would save time." Mrs. Knight moved past to turn on the bath. Then she glanced back over her shoulder. "Did they send up the hotplate for your tonic? I can get that started if you like."

"No need," Mrs. Jackson said. "When I was at the specialist surgeon's, they did tests on my blood! To see one's own blood in a vial is the most peculiar feeling."

Mrs. Knight sat on the edge of the tub, her eyes widening. "I imagine."

"But the doctor said everything's in order! I won't need the tonic for now. I'm to return in a year for a recheck, but," she shrugged, "it seems I'm recovered!"

Mrs. Knight beamed. "I'm so very happy for you."

It still felt odd not to take her tonic every day. Mrs. Jackson took a deep breath. It felt like a new chance.

"I'll have them take the hotplate away, then," was all Mrs. Knight said on the subject. Mrs. Knight clearly wished to ask why she'd needed the tonic in the first place, but had never said a word, for which Mrs. Jackson felt grateful.

***

After the couple had been dressed, Mr. Jackson led his wife down to breakfast. The long dining room was almost at capacity, waiters and maids coming and going around large round tables holding people in various stages of their meals. An attractive young man played upon the grand piano on its dais in the midst of the room, his soft music filling the air.

Mr. Jackson spied George across the room hard at work, dressed in his waiter's uniform. Their eyes met; George gave him a quick smile and a nod.

Mr. Jackson smiled fondly at him. Could they possibly sneak in one more boating trip before the cold weather hit?

The dowager Duchess Cordelia Stayman sat at one of the many large round tables, that particular one half full. Glancing up, she wiped her mouth then hurried over, the beads on her pale tan morning gown rattling. "Oh, my dear Mrs. Jackson! And Mr. Jackson! I have been counting the days!" She took each of their arms in hers, escorting them back to her table. "You must sit with me and tell me everything of your journey!"

The other guests at her table smiled to themselves.

Several seats around the dowager were empty. Mr. Jackson gestured for his wife to sit next to the dowager, then sat to the right of his wife. "I hope you're well?"

The dowager blushed. "Quite well, sir. And you?"

"Got in late last night."

A waiter came up. His name-tag said: Will. "Care for some drinks, sir?"

"Ah, yes," Mr. Jackson said. "Coffee for me, heavy cream, no sugar." He turned to his wife. "Tea?"

"Yes, I'll have tea, thank you."

A woman across the table said, "It was nice meeting you, ma'am. We're off to the station." She and several of the guests rose, so Mr. Jackson did too.

"Goodbye," the dowager said, waving to them as they left. Then she turned to the couple. "Such lovely people. Only stayed overnight, more's the pity." Her manner became enthusiastic. "Now you must positively tell me about your trip! How is your arm? Did you see the surgeon?

As a busboy moved in to clear the remaining plates across the table, Mr. Jackson resumed his seat.

Mrs. Jackson said, "I did!" She held out her right arm, bending and straightening in under its long sleeve. "Good as new!"

Duchess Cordelia seemed to relax. "I'm so glad. I've worried this entire time."

"That's very kind of you," Mr. Jackson said. "But there was no need to fret." He rested an arm around his wife's shoulders. "I've taken good care of her."

His wife nodded, her deep blue eyes twinkling. "He has! Oh, you should see our little villa in Tuscany. It's gorgeous. We would love to have you come visit. And the view!"

He felt glad the two continued their chatter, as he had no words. The fact that she said "our villa" instead of "his villa" moved him no end.

She's finally accepted me.

Something in the trip over on the steamer to Europe had calmed the nights of weeping in his arms for the husband and little son she'd so suddenly lost. For many nights in Tuscany, though, she lay beside him, eyes open, unmoving.

It was only on the long days back that she seemed to truly recover from her ordeal. He'd find her on deck, staring out over the water hat in hand, heedless of the wind or rain. But she'd turn to him and smile, and all would be right again.

"Your coffee, sir," the waiter said.

Yet she'd never spoken about what happened.

As he took his arm from around his wife's shoulders, she turned to him. "You're awfully quiet."

Mr. Jackson smiled at her. "So I am." Then he said to the dowager, "What news?"

Duchess Cordelia had lived at the Myriad Hotel for over three years, and was — at least in her own mind — the absolute expert on the goings-on there.

"Oh, the new Chef is simply marvelous," Duchess Cordelia said, beaming.

A passing waiter smiled at her, then continued on.

Duchess Cordelia fanned herself. "And so good looking, too!"

Out of the corner of his eye, Mr. Jackson saw his wife give a bemused smile. He said, "I'd heard he's done well, but —"

"You have no idea," Duchess Cordelia said. "Simply magnificent!"

Seeing their waiter approach, Mr. Jackson said, "Then I'm excited to see breakfast!"

Will chuckled as he put down the plates. "Good timing then, sir."

Mr. Jackson said, "Indeed!" He cut off a small piece and took a bite: Eggs Mornay, the thick white cheese sauce lightly spiced. "Delicious!"

Mrs. Jackson, mouth full, nodded. "Mm-hmm."

As they ate, Duchess Cordelia spoke at length about some scandal involving a young — unmarried — couple found after hours in the back of the library. It was most amusing, although their parents must have found it less so. Then the dowager said, "You simply must see the new collection. They have a whole set of historicals!"

Mr. Jackson wiped his mouth. "We have plenty of time. I don't plan to leave this hotel ever again, if I can manage it." While he enjoyed their travels, he hadn't realized how much he missed George until their reunion.

Duchess Cordelia said, "And you simply must come tonight after dinner and play dominoes."

Mrs. Jackson shrugged. "I've never played."

At the same time, Mr. Jackson said, "Really? Are you certain? We'd hate to intrude."

"You'd be the guests of honor!" Her smile slipped. "Even though my poor Albert's not with us anymore, he insisted we keep up the game." After a moment, her enthusiasm returned. "Please join us. I moved it to Tuesday nights: it's the slowest day, so the most people can participate. We all play — the maids, the waiters, anyone who wishes. I'm certain he'd want you there."

Mr. Jackson nodded, feeling a twinge of sadness. He missed Albert as well. "Then we'll be happy to attend."

***

Mrs. Jackson saw the sadness in his eyes, and patted his hand. He'd formed a bond with the dowager's husband the last time they'd been here.

A pity, how that all turned out.

She turned back to the old woman. "Do they ride bicycles here?"

Duchess Cordelia seemed surprised. "Of course! Although I haven't ridden in some time. I used to love it as a child." She drew back, hand to her chin. "They say you never forget!"

Mrs. Jackson chuckled. "Well, I have learned how. My Mr. Jackson here taught me." She reached beside her to squeeze his hand. "Taught me to swim as well." Where she'd come from, only men and boys actually went full into the water.

Duchess Cordelia gasped. "You never learned to swim? Or ride a bicycle? Well, my dear, it seems your education is lacking! What else do you not know?"

Mr. Jackson laughed. "Now, my Lady, how would she know what she didn't know?"

Mrs. Jackson thought that insight quite amusing.

Duchess Cordelia gained a new energy. "Then I shall make your education a project —"

At that, Mrs. Jackson laughed. A project!

"— because no young woman should go without experiencing all the world has to offer! You don't want to get to be my age and regret missing out."

"She does have a point," Mr. Jackson said.

Duchess Cordelia beamed. "I shall begin by teaching you dominoes!"

Mrs. Jackson found that most amusing.

Will hovered past Mr. Jackson. "May I take your plates, sir?"

He turned to the man. "Why yes." Then he glanced at them. "I think we're done here, are we not?"

Mrs. Jackson nodded, then spoke to the waiter. "When does your Chef arrive? We'd like to meet him."

"He's been here all morning, ma'am. You've caught us at a busy time, what with the tourists and all." He glanced aside, then back. "And we're a bit short-staffed this week."

"We don't wish to intrude," Mrs. Jackson said. "When would be the best time to greet him?"

"The staff sits for dinner at 7. We do the cooking to give him a rest. If you come by at, say, 6:30, he should be available."

Mrs. Jackson felt excited. "Wonderful!" Then she held up her hand. "Don't tell him we're here, if you would. I'd like it to be a surprise."

"Won't hear of it from me."

Duchess Cordelia's eyes were wide. "You know him, then?"

Mrs. Jackson smiled to herself. "You might say that."

After breakfast, Duchess Cordelia insisted they tour the library, so the couple did. Mrs. Jackson and the dowager moved to the velvet-bound rosewood seats and relaxed into them.

Mr. Jackson didn't join them. "I must fetch Bessie."

Mrs. Jackson smiled up at him fondly. He'd certainly warmed to her little dog since they'd found the poor thing starving outside the hotel. She took his hand. "Thank you."

"Of course. We don't want our 'Queen Bess' to overstay her welcome!" He winked at her, then left.

A laugh burst from Duchess Cordelia: heads turned towards them. She said more quietly, "Queen Bess?"

"Just something I made up this morning."

"It does fit." Then she sat up straighter. "Now you must tell me about your trip!"

Mrs. Jackson chuckled. "Have I not been telling you this entire morning? Very well. These cities are a marvel! So many sights, the people!" Having spent her entire life before her marriage to Mr. Jackson in one backwater town, she still felt astonished at it all. "We met with the specialist surgeon, but apparently the man is quite in demand — it took almost a month to have the surgery."

She extended and bent her right arm, going over it with her left hand. "Then we took a steamer ship to Tuscany. I've never seen so much water in my life!"

Duchess Cordelia nodded. "I remember our travels, Albert and I — before we came here."

From her face, Mrs. Jackson guessed the memory was now bittersweet. She put a hand on the dowager's.

But the old woman's face brightened. "It was a good time." She pulled her hand back, straightened her clothes, dusted off her dress. "Don't mind me; I just wish he were here."

Mrs. Jackson nodded. Wishing to change the subject for Duchess Cordelia's sake, she continued: "I was almost well when we got to Tuscany. Which was a good thing!" She smiled to herself, recalling their time in the sun. "But after a while, we both felt ready to return."

"I'm glad you did." She reached out to rest her hand on Mrs. Jackson's. "I missed you both terribly."

Mrs. Jackson felt moved at this, turning to put her other hand on top of Duchess Cordelia's. "I've missed you, too."

They sat together, both having endured and lost so much, yet even now able to find comfort in friendship and joy in a pleasure shared.

Mrs. Jackson said finally, "Which of those new books do you think I should read first?"

"Well, since you like Emerson, perhaps Thoreau?"

Mr. Jackson and Bessie approached then. He sat across the low round table from them, resting Bessie on his lap, where she settled in. "Are you two enjoying yourselves?"

"Let me get that book for you." Duchess Cordelia left for the stacks.

"We are," Mrs. Jackson said. "Did our girl receive a good report?"

Bessie's eyes were closed.

Mr. Jackson chuckled, smoothing the little dog's hair. "I think those boys tired her out." The veterinarian had several boys ranging from ten to sixteen, who adored their "little Bessie."

"Here you are," the dowager said, book in hand. "I've heard good things about this one."

Mrs. Jackson took the copy of Walden, Or Life in the Woods from Duchess Cordelia. The cover looked a bit dreary, so she set it in the space between herself and the armrest. "I'll check it out to read in my rooms."

Mr. Jackson said, "Where shall we have luncheon?"

Mrs. Jackson chuckled. "Do you need to ask? We simply must visit Miss Goldie Jean!"

The dowager clapped her hands. "Splendid!"

Several of the other library patrons glanced over.

Duchess Cordelia lowered her voice, cheeks coloring. "You will completely enjoy it. She's gotten ever so much commerce, she needs to expand."

Mrs. Jackson felt surprised: the shop had barely opened. "Already?"

"Why, yes! She plans an entirely new and larger kitchen." She leaned over to speak in conspiratorial tones. "Mr. Carlo has been ever so helpful in 'persuading' the city to speed up the process."

Mr. Jackson chuckled. "Why am I not surprised?" He ran a hand over Bessie's hair. "Then we shall visit." He smiled to himself. "Hopefully without seeing Mr. Carlo."

This amused Mrs. Jackson no end. "And here I thought you loved everyone."

Mr. Jackson rolled his eyes, then picked up a book from the stack on the table. "Hardly."

"I suppose I don't blame you." She picked up a book from the table which looked interesting then turned to Duchess Cordelia. "Will you be coming with us?"

"Only if it's no bother."

Mr. Jackson looked up from his book. "Not at all! We insist." He closed the book, then put it on one side and moved Bessie to the other, leaning forward. "I promised dear old Albert I'd look after you, and you must be properly fed."

This seemed to delight the old woman. "Then I shall be honored."

Mrs. Jackson relaxed into her chair with a sigh. It felt good to be back, here in the hotel library she'd come to love so well.

The three read together in silence for some time. Then the clock struck half past eleven.

Mr. Jackson closed his book. "I think it best to go early, before the rush. Meet in the lobby at noon?"

Duchess Cordelia nodded. "I'll ring for Effie to help me get changed."

Mrs. Jackson checked out her books and the couple returned to their suite so she might put on her shawl. It was becoming chilly out. "We'll need winter jackets if we're to stay here for very long."

4

Mrs. Jackson followed Mr. Jackson and the dowager Duchess to a bistro with a gleaming glass storefront edged in brass.

Inside, small round tables and wooden chairs with delicate curved backs were set around the room, which was half-full. To the right, a long glass counter displayed a tempting delicatessen: meats, pastries, breads, fruit, and various cooked dishes. A sign on the counter read:

Buy Here, Eat There!
Quick, Easy Take-Out

Mrs. Jackson felt amazed. "What a novel concept!"

A woman with brown hair who appeared to be in her forties stood behind this counter. When she glanced over, she smiled, passing through a swinging door which came to her hips, and approached them, arms wide. "Goodness gracious! You should have told me you were in town."

Mrs. Jackson hugged her, then drew back to survey her. "Miss Goldie Jean. How splendid you look! And your shop!"

Her cheeks colored and she gave a shy smile. "I'm so glad you like it." She quickly recovered, though. "Come, sit wherever you like. Menus are on the tables. Just let me know when you're ready to order."

The room was brightly lit and cheerful. The couple chose a table across from the counter, along the wall.

Once they'd gotten their meals, Mrs. Jackson turned to Duchess Cordelia. "Now you must tell us everything which has gone on."

"I'm afraid my life has been uneventful. It's awfully lonesome these days with Albert gone. I like to visit the garden: it makes me feel closer to him."

Mrs. Jackson nodded.

"But something's happened at the Hotel. I'm certain of it."

Mr. Jackson said, "Going on?"

"Yes! Whispers and looking about this entire past week." Duchess Cordelia glanced around then leaned forward. "I'm hoping someone will spill the beans at dominoes tonight."

"It sounds most intriguing." Mr. Jackson took a sip of his coffee. "Hopefully it'll be something pleasant."

After lunch, the couple returned the Duchess to the Hotel, then went shopping for winter clothing. Mrs. Jackson especially loved the soft warm coats.

She found a cute little tan beaded handbag which matched the dresses she'd bought so far. She particularly liked its zippered pouch inside. So useful!

Around tea-time, they (and Bessie, and all their packages) went to a little stand and got something she'd never had before: the "hot dog". At first she felt dubious about the name. "What kind of meat is that?"

From the amused look on Mr. Jackson's face, he knew what she'd been thinking.

"These are entirely beef. You want pork, they got 'em around the corner." The man didn't seem to approve of his competitor's product. He turned to the next fellow. "You ready?"

She watched him put the meat in a bun and pile on vegetables and sauce. They smelled good. She turned to Mr. Jackson. "Let's split one."

So they did. "This is delicious," she said. "Why did they never sell these back home?"

Mr. Jackson just smiled at her.

Once, she'd thought her city was the center of the world. But now, seeing the sights, tasting all the delicious foods, doing things no one would ever have thought of there ... it made her almost glad she could never go back.

"What are you thinking about?"

She took his hand. "I love being here with you."

His cheeks colored, a shy smile upon his face. Yet his eyes grew moist. "That's the most wonderful thing anyone's ever told me."

She squeezed his hand. "Well, it's true." She slipped the little pinched end of her meat to Bessie, who set to it with vigor. "You've been here before in winter. What do you think we still need to buy?"

***

When the taxi pulled up to the Hotel, Harry was there to meet them. "I'll have Melvin bring these packages to your rooms."

"That's very kind of you," Mrs. Jackson said.

As Melvin and Harry piled the packages onto Melvin's cart, Mr. Jackson turned to her. "Want a soda?"

She did feel thirsty. "Yes, let's get one! I want to try strawberry this time."

Bessie kept pulling towards the other end of the circle drive. So Mrs. Jackson picked her up. "Come on, Bessie," she said, and they went inside, to the soda shop on the right end of the lobby.

The last time they'd visited the Hotel, her Mr. Jackson had discovered the secret of the stuffed owl in the soda shop's far ceiling corner: when it blinked, this meant that a shipment of liquor had been delivered!

Neither of them had yet seen the speakeasy which must be somewhere below, but Mrs. Jackson felt sure it would be just as grand as what they'd seen so far.

As they sat at one of the cute little round tables sipping their sodas. Mrs. Jackson said, "May I ask something?"

Mr. Jackson set down his drink. "By all means."

"How did you know to meet me at the station?"

He chuckled. "The night we left home? My brother-in-law found out all about it and sent me word."

Mrs. Jackson glanced up to see him watching her, and his manner felt different than it had. It seemed as if he waited for her to explain what happened, why she went there. She sighed, feeling glum.

"You don't have to tell me if you don't want to," he said. "Just know that if you do want to, I'm here." His hand felt warm upon hers. "I care for you very much."

She nodded, yet felt a certain fear. She picked up Bessie from the floor and gave her a hug, eyes stinging.

She felt his hand warm upon hers. When she opened her eyes, he stood beside her. "It's almost time. You still want to see your friend?"

Mrs. Jackson smiled to herself. "I would." She set Bessie down, who had begun to struggle free. "Let's see how he's fared."

She felt excited at the prospect of seeing the new Chef, as well as a bit daunted. Would he remember her? And if he did, would he be glad to see her, or dismayed?

She and Mr. Jackson waited to one side of the staff's dining room as maids placed bowls of cut flowers upon the long trestle tables. Then the great Chef appeared.

He'd matured since last she saw him. He strode in, tall, confident, wearing a sky blue and white plaid shirt and black trousers. "You wished to see me?" Then realization dawned. "Mrs. —"

Mrs. Jackson quickly held up her hand. "Monsieur, please — here, we're called Mr. and Mrs. Jackson."

The young man stared at the two, mouth open. "Is what they're saying true? Did you kill him?"

The horrible night not so long past came crashing in. *People think I killed him?* "No," she finally said. "But I was there. I — I was with him." What could she possibly give this man? "He didn't die alone."

The young Chef nodded, face downcast. "Thank you for telling me." Then he grasped her upper right arm, his eyes kind. "I'm so sorry for your loss."

For all the time that had passed, all the tears she'd cried, Mrs. Jackson still felt numb, as if perhaps it had been all a bad dream. "Thank you."

"Let's sit," the young Chef said, so they did. He clasped his hands on the table in front of him. "I've wanted to thank you for the opportunity to come here."

Mrs. Jackson glanced at Mr. Jackson, who smiled softly. "When my wife told me about you, it seemed the perfect solution to the Hotel's difficulty."

Mrs. Jackson leaned forward, and in an instant she knew what she needed. "Are you happy?"

The young Monsieur seemed to consider this most seriously. "I am."

He leaned back, and in his voice lay a hint of his time in Paris. "The first few days were difficult, me being young enough to be their child. Grand-child, for some. And for all my years of experience, this was my first time to be in actual charge of the kitchens. A few thought it wrong to let the former Cook go, and they put their anger upon me."

He glanced aside, a small smile upon his face. "But I gathered my entire staff together the day I took charge and said, 'I was brought here to prosper you. If you can't take my commands, speak before we close today, and I'll release you with a good recommendation. Defy me henceforth, and matters won't go so well.'"

Mrs. Jackson gasped. "How did you dare speak so?"

The young Chef smiled to himself. "I merely considered what the men I'd trained under since I was a boy would have said, then softened it by half." He chuckled at that. "My masters have been fierce, formidable men. But wise, for the most part." He glanced away. "And we've prospered, for which I'm grateful."

"As are we," Mr. Jackson said. "I know we've never met before, Monsieur, but my wife has spoken of you enough that I feel I know you."

This seemed to amuse the young Chef no end. "I hope your opinion of me is mostly good."

"It is," Mr. Jackson said.

Good smells came from the kitchen, and men began setting the tables, George among them.

Mrs. Jackson rose, and the men did as well. "We should let you get your dinner." On impulse, she hugged the Chef, recalling the first time she'd met him, long ago. "I'm very, very proud of you."

He smiled shyly, eyes reddening. "I wouldn't be here except for you. For that, I'm forever grateful."

5

Mr. Raymond arrived right on time to dress Mr. Jackson for dinner. He laid out his shaving kit, selected Mr. Jackson's dinner suit, and prepared a hot towel just as usual. But after Mr. Jackson seated himself for the shave, Mr. Raymond frowned.

"What is it?"

"Your neck." He fished out a small mirror. "A blemish has formed there."

Mr. Jackson felt amused. "I haven't had one of those since I was a boy."

"You're very fortunate." He applied the hot towel, then turned to his kit, took out some instruments, and small jars of various colors. "It's happens a lot, especially in men with such coiled hair as yours."

Mr. Jackson relaxed into the chair as Mr. Raymond lathered his face, sharpened his straight razor, and began his work.

Mr. Raymond finally said, "There! Good as new."

Mr. Jackson took up the mirror. The blemished area was reduced in size and had been covered by a paste closely matching his dark skin. "Must I do anything?"

"Wash your neck with soap and apply another hot towel before bed. That and a good night's sleep should take care of it. But I'll check on it in the morning."

***

The couple, having been suitably attired, went down to dinner. To Mrs. Jackson's surprise and delight, the Chef sent out a special plate with her favorite foods: roasted ham glazed with honey and cloves, potatoes mashed with garlic and butter, sweet pickles, and a fine crystal cup holding lime sorbet.

After dinner, the couple joined Duchess Cordelia in her suite for dominoes.

Many of the maids, waiters, and other staff were there, most already seated around the spacious parlor. Their waiter for breakfast, Will, was there. And George Neuberg, of course, as well as their bellhop Melvin and the red-haired valet they'd seen parking cars the other night, whose name turned out to be Harry.

Other friends were there as well. Helen ran a nearby pastry shop, and was newly married to Mr. Jackson's friend Eugene, who did the "dirty work" around the Hotel. Duchess Cordelia introduced Effie, the maid for their floor, who doubled as her lady's maid.

Mr. Jackson introduced a young man named Stanley — who happened to be Effie's older brother — as his new manservant. Bessie immediately went to Stanley and put her little paws up on his shin, tail wagging.

He gave Bessie a fond smile and petted her head.

"You're the fellow who lost the gem in your tie-clasp," Mrs. Jackson said. "A pleasure to meet you."

"Yes, ma'am," Stanley said.

"Well, we've looked all round," Mrs. Jackson said.

"As did I," said Effie.

"I'm sure it'll turn up," Mr. Jackson said.

But not everyone was there. Mr. Lee Francis was home with his wife and new son. The young Head Chef had begged off, saying he did little after close and cleanup but to fall into his bed. "The work is entirely taxing. But I feel stronger with each day. Perhaps in the future, I'll join you."

"It seems everyone knows everyone," Mrs. Jackson said, a bit daunted by the thought. Somehow, her Mr. Jackson seemed to know them all already. How did he do it?

Effie smiled at her, holding out a hand. "Well, now you know us all too. Come, sit here by us."

So she did! Mrs. Jackson had never played dominoes before, but the rules weren't difficult to learn and she was soon winning from time to time. She noticed her Mr. Jackson and George whispering together through most of the game, and she suspected he didn't know how to play any more than she had.

Bessie had the run of the suite until she put her paws up on Melvin, who shied away from her. "I don't like dogs much."

"Forgive me," Mrs. Jackson said. "Bessie! Over here." She picked up the little dog and clipped on the leash, keeping her close by.

The party seemed quite the success. Those there were full of gossip about the doings in the Hotel, which Mrs. Jackson found mostly amusing.

When someone mentioned the Hotel manager, though, the dowager Duchess frowned, crossing her arms in front of her. "I'd prefer not to speak of that man, if you please."

The others glanced at each other and fell silent. It seemed clear that Duchess Cordelia Stayman still blamed Mr. Flannery Davis for the unfortunate events which took place during the last time the couple had stayed at the Hotel.

But soon everyone was talking and laughing again. And the biggest topic of discussion was the Head Valet: the man, it seemed, had gone missing.

6

Mrs. Jackson said, "I've seen him, but I don't believe we've ever been introduced."

Mr. Raymond said, "His name's Earl Vincenzo. Odious fellow."

"He is not," Effie said in a teasing tone. "Lately, he's been rather sweet. Besides, I thought you were friends."

Mr. Raymond rolled his eyes and crossed his arms.

George said, "Vincenzo's still not back?"

Many shook their heads.

Eugene leaned forward. "And no one will say anything about it."

"One minute he was there," Harry said, "the next, he was gone." He seemed daunted by this.

Mrs. Jackson said, "And no one's seen him since?" It seemed a mystery, to be sure.

"Good riddance." Maria had been promoted to Head Maid since last the couple had visited. "Always come in barking at people like he owned the place. And always bothering my maids." She gave Effie a quick glance. "Probably run off with some girl or other."

Effie looked uncomfortable.

Melvin pushed up his round spectacles. "Wonder who'll replace him."

"They better do it soon," Harry said. "It's been a week now, and all confusion since."

How strange, Mrs. Jackson thought. "Does he often go missing?"

They all looked at each other.

Eugene said, "No, come to think of it. He never has."

***

Mr. Jackson watched his wife as she played. The change that had come over her since they left for their trip amazed him. She smiled now. She even seemed to be making friends here.

He recalled how her face crumpled at the young Chef's mere mention of the night her first husband died.

She's still not recovered, he thought.

Nor should she be, he decided, recalling his own terrible loss long before.

Travel seemed good for her. He'd not wanted to leave. But might more travel help her?

After several rounds of dominoes, a knock came at the parlor door. Room service had arrived, with various sorts of food and drink. Duchess Cordelia announced a refreshment break, instructing the waiters to place the assortment upon the table and dresser in the bedroom.

Mr. Jackson stood, stretching. The games were lively and the conversation good, but he needed to move about. He found George by the drink table, setting out the cups. "There you are!"

George turned to him with a smile. "That last play was a good one!" His face turned mischievous and sly. "But I'll win next time!"

Mr. Jackson laughed. "I take up the challenge, sir!" Then he sobered. "Let me ask you something: how about you come with us on our next trip?"

George's manner cooled; he glanced away, giving a half-hearted shrug. "I don't know ..."

"Can't you get off work?"

George's shoulders twitched. He stuck his hands in his pockets, eyes upon the floor. "Sure, I could, but ..."

Mr. Jackson wasn't sure what was wrong. "You don't have to answer now. I'm not even sure where we'll be off to next." He smiled to himself. "We'll probably be here for a while. Just wanted to make the offer."

George nodded, eyes still upon the floor. "Thanks." He clapped Mr. Jackson on the arm, not looking at him. "Be right back." He went towards the bathroom.

Mr. Jackson loitered there at the table for several minutes. When George didn't return, Mr. Jackson knocked on the door. "You all right in there?"

"Go on, you goof," George said lightly. "I'm fine."

Smiling to himself, Mr. Jackson went to check on his wife.

Mrs. Jackson stood out on the parlor balcony smoking, gazing out over the lake-shore. Bessie lay curled up at her feet. She turned at his approach. "Enjoying yourself?"

He put an arm over her shoulder. "I am." Then he recalled he'd never asked her. "You mind if we bring George with us the next time we travel?"

His wife chuckled. "I thought you wanted never to ever leave."

He turned to face her, leaning on the wrought iron railing. "Well ... it depends."

She gave him a wry, knowing smile. "I see!" She let out a short laugh. "Sure! Bring him along! I like George."

"Do you?"

"Very much." She took a drag on her cigarette, blew out smoke, staring out over the shoreline. "He reminds me a bit of myself at that age." She turned to face him, leaning upon the rail. "Hopefully, he'll turn out better than I did."

Mr. Jackson studied the lovely curves of her face, lit by both the room behind and the buildings before her. He tucked a curl around her ear. "I don't think you turned out so badly."

He loved watching her blush, the barely shy smile.

Cordelia called out, "Want to play more?"

They went inside. Mr. Jackson looked around. "Where's George?"

Cordelia said, "Wasn't feeling well, the poor dear. He went home."

Mr. Jackson said, "I'm sorry to hear that."

He seemed okay a few minutes back, Mr. Jackson thought. *If he's not here tomorrow, I'll look in on him.*

"It's your play, sir," Cordelia said, and all thoughts on the matter were forgotten.

***

When the couple returned to their suite, they sat for a time in the parlor, Bessie curled up on the floor between them. Mrs. Jackson said, "What do you think about this missing Head Valet?"

Mr. Jackson shrugged. "It's really none of our concern. My only hope is that the Hotel will choose someone a bit more agreeable next time."

"You don't like him?"

He seemed to seriously consider this. "I've only come across him twice now, yet each time I felt uneasy." He shook his head, gave a one-shoulder shrug. "He's done nothing to offend. It's just ..."

Mrs. Jackson nodded, not understanding but trying to. Mr. Jackson's mind often seemed to run in different circles than hers. "How's your new manservant?"

"Perfectly well. I prefer Mr. Vienna, but this man is capable enough."

Something about the way he'd said it ... "Yet he also makes you uneasy."

Mr. Jackson straightened, took a deep breath and let it out. "Well, to be honest, yes." He shrugged, then smiled down at their little dog, who'd put her paws upon his leg. "Bessie seems to like him, at any rate."

He reached down to smooth her hair, then set the little dog beside him. "It's nothing I can pin on the man, but I'll be very glad when Mr. Vienna returns. Perhaps it's just that I'm more used to him."

"When Mr. Vienna does return, you should request him on a more permanent basis."

Mr. Jackson's face brightened. "An excellent idea! Yes, that would be splendid. I'll speak with Mr. Vienna about it the moment he arrives."

***

The next morning, Mr. Jackson felt more rested, and in a much better humor. But instead of getting better, his neck now had several blemishes upon it.

Mr. Raymond shook his head. "I can try an oil treatment. But in cases like this the best course is to let the hair grow. Have you ever fancied a beard?"

Mr. Jackson shrugged. "Never considered it. But if you think it'll help ..."

"I do."

"Then just trim round the edges as you can."

When the couple went down to breakfast, the tables in the back third of the room had been changed. Instead of the usual large round tables, there now sat dozens of square tables which seated four. The dining room was packed: they got the last two seats in a round table of sallow-faced men who chattered to each other in a language he didn't understand.

George was there that morning, stationed far across the room. Yet he looked haggard, and too focused upon his work, as if he'd not slept.

"I hope he's well," Mr. Jackson said.

"We all have our down times," his wife said. "He'll be his old self again."

Mr. Jackson thought about that. "Duchess Cordelia said he went home ill. You don't think so?"

His wife shrugged. "You know him better than I."

He considered this the entire meal, running back over the conversation he'd had with George in his mind. He couldn't think of what he might have said which would trouble George so. Perhaps he was feeling ill even then, and didn't wish to speak of it.

Mr. Jackson sipped his coffee, which tasted especially good this morning. *You're fussing like an old woman.* His wife had been entirely correct: whatever was the matter, George would soon be well.

He chuckled at himself. In any case, if he'd said something to offend, George would surely say so.

His wife said, "What amuses you?"

"Oh, it seems people act in their own certain way. We're all quite predictable."

She gave an ironic little snort of amusement. "Until we're not."

"Oh?"

"That Head Valet, for example. Everyone's saying he'd never run off, yet there he's gone." She raised her hand for the waiter. "Might I get more tea?"

Mr. Jackson mused upon what his wife had said, then he took up her hand and kissed it. "These puzzles do occupy your mind." Was she so focused on this Head Valet simply to forget her own sorrows?

She smiled warmly at him. "Are you feeling neglected, sir?"

The group of travelers rose, so he did as well. They left without so much as acknowledging him, which seemed rather rude. He sat, finishing his coffee as he pondered his wife's question. "Not that I can detect."

She leaned towards him. "Let's spend the day together, as we did before we left here last."

"That sounds like an excellent idea."

After breakfast, the couple decided to go for a stroll in the park near to the Hotel. Bessie was quite enthusiastic about this idea.

Mr. Jackson said, "Did you enjoy the time last night?"

His wife blew out smoke and tapped the ashes from her cigarette. "I did. I'm looking forward to playing again next week."

Bessie's curly black hair had been last cut several weeks back. "When we get back, let's see if the groomer has room for our girl today."

His wife looked down and laughed. "She is looking a bit mop-like, isn't she?"

The day was bright and cool, the sun having a touch of orange to it even at this early hour. He'd only been here once in winter, and that only for a day.

Perhaps they'd go south this trip, he thought. That is, when George was feeling well again. The Caribbean was said to be lovely this time of year. They'd have to go before the weather turned bad ...

"Did you want to go there now?"

With a start, Mr. Jackson realized they'd come round the park. It was either around once more, or back to the hotel. He checked his watch: half past eleven. "Let's see if they can fit her in."

They walked back to the Hotel and across the wide lobby to the right, where a hallway led past the elevators. A hall on the right read:

Dog Grooming & Veterinary Services

The veterinarian stood at the counter rifling through papers. He glanced up when they entered. "Good morning! I hope all's well?"

"Certainly," Mrs. Jackson said. "Might we get Bessie a trim?"

The man beamed. "Right this way!"

The veterinarian's wife was the groomer. When they entered her back room, she was leading a Great Dane to his owner. That done, she smiled at them then said to Bessie, "Time for your bath?"

Mr. Jackson handed over the leash. "As the youngsters say, she needs a hairdo."

The woman said, "I'll take care of everything."

He said, "When shall we return?"

"Oh, a bath and a clip won't be more than an hour. But take all the time you need. My boys'll look after her."

The couple went back to the lobby, intending to look around the gift shop, which they'd not yet had a chance to visit. But the owner of the Hotel spied them, striding purposefully in their direction.

"I wonder what he wants," Mr. Jackson said, feeling disgruntled.

"Now, now," his wife said. "No need to keep grudges."

He thought that possibly right. Yet the man was insufferable!

Mr. Montgomery Carlo was a swarthy heavyset man with hooded brown eyes, who held a black walking-stick tipped in brass. "So good to see you again!" He held out his hand. "Might I have a word with you — just for a moment?"

Mr. Jackson shook the man's hand, if a bit grudgingly. "Very well."

The couple followed Mr. Carlo out to the front. This time of day, traffic in the street was brisk and noisy. Yet in the circle drive there was little activity.

Two valets he hadn't met yet, one black-haired, the other blond, stood talking. Harry leaned on the Head Valet's podium ten feet away, nodding to them when they glanced over.

Mr. Jackson said to Mr. Carlo, "How may we help?"

"I'm sure you've heard by now about my missing Head Valet."

"We have," Mr. Jackson said.

Mr. Carlo shook his head. "The police have absolutely no interest in the matter. And he's been gone over a week!"

Mrs. Jackson sounded impressed. "It's very kind of you to have such concern for your employees."

"It's more than that. Earl's my first cousin —"

Mrs. Jackson said, "Oh?"

" — and he wouldn't run off. Not in the middle of a shift, and certainly not without telling someone where he'd gone."

Two cars drove up past them and parked just past the Head Valet's podium. Harry pressed a button there.

Mrs. Jackson nodded. "I understand, sir. And I sympathize! But it's not unusual for Missing Persons cases to be of low priority. In adults, that is."

Mr. Jackson felt a flash of pride in her knowledge of such matters.

Mr. Carlo drew back, chagrined. "So what can I do?" Then his face turned determined. "You must help me."

Melvin came outside, hurrying up to the first car. A second bellhop followed.

Mr. Jackson spoke quietly. "The last time we helped you, Mr. Carlo, you tried to blackmail us. Why should we help you now?"

Mrs. Jackson stared at him as if he'd gone mad.

But it was true!

Mr. Carlo said, "Sir, I — I humbly apologize for my behavior. Please forgive me."

The man must really be worried. "Oh, very well."

Mr. Carlo looked relieved.

"But only if we're kept entirely out of any publicity."

"You have my word," said Mr. Carlo.

Mrs. Jackson said, "Where was he last seen?"

Mr. Carlo gestured to the other end of the circle drive some thirty feet off, where cars would leave to merge onto the city street. A third car had pulled up behind the first two. "He went into the alleyway there and hasn't been seen since."

Mrs. Jackson said, "Then we must see this alleyway!"

His wife was all too eager to solve a puzzle. At times, it amused him. Today, he felt annoyed.

I'm still angry at Mr. Carlo, he thought.

He took a deep breath, let it out. The man's family had disappeared. He should at least look.

Harry came jogging into view. A large group streamed out of the Hotel, turning towards them.

So Mr. Jackson followed Mr. Carlo past the cars, the young valets, the crowd of people, the bellhops and their loads of luggage, to stand on the sidewalk in front of a long, graveled alleyway.

The alley went straight through to the far street past two stretches of wall. The wall on the left was three stories of brick, the hotel's wall on the right was stone, thirty-three stories high. The alley ran for a good city block, with not so much as a window on either side until he looked up. Six stories above them, the Hotel's balconies began.

Mr. Jackson felt astonished. Where could the man have gone? "Are you certain he went this way?"

"Three of my valets saw him turn the corner," Mr. Carlo said. Then he looked up at each side. "I've even had men go to the roof and balconies to look for rope." He shook his head. "Nothing." Mr. Carlo poked his walking-stick into the gravel. "Only goes down a few inches — hardly enough to hide a body."

"Oh, dear," Mrs. Jackson said. "Don't think that, not yet."

Mr. Jackson took his wife's arm. "Very well. Let's see this alleyway. Perhaps there's something about it we're missing."

***

Mrs. Jackson clung to Mr. Jackson's arm as they crunched over the gravel. Where could the man have possibly gone to?

The alley ran without break: walls, gravel, sky.

It was as if the man had disappeared.

She'd seen gravel many a time. Yet she'd never walked on the stuff before, and she hated the way it gave way beneath her feet. It shifted, made unpleasant sounds as she moved. "Surely someone heard him walk on this."

Mr. Jackson said, "At mid-day, with traffic like it is? Hardly. Listen."

They stopped, and from here — perhaps twenty yards down — they could barely hear the traffic.

A chill came over her. A man could have shouted, screamed, and not been heard.

The three crunched along to the end of the long alley. No grates lay on either side.

Did this alley have no drainage?

She decided a grate would have let the gravel just drop through. The path ran smooth and complete.

Perhaps they put down gravel to cover up flooding, she thought, so it wouldn't be muddy.

Along the left was brick all the way to the wide, tree-lined street. But the fine stone of the Hotel ended some thirty yards to the right along the drop down to the dock, with a metal railing painted black spanning the distance. Far below, men and trucks and loads moved in a flurry of activity.

They crunched over to the sidewalk and turning round it, surveyed the dock. From this vantage, there were three levels. A platform at street level had stairs descending fifteen feet on either side to the parking lot.

To the left, several trucks were parked at a loading dock. A truck pulled up a driveway on the far side of the lot and turned to drive away.

To the right, another truck backed down an underground driveway to a second loading dock large enough to fit three trucks there.

"He was supposed to meet some of my dockworkers there." Mr. Carlo pointed across to the platform. "They were to have lunch together —"

Mrs. Jackson noticed several electric lamps above the platform. Of course, they were turned off at this time of day, but what surprised her was that one of the glass covers was blue!

"— but he never arrived. Twenty minutes they waited. But when they walked through to the front to find him, he was gone."

It didn't take twenty minutes to walk back here. Surely someone would have seen Mr. Vincenzo if he'd emerged. Mrs. Jackson gazed down the alleyway. "I have no answer for you, sir."

This seemed a puzzle greater than any she'd solved yet. "Men don't just disappear. There must be something else going on."

"I'll walk back with you," Mr. Carlo said. "Through the alley, or brave the docks?"

The docks seemed all a-flurry. Another truck passed them to turn into the driveway. Men were carrying boxes up the steps to the platform on both sides.

"Perhaps the alley," Mr. Jackson said.

A car came slowly crunching up the alley, and as it approached, they stepped aside to let it pass. Mrs. Jackson said, "Does this way have much traffic?"

"No," Mr. Carlo said. "It's too sharp a corner to turn the trucks into the dock, so most go the long way round. Just the occasional car."

A family sat in the car: three children and a couple. The husband hunched over the steering wheel, peering this way and that before turning left.

Mr. Carlo chuckled. "It's likely that he's lost."

As they retraced their steps, Mrs. Jackson remembered the brochure she'd seen when they arrived to the Hotel. "Didn't this alley used to have cobblestones?"

Mr. Carlo shrugged. "I suppose the City Planning Office might know."

Mrs. Jackson felt her foot suddenly slip into the gravel, and something grated along the heel of her right shoe. She stopped, lifted her foot. A deep gouge over a half-inch long rose up along the leather covering her heel. "My shoes are ruined by this stuff!"

Mr. Jackson said, "We'll get you another pair."

"I suppose." She trudged along, feeling disgruntled. She liked those shoes. "But why would Mr. Vincenzo come down this alley at mid-day wearing his good shoes when he could have just gone through the Hotel?"

Mr. Carlo stopped, astonishment on his face. "You're right!"

"You know, I'd never considered that," Mr. Jackson said, at almost the same time.

They stared at each other.

Mrs. Jackson struggled along through the gravel, clinging to Mr. Jackson's arm. "There must have been some reason for it." She peered up at the blank walls beside them, feeling as though she missed something.

When they arrived back at the front of the Hotel, Mrs. Jackson said, "Might I speak to the valets here? With your permission, Mr. Carlo, of course."

Mr. Carlo said, "Whatever you need." Then he disappeared into the Hotel.

"Let's get you into some other shoes," Mr. Jackson said, "then we can pick up Bessie."

While she put on a new pair, Mr. Jackson leaned against her dresser, her damaged shoes in hand. "If you really like these shoes, I can have them repaired. Whatever makes you happy."

He was a dear man. "Only if it's no trouble."

"None at all! I'll call right down. They can send the maid for our floor to have it taken care of."

Mrs. Jackson smiled at him. "I appreciate it."

When the couple came out of the elevators, they went left, then turned down the narrower hall to their right to retrieve Bessie from the groomer.

Mrs. Jackson felt a great fondness for her little dog. "Why, you've had a haircut! Don't you look pretty?"

Bessie danced with excitement.

Returning to the larger hallway, the three turned left past the elevators. They then went to the lobby and the gift shop which lay in its left corner, close to the street.

The gift shop had all sorts of items one might expect: souvenirs of the Hotel, as well as of the city. Toiletries and patent medicines, fresh flowers, small gifts. After so much travel, to her it seemed ordinary. But Mr. Jackson appeared enthralled, examining each item in turn.

Mrs. Jackson handed Bessie's leash to him. "You stay as long as you like. I think I'll talk with the valets."

Mr. Jackson gave her a happy smile, then went back to examining a golden wristwatch.

So Mrs. Jackson returned to the front of the hotel. Traffic had slowed in the time they'd been gone. Harry waited alone at the valet box, so she approached him. "Sir, might I have a word? Mr. Carlo has approved it."

"Of course."

"You said last night that Mr. Vincenzo was there last week," she pointed the way she'd just come, "and then he was gone."

"Yes, ma'am. I saw him standing there. Well, it was back closer to the wall. Then a car came up, and I took the man's keys. When I looked back, Mr. Earl was gone."

"What happened then? Anything unusual?"

The young man stood in thought for a moment. "When I pulled out to park the car, a truck turned in front of me into the alley. It was all very sudden: he didn't signal or nothing. I had to slam on my brakes."

"One of yours?"

"Yeah," he said, as if he hadn't realized it before. "It was strange. No one drives trucks down there. Even with the small ones you have to do a three-point turn to get into the dock."

Mrs. Jackson had never driven a car, but she understood what he meant. Something definitely wasn't right. "Did you happen to look down the alley?"

"No, ma'am, I didn't. It was busy out. You have to keep your wits about you to get parking here!"

Right then, Mr. Carlo, Mr. Jackson, and Bessie came out through the front doors to the Hotel. Bessie seemed very happy to see her!

A car pulled up. Harry said, "I best get back to work."

"Thanks for your help."

The three approached her. Mr. Carlo said, "Did you learn anything?"

"Well, yes," Mrs. Jackson said. "A truck went down the alley a short time after Mr. Vincenzo did."

Mr. Jackson put his hand to his chin, "So they could have picked up Mr. Vincenzo or seen what happened."

Mrs. Jackson gestured to Harry, who stood with an older gentleman beside a gleaming new car. "He said the truck was one of yours. He should be able to tell you which one."

Harry got into the car and drove off.

"I'll speak with him when he returns," Mr. Carlo said. "Each truck is assigned to a crew. They should be able to tell me what they saw, if anything."

Mrs. Jackson said to Mr. Jackson, "Did you end up getting anything?"

He gave Mr. Carlo a quick glance. "A gift for a friend. I had it sent up to the room."

Bessie began sniffing their shoes, then pulled towards the graveled alley, whining.

"You know, she's done that twice since we arrived," Mrs. Jackson said. "I wonder what she smells."

The three of them followed Bessie to the gravel, then down the alleyway. About ten yards along, Bessie moved to the center of the alleyway and began growling.

When Bessie began to dig, Mrs. Jackson snatched the little dog away from the sharp gravel. "No, Bessie, dear, you'll hurt yourself!"

Mr. Jackson stood staring at the place Bessie had been digging, horror on his face. "We need a shovel." He turned, running towards the street.

Mrs. Jackson took a step back. "Mr. Carlo, perhaps you should join him." She looked over at the man, who'd gone pale. "If your cousin is in there, you don't want to see him."

Bessie strained in her arms, growling, barking.

"Hush," Mrs. Jackson said, petting her little dog. "You've done your duty, and that very well."

The black and brass walking-stick clattered to the ground. Mr. Carlo retreated to the wall, hands clasped to his face.

Soon men came with shovels, and under the gravel there was a manhole, propped open with a bit of gravel. They then called for crowbars, and after some effort, removed the cover.

Underneath, it was as they'd feared.

Mr. Earl Vincenzo lay below, gravel all around him, dead.

7

Mrs. Jackson held Bessie as she, Mr. Jackson, and Mr. Carlo stood on the sidewalk watching the crime scene.

Mr. Carlo had his fists firmly planted on his hips. "So **now** the police are interested," he said bitterly. "If they'd done their job, my cousin might've been found the day he disappeared. Perhaps even alive!"

The alleyway had been cordoned off at the street on both ends, with officers directing curious passerby around the area. Inside the cordon, a truck marked "Coroner" sat parked facing the street. In the alley beyond, a flurry of activity.

Sergeant Benjamin Nestor approached the couple, shaking his head. "You again."

Mr. Carlo pressed forward. "What happened?"

"Hit on the head, looks like," the sergeant said. "But it's a good ten feet down there. Still don't know if it was the blow to the head or the fall that killed him. The coroner will have his report to us in a few days."

"I'm calling his wife," Mr. Carlo said.

The sergeant watched him leave. "All this time I thought he'd run off."

"You're a homicide man," Mr. Jackson said. "How'd you know about this?"

"Carlo had me on the phone not thirty seconds after my patrolman left, wanting to make sure he got proper service." The sergeant let out a short laugh, then sobered. "I suppose he's got you two investigating now."

"Only just," said Mr. Jackson. "But my wife did learn something useful."

Mrs. Jackson felt amused at the dubious expression on the sergeant's face. "I spoke with one of the valets. A Hotel truck went down the alley minutes after the man did. It's a full block to the other side: surely whoever drove that truck saw him."

The sergeant nodded. "I'll have my men talk with them. I've also sent men to see where those tunnels go. If he climbed down and someone killed him, there'll be some sign of them along the way."

Mrs. Jackson shook her head. "Someone replaced the manhole, filled in around it, and smoothed it out. That took time. Whoever was on that truck either saw Mr. Vincenzo and the man who killed him, or did the deed themselves."

Mr. Jackson had been frowning, hand to chin. "The hole isn't that very far from the street. Surely someone saw something."

To Mrs. Jackson's dismay, the sergeant laughed. "Here? Even if someone were to watch the entire deed, they'd not tell me. No, sir, while we police do our best, the Mob has too much influence here." He shrugged. "For all we know, they could have done this themselves."

Mr. Jackson said, "Mr. Carlo has asked us to help. But what would you have us do?"

"As little as you must," the sergeant said. "But if you do learn something, bring it to me first. Carlo's too invested in this matter to be rational."

Mrs. Jackson nodded. In his state, Mr. Carlo might shoot someone they merely considered a suspect.

Then the sergeant twitched. "There is one thing. The wife. I'm sure she knows something, but she won't talk to me."

Mrs. Jackson felt surprised. "You want me to?"

"If you would. Perhaps she'd talk to you."

Mrs. Jackson took a step back, heart pounding. Talk to a grieving widow about her murdered husband? Her voice shook. "I don't know if I can."

Sergeant Nestor frowned. "You're ever the sticky-beak when it's not wanted. Now I actually need your help and you say no?"

Bessie struggled a bit in her arms, growling.

To her surprise, Mr. Jackson said, "I won't have my wife harassed! She's still in mourning!"

Sergeant Nestor's eyes narrowed, as if trying to recall something.

"You've asked," Mr. Jackson said sternly. "If and when she feels able, she'll do so." He put his arm around her shoulders. "Until then, good day to you."

"Well, then," the sergeant said, and it seemed clear he felt disgruntled. "I should return to work."

Mrs. Jackson set Bessie down, the leash looped around her wrist. Overwhelmed with grief and remorse, she buried her face in Mr. Jackson's chest.

His arms went warm around her. "I'm sorry he did that. It was thoughtless and unfair."

She turned her head to one side, another wave of grief washing over her before she could speak. "Thank you for defending me." It was so different from the man she once thought him to be. She put her arms round him, eyes shut, listening to the people passing by on all sides. Then she took a handkerchief from her pocket and wiped underneath her eyes.

He smiled fondly at her, then took her face in his hands and kissed her forehead. "We'll get through this." He glanced down. "Won't we, Bessie?"

Smiling to herself, Mrs. Jackson stuffed the handkerchief back into her pocket.

The couple turned arm in arm to face the lake, and slowly, her mind began to clear. Her gaze fell across the wide Lake Shore Drive and onto the lovely benches stationed there. She nudged Mr. Jackson, gesturing towards them. "Are you thinking what I'm thinking?"

"I believe I am."

For the next few days, the couple took Bessie down to the stoplight, across Lake Shore Drive, then back. They sat upon the benches at the time the murder must have occurred.

But while they saw many a person cross the graveled alley, only one crossed every day: a young woman wearing a cloche hat and coat the color of dark mustard.

The next day, Mrs. Jackson followed her.

8

The woman was short with strawberry blonde curls. She walked quickly, with purpose, never looking back, then darted between two buildings.

When Mrs. Jackson peered around the corner into the cobblestone alleyway, the woman stood right there, arms crossed.

Mrs. Jackson jumped back, startled. "Oh!"

She was young, perhaps twenty, with hazel eyes. "I thought you were checking on me," the woman said, "rather than just going my way. Who are you? And why are you following?"

"I mean you no harm." Mrs. Jackson stepped forward, out of view of the street. "But you go past the Hotel every day. In that alley where the police have been, did you see anything go on last week?"

A cynical look crossed the woman's face. "With the police, are you?"

"Not actually," Mrs. Jackson said. "The family asked me to help." For a moment, she'd forgotten what she was called here. But then she held out a hand. "Pamela Jackson."

The woman's eyebrows raised, but she briefly took Mrs. Jackson's hand, her unbuttoned coat falling open. "A lady investigator? You don't see that every day."

"Mostly retired." This girl wasn't one of the waifs displayed in the papers: a fine form lay under that cute little dress she wore. "But my Mr. Jackson and I are acquainted with the family, so —"

The woman let out a soft chuckle. "You've been pressed into service." She gave a quick flick of her chin. "The husband works with you, I take it?"

Mrs. Jackson shrugged. "We're just newly married."

The woman appraised her. "You seem a decent enough sort. Sure, I saw a truck there last week. I noticed it because there hasn't been one there for a long while."

"Now that is interesting. How long ago were other trucks there?"

The woman smiled. "Oh, back when there used to be cobbles in that alley. And that's all I'll say on that topic, thank you very much."

Hmm, Mrs. Jackson thought.

"Don't look for me later. I'll be taking a new route to work from now on."

Mrs. Jackson blurted out, "Then I shall be grieved. You're the most interesting person I've met here so far."

The woman's cheeks colored, and she gave a wry little smile. "Am I now?" For an instant, the woman surveyed her. "Perhaps I might not disappear entirely."

For the first time in a long while, Mrs. Jackson felt flustered. "Please don't. I beg you, pray join us for dinner. As amends for having caused you distress."

"Dinner? At that grand hotel?" The woman chuckled. "I'd have nothing to wear."

"Luncheon?"

The woman considered it. "Perhaps." Then she straightened, spoke with confidence. "I believe I will."

Mrs. Jackson felt relieved. "Tomorrow, then? Just give your name to the Headwaiter."

"It would be a pleasure."

"I'm truly sorry to have disturbed you."

The woman gave a soft smile. "The name's Ophelia. Denton. But if anyone else comes looking, I never saw you in my life."

***

While Mrs. Jackson was following Miss Ophelia Denton, Mr. Jackson decided to speak to the Hotel's manager.

Mr. Flannery Davis sat behind his desk, glancing up at Mr. Jackson's knock upon the open door. "Good day, sir. How may I help?"

Mr. Jackson tucked Bessie under his left arm. "Might we speak privately, sir?"

"Of course. Close the door, there, will you?"

Mr. Jackson closed the door and sat across the desk from the man, settling Bessie on his lap. "I know about your little speakeasy downstairs."

300

The man paled for a moment, but quickly recovered. "Are you going to tell the Feds?"

"Certainly not!" Mr. Jackson and his wife wanted nothing to do with the Feds. "Yet I also know that your former Head Valet had some dealings with those supplying you."

"Oh," the manager said, realization dawning in his face. "And you think he may have offended them?"

"Hard to say, not knowing what his involvement was. But Mr. Carlo's quite anxious to learn who's done this, so —"

"You're here on his behalf."

"I felt it better to speak with you about this, rather than him. The whole thing must be a terrible ordeal."

"Indeed." The manager nodded slowly, eyes on his desk. Then he raised his head. "When a shipment comes in, we have a signal —"

The blinking owl in the soda shop.

"— which Mr. Vincenzo can — um, could — see from his station. At that point, he collected the staff together to unload the trucks."

"So the entire staff is in on this?"

"Most believe it's a delivery like any other. Many of the youngsters know about the speakeasy, but —"

"Not that they're helping to supply it."

"No. Only our most trusted men know what's in the crates we receive."

"Let me get this straight. Mr. Vincenzo was simply in charge of collecting workers to unload trucks. Am I correct? Or did he have a bigger role?"

"Well ... he'd look out for the Feds, or anyone he suspected of being with them. There's a blue light out back. If that goes on —"

Mr. Jackson recalled the trucks backing down to the lower dock. "The trucks drive away."

"Exactly."

It sounded as if the only people who might take offense at what the man was doing were the Feds themselves. Hardly the sort of fellows who'd knock a man senseless then throw him into the sewers. "Well, thanks for speaking with me."

"My pleasure."

"And thank you for your kindness."

"Oh, that, sir. Never you mind. Mr. Carlo's family first came here as outsiders, and he saw how your people — and his — were treated first thing. We had a talk about it when I was hired. You have money, you are more than welcome here."

Mr. Jackson smiled, but he didn't feel it. He'd first come here after he had his men investigate the place, and while it was indeed as fine as it seemed, his first few visits — while comfortable indeed — had not been nearly so welcoming.

When he first brought his wife here, injured as she was, it was the best he might manage on such short notice. But her accompanying him seemed to have made all the difference. "Very good." He rose, setting Bessie onto the floor. "I'll let you get back to work."

***

Mrs. Jackson met back with Mr. Jackson for an early luncheon, which they took in the Hotel dining room. But before they might share all they'd learned, the dowager Duchess appeared!

"Oh, my dear friends! You should have told me you were coming early! I would have met you at once." She surveyed Mr. Jackson's face. "Oh, I do love the beard!"

Mrs. Jackson smiled to herself. "Won't you join us?"

"Only if it won't be an imposition," Duchess Cordelia said.

"We insist," Mr. Jackson said. "In fact, I would welcome your thoughts on a matter."

Duchess Cordelia sat beside Mr. Jackson. "What matter?"

Mrs. Jackson was about to speak, but Mr. Jackson held up a hand. "You must promise to tell no one —"

Ah, Mrs. Jackson thought. That would be like telling the wind not to blow.

"— but the police believe that the Head Valet was murdered!"

Duchess Cordelia gasped, pressing her lined hands to her mouth. "Goodness!" She leaned forward, glancing around. "Do you think we're in any danger?"

"Surely not," Mr. Jackson said. "But who would want to murder him? He seemed a decent enough chap."

Mrs. Jackson snorted quietly, amused.

Yet his words seemed to draw some recollection from the dowager, who leaned forward to speak in hushed tones. "Did you know that he was an awful flirt? With married women, no less!" She leaned back. "One of the husbands, that's who I'd put my money on." She gave a self-satisfied nod. But then her face turned sad. "Poor Effie —"

Mrs. Jackson said, "Why Effie?"

"Oh, my dear ... you really must not mention it. But she got entangled with the man. He broke her heart some time back, and I believe she still carries a torch for him." The old woman's head drooped as she shook it sorrowfully. "She looks cheery enough, but when she thinks no one's looking ..."

"What a pity." Mr. Jackson seemed to truly mean it.

This brought back uncomfortable memories of herself becoming entangled with the wrong man, which Mrs. Jackson pushed aside. "Do you know who any of these husbands might be?"

Duchess Cordelia gained a new energy. "I shall write you a list. It will probably not be complete, but —"

Mr. Jackson chuckled. "Why in the world a list?"

"Hush, dear," Mrs. Jackson said, not wanting him to dissuade the woman when she'd finally given them something useful. "A list would be lovely."

"Well," Duchess Cordelia said, "I know you're investigators. I was going to ask Mrs. Jackson to the library with me, but I saw our Mr. Carlo hurry over to speak with you. And of course everyone knows Mr. Vincenzo is Mr. Carlo's cousin, and so —"

Mr. Jackson said, "You really are remarkable."

Duchess Cordelia blushed, giving him a shy smile. "Why, thank you, sir."

Mrs. Jackson chuckled, amused. "Your list would be ever so helpful."

The waiter brought Duchess Cordelia's meal to her.

"I do hope so," she said, in between bites. "My main hope is that the culprit is someone from outside the Hotel. We've had enough scandal here to last a lifetime."

***

After their plates were taken away, Mr. Jackson asked for pen and paper so Duchess Cordelia might write. As she wrote, the waiters cleared the huge dining room, removing the plates, the silverware, the centerpieces, the tablecloths. Maids with vacuum cleaners began working over the carpeting.

Had Mr. Carlo been aware of what his cousin was up to?

Perhaps he didn't want to see what everyone around him did, Mr. Jackson thought. He'd had this experience himself, in other matters.

Duchess Cordelia hesitated for just a moment, wrote one more name, then set the pen down with a smack. "There! You have learned all I know on the topic."

"You have our sincere thanks," he said.

"This will be ever so helpful," said his wife.

The dowager beamed. "You simply must tell me all about it when you catch the man."

He could feel his wife withdraw into herself. "These matters are confidential. Imagine if we'd told everyone about what happened the last time the Hotel had this sort of thing go on."

"Oh," Duchess Cordelia said, seeming dismayed.

"You see," his wife continued, "some things are best left silent."

Mr. Jackson heartily agreed. "Never fear, my Lady, you'll learn who did the deed soon enough." He took the paper from her and glanced quickly over it: relatively small print, both sides. "Assuming we can."

Bessie began pawing at his leg, and he smiled down at her. "Ready to go outside again?"

***

Mrs. Jackson held onto Mr. Jackson's arm as the couple strolled down Lake Shore Drive with Bessie, looking at the shops.

They'd not been out much the first time they'd been here, what with her injury and all. Then after they'd solved the unpleasantness at the Hotel, her Mr. Jackson had been focused on seeing the sights. Duchess Cordelia, of course, had wanted them to see "everything."

That made her giggle.

"What amuses you?"

Mrs. Jackson smiled to herself. "Just thinking of our Duchess. She does so love this place."

"Ah," he said. "Then you were thinking of our last visit here."

He did that on relatively little information. She took his hand. "You know, you're quite remarkable yourself."

She loved to see his blush, his little smile.

The she realized the truth: she was becoming fond of him. She was becoming enamored.

And it frightened her.

When she agreed to marry him, she'd been fleeing the devastation of her past life. His offer seemed for the best, but she only accepted because she didn't think it anything other than a suitable arrangement.

They'd been bitter rivals for over a decade. She knew of his fondness for men. And while recently he'd been more congenial, she'd thought him to be such a scoundrel that she didn't care if he died, as everyone else had who she'd let into her life.

And as he'd said: *it might make life easier for you.*

But then it turned out he'd been in love with her.

She squeezed his arm tightly. "You must take care. We mustn't be seen to have too much interest in police matters, not so close to the Hotel."

He smiled to himself. "My dear girl. You worry yourself far too much. We have Sergeant Nestor, and Mr. Carlo, and a host of others here who'll protect us." Then he turned to face her, people streaming back and forth around them. "Not to mention my men."

She'd forgotten about them.

He took her hands. "So you see, we shall be just fine." He offered his arm, and they continued to stroll along. "There's not a man in the world who can hurt us."

9

The couple took tea in their rooms. Mr. Jackson sat with his wife reading the books they'd gotten from the library earlier, until Mr. Raymond came to dress him for dinner.

Mr. Raymond examined the blemishes on his neck closely. "Your skin seems to still be agitating itself there." He drew back, hand to his chin. "It's strange: usually letting the hair grow does the trick."

He went to the bathroom to wash his hands, leaving the water running. When he returned, he opened his kit. "I'll do another heat treatment after the ointment, to open the pores. That will help drive the medication in."

Mr. Jackson nodded. Despite still feeling uneasy about him for some reason, the man seemed most competent. And quite sanitary. "Sounds good."

Mr. Jackson watched as Mr. Raymond prepared to work. The man had a medium build, but his arms strained the shirt he wore, particularly when he did his mixing. "You look like a man who values his exercise."

Mr. Raymond grinned. "I've done a fair amount in my time. But I had to help after my father died."

"I'm sorry to hear about it."

Mr. Raymond shrugged, glancing away, and spoke lightly. "No matter. He died when I was a boy."

A boy? Mr. Jackson recalled when his own father died. Even as a grown man, it'd been painful. "That must have been difficult."

Mr. Raymond began applying the ointment. "Yeah, well, that was life. I started sweeping for the neighbor's shop, then when I got old enough, I worked as a messenger boy. Then later on, I took up boxing."

"Boxing? You managed not to get hit too badly."

Mr. Raymond let out a laugh. "Got my nose broke once. The doctor who fixed me said I should get out before I got concussed, or worse. I signed up for valet training at his advice."

"That was quite kind of him."

He seemed surprised. "Never thought of it that way. It did come in handy: during the war, only those with valet training got to tend the officers."

"How was the training?"

Mr. Raymond shrugged. "Hard at first. I didn't have the schooling that some did. But I like it."

He went into the bathroom, turned off the water, then returned with a steaming towel. "I still do the boxer training on the side. And I particularly like the lifting of weights. It relaxes me."

The hot, moist towel on Mr. Jackson's face seemed quite relaxing. He looked forward to dinner with the

Neubergs tonight. Their dinner upon the yacht six days earlier seemed a century past. "Say, would you care for dinner with us sometime?"

Mr. Raymond's eyes widened. "That's very much appreciated, sir! But fraternizing with clients isn't allowed. Company policy. I wouldn't have gone to play dominoes if I'd have known you'd be there."

"Well, I don't want you in trouble. But I don't want you not to play alongside your sister on our account. Would it be all right if we stayed at separate tables?"

Mr. Raymond considered this. "I'll ask, sir. I don't see why not."

Some time later, Mr. Jackson met George Neuberg and his parents in the lobby. He felt pleased to see them, particularly George, who he hadn't gotten a chance to speak with since the dominoes game.

George looked more rested, back to his old self, and his parents seemed well. But when they met in the lobby, Bessie barked at Mr. Neuberg until Mrs. Jackson brought the dog away to be watched during dinner.

As she left, Mr. Jackson turned to the Neubergs. "I'm terribly sorry; I don't know what's come over her."

Mr. Neuberg shrugged. "Dogs don't seem to like me, and I have no idea why."

That amused Mr. Jackson. "Who knows what might go on in the mind of a dog?"

"True," Mr. Neuberg said. "Say, I like the beard. It suits you."

"Thanks." Mr. Jackson wasn't so fond of it. If only his skin would heal so he might have a proper shave!

Mrs. Jackson walked up. "She's all settled in with her dinner. They said to take as long as we like."

"Well done," Mr. Jackson said. Then he turned to his guests. "Come, our table's waiting."

It'd been a good idea to reserve the table: not an empty seat remained save for the ones around theirs.

George gave Will a bemused grin when the waiter showed up to take their order.

"Well, aren't we spiffy," Will said to George, then nudged him. "Out with the big cheese, are we?"

George said, "These are my parents."

"Oh." Will rushed to slide in Mr. Neuberg's chair, then Mr. Jackson's, then George's, who for some reason had placed himself directly across the table. "No harm meant, sir."

George laughed. "Don't 'sir' me, ya whisk broom, get us our menus."

"Right away." Will went off, feeling his chin. There really wasn't much there, but he'd evidently forgotten to shave before dinner.

"Your dining room is spectacular," Mrs. Neuberg said. "And your friends seem very nice."

George smiled to himself.

Will came back with the menus and began passing them around.

Mr. Jackson said, "Order whatever you like; the food is magnificent."

George said, "But —"

Mr. Jackson raised his hand. "I insist. I invited you. It's only fair."

George's eyes narrowed, but he said nothing further.

What could possibly be bothering him? Mr. Jackson resolved to speak to him about it later.

But the conversation and the food pushed it out of his mind, and it wasn't until he lay in bed that evening that he remembered. *Oh, well*, he thought. *I'll have plenty of chance to speak to him about it later.*

***

The next day at lunch, Mrs. Jackson made sure to sit facing the dining room door. She generally did as a matter of course — an investigator would never want someone to approach from behind unseen.

But today, she felt all a-flutter.

Would Miss Ophelia attend? Would she and Mr. Jackson get along? Would Bessie like her?

"I've never seen you so unsettled," Mr. Jackson said, yet in a good-natured way. He took her left hand. "I'm sure all will go well."

The table was almost full, their choice made on purpose so as not to have the conversation occupied too much by the old dowager's reminiscing.

Miss Ophelia Denton appeared then, and was shown to their table. Mrs. Jackson rose. "Come round and sit here."

Bessie, who'd been lying on the floor beside Mrs. Jackson's chair, perked up her ears.

"Mr. Hector Jackson," Mrs. Jackson said, "may I introduce Miss Ophelia Denton."

Ophelia held out her hand. "A pleasure, sir."

Mr. Jackson said, "My wife has told me much about you." He gestured down. "And this is Bessie."

"Hello, Bessie," Ophelia said.

Bessie's eyes were bright, her tail wagging.

They sat and placed their orders. A waiter poured their tea.

"This hotel is lovely," Ophelia said. "I've passed it for years now, but never dared step inside."

"Oh! You must see the entirety," Mrs. Jackson said, then felt foolish. She sounded like Duchess Cordelia!

Ophelia gave her a wry smile. "The grand tour? I'd not miss that."

Mr. Jackson said, "What is it you do, Miss Denton? To pass by our hotel every day."

Ophelia grinned. "Oh, I'm a dancer over at Club Patruni." She leaned back. "Don't suppose you folks have ever heard of it."

Mrs. Jackson shook her head, glanced at Mr. Jackson, who shrugged. Then she turned back to Ophelia. "Do you like it there?"

It was Ophelia's turn to shrug. "I don't have to cook and I don't have to clean. I stay on stage, so no flippers on the fanny. And I don't have to muck about with children." She grinned. "Suits me just fine."

The mention of children sparked a pang in Mrs. Jackson's chest. She missed her little son terribly. How she wished things might have gone differently!

But she had to accept it: he was gone. She could never see him, never hold him again.

Mr. Jackson's hand grasped hers. "My wife's in mourning for her child."

Ophelia grimaced. "I'm so very sorry. I had no idea!" Her hand was soft, holding hers. Then she opened her napkin. "We'll not speak on the topic again."

That made Mrs. Jackson smile a bit. "You know, I think we might get along just fine."

They fell silent, yet it didn't feel awkward the way such silences often do.

Mrs. Jackson felt interested in Ophelia's work. "What's the Club Patruni like?"

"Fun place," Ophelia said. "Ground floor's got dinner and a regular show. But there's this area downstairs —"

"Ah," Mr. Jackson said, as if now he understood everything. "You work there."

"Yeah," Ophelia said, her tone approving. "You know your onions, don't ya?"

Mr. Jackson grinned.

The waiters set down their plates. Mrs. Jackson got the gist of the conversation, but the talk here was still strange to her. "What kind of dancing do you do?"

Ophelia gave her a wink and a grin. "You'll have to come by and see."

Mr. Jackson stirred. "So what does your mother think of —"

At the word "mother," Ophelia's face fell.

"Oh, dear," Mr. Jackson said. "Forgive me."

Ophelia didn't look at either of them. "What the war didn't get, the flu did." She raised her head, squaring her shoulders. "I like to think she'd want me happy." She turned to face her food. "You gotta live life today is my motto. Tomorrow's just a word, not a guarantee."

Mr. Jackson nodded. "Well said."

Ophelia picked up her fork. "Don't know about you, but I'm hungry."

Mr. Jackson laughed, then unfurled his cloth napkin, setting it on his lap.

Mrs. Jackson began poking at her food. *You gotta live life today.*

She wasn't entirely sure she knew how.

***

It turned out that Miss Denton had the day off. So after they'd eaten, Mr. Jackson proposed a tour of the Hotel.

The three of them walked the gardens, peered at the spa area, looked out over the docks. They even climbed the grand staircase and walked round looking at the sights there. But Miss Denton seemed most fascinated by the elevators.

After a few rides up and down, Mr. Jackson said, "There's another swimming pool and garden on the roof. If you'd like to join us, we could have tea there. Or we could have it brought to our suite instead."

"Is it that late?" Miss Denton seemed surprised at the time, rather than worried about having somewhere to be. "Let's see your suite."

She gasped in delight at their parlor. "It's gorgeous!" Rushing to the parlor's French doors, she flung them open and stepped upon the balcony. "And the view!"

Mr. Jackson went to the telephone in the corner.

"Room Service, may I assist you?"

"Full tea service to 3205, the parlor door."

"Right away, sir."

He went out to the balcony.

Miss Denton said, "— and the fellow had snuck his way right under the costume rack! Oh, you should have seen his face when the bouncers arrived."

His wife laughed, the sun on her face, her hair flowing free.

How fortunate I am, he thought.

She glanced over at him with a happy smile, her cheeks coloring, and he thought his heart might seize up within him. *She's so beautiful.*

A movement out of the corner of his eye. Miss Denton looked between them, her face guarded.

He smiled at her. For an instant, he felt moved. "It's good for my wife to have friends here."

The girl's delightfully wry smile returned. "Do you not have many friends here?"

His wife gave a one-shoulder shrug. "Acquaintances, many. Friends?" She glanced at him, took his hand. "I suppose our dowager Duchess is friendly to us."

Miss Denton's eyes widened. "A Duchess? Here?"

He said, "She lives down the hall. We made her acquaintance the last time we stayed."

His wife grinned. "She's a lovely old lady. I'll introduce you. But she'll talk your ear off if you let her."

The parlor door bell rang. "Ah," Mr. Jackson said, "tea's here." He went to the door, Bessie following. To his surprise, George stood there! "Come in!"

George chuckled. "Didn't expect me here, did you?"

"Not at all."

He wheeled the cart into the room. "They've got us rotating jobs. Want it set up on the table there?"

"Certainly." Mr. Jackson said.

The two women came into the room. His wife said, "George! You must meet our new friend. This is Miss Ophelia Denton." She then gestured to George. "George Neuberg and my Mr. Jackson are dear friends."

A wry smile. "Are you now?" Miss Denton held out her hand. "Pleasure to meet ya."

The four of them got the table set up, Bessie sniffing the cart and whining. George laughed. "This goes much faster with four!"

"Sit with us for a bit, then," Mr. Jackson said, "since you have the extra time."

George grinned. "I do believe I will."

Miss Denton looked between himself and George, more than a bit puzzled, it seemed, at the sight of a waiter sitting with Hotel guests.

Mr. Jackson said to George, "How did your parents like dinner last night?"

George's easy attitude disappeared. "They enjoyed it very much. They asked me to offer their thanks."

What was wrong? "Think nothing of it! They've hosted us more than once. It was my pleasure."

George rose. "I best be off, before they send someone looking." He nodded to Miss Denton. "A pleasure to meet you." Then he took the cart and left.

Miss Denton said, "You've got interesting friends."

Mr. Jackson said, "I suppose we do." But his mind was on George. He'd been acting odd last night at dinner, too.

Perhaps he'd had an argument with his parents. His father could be overbearing, his mother, clingy. It would irritate any man after too long.

His wife and Miss Denton were eating, drinking tea, and chatting. Bessie seemed intent upon a couple of sandwiches his wife had emptied onto a saucer.

Miss Denton looked over at him. "So if you don't mind me asking, what was all that business in the alley about, anyway?"

He and his wife exchanged a glance, and he recalled her words to Duchess Cordelia. "I don't think we should say, not now."

His wife gave him an amused smile. "A man was attacked. We're still trying to figure out who did it."

Miss Denton's eyes widened. "Attacked? Next to this rich hotel?" She sounded dismayed. "Right near where I walk every day!"

His wife looked chagrined. "I didn't consider that."

Miss Denton smiled at her. "Never fear, I always stay to public roads. No alleys for me!"

It turned out that Miss Denton lived in a boarding house not too far off. "It's not bad. Room and board with a bath down the hall."

His wife said, "That sounds near where that old lady died a few months back."

"I knew your dog looked familiar," Miss Denton said. "It was right next door. This little gal used to follow me along the fence when I'd go off to work." She smiled under the table. "Fancy meeting you here!"

Bessie looked up, wagging her tail, then set back upon her meal.

The dog had an unusually good appetite these days. But she didn't seem to be getting any bigger. At least, not that he could see.

Perhaps it's some instinct, he thought. He'd heard that animals sensed the coming of winter.

His reverie was broken as Miss Denton rose. He scrambled to his feet. "Must you go?"

She chuckled. "If I don't show up for dinner on my days off, my landlady'll toss me out."

"Well, we don't want that," Mr. Jackson said, amused. "Let's be away then. I'll call down for a taxi."

"That's not necessary," Miss Denton said. "It's really not far."

"I insist," he said. The sky was beginning to darken. "I'll not have you out walking at night, and that's final."

As he went to telephone, Miss Denton said to his wife, "Guess I better not tell Grandpa my last show ends at two A.M."

His wife giggled. Giggled!

Grandpa? Good grief, he thought. I'm only thirty-three. "Yes," he said into the telephone, "a taxi. We'll be down in five minutes."

As they waited for the elevator, his wife said, "Would you like to play dominoes with us later tonight?"

Miss Denton tipped her head to the side a bit. "Never played." She shrugged. "Wouldn't know how."

He said, "Neither of us had played before last week's game. And you can meet Duchess Cordelia. We play in her suite."

Miss Denton hesitated, eyes wide. Then she smiled in a devil-may-care fashion. "Why not?"

His wife said, "It's after dinner. Around ten?"

"I'll meet you in the lobby at half past nine," Miss Denton said. "Unless you want to tell me the number."

The elevator door opened. He said, "We'll be happy to meet you down there. I'll send a taxi for you." He felt amused at the puzzled expression that crossed the girl's face, then her slow nod as she figured it all out. "It's settled then."

After they put Miss Denton into a cab and sent her on her way, his wife took his arm. "Thank you for being so kind to her."

He felt moved, so much so that they were back into the lobby before he might speak. "You've been very kind to George as well."

She gave a little pleased-with-herself smile and squeezed his arm. "We all need friends here."

They'd reached the elevator. "Indeed we do." The elevator opened and they went in. "Thirty-two, please."

The man at the controls nodded. "Yes, sir."

The couple stood in silence as the elevator moved upward. Right before they reached their floor, his wife said, "I wonder what friends our man had."

"It's a fair question."

***

When the couple returned to their parlor and the door firmly shut, Mrs. Jackson let Bessie off her leash to sniff about once more.

Yet Mr. Jackson stood in the center of the room.

She said, "What is it?"

"If Mr. Earl Vincenzo had offended someone so mortally as to have them kill him this way, wouldn't he know? Why would he ruin his shoes, as you put it, to meet up with someone in an alley, alone, that he knew wanted him dead?"

She had no idea.

"And in broad daylight, too? Nothing about this is making sense."

"It feels personal," she said. "Why not shoot the man? To hit him on the head ... go to all the work of putting him into the sewers —"

A look of horror crossed his face. "Mr. Vincenzo had to have helped dig out the manhole cover. Or at least be standing there when they did so."

"What do you mean?"

"Just picture it. Mr. Vincenzo goes down the alley. Moments later, the other valet almost hits a truck going in after him. So we have the head valet and the truck in the alley. Am I right?"

"I suppose."

"So whoever is driving the truck — let's say our two men — get out and talk to the valet. Now, the alley is still covered in gravel."

She nodded. "So they were there for some time."

"Yes. But they had plenty to spare. I'll wager if we find another witness, they'll merely say they saw the truck parked there. And if they passed on the other end, all they'd see were men and a truck. And even if they saw the murder take place, it'd be difficult for someone standing a full block away to identify them, not unless they knew them well."

Realization dawned. "They had to have parked behind the manhole! So there must be some way to mark its location that we missed."

"Very true! Well done. So the men are there. Perhaps the Head Valet believes there's something under there that he wants."

She recalled the way the gravel had crunched and slipped as they walked through it. "Important enough for him to ruin his shoes over."

He chuckled. "Indeed." Then his mirth faded. "But the callousness of those men! All that time, knowing the Head Valet's fate, yet allowing him to stand there."

She pictured the scene. "Or worse, help perform his own death."

Mr. Jackson nodded.

"So we look for at least two shovels," she said. "One is sure to be what hit him."

"You think so?"

She shrugged. "Seems reasonable. If you're going to hit someone after digging, and you both need to dig, you won't come up to them carrying a gun."

He seemed to gain a new energy. "I'll speak with the manager tomorrow about the shovels. Care to join me?"

She shook her head. She didn't like it. She didn't want to do it. But she now knew what she had to do. "Perhaps I will speak with the man's wife. She would know of his friends. And who hated him so fiercely."

10

The next day, Mrs. Jackson left Bessie with the veterinarian's boys and took a taxi to the Head Valet's home, arriving precisely at eleven. "Wait here, if you please," she said to the driver. "I shouldn't be long."

Mrs. Vincenzo lived in an area far too rich for the salary of a valet, even the Head Valet of a hotel so grand as the Myriad. A maid answered the door, ushering Mrs. Jackson to a spacious parlor. "She'll be right with you."

Mrs. Vincenzo was a tall, elegant woman, perhaps forty, with long black hair done up into a swirling bun reminiscent of days past. She took Mrs. Jackson's hand briefly then sat on a chair across the gilt-edged coffee table. "Thank you for visiting, ma'am. I admit to being surprised by your call."

"My husband and I are helping Mr. Carlo learn who hurt your husband," Mrs. Jackson said. "But I did want to express our condolences as well."

"Thank you," she said. Then her head drooped as she looked away. "How may I help you?"

"I know the police have asked these things," Mrs. Jackson said. "But perhaps you might have recalled something since then. Would anyone have reason to harm your husband?"

"Many have such reason." Mrs. Vincenzo let out a small amused snort, lips curling up at the corners. "I suppose I'm a suspect, even."

"You?"

She breathed deeply: in, then out. "My husband could be a violent man when provoked. And I seemed to ever provoke him. But I didn't do it."

"No one thinks you did," Mrs. Jackson said gently. "We'd like to learn who might have, though."

Mrs. Vincenzo nodded slowly. "I have a fear —"

At the way the woman stopped so suddenly, Mrs. Jackson felt a chill. "Of what?"

The words seemed ripped from Mrs. Vincenzo. "Let it not be!" She pressed her hands to her face.

Mrs. Jackson leaned forward. "What is it you fear?"

"My father. Could he have done this?"

Mrs. Jackson leaned back, mind whirling. Of course, she thought. What man wouldn't do anything to protect his daughter? And this had to be why she didn't want to speak with the police.

"Oh, that I'd said nothing, showed him no injuries, made no complaint! He's threatened to kill my husband more than once." The woman dropped her hands; tears lay on her face. "To lose my husband and father both!"

"We don't know anything yet. Could he do this?"

"I don't know!" Mrs.Vincenzo seemed despondent. "Which is worse? To know the fact of his good or bad, or to doubt him? My own father!" She began weeping.

Mrs. Jackson sat beside her, rested her hand upon Mrs. Vincenzo's back. "I'm glad you told me. Now we can clear your mind once and for all. My husband and I will learn the truth."

Mrs. Vincenzo wiped her eyes. "Thank you."

"And your father's name is?"

"Oh, yes, forgive me. Leo Trappola."

Mrs. Jackson retrieved a pad and pencil from her handbag and wrote the name down. Then she recalled what Ophelia had said, and decided to take a different tack. "Did your husband have many friends? Or people your children —?"

She shrugged. "We have no children. We lived separate lives. If he had friends, I knew nothing of it."

"He never mentioned anyone? No one came over?"

Her face pinched in concentration. "There was some tradesman who came by a few weeks back. They talked in here. An older man."

"Do you recall his name?"

She hesitated. "Newman? Newport?"

A chill ran down Mrs. Jackson's back. "Neuberg?"

"Yes, that's the name. I'm sure of it."

Oh, dear. "You said many people had reason to wish your husband harm. Who else?"

Mrs. Vincenzo peered at her hands. "He's not been a good man, Mrs. Jackson. Even from his youth." She sighed. "When I first met him, he was what the kids these days call a hoodlum. I was young and stupidly in love, but even then, I should have known he'd meet an untimely end."

"Was he with the Mob?"

She shrugged. "Not any of the bigger groups. But yes, though he tried to keep me from knowing. And of course, now he's working with Monty, who's always into something. Earl told me once not long ago that he wanted to get his life right —" at this, she shook her head. "Now I suppose I'll never know for sure."

"But you don't know the specifics? What gang?"

She shook her head. "I'd tell you if I did, I swear."

Even after all he'd done, she still loved him. Mrs. Jackson put her hand upon Mrs. Vincenzo's, feeling a surge of grief. "I'm ever so sorry for your loss."

***

On the way home, Mrs. Jackson considered the matter. Why would George's father come here? Surely he didn't have anything to do with a murder. Did he?

Bessie didn't like him. But that didn't mean he was a murderer. What possible motive might he have?

And though she felt Mr. Leo Trappola to be a likely suspect, something about the idea of either one being involved bothered her. The Chicago waterfront was wide, the countryside vast. Why kill Mr. Vincenzo in the middle of the city, risking discovery?

And there were much easier ways to dispose of a body. Shoveling gravel and hoisting manholes at noon seemed a bit much for men who had to be at least sixty.

Could either one have hired others to do it?

First things first, she thought. She didn't even know Mr. Neuberg's line of work.

She decided to begin there. The man could have a perfectly reasonable explanation for visiting.

Then there was the other matter.

Mrs. Jackson let out a sigh. She'd worked as a private investigator for many years. But the thought of tracking down Mr. Leo Trappola made her weary.

I'm too old for this.

Sergeant Nestor wanted her to get information from this woman, and she'd done it. Next time she saw him, she'd pass it along and see what he thought. For all she knew, he might already have spoken to the man.

She chuckled softly to herself as she got out of the taxi in front of the Hotel. At least now old Nestor had to admit she was useful.

***

Earlier that morning, Mr. Jackson had put on his scuffed shoes before accompanying his wife downstairs. When they parted in the lobby, Mr. Jackson stood for a moment watching the enormous fountain in the center there. He

330

felt as if pieces were still missing to this puzzle they'd been handed. But what?

No answer appearing, he went to see the manager, who left to investigate whether shovels were missing.

In the lobby once more, Mr. Jackson still had no ideas arise. So he decided to look at the alley.

The way was entirely bare. A few police stood at each end of it, but apparently Sergeant Nestor had told them about him, because they allowed him to pass.

Mr. Jackson stood ten feet from the open manhole. No marks stood on the walls beside it, nor anywhere along the route from the street.

Mr. Jackson approached a uniformed officer, a pale young man with big ears and freckles. "Were there any objects found in the alleyway?"

The officer blinked, shaking his head. "Don't rightly know. Forensics would have all that."

Mr. Jackson nodded. "Thank you, sir."

The officer nodded. "I seen you before, that night the waiter got sick. I was keeping the swells out the crime scene. You the house dick now?"

"I beg your pardon?"

"The hotel detective."

Mr. Jackson felt surprised at the idea. "I hadn't considered the matter."

The young officer chuckled. "Is Carlo at least paying you to come out here?"

Mr. Jackson considered the fact that he and his wife had lived in this magnificent hotel twice now, and so far, for free. "In a sense, yes!"

The officer grinned. "Then good for you."

Mr. Jackson fetched Bessie from the veterinarian's boys, who'd been playing with her, and returned to his suite. His wife was still with Mrs. Vincenzo, so he took off his scuffed-up shoes and stretched out on his bed.

Bessie began sniffing every bit of the room, as usual.

He let out a weary sigh. His wife was so incredibly brave to meet with that woman, after all she'd been through. Even though he didn't know the details of what happened the night before they'd married, he knew enough. She'd been hurt terribly, more in her heart than even that huge scar upon her arm, and he had to think of a way to help her recover.

He felt relieved that she and Miss Denton were getting along. From what he'd seen so far, this girl would provide quite a bit of diversion on her own.

The rash under his beard still felt tender. If anything, it seemed to be getting worse. He'd never had such an extensive rash before, not even as a boy.

Could it be something he ate? They'd eaten well on the steamer, but this new Chef's cooking was quite rich. He'd heard of people reacting in this way to new foods, although it'd never happened to him.

He patted his belly, which he'd let go a bit. Maybe he needed to start keeping better watch over his diet. And getting more exercise as well.

He sat up. "Here, Bessie, let's go for a walk."

They took the elevator down to the main floor, but instead of going to the right and out to the lobby, Mr. Jackson decided to turn left, past the veterinary and the gardens, then left again to the hallway from the kitchens to the platform out back.

George stood leaning against the wall outside the kitchens, tying his shoe. He glanced up. "What are you doing here?"

"Just walking about." He went to George. "Is everything okay?"

George glanced away. "Fine. Did your friend enjoy the day?"

For a moment, Mr. Jackson was at a loss. "Oh, the girl. Yes, Miss Denton had a grand time. Stayed almost to dinner."

George raised his eyebrows.

Mr. Jackson chuckled. "She's lively, that one. Be good for my wife to have someone closer to her age than Duchess Cordelia to spend time with."

George nodded slowly.

"Say," Mr. Jackson said, "do you want to see Miss Denton's show? I was thinking the three of us could have dinner there."

"Don't you want to play dominoes tonight?"

"Good grief. I completely forgot. Tomorrow, then?"

"You're lucky I'm scheduled early. Where at?"

Then Mr. Jackson had to recall. "Club Patruni?"

George laughed. "It's been a while since I've been there. Sure, I think I can swing it."

"Let's meet in the lobby tomorrow night at seven."

***

When Mrs. Jackson's taxi pulled up to the Hotel, Mr. Jackson and little Bessie were there, walking along past the doors. She paid the driver as Harry opened the door for her.

Her Mr. Jackson glanced back, reversing course to meet her. He kissed her cheek. "Did it go well?"

"Well enough. What have you been up to?"

"This and that. Took our Queen Bess for a stroll. Want to have lunch here?"

"Let's go up to the suite first: I need to freshen up."

So the couple took the elevator to their floor.

Effie's maid cart was outside their suite, the parlor door open.

Mrs. Jackson knocked.

Effie's voice emerged from Mr. Jackson's bedroom. "Come in."

Mrs. Jackson turned to him. "I'll just be a moment."

After combing out her hair and other such matters, she returned to find Effie plumping the sofa cushions in the parlor. "There! All done," Effie said.

"You do a marvelous job," Mrs. Jackson said.

"Thank you, ma'am."

"You seem in good spirits today. What news?"

Effie blushed. She glanced around, lowering her voice. "I've been proposed to."

"Congratulations." Mrs. Jackson kept her voice low also. "Who's the lucky fellow?"

She beamed. "Mr. Clifton Strait. The Headwaiter."

Why would she want to hide her happiness? "Do you have a date planned?"

She hesitated. "I've not answered yet."

Mrs. Jackson said, "I see." A quick glance at the door: Mr. Jackson stood out in the hall still, turned away.

"I want to marry him, ma'am," Effie said, "truly." She bit her lip. "We just need some discussion first."

"Hmm." Mrs. Jackson entirely understood. But she'd kept far too many secrets in her day. "If you trust this man, if you truly love him, tell him every bit. If you don't, walk away and don't look back."

Effie's eyes widened. Then she nodded.

Mrs. Jackson smiled at her. "Either way, your conscience will be clear. Believe me: it's the best way to live." Her conscience was entirely clear, and had been so for some time. Every secret she'd ever had was revealed in public, long ago. She hoped no woman would ever have to go through that.

Effie peered downward for a moment. Then her head rose. "I will, ma'am, thank you."

Mrs. Jackson raised her voice then. "Let me know how it all turns out."

After Effie left, Mrs. Jackson let Bessie loose to inspect matters.

Mr. Jackson said, "What was all that about?"

She gave him a grin and a giggle. "Didn't your mother tell you not to pry?"

He let out a little "hmph". Then he laughed. "My mother told me quite a few things, most of which I ignored. Keep your secret, then."

"It's not my secret to tell." Yet she considered the conversation she'd just had with the woman. Could Effie's hesitation to accept the Headwaiter's proposal be due to not wanting to reveal her prior entanglement with the Head Valet?

But if the man already knew of it ... the timing of his offer was much too much of a coincidence. "Suppose a man's death put you at an advantage. Would that not make you a suspect?"

"I'd say it would."

Mrs. Jackson nodded to herself. Yet to reveal it now, just after Effie confided in her ... if the man were innocent, it would be dreadful for them both. "Too many people benefited from Mr. Vincenzo's death. It's a wonder the man lived as long as he did."

11

That evening, as usual, Mr. Jackson's valet arrived to dress him for dinner. After examining the skin under his beard, though, the valet proposed a more intensive treatment.

Mr. Jackson lay on his bed propped up by many pillows, a hot towel covering his beard. "How long have you worked here?"

Mr. Raymond stood by a small folding table, mixing something in a cup. "Off and on for a little over a year. Just luck of the draw where you're sent."

"I didn't realize."

"Yes, sir."

"Your sister works here. Do you get to know the people here much?"

Mr. Raymond began to whip the cup's contents. "Just who I meet here and there." He gave a quick glance over. "That night you were there was my first night at dominoes, too."

Mr. Jackson felt pleased. "Well, fancy that!"

Mr. Raymond took the towel off and began applying whatever was in the cup to Mr. Jackson's face, massaging it in. "This should help strengthen the skin."

Having his face massaged felt pleasant. After the massage was completed and another hot towel applied, Mr. Jackson said, "We plan to stay for a little while."

"I'm sure Effie will be glad for that, sir. She's fond of you both."

Mr. Jackson smiled to himself. "But it doesn't feel right to live somewhere and not know the names of your staff. I've gotten to meet some of the back men so far, but not any of the drivers. Do you know them?"

His valet tensed up, just a bit. "Yeah, a couple. Here, come sit in the chair and I'll do a comb-out and trim."

Mr. Jackson moved to the chair. "Forgive me; I don't mean to pry."

Mr. Raymond focused on his combing, then brought out the scissors and began snipping. "Well, the two I know are the ones being talked about. For that murder."

"I see."

"I don't want to get mixed up in any of it."

Mr. Jackson couldn't blame him. Yet it seemed Mr. Raymond might already be mixed up in it, if what Duchess Cordelia had told him of the closeness between his sister and the dead man were true. "I don't blame you: it must be horrible for everyone."

Mr. Raymond moved to the other side of the chair, eyes downcast. "It has been."

Mr. Jackson felt sorry for the man. His sister must be going through a multitude of feelings about the man's death. And who wouldn't want to comfort and protect their sister? "Cheer up; things will improve, I feel certain of it."

***

That night after dinner, Duchess Cordelia's suite overflowed with players, so much so that she had to call for extra tables. The Headwaiter was there, a powerfully built man who resembled the Head Valet. Ophelia was there, as was George.

The dowager insisted the couple sit with her, and to round out the table she invited Will to sit with them also.

Mrs. Jackson glanced over at the next table. Effie seemed as much in conversation with the Headwaiter as she was attending to her tiles. Her brother Stanley sat beside her, looking glum.

"So many here tonight!" Duchess Cordelia set a tile. "If this keeps up, I'll have to order another box!"

Mr. Jackson laid a double. "Nice problem to have."

The way he smiled to himself made Mrs. Jackson think he had an idea brewing.

Duchess Cordelia beamed, raising her voice a bit. "I do so love having everyone here. It gives me something to look forward to."

At the break, the others drifted off to eat, drink, and so on. Mr. Jackson said, "Miss Denton, we'd like to visit sometime. Is there anything we should know?"

Ophelia blushed all the way to her hairline. "You sure you want to do that?"

Mr. Jackson said, "We're sure."

"Then don't go in the front. Come round to the side door and knock three times. When they open up, tell them you're friends with Carrie."

Mrs. Jackson said, "Carrie?"

"Yeah. That's the code this month. If they ask, say you just met."

Mr. Jackson grinned. "Got it."

"You really want to see me?"

Mrs. Jackson said, "Of course we do."

Mr. Jackson excused himself, and Ophelia said she was getting a drink.

Mrs. Jackson found George off in a corner, eating a large sandwich. "May I join you?"

George gestured to a chair beside him.

She could sure use a cigarette. But she didn't know whether the dowager allowed smoking in her suite.

"What can I do for you?"

Mrs. Jackson smiled. "Nothing, really. But I was wondering. Your father seems quite wealthy. What does he do?"

George nodded as he chewed. Then he swallowed. "Builds boats. Our family business, really. He took over from my grandpa, who took over from his." He shrugged. "I grew up on boats as much as on land, now that I think of it."

"Does he buy boats as well?"

George set his sandwich down. "Sometimes. Why?"

"I learned something curious about your father today, that's all. He visited Mr. Vincenzo's home a few weeks back."

"Why is that curious?"

"Because according to his wife, your Head Valet didn't get many visitors."

George nodded soberly. "Is my father a suspect?"

Mrs. Jackson shrugged. "Not really."

George snorted. "I should hope not. My father's a forceful, strong-willed man, but he faints dead away at the sight of blood."

"That must have made for an interesting childhood."

"I learned to go to my mother after a tussle if I wanted tending."

"Rather than having to tend to him."

George let out a laugh. "Yeah."

***

They were at Duchess Cordelia's until late. The next morning, the couple decided to have breakfast in their rooms. As they ate, Mrs. Jackson said, "When I spoke with Ophelia, back when I followed her, she mentioned something strange."

"Oh?"

"Well, the brochure at the front desk clearly showed large cobblestones in that alley. And she mentioned a time when the alley was cobbles rather than gravel. But

341

she mentioned it in a way which makes me think that there's more to it."

Mr. Jackson leaned back, coffee in hand. "Why put gravel over perfectly good cobblestones?"

Mrs. Jackson snorted, amused. Her Mr. Jackson was intelligent indeed, but he knew little about the common man. "What if those nice large cobblestones are worth ever so much more than gravel?"

Mr. Jackson slowly nodded. "You think someone pried out the stones to sell?"

"I do. And who better to look the other way than our Head Valet?"

"Which means another set of suspects, should he have threatened to speak of it." Mr. Jackson downed his coffee and rose. "This is too dangerous a matter for us to investigate. I believe we should make an appointment with the sergeant."

12

Mr. Jackson felt surprised to be told they might visit the sergeant at their convenience. So he and his wife dressed, left their dog with her minders, and took a taxi to the police station.

Mr. Jackson walked in to find a flurry of activity. Men wheeled carts full of folders and mail. Uniformed officers sat typing reports, while another uniformed group brought in a few rough-looking men in handcuffs, moving them quickly past.

He took his wife's arm, leading her to the main desk. "Hector Jackson for Sergeant Nestor, please."

The man checked a clipboard, then gestured to the right. "That way."

The sergeant rose when they entered, offering his hand. "What can I do for you?"

"My wife has learned something which you may find of interest."

"Oh?"

His wife said, "Our dead valet was looking the other way as men sold the cobbles in that alleyway and replaced them with gravel. I'm not sure which group was involved, but that's more your domain."

"I see. And where did you learn this?"

His wife bristled, probably at the man's tone.

Mr. Jackson stepped in. "You know we can't reveal our sources, sir. But it involves an eyewitness who wishes to remain anonymous."

The sergeant nodded slowly. "And this witness believes ... what?"

Mrs. Jackson said, "She implied that your Mob was involved."

Sergeant Nestor gave out an amused "Heh." Then he leaned his elbows on the desk. "There are a half-dozen such groups out there, Mrs. Jackson, and dozens more petty gangs who might think up such a scheme. But I'll have my men ask around." He leaned back, hand to his chin. "If Mr. Vincenzo tried to blackmail them ..."

They'd not hesitate to destroy those who opposed them. "I thought it best to bring this to you."

"As was wise." The sergeant rose, so Mr. Jackson and his wife did too. "Thanks. I'll look into it."

Mr. Jackson felt curious. "Were you able to speak with the men waiting for Mr. Vincenzo?"

"I did," the sergeant said. Then he looked at Mrs. Jackson. "Carlo relayed your discussion to me. You were right about one thing: the man hated gravel. He'd never go that way. They were waiting for him on the platform there by the back steps."

Mr. Jackson watched his wife as she slowly nodded, eyes narrowing. "So he had some vital reason to go down the alley," his wife said. "He was lured there, or intended to meet someone. It had to be something recent, a change of plan."

Sergeant Nestor shrugged. "If so, no one's talking. The valets swear that, other than him leaving, they never saw a thing. The men assigned to that truck went on vacation the day prior. They'd saved up for years, three weeks time off each. We're still tracking them down."

"That's convenient," Mrs. Jackson said, and the way she said it almost made Mr. Jackson laugh.

"Indeed," the sergeant said. "But we have clear evidence of where the two men went: train tickets, reservations. They took their families: the children were taken from sports, the wives hired housekeepers." He paused, hands clasped on the desk in front of him, glancing aside, then back. "They aren't acting like felons fleeing some impulsive act. Either this murder was very well-planned — and from all accounts, these two aren't highly intellectual men —"

Mrs. Jackson snorted, evidently amused.

Mr. Jackson said, "Or they weren't involved at all."

The sergeant shook his head. "We should know the truth soon enough."

"Oh, that reminds me." His wife fished about in her handbag. "I managed to get a list of the men whose wives Mr. Vincenzo had been ..."

The sergeant looked amused. "I see."

"And I would add a Mr. Clifton Strait to your inquiries. He's the Hotel's Headwaiter. Mr. Vincenzo's death put him at an advantage in certain personal dealings."

The sergeant's face didn't change. "What dealings?"

"The matter's complex, sir, and involves a personal item told to me in confidence. But at least ensure this man has an alibi."

Sergeant Nestor's eyes narrowed. "You know it's a crime to withhold evidence."

Mr. Jackson leaned forward, yet he kept his tone even. "Are you threatening my wife, sir?"

His wife raised a hand. "I wish to find this man as much as you do. I have no real proof of any wrongdoing, only a suspicion. And it's a delicate matter, one which I might be within my rights not to have mentioned at all. I'm only sharing it in order to help."

Uncertainty crossed Sergeant Nestor's face then.

"All you must know," Mrs. Jackson said, "is that the man could have motive."

The sergeant crossed his arms, leaning back. "Very well. But if I find you're holding out on me, I'll drag you both in."

Mr. Jackson thought the man to be blustering more than anything at this point. But he did wonder what the Headwaiter was involved with and how his wife had learned of it!

Mrs. Jackson said, "One more thing: Mrs. Vincenzo had concerns about her father. He hated the man and had threatened to kill him."

The sergeant let out a snort. "Not hard to see why." He leaned both hands on his desk. "Well, you can let Mrs. Vincenzo know her father's not a suspect. He was at a charity event when the crime happened."

Mr. Jackson felt astonished. "However did you learn this so quickly?"

Sergeant Nestor grinned. "My boys were assigned to the event."

This seemed most curious. "Aren't you a homicide detective?"

"Sure I am. But three of my sons stand guard at events. I went by to bring one of them something and saw the man." He let out a short laugh. "You've been around as long as I have, you get to know the big shots."

Mrs. Jackson nodded. "Was there anything else I should ask? When I talk to the wife?"

Sergeant Nestor squinted at her a bit, his lips pursing. "He'd been gone for a while. But the really interesting thing about her is that she wasn't the one who reported him missing."

13

After speaking with Sergeant Nestor, the couple returned to the Hotel and collected Bessie.

But Mrs. Jackson didn't want to wait — she left Bessie with Mr. Jackson and took a taxi to visit Mrs. Vincenzo once more.

On returning to Mrs. Vincenzo's mansion, Mrs. Jackson found a number of fine automobiles parked out front. Just then, a great number of persons — including Mr. Carlo — emerged. If Mr. Carlo noticed her, he didn't acknowledge it.

She waited until the entryway was clear to announce herself to the butler.

After being left standing on the step for a while, the butler returned. "Mrs. Vincenzo is with her attorney at present, but bids you wait in her parlor."

"I'd be happy to."

As she'd not been invited to sit, Mrs. Jackson amused herself by looking around at the photographs. Some were of older people, with and without Mrs. Vincenzo. A photo of a large group of the workers at the Hotel, taken in what looked like a park, sat framed on the mantel. It was a rather informal photo: Mr. Vincenzo had his arms around the shoulders of both Mr. Montgomery Carlo and Miss Effie Raymond.

After perhaps ten minutes, Mrs. Vincenzo appeared, rushing over. "What news?"

"I've confirmed that your father's not a suspect."

The woman sagged; Mrs. Jackson grabbed hold of an arm as she helped her to a seat. She took the chair beside her. "Just rest there. All will be well."

Mrs. Vincenzo covered her face with her hands. "One bit of good news in all this horror." She leaned back, eyes closed as if exhausted. "That was the will being read. Out loud, in front of all those men." She opened her eyes, and tears lay in them. "My husband left three thousand dollars to some girl up north."

Mrs. Jackson gasped. Three thousand dollars?

"The humiliation of it! I feel as though he's killed me instead of dying."

Men had been killed for less. "I know you don't want to speak of this, but I must ask. What's her name?"

"Miss Mary Bluff."

"And you have no idea who this woman is?"

"None." She gazed off into the distance. "That must have been who he meant."

"I beg your pardon?"

She sighed. "He left a note."

What?

"I didn't tell the police. I'm sorry. But his car, his clothes, and his luggage were gone. He said he couldn't stand to be apart from her any longer."

"Where is it?"

"I threw it in the fire. But then Monty wouldn't believe Earl ran off. And when they found him dead —"

"It no longer seemed important."

Her words turned bitter. "Three thousand dollars. I hope the hussy chokes on it."

One more thing for Sergeant Nestor to look into. "I'm so sorry."

Mrs. Vincenzo smiled, patting Mrs. Jackson's hand. "I'll manage." She let out a sigh. "This place was always too big for me. But he seemed so proud of it that I never wanted to say so. I think I'll sell and move to the seaside." She sat straighter, her cheeks gaining their color. "Yes, I think a change would do me some good."

***

When Mrs. Jackson returned, her suite was empty.

She telephoned the police station. It took a while to be connected with Sergeant Nestor, but he seemed fascinated with what she had to say. "Three thousand dollars? That's quite a motive! Did she happen to say where the woman lived?"

"Just up north somewhere. But I'm sure her lawyer must know."

"Right," Sergeant Nestor said. "Thanks."

After Mrs. Jackson hung up the phone, she heard Mr. Jackson and Bessie come in through the parlor door. "I'm in here," she called out, then went to meet them.

But Mr. Jackson did not appear happy. "How could you possibly think that George or his father would be responsible for the Head Valet's death?"

Mrs. Jackson felt entirely confused. "Wait. What happened?"

"I took Bessie for a walk around the block and George was standing out back on the platform. Smoking! I asked why in the world he would start smoking. He said he heard it calmed the nerves. I had to drag it out of him that you'd been asking about his father."

"I asked about his father, yes. But I never accused either one of them of anything. I learned from Mrs. Vincenzo the first time I spoke to her that he'd been there in the weeks before her husband's death, so at dominoes I inquired as to what his father did for a living. He asked if I suspected his father and I told him no."

Silence fell between them.

"This isn't like him," Mr. Jackson finally said. "If he lied to me about this, then he must feel he can't share the truth of whatever troubles him."

For a man as open and honest as her Mr. Jackson was, this must be distressing. "Then you mustn't press him on it any further. He'll speak of it when he's ready."

He seemed disgruntled. "I suppose." Then his face brightened. "Want to have lunch now?"

She grinned, taking his arm. "I would indeed."

On the elevator, Mr. Jackson said, "Would you like to see Miss Denton's show tonight?"

This sounded exciting. "I'd love to!"

The elevator doors opened and they started down the hall. "Very good. We're meeting George in the lobby at seven; we can have dinner there."

It sounded as if the matter had already been arranged. "And what if I'd said no?"

Mr. Jackson shrugged. "Then we'd go another time." He stopped there in the hallway, taking her hand. "I don't mean to intrude upon your life. I just want to make you happy."

She smiled to herself at his words. "I'd be glad to go with you. But we'd better call Mr. Raymond and Mrs. Knight to make sure they can be there early."

He smiled at her fondly. "Already done."

The dining room was as packed full as ever. While they were finishing their meals, the dowager Duchess approached. "Did you enjoy the games last evening?"

Mrs. Jackson smiled at her. "We did!"

"What are you doing after lunch?"

The couple looked at each other, then back at her. "We have nothing planned," Mr. Jackson said.

"Would you like to visit the library?"

"That sounds good," Mr. Jackson said. The couple rose, following the dowager Duchess out to the lobby.

"That reminds me," Mrs. Jackson said, "I haven't returned the books I checked out the last time."

"How did you find the one I showed you?"

"Walden? Pretentious, boring, and in some parts, offensive. I didn't finish it."

"I'm sorry to hear that," Duchess Cordelia said. "It's said to be a classic work."

Mr. Jackson laughed. "Let's return this 'classic work' and find you something more suitable."

The three turned towards the grand fountain to cross the wide lobby, but in came Sergeant Nestor and two of his men, all dressed for the street. The sergeant strode straight towards them.

"Good day, sir," Mr. Jackson said.

The sergeant said, "Who gave you that list?"

Out of the corner of her eye, she saw Mr. Jackson glance towards the dowager. "Why do you ask?"

But he went straight past them to Duchess Cordelia. "I ought to arrest you right now."

"Sergeant Nestor," Mr. Jackson said, "may I ask what's wrong?"

"You may," he replied. "Did you happen to read that list before you gave it to me?"

The couple glanced at each other. "Sorry to say," Mrs. Jackson said, with some chagrin, "I didn't."

"Well, the last entry was Mr. Flannery Davis."

Mr. Jackson frowned. "The Hotel's manager?"

"Yes. And not only was Mr. Davis undergoing minor surgery at the time of the incident, his wife was horrified at the accusation that she'd been entangled with his Hotel's Head Valet." He turned to Duchess Cordelia. "How could you make such a claim? Interfere with someone's marriage like that? Not to mention waste the time of this investigation?"

Duchess Cordelia's eyes reddened, her lip quivering. "My poor Albert would be here today, comfortable and well, if not for that man's bullying. Do you not think my marriage has been interfered with? My time wasted? My life beset by accusation? All because Mr. Flannery Davis felt compelled to make my husband's life a misery. Well, now Mr. Davis knows how it feels."

Sergeant Nestor, for once, had nothing to say.

The dowager thrust her hands out, head turned away. "Put me in a cell if you must."

"My Lady, I don't think that'll be necessary. But the next time you want revenge, think of who else it might harm. I believe you owe Mrs. Davis an apology."

Duchess Cordelia's face fell. "I do regret that. I never meant harm upon her." She glanced at the couple, embarrassment on her face. "I'm sorry to involve you in this. I'll go wait in the library."

Mrs. Jackson felt embarrassed as well. What must this sergeant think? "I'd have never given you the list if I knew any item on it was false."

"Well, the information Mrs. Vincenzo gave you seems to be correct, at any rate," Sergeant Nestor said. "We found Mr. Vincenzo's car."

Mrs. Jackson said, "Where was it?"

"In a tow lot nearby. It'd been picked up around the corner for being parked too long. His luggage was in the back. We're checking everything for fingerprints."

So he did intend to leave, as his wife said. "Mr. Carlo seemed convinced Mr. Vincenzo wouldn't leave the Hotel. But I wonder ... if he meant to leave his wife that day he was murdered, where he planned to go."

14

When Mr. Raymond came to dress Mr. Jackson, he examined the hair under his beard and sighed. "Your rash seems, if anything, worse."

"What could possibly be causing this?"

"I've done all I know." He began carefully combing Mr. Jackson's beard, trimming it as he went. "Just keep with the hot towels before bed. If it doesn't improve in a few days, we might need to consult a doctor."

"It seems a good plan," Mr. Jackson said. "I've been wondering: do you think exercise might help?"

Mr. Raymond considered this. "It certainly couldn't hurt. I know of several fitness clubs nearby. I'll leave a list at the front desk for you."

"Splendid!" He still didn't feel entirely comfortable around the man, but the more he'd gotten to know him, the more he approved. Very professional.

Mr. Raymond brushed off Mr. Jackson's jacket. "There! Have a wonderful evening."

***

Club Patruni certainly looked impressive. A grand marquee, lit all round by electric bulbs of gleaming gold. Past the sidewalk, the entry was tiled in marble.

But they didn't go in that way. Mrs. Jackson let the men lead her to the side entrance, labeled "Private."

The door opened on Mr. Jackson's triple knock.

"We're friends of Carrie," Mr. Jackson said.

The man who opened the door was very well dressed, yet burly. "Yeah?"

Mr. Jackson gave the man a winning, slightly embarrassed smile. "Well, we've only just met."

The man gave him an amused grin. "In you go."

As they followed the man down a long flight of stairs then along a narrow hallway, Mrs. Jackson whispered, "You'd do well on the stage."

She felt pleased to hear Mr. Jackson chuckle in reply.

Another equally well-dressed man stood guard over a second door. The first said, "Front row."

Beyond this second door lay a large hall. Dozens of small round tables, beautifully set, lit by small candles in the center. Waiters moved here and there in the glow of a wide stage an easy step up. Behind it, a jazz orchestra on a platform another easy step up finished a set. The room burst into applause.

The second man spoke into the ear of a third. This man turned to them. "Your hats, sirs?" After George and Mr. Jackson exchanged their fedoras for tickets, the man escorted the three to a front row table.

A waiter came up. "What will you be having?"

Mrs. Jackson said, "Tea for me, thanks."

"Coffee, heavy cream," said Mr. Jackson.

George stared at them. "You're in a speakeasy and not drinking?"

The couple glanced at each other, Mrs. Jackson unsure how much to reveal. Mr. Jackson said lightly, "Neither of us drink alcohol, but feel free to if you wish."

George looked put out. The waiter stood there.

"Gimme a whiskey sour, then," George finally said. "And separate checks, if you please."

"That's entirely unnecessary," Mr. Jackson said once the waiter left. "I invited you."

"I know you invited me. But I pay my own way."

Mr. Jackson shrugged, then leaned close to speak into her ear. "I should've told him we don't drink."

She nodded. "All's well."

A few minutes later their drinks arrived. The music was perfect, the food, delicious. But Mrs. Jackson's real interest was in seeing Ophelia's show.

A heavyset, dark-haired man stepped up on the stage. "And now, the show you've all been waiting for: The Patruni Girls!"

Two rows of women came out wearing high sequined headpieces and gossamer robes, much like the one she'd worn on the yacht. Yet the robes were adorned with sequins and gems, and so were the gowns they wore underneath. The women met in the center then twirled round to all corners of the stage, their robes flying out around them.

The crowd cheered and whistled, and one by one, the women spun, casting their robes just past the edge of the stage to slide off onto the floor. Their sleeveless gowns came to their ankles, glittering golden and red. Now that the robes were off, the sheerness of the gowns showed the scanty undergarments beneath.

The cheers grew ever louder! The ladies began to dance, making elegant circles, moving forward and back in rows, then combining to cross the rows.

Someone nudged her. "Look there," Mr. Jackson said in her ear.

Yes! There in the third row danced Ophelia, wearing so much makeup that at first Mrs. Jackson didn't recognize her.

Now forming one dancing row, the group began to unclasp their gowns, twirling out of them at the right back corner of the stage, then skipping along. These new garments covered what underwear might, yet these were bedazzled with gems and tassels, which danced as much as they did.

The women danced for some time, kicked up as one, then posed in a grand finale.

Mrs. Jackson shouted, "Bravo!" as the crowd roared their approval.

A pair of older women began collecting the scattered garments as the dancers lined out.

Mrs. Jackson turned to the men. "What a show!"

"They certainly don't have anything like that back home," Mr. Jackson said.

George shrugged. "I prefer the acrobatic ones."

"Oh, you," Mrs. Jackson said, feeling playful. "We can go see one of those sometime if we must."

George leaned back with a drink and chuckled.

The heavyset man stepped casually up to the stage and spread his arms wide. "Ladies and gentlemen," he boomed, "the floor is yours!"

The orchestra struck up a new piece, and couples began stepping up to the stage to dance. The man making the announcement stepped down and approached their table. "I heard this was your first time here. How do you like it?"

Mrs. Jackson wondered a bit about the man not introducing himself.

But Mr. Jackson only said, "Splendid!" He rose, extending a hand. "Hector Jackson, sir, at your service."

The man shook it. "Leo Trappola. The proprietor."

George stood. "Nice place you have here."

Of course, she clasped the man's hand as well. But her mind was on other things. She scrutinized Mr. Trappola's face. *This is the father.*

He had the best alibi one might possibly have: the sergeant being there right when the man walked by, just as Mr. Vincenzo was being murdered.

Yet the timing of it seemed curious. Could Mr. Trappola have had Mr. Vincenzo murdered to avenge his daughter?

15

Just then, Ophelia came up, wearing her dark mustard coat, a black sequined headband over sweaty reddish-blonde hair. "You made it!"

Mr. Trappola gave a thin smile, moving on to the next table.

Greetings all round, and Ophelia sat in the empty chair next to Mrs. Jackson. "I have two more shows to do: eleven and one. You're welcome to stay if you like, but it's not necessary."

"Are the shows different?"

Ophelia shrugged. "Yes and no. We have six dance numbers. Sometimes we get new costumes. You'd probably like that part."

"I'd love to see them all." Mrs. Jackson took her hand. "You were magnificent. But we were up late last night. Perhaps a rain check?"

"Of course." Ophelia gave her a warm smile, squeezing her hand. "I'd love for you to see them."

"You both should come by next week," Mrs. Jackson said. "On Monday, when you're both off. We can have tea in our parlor."

George said, "It'll have to be Tuesday: no one gets time off this weekend."

"Oh," Mr. Jackson said. "Labor Day weekend. I'd forgotten."

"That seems unfair," Mrs. Jackson said.

George shrugged.

"Tuesday it is, then," Mr. Jackson said. "Come by after luncheon."

Ophelia said, "That would be ducky!"

Mrs. Jackson smiled fondly at her.

Mr. Jackson said, "How long do you have? Before you have to return?"

Ophelia glanced at Mr. Trappola standing a few tables off, then stretched her legs under the table with a smile. "Until ten-thirty, I'm free as a bird."

"Let's get you some refreshment, then," Mr. Jackson said. He waved a waiter over. "Give the young lady whatever she likes, and put it on our tab."

Mr. Trappola nudged the waiter and spoke in his ear. The waiter leaned over then and said something to Mr. Jackson, whose face lit up in surprise. "How very kind!" He turned to Mr. Trappola and nodded.

While the waiter took Ophelia's order, Mrs. Jackson spoke in Mr. Jackson's ear. "What was all that about?"

Mr. Jackson said quietly, "Apparently Mr. Carlo discovered we were here. He's asked Mr. Trappola to send him the bill for tonight's outing."

"Interesting." It was particularly interesting if Mr. Trappola had murdered Mr. Carlo's cousin. "But fortunate for us."

Mr. Jackson laughed. "Indeed it is."

She watched Mr. Jackson talk and laugh with the others. What would it have been like, to grow up never having a moment's worry about money? Yet it didn't seem to have spoiled and hardened his character, like the over-application of money to children so often did.

She said to Ophelia, "Where's the Ladies' Room?"

Ophelia grabbed her hand. "I'll show you."

Mrs. Jackson told the men, "We'll be right back."

The Ladies' Room was just as fine as the hall: a row of mirrored dressing-seats, the floor tan marble. As Mrs. Jackson put on new lipstick, Ophelia said, "How did you like the show, really?"

"Didn't you hear what I said? I loved it!"

Ophelia shook her head in disbelief. "You're a strange one."

"Whatever do you mean?"

"You talk and act so old-fashioned. Yet when you see me dressed like this," she opened her coat to show off her sequined undergarment-looking outfit, "you don't bat an eye."

Mrs. Jackson let out a laugh, feeling coy. "Well, I suppose I'm not your ordinary woman." Her cheeks heated up as she looked into Ophelia's eyes. "And I think you're beautiful."

Ophelia blushed, wrapping her coat around her. "We best get back before they start looking for us."

The two went back to their table and listened to the music once more. Yet Ophelia seemed to be looking at them more than at the show.

After a time, Ophelia leaned over. "Do you really like me?"

Mrs. Jackson smiled to herself. "I do."

"And you really like him?"

She considered the matter. "I do."

Ophelia seemed a bit pensive after that.

When the music paused, Mr. Jackson said, "I'll send a taxi for you after your work from now on. What time will you be ready?"

Ophelia gaped at him. "Um ... we have to help clean up after. Half past two?"

He smiled broadly. "Half past two it is."

She seemed at a loss for words. "Thanks!" Then she kissed Mrs. Jackson on the cheek, whispering, "I like you too." She waved to the others. "Goodbye!"

Mrs. Jackson felt touched at Ophelia's declaration.

The table rang forth with farewells, then George called for the check. Yet he seemed dismayed at the total. "Did I really have that many drinks?"

He had drunk quite a few ...

Mr. Jackson said, "Just have them combine checks."

George's face darkened. "I won't do that."

Mrs. Jackson leaned forward. She realized he didn't know the situation. "But —"

"No," George said, "and that's final."

Mr. Jackson said, "Can I spot you the difference?"

"I suppose," George said, clearly disgruntled.

Mr. Jackson got out his wallet and handed over a fiver. "That enough?"

"More than," George said. He waved over the waiter and paid the bill.

When he made to hand back the change, Mr. Jackson waved him off. "You might need that. Just pay me back when you can."

George crossed his arms and looked away.

"Well, then," Mr. Jackson said, "shall we be off?"

George said nothing on the cab ride home.

The couple got out at the Hotel. George did say goodbye, at least. "It was a lovely evening."

"See you tomorrow," they called out, and returned to their suite.

"I'm sorry about George," Mr. Jackson said. "I think he's had too much to drink."

Mrs. Jackson nodded. Clearly something was bothering him. But she figured that whatever it was, he'd talk about it sooner or later.

"I have a surprise for you," Mr. Jackson said. He brought out a box. Inside were her shoes, good as new!

"Oh, thank you." She threw her arms around his neck. "They look perfect!"

That night, Mr. Jackson lay thinking about how such small things as fixing a pair of shoes brightened his wife's day.

But this gave him an idea. This young Chef had known his wife. Perhaps he might be able to speak with her, see how she was really faring. He might even have some idea as to how best to help her.

The next morning, he woke early, well before breakfast, excited about his idea. "Come on, Bessie." Clipping on her leash, he headed down to the kitchen.

After allowing Bessie to do her business outside, Mr. Jackson stood by the back entry to the kitchen, which was well down the hall from the door to the docks.

The kitchen seemed to be busy, yet not frantic. The aroma of freshly-brewed coffee filled the air. A few were slicing fruit and chopping vegetables, but most of the staff there were placing cloths and silverware rolled up in napkins upon rows of meal carts.

To Mr. Jackson's surprise, George came up, taking off his apron.

George seemed just as surprised to see him. "What are you doing here?"

"I could say the same of you."

George let out a laugh. "The Headwaiter telephoned late last night: wanted me to cover breakfast instead of dinner this week."

"Well, that's good, I suppose." Then he remembered why he'd ventured here. "Might I speak with your Monsieur for a moment?"

"Let me check."

All this time, Bessie had been sniffing the area, and right as George was leaving, she let out a sneeze.

George glanced back. "Bless you!"

Her ears went up, tail wagging.

Mr. Jackson scooped Bessie into his arms. "I hope you haven't caught a cold."

Leaning against the entryway, he pondered this. Did dogs get colds?

Perhaps he should keep an eye on her.

George returned. "Follow me."

Still carrying Bessie, Mr. Jackson followed George past rows of sparkling marble counters, a maid counting napkins, and several others sorting clean silverware.

In the very back, an office door stood open. A large chalkboard hung beside it upon the wall with the day's menu written upon it.

Mr. Jackson peeked around the threshold. The office was small, with cabinets and shelves everywhere.

In the midst of this, the Monsieur sat at a desk writing into a ledger, a stack of papers beside it. He glanced up, surprise on his face. "Please, sit down!"

Mr. Jackson turned to George. "Thanks!" Then Mr. Jackson sat, resting Bessie on his lap. He said to the Chef, "I hope I'm not disturbing you."

The young Monsieur set his pen down, leaned back, hands behind his head, and smiled. "I could use a break." Then he leaned forward. "How may I help?"

How to begin? "I'm sure you know as well as anyone the trials my wife has faced."

The Chef shrugged. "Only a few. She seemed well when last I saw her, before leaving for Paris. We hadn't seen each other for a few years until the other day."

Mr. Jackson felt dismayed.

"Would you like me to speak with her?"

"If you might. I know it's not been very long since her calamity. But she's grieving, and I honestly don't know how to help."

Monsieur rested his elbows upon his desk, hands bridging in front of his chin. "What exactly happened there? Do you know?"

"Only what it said in the papers. She's not spoken a word about it."

Hesitation crossed his face. "I was in Paris at the time. I heard nothing until the police contacted me, just before the Hotel did."

"The police?"

"Yes, well, from their interviews, they learned my connection with him." He let out a breath. "I don't believe I was a serious suspect, being in Paris the entire time, yet I can see why they might think I could be involved." But then he shook his head. "But even if I wished to harm the man, I wouldn't. Revenge is bitter from beginning to end, leaving nothing for the future."

"Forgive me, sir." This man was a decade younger. Yet Mr. Jackson had never up to then felt so unsure. What could he say? What should he say? "What I know for fact is that she witnessed her husband's murder, becoming injured during the battle. I found her at the station and persuaded her to let me accompany her." Recalling her surprise at seeing him by the ticket counter amused him even now. "That's all I know."

He blinked, confusion upon his face. "And ... you're truly married?"

Mr. Jackson nodded. "It seemed the best way to protect her." He pictured the happiness in her smile. "It's only been a few months, but I think it's worked well."

"I wish I had more for you. Perhaps my parents —"

Mr. Jackson raised a hand to stop him. "Please, sir, no. If word got out that we were here, it would put her into danger."

The Chef blinked. "Of course, but —"

"I trust you to be discreet because my wife does. But I don't know these others."

The young Monsieur nodded quickly. "I understand. I'll not speak of her to anyone."

Relief washed over him: they were still safe here.

"I leave for the local markets at four-thirty; have her give a note to the Headwaiter the night before if she'd like to accompany me. Or if that's too early, she can meet me at the roof gardens. I'm usually there by seven: I like to watch the sun rise."

Mr. Jackson thought she'd never want to get up that early in either case, but he said, "I'll let her know."

The Chef smiled to himself. "Or if that's still too early, this time of day would work well." He glanced aside. "The nice part of being Head Chef is that much of the preparation is done by others." Then he chuckled, looking down at the open ledger before him. "The bad part is paperwork."

Mr. Jackson grinned. "I'll leave you to it, then. Thank you, sir."

***

As a peace offering to Sergeant Nestor, Mrs. Jackson volunteered to call the names on Duchess Cordelia's list.

It was tedious but necessary work, taking several days. During this time, her Mr. Jackson had suddenly decided to take up sport. He'd gone to several fitness clubs to tour the premises and interview the proprietors.

She wasn't sure why he might not just have his men do that, but it seemed to make him happy. When he returned each time, Bessie would do her usual sniffing about the entire suite then flop into her little bed, eyes shut. He, on the other hand, returned invigorated, full of ideas about topics from their next trip to what he and George might do on the man's next days off.

Mrs. Jackson loved to see her Mr. Jackson beaming with enthusiasm each day. And he seemed genuinely concerned for her well-being. How am I so fortunate, she thought, to have found such a partner in life?

It presented such a contrast: none of the men on Duchess Cordelia's list seemed happy. Most were angry at both their wives and Mr. Vincenzo, some expressing relief or even gladness at his death. All but three, however, had alibis for their whereabouts.

Sergeant Nestor came to call the morning of Labor Day, dressed more casually than ever before.

"I don't suppose you police get the day off?"

He chuckled. "Actually, at my level, I do. I was on my way to a barbecue."

When she presented the many pages of notes to him, he actually appeared impressed, as well as sobered. "I've misjudged you: this is excellent work."

She felt amused at his admission. "We've both wanted the same thing all along: to solve this crime, each for our own reasons."

This brought a suspicious gleam to his eye. "What are your reasons for doing this?"

For an instant, this took her aback. "I suppose I enjoy puzzles," she finally said. "I find the entire matter most curious. And your shelter and care of us here has been more than enough payment."

She regretted saying that last sentence as soon as the words came forth: he'd be reminded of how they got into this camaraderie.

It seemed the Feds still wished to question her about her first husband's murder. She wasn't sure what story her Mr. Jackson had given the last time they'd stayed here, but Sergeant Nestor and Mr. Carlo had helped hide her. In exchange, of course, for the couple's assistance in solving several deaths right here in the Hotel.

After the terrible night she'd fled her city, she'd had many reasons to hide. She was the only living witness to what had happened. If the men associated with those who killed her husband searched for her out in the wide world, then those she cared about back home might remain safe, or at the very least, alive.

They'd be watched, for certain, in case she might try to make contact. But eventually, those men would grow tired of watching, tired of searching for her. So the longer she stayed away, the safer the people she loved would be.

And as long as men like Mr. Carlo, Sergeant Nestor, Mr. Jackson, and his men continued to protect her, she'd be safe here as well.

Sergeant Nestor laughed. "Never fear, Mrs. Jackson, I have no wish to bring myself under any further scrutiny than I must. You'll not be called as witness to any of it."

"I'm relieved," she said. "As I'm sure your budget office will be."

He grinned. "I do believe you're right."

***

The next afternoon was warm, yet high storm-clouds gathered. The sun peeked out from time to time, bathing the room with light.

Mr. and Mrs. Jackson, George and Ophelia sat round the rosewood table in the parlor sipping lemonade.

Mrs. Jackson thought the parlor quite lovely, with its black, cobalt, rosewood, and brass decor. Along with the perfect shade of white upon the walls, the room seemed quite airy.

The clock on the parlor mantle struck three. They'd been chatting for some time, yet George seemed moody, unusually quiet.

Mr. Jackson stirred, bringing out a smallish black velvet box. "In honor of George's birthday," he said, handing the box to him.

At first, George appeared taken aback. He opened the box, and in it was the gold watch her Mr. Jackson had been admiring at the gift shop.

George got very still, then his face turned angry. He set the box down.

Mr. Jackson said, "What's the matter?"

George stood, pushing back his chair. "If I wanted to be some rich man's pet, I'd have stayed home with my father!" He left the box on the table, closing the door to the hallway more forcefully than needed.

Ophelia said, "What was that all about?"

Mrs. Jackson had no idea.

Mr. Jackson sat, mouth open, then it looked as if he'd come to some insight. "Pardon me," he said, then left as well.

Ophelia leaned over with a wry grin. "Never fear: I'll be your pet anytime."

This made Mrs. Jackson laugh. She patted Ophelia's hand. "Then my Pet you shall be!" Although she felt sure Ophelia must be joking, she hastened to say, "Mr. Jackson's a kind and generous man of great wealth. I, on the other hand, have very little to my name." Everything she'd built had been lost when she fled her past life. "I'm quite grateful for his regard."

Ophelia chuckled. "How else might it be, even for such a modern woman as you?"

"I thought you said I was old-fashioned."

"We all have to change sometime." Ophelia leaned back, lemonade in hand. "You strike me as someone who's made many a change in your day."

Had she? "The biggest one, of course, was coming here." She leaned towards Ophelia upon an elbow, chin upon her hand. "But perhaps my second was inviting you to luncheon."

"Oh," Ophelia said. Then she smiled as if she'd made quite the achievement. "Then I'm grateful I happened to notice you following me." But then the young woman sobered. "I hope George is well. He seems a decent sort."

Mrs. Jackson nodded. "I think he is."

Ophelia said, "Do you really like my show?"

"I thought it was lovely." Why keep asking this? "The real question is do you like performing it it?"

"I do. But when Mr. Jackson asked about my mother, I ... I wonder if she'd approve."

"You told me she'd want you to be happy."

Ophelia gazed at the floor, nodding slowly. "I think she would."

"Of course she would. Are you happy there?"

"I do. But I miss spending time with you."

Mrs. Jackson felt moved. "I miss spending time with you as well. We should go holiday shopping."

"I'm not sure who I might shop for," Ophelia said. "But I'll make myself a list."

"We can do whatever you like."

Ophelia smiled, her cheeks coloring. Then she glanced at the clock, and her face turned alarmed. "I need to go. My friend's out of town, and I promised I'd look in on her mother. I'd best hurry if I'm to be back home in time for dinner."

Mrs. Jackson rose, kissing Ophelia's cheek. "Then you should go. Have a wonderful afternoon."

***

It didn't take long for Mr. Jackson to catch up to George: he stood leaning against the railing on the platform outside the kitchens, head down.

The noises of the dock must have made it so George didn't hear him approach, because he jumped a bit when

Mr. Jackson leaned upon the railing beside him. He spoke sharply. "What do you want?"

"I just want to know what's going on."

"Well, I'd like to know the same thing."

"What do you mean?"

"Do you get your kicks off of rescuing puppies?"

Thinking of Bessie, Mr. Jackson let out a laugh. "I don't know what you mean."

"You clean up after me on the boat, you pay for my dinner, you get me this much too expensive watch. You 'spot me' an entire week's pay. You want me to go on this huge trip with you. Do you buy all your friends?"

"What? No!" Mr. Jackson felt dismayed. "It's not like that at all."

George turned to stare out over the parking lot. "My father told me since I was small to be my own man. Now he demands I return home and take over the business. Well, I won't be handed my lot in life. And I won't be beholden to him, you, or anyone else."

Mr. Jackson couldn't believe what he was hearing. "Beholden?" For an instant, he had no idea what to say.

"Your wife saved my life earlier this year, and for that I'm grateful. But I'm not a child. And I won't be owned by anyone."

He moved away, and Mr. Jackson grabbed his arm. "George, wait."

George shook off his grasp, hard. "What." His face said: *I can't fight you or I'll lose my job.* His stance said: *But I will if I have to.*

Eugene stood in the parking lot at the bottom of the left set of stairs. "You boys all right up there?"

George glared at him. "Yeah."

Eugene looked to Mr. Jackson, who nodded.

Then Mr. Jackson turned to George. "Please don't do this." How might he say it? "I never meant to make you feel this way." In spite of how awful he felt, he blurted out, "I guess I'm just a generous guy."

Whether it was what he said or how he said it, a laugh burst from George. He returned to the railing. "Too generous, by half." Then he said, "I could never wear that watch. I'd be looking over my shoulder all the time."

Mr. Jackson smiled to himself. "Then let's get one you like better."

***

Mrs. Jackson felt glad when both men returned to the suite. From their faces, it seemed that George and Mr. Jackson had resolved their differences.

And since the men were off to purchase a watch, Mrs. Jackson decided to see what she might learn about the mysterious truck.

She brought Bessie to the lobby level then turned left, then right down the hall to the veterinarian's. One of his boys was on duty, a lad of perhaps fifteen. "Might you watch Bessie for an hour?"

The boy beamed. "I'd be happy to!"

Returning to the main hallway, Mrs. Jackson recalled what Mr. Jackson had said the last time they'd stayed here about the layout of this place. She turned right, walking past the windows displaying the gardens, then turned left.

The smell of food and the noise of trucks increased as she went until she reached the intersection her Mr. Jackson had told her about. To the left was the kitchen, to the right, an elevator and the door to the platform she'd seen from the street.

She went through the door to stand upon the balcony there. Far across the parking lot, a truck stood parked. Other trucks had backed up to the loading dock to her right. A truck emerged from the underground dock to her left, then went up the driveway.

"Can I help you?"

With a start, she turned to face the man who'd been at the dominoes game. "Yes ... Eugene, am I right?"

His name was right on his coveralls.

He grinned. "I remember you, Mrs. Jackson."

She gave the truck parked across the way a quick glance. "Have the police done with that yet?"

"I believe so."

No one stood guard. "Might I look at it?"

"Be happy to escort you."

Mrs. Jackson followed Eugene down the stairs on the left and across the lot to the truck. It had no doors, room for two up front, and a flat area in back with wooden sides.

She didn't approach the truck, just peered at it. It looked new. "What kind of truck is this?"

"Model TT. Pricey, but good at hauling heavy stuff."

"You know a lot about it."

Eugene let out a short laugh. "I better: I'm the one who's gonna fix it when it breaks."

The back area was empty except some gravel in the corners. "What kind of men drive this one?"

"They keep to themselves, don't complain." He shrugged. "Not much to say."

She moved to the passenger side and leaned into the cab. The foot rest was curved, going to a padded bench seat. If anything small were dropped, it'd get wedged …

A reddish glint caught her eye. "You have a knife?"

"Sure." Eugene fished out a pocketknife and opened it for her. "See something?"

"I do." Dusting off the floorboard, she sat upon it and carefully worked the tip of Eugene's knife under the glinting area.

A small red gemstone.

Heart pounding, she folded the knife and handed it back to Eugene.

The gemstone sat on the floorboard, murky red.

Was Mr. Jackson's valet involved in Mr. Vincenzo's murder?

"You okay, Mrs. Jackson?"

Was Mr. Jackson in danger?

16

She picked up the gem and put it into the zippered area of her handbag. "I'm fine." She stood, dusted herself off. "Let's look at the tires."

The tires had gravel stuck in them. Eugene shook his head in distaste. "They were supposed to clean this out before they left for vacation."

"Were they now."

"Yeah. I've never seen them leave a truck like this."

"That's very interesting."

Eugene stood there a moment. "You think someone drove this without permission?"

Mrs. Jackson nodded. "It's very likely." Equally likely was that these men gave the keys to whoever drove it.

The two returned to the platform. "Thanks so much for letting me look at it," Mrs. Jackson said. "This has been very helpful."

Eugene tipped his cap. "Glad to be of service."

"And say hello to your wife for me, will you?"

He beamed, cheeks coloring. "I surely will."

She smiled as she watched him bounce down the steps. *Men in love are all the same,* someone told her once. And it was true.

Mrs. Jackson retrieved Bessie and returned to their suite. When she got to her rooms, Mr. Jackson hadn't returned, but it wasn't yet time for tea. Bessie began her usual sniffing of every inch of the suite.

Mr. Jackson didn't like for her to smoke in their rooms, so Mrs. Jackson stood out on the balcony instead.

She loved looking out over the water. Being out on the open water these past few months had cured much of what ailed her. Helped her begin to grieve.

And the thought that Mr. Jackson might now be in danger terrified her. It was as if her worst nightmare had come to pass.

Why was that gemstone in the truck? And what did it mean?

Mr. Jackson had told her his valet knew the two men who drove the truck. During a ride, or even just sitting in the truck, he could have lost the gem.

The valet could have borrowed the truck for some quite innocent reason and lost the gem then.

Or Mr. Stanley Raymond could be Mr. Vincenzo's murderer.

The man didn't look like a murderer. While he seemed to dislike Mr. Vincenzo, many people did — including her Mr. Jackson. And Mr. Raymond didn't look strong enough to move a manhole cover it'd taken three men to pry out.

Besides, Bessie liked him.

Whether this valet of his was involved with Mr. Vincenzo's murder or not, she couldn't tell Mr. Jackson what she'd discovered.

She knew him well enough to know he wasn't the kind of man who could hide his true feelings. He'd act differently. If Mr. Raymond was innocent, it'd surely offend him. If he were guilty, it'd tip the man off and he'd flee.

So she had to learn the truth herself, and soon.

She put out the cigarette and went to the phone. "The police, please, non-emergency line."

It took a while to get Sergeant Nestor on the line. "What can I do for you, Mrs. Jackson?"

"I just learned something which may interest you. The two men who drove the truck were supposed to clean the truck entirely before they left on vacation, down to prying the gravel from the tires. One of his coworkers said that they'd never left a truck in this condition before."

"Well, that's interesting. Explains the fingerprints."

"Oh?"

"Let's just say that they're not those of our drivers."

"So you did find the men."

"Yeah, and you won't believe what they're saying."

"What's that?"

"They think they're being set up."

"Well, that is interesting. Are they saying by who?"

"No, they won't say. I'm not sure they know. But we know where they are now, and I have local officers watching them."

Mrs. Jackson considered telling Sergeant Nestor about the gem. But even if they might prove the gem belonged to Mr. Raymond, it only showed he was in the truck before they arrived here. So the gem proved nothing. She needed more.

***

While Mrs. Jackson pondered the true meaning of the gemstone, Mr. Jackson was taking George Neuberg out to buy a watch.

When they entered the watch store, the proprietor hurried behind the counter to greet them. "Welcome, good sirs. Did you have something special in mind?"

George took off his old, beaten-up watch. "I'd like to replace this in a similar style."

"I have a selection of leather-strap watches right here." He went around behind the U-shaped glass counter to the far left, sliding open the glass. He lifted a long display board, resting it to stand upon the counter.

Mr. Jackson thought privately that they all looked much the same, but after some consideration, George chose one along with some leather oil for the strap.

George stretched his arm out to admire his new purchase. "This is just what I wanted."

"My pleasure," Mr. Jackson said, and the two shook hands. "Happy birthday."

Leaving the old tattered watch with the proprietor, they went to a bistro nearby, taking one of the small tables near the window. The waiter came up. "What can I get for you, sirs?"

"Tea and toast," George said. "And separate checks, if you please."

"Coffee for me, heavy cream." Mr. Jackson felt amused. If the man wanted to pay his own way, he'd certainly allow him to.

And after the waiter had left, George lowered his voice. "I didn't know you don't drink."

Mr. Jackson shrugged. "Never cared for it. And my wife came to grief over it long before we were married."

George's eyes widened. "Sorry to hear that."

The obvious question hung in the air. "I don't believe she minds if you drink in front of her, but you'd have to ask."

The waiter set their orders down, along with their checks, then moved on.

Mr. Jackson poured his cream, then took a sip. Not bad. "I've been thinking about what you said that day upon the platform." How might he say this? "My situation is unlikely to change. I daresay, I hope it never does. Yet I realize it puts you in a dilemma."

George snorted quietly.

"As it turns out, my wife's quite the modern woman." He smiled to himself, a surge of fondness coming over him. "And she very much looks forward to you joining us when we travel."

Instead of answering, George spread jam upon his toast and took a bite.

He'd felt shocked when George told him how little he made for all the work he did. "Have you enjoyed being a waiter?"

George considered this as he chewed, swallowed. "It sounds strange to say it, but I do. Yet I see the need for improvement in the way the front house is run."

Mr. Jackson nodded. "What things might you do?"

As George began outlining his plans for improving the Hotel's restaurant service, Mr. Jackson watched him. And he saw his error.

He'd wanted to smooth the way for the younger man, offer experiences that George might never get on his own. Yet for George, the adventure lay in overcoming the obstacles to his personal success.

"So what do you think?" George took up his teacup and over the edge of it, their eyes met.

He loved the way George's cheeks colored. "I think I owe you an apology."

George set the cup down.

"But we can't be pals if you're going to lie to me."

George's face fell. Then he nodded.

"There we have it." Mr. Jackson smiled, feeling relieved. "I've decided to join a fitness club. I get a free pass each month. Want to join me next week for tennis?"

"I've never played."

Mr. Jackson fancied himself quite accomplished at it. "You taught me dominoes: it's only fitting that I return the favor."

***

Mrs. Jackson felt relieved when Mr. Jackson returned safely to their rooms. "How was your trip?"

He seemed more relaxed than she'd seen him in some time. "Quite productive, I'd say."

She went to him, putting her arms around his waist. "Let's stay in for dinner."

He smiled at her. "I'd love to. Just let me call down to let them know we won't need Mr. Raymond or Mrs. Knight this evening."

She'd forgotten that they were assigned through the front desk. This was perfect. If Mr. Raymond inquired, the desk clerk could say he spoke with Mr. Jackson and all was well.

"Have them send up the evening news as well," she heard Mr. Jackson say.

She kicked off her shoes, stretching out upon a chair. "Oh, before you hang up — have them give me a wakeup call for six."

He did so, then put down the receiver. "You're meeting with le Monsieur Chef tomorrow, then."

She smiled at him. "Indeed I am."

It wasn't that she hadn't wanted to meet with the Chef up to now, but each day, the work with Duchess Cordelia's list had left her fatigued. Now that it was completed, and she'd had a chance to recover, she felt intrigued to see what the young man had to say to her.

Duchess Cordelia had been subdued for the past days since her embarrassment, almost quiet. At first, the old woman's rage at her husband's fate felt startling, but as Mrs. Jackson considered the matter, she'd come to understand. She'd made certain to reassure the dowager that things were still well between them.

Mr. Jackson sat beside her. "Why so pensive?"

"Just thinking of Duchess Cordelia. You know, every one of the names on that list was true, but —"

"Sergeant Nestor will only remember the false one."

"Yes. I feel bad for her, though I know I shouldn't."

"She's dependent on the Hotel. It must be a difficult way to live, having been in such wealth as she was."

Mrs. Jackson sighed. That was the way of it for women — always dependent on someone to survive.

"Something's wrong."

She considered the matter. "Do you think it wise to withhold information when it might be harmful?"

Mr. Jackson shrugged. "To a child, certainly."

His meaning was plain: adults had the right to be told. What should she do?

He knelt before her, took her hands. "My dear girl, I'm not a child. Whatever this information is, it can't harm me. And I'm not going anywhere. Remember what I promised? If you ever decided you'd rather be free, I'd release you at once. Though if you said that," he took a deep breath and let it out, eyes moist, "I'd truly mourn."

"It's not that." She rested her hand on his soft scratchy black beard. "I fear for you."

Surprised, he drew back. "For me? Why?"

At present, she was out of new ideas. And he was ever so good at them. So she told him about the truck and the gem.

Mr. Jackson sat on the floor tailor-seat for a full minute in silence. Then he leaned back, hands behind him, and looked up at her. "You feared he'd learn of what you found through my reactions."

She nodded.

"Thus staying in for dinner."

She grinned, chuckling, yet tears welled up. She tried one answer then another, yet none seemed suitable.

"Come here." he said, and she sat on the floor beside him. He wrapped his arms around her; she rested her head on his chest. "You're probably right. I'm not nearly as good as hiding things as you are. But I'm grateful I've never had to." He kissed the top of her head. "Whether this man has done something wrong or not, I'm sorry now that I kept Mr. Raymond on. I've not felt comfortable with him. And instead of acting to secure a different man that very first day, I continued in spite of it. And now we're in a pickle."

"Don't say that. I won't have you blame yourself."

"But I do, for the main reason that now you're in tears on my account." He turned to face her, taking her hands. "I am not going anywhere, I promise. I have no plans to die, and if for some reason I dropped dead this instant, it wouldn't be because of anything you've done. Please stop fearing for our future."

It'd been so long since she dared to believe she had a future that she began to cry.

He kissed her hands, then leaned his elbows upon his knees, her knuckles upon his forehead. Then his head rose, and he kissed her hands again, his eyes red. "We'll get through this," he whispered, a wry smile on his face, "whether you believe me or not."

The absurdity of the whole thing made her laugh. All over a gemstone! "We shouldn't dismiss the man. But until we learn the truth, he mustn't come here."

Mr. Jackson nodded, his face sober. Then he rose. "I'm tired of sitting on the floor."

She laughed. They sat around the table to wait for their dinner to arrive.

"I'll learn the truth," Mrs. Jackson said, wiping her eyes. "Surely someone must know one way or the other what went on that day."

"That the police haven't already questioned?"

"Eugene said the truck's drivers would never have left it in the state it's in. Less than a day went between the time the men left and the killer took the truck. So assuming the men really did clean the truck before leaving on vacation, the fingerprints on it have to be those of the killer."

"That would be reasonable."

"So how did the killers get the keys? Sergeant Nestor says the men believe they've been set up, but don't know by who."

"Interesting. So it's reasonable to assume these men didn't give the keys to anyone."

"Not if they're innocent. And Sergeant Nestor says the fingerprints don't match those of the men."

Mr. Jackson rocked backwards a bit, blinking. "The killers stole the keys."

"And I can't imagine the keys were left for anyone to take. They must be under lock themselves. So unless these killers are also master lock-pickers, they left a trace of their crime." She nodded to herself. "Eugene would know if anything was broken." She glanced at the clock. "He's gone home for the day, but I can speak with him tomorrow."

The parlor bell rang, and Mr. Jackson rose. "That would be our dinner."

She smiled up at him. "I'm glad we stayed in now."

***

The next morning, Mrs. Jackson and Bessie emerged from the elevator onto the roof as the sun peeked over the horizon. The Chef stood dressed in dark blue facing the sun, his hands behind his back.

Peace radiated from him, so different from the bitter, angry young man he'd been.

She moved toward him; he turned to her and smiled. "I hoped you'd visit."

A large garden stretched before them, planted in large, decorative boxes, raised to knee high and carved with intricate patterns. Many stood free, yet many were covered in cloth. Some plants she could identify, others left her baffled. Yet each was beautifully tended and lushly growing. "You come here every day?"

"Indeed I do." He gestured out over the plants. "The best way to eat is food you tend yourself." A thin smile touched his lips. "The garden had been sadly neglected when I arrived. But it's recovered somewhat, with a bit of love."

Mrs. Jackson felt surprised, sure that the dowager's husband — who loved gardens — would have tended it.

Had he been gone that long? All that happened seemed like yesterday. "And you went to the market at half past four?"

He smiled fondly. "I did. You see, I've been rising at four since I was a boy. The kitchens don't tend themselves." The Chef stretched out his hand to her. "Come, there's much to do."

According to him, they'd had unseasonably hot weather up to now, but a freeze was predicted. "If the tomatoes are left out tonight, they'll spoil, and the plants will die. We must gather every one and bring the plants inside for the winter."

So she let Bessie roam around the large outdoor swimming pool — now covered — and sniff the various area of the roof. In the meantime, they went among the boxes, removing the cloth, gathering tomatoes into large trays upon wheeled carts as they went. For a time, she got lost in the work, focused on collecting each of the round little fruits.

"Your husband has been concerned for you," the Chef said.

She smiled to herself. "I gathered."

A silence fell as they moved the full carts over to the elevators and selected empty ones, then returned to collect the remaining tomatoes. Far below, a distant hum of traffic, the chirp of a bird, Bessie's soft noises as she went here and there, the opening of the elevator door, the sound of feet.

His voice broke the quiet. "I don't wish to presume."

Bessie came and sat nearby. Men wheeled large barrels out, and began to dig out the bare tomato plants, setting them gently into the barrels, dirt and all. After they'd placed several into one barrel, they'd bring out another. She felt fascinated by their work, yet she turned to the Chef. "Say what you wish, sir."

His face fell. "I don't mean to offend. Yet ... if any harm has come to my life, it was in the bottled-up secrets of others exploding into vengeance. And I've learned it can cause more harm, even if the secret be hurtful, to keep sorrow hidden rather than share it with those who love you."

For some reason, this made Mrs. Jackson blush.

The young Chef seemed not to notice. "Your husband seems a good man. But if you can't speak to him about your sorrows — and they don't involve him — find someone you can speak with. Anyone will do." He placed the last tomato into the cart, dusted his hands off and laid his hand upon her shoulder. "Don't let what happened then destroy your life now."

They wheeled the last cart over, then the Chef took up a large basket. It was then she noticed the short black apron he wore. Retrieving a knife and a pair of gloves from the apron, he handed her the basket. Then they moved past a long box full of cabbages to another grown thickly with foot-tall leafy plants. He began working quickly, cutting the plants off at the base and putting them into the basket she held.

"What's this called?"

"Endive. Freezing will damage it as well. Tonight, I'll include it in a salad and an appetizer. Whatever remains will be soup tomorrow."

"That's very wise."

"The Hotel is lush and expensive and grand," he cut off a plant and put it into the basket, "but it's also a business." He moved to the next plant, cut it off. "We have to use every bit we have if we're to prosper in the future."

"You really care about the Hotel."

He seemed taken aback. "Why come here then attach my name and reputation to it if I didn't?"

She hadn't thought of it that way before. "Then the situation with the Head Valet must trouble you."

He dropped the plant into the basket. "I've heard nothing of it. What happened?"

"He was murdered just outside the Hotel."

His jaw dropped, eyes widening. "How horrible! Do they know who did it?"

She shook her head. A whole long line of people had gone along hating the man for years. What could have possibly caused the men who murdered Mr. Vincenzo to do so now?

17

Mrs. Jackson and Bessie returned to her suite to find Mr. Jackson fast asleep. After calling down their breakfast order, she asked the desk clerk to notify Mr. Raymond and Mrs. Knight they wouldn't be needed this morning. Then she sat at the table near the lovely balcony in his bedroom, watching his dear sleeping face.

And her mind drifted to the conversation she'd just had. There was so much she didn't know, it seemed, about the young man who now stood as Head Chef here. Yet she felt pleased at how he'd turned out.

Mr. Jackson had worried for her. Her heart clenched at the thought. *He cares for me.*

The thought brought a certain anxiety. Although he'd assured her time and time again that they were safe here, the thought that he might be taken from her ... somehow ... hadn't left her.

Being so early, she didn't expect their tray for at least an hour yet. So she had a leisurely read of the thick morning newspaper, Bessie nestled beside her.

She'd asked for the tray to be delivered to her bedroom so as not to wake him. But when she returned from answering the door, Bessie following behind, he smiled up at her.

"I thought I'd let you sleep a bit." She sat on the edge of the bed beside him and kissed his forehead.

He wrapped his arm round her. "Something smells wonderful."

"Are you hungry?"

His face turned playful. "Ravenous." He pulled her close, pretending to gnaw her ear.

It tickled. "Well, then, I better make sure you're properly fed!" She went to the other room, rolling the cart over by the table. Mr. Jackson had put on his robe, and stood by watching. She lifted the lid.

"Oooo," he said. "Bacon."

She put the plates on the table. Besides the bacon, there was an omelet, crisply roasted cherry tomatoes with herbs scattered atop them, hashed and browned potatoes, and toast.

A carafe of orange juice, another one with water in it, a coffeepot, and a teapot stood on the shelf underneath. All the trimmings of a proper breakfast sat beside them, with a small plate of chipped beef and a narrow bone set aside for Bessie. "My, this is magnificent." She felt touched that they remembered her little dog.

Mr. Jackson helped her set up the table, then set to his meal with a good appetite.

The food was delicious, every bite. She gazed over at him fondly. "Thank you for being concerned for me."

He took a sip of his coffee. "So you did speak with the Chef this morning."

"I did. The view from the rooftop is lovely. And the garden! He let me help in it."

"Oh?"

"I picked those tomatoes!" She felt rather pleased with herself.

He smiled fondly at her. "I'm glad you enjoyed it."

She considered the entire morning. "I did! I don't normally rise so early. But ... I believe I will again." It'd been so peaceful up there.

And she realized this was what she wanted: peace, and some real work to do that meant something.

For some reason this feeling of peace made her think of Ophelia. She felt at home with her. Like they'd been friends forever, and instead of learning each other new, were just picking up where they left off.

Bessie put her paws up on Mrs. Jackson's legs, and she nestled the little dog on her lap. "Sorry to tell you: it's supposed to freeze tonight."

"A pity," he said. "I guess more sailing this year's out of the question."

"I didn't consider that. George's parents will be heartbroken."

"I imagine they'll invite us over sometime during the holidays."

"I hope so. And we can leave Bessie here with people she doesn't feel compelled to bark at."

He laughed.

"How's your neck?"

"Whatever Mr. Raymond's been doing must be working: it's better today."

She didn't know why, but the news gave her a great sense of relief. "I'll feel terrible if he's truly done nothing wrong. It's horrible to suspect someone."

Mr. Jackson nodded. "This may sound strange." He touched his neck. "Yet I felt better at once when you said we'd not have him here again."

The thought of a man who might murder someone with a straight razor to her Mr. Jackson's neck made her shudder. "This is maddening. I must learn the truth. I don't believe I'll rest until I do."

He smiled at her, opening up his the morning news. "Go speak with Eugene, then. Bessie and I will hold down the fort."

But first there was something she wanted to do.

She found the Chef standing out on the platform in back, gazing out over the parking lot and the trees beyond. He twitched when she stepped up beside him. "I didn't hear you!"

"It's noisy out here, isn't it?"

"I admit to being a bit caught up in my thoughts," he said. "How may I help you?"

"I wanted to thank you for speaking with me this morning. I enjoyed it very much."

He smiled. "I did, too."

400

"Have you seen Eugene? The maintenance man."

"Sorry, I don't know many of the names here."

"I'm sure he'll be by soon." She stood with the young Chef, listening to the sounds of the trucks and men. "There's something you should know."

He nodded soberly.

"You and my former husband may have had your differences, but from the moment I learned of his relation to you, I looked on you as family."

He took a deep breath, in and out. "I seem to have found my family wherever I went. Each cared for me as they could, then let me make my way as I might."

"That's very charitable of you, all things considered."

He laughed. "How many have people all over the world who love them? I hardly consider anymore the few who felt glad to see my back." He checked his watch. "I best return to work — I'm sure they have a whole line of plates for me to check."

She grinned at him. "Enjoy your morning."

"I will."

Right then, Eugene passed by down below, and she waved to him. He jogged his way up the steps. "What can I do for you?"

"I'm curious about the trucks. Do you secure the keys here in any way, or can anyone access them?"

He leaned upon the railing. "Now, that's an interesting question."

"Why do you say so?"

"Because a week before you returned here, someone broke the lock to the key rack. It must have been after all the drivers picked up their keys in the morning."

"Why do you say that?"

"I only learned about it because the man who locks up at the end of the day came to me worried about his truck. The key rack being broke open like that and all. None of the keys were missing, so after I fixed the lock, I forgot all about it."

She considered the matter. "And no one saw who did it?"

Eugene shook his head. "I don't know why that darn fool Davis let those two drivers take three weeks off this time of year. Between the Head Valet walking off in the middle of his shift, a truck out of commission and the tourist rush, we've been so busy a crowd could have carried the truck off without anyone seeing it."

And in the three weeks in between, any fingerprints on the key rack would be long gone. "Thanks, this has been really helpful."

"You think someone here killed Mr. Earl?"

She sighed. "It's looking more like that every day." And just in case Eugene took it on himself to talk about it, she added, "But we still don't have enough to pin it on anyone."

He shrugged. "I just work here."

After speaking with Eugene, Mrs. Jackson returned to her suite.

Mr. Jackson was in knickers and an undershirt doing calisthenics in his room as Bessie ran back and forth around him.

She laughed. "What a sight you two make!"

He straightened, a grin upon his face. "I'm glad we provide you with some entertainment."

"What's spurred on this interest in exercise?"

He took up a towel which lay upon the bed and wiped his brow. "I thought that perhaps it was time for me to begin paying more attention to my health."

"That seems wise; carry on." She went to her bedroom to call for lunch to be delivered to their suite. It came about the time Mr. Jackson emerged from his bath. "Shall I have this set up in your room or the parlor?"

Mr. Jackson's voice emerged from his rooms. "In here is fine."

To Mrs. Jackson's delight, a spicy endive and tomato salad accompanied the meal. "This smells delicious!"

"It does," Mr. Jackson said. "One thing about exercise — it does improve the appetite."

Mrs. Jackson set up a plate on the floor for Bessie, and returned to her lunch, which was delicious.

The couple ate, and talked, and eventually a waiter came and took their plates away.

Bessie, who'd been lying upon the carpet the entire time, suddenly ran off into Mr. Jackson's bathroom.

He turned his head to follow. "I wonder what she wants in there?"

A few moments later, a strange noise came from Mr. Jackson's bathroom. He got up and went there. "Oh, dear. She's gotten sick!"

Mrs. Jackson found him wiping the floor with a damp towel. Bessie lay close by, head on her paws. "Poor little thing."

He rinsed out the washcloth and wiped the floor again. "She probably ate too much."

Bessie didn't look right. "I don't know ... she's never done this before. Stay here: I'm taking her down to have the vet look at her." She scooped the little dog up in a clean towel and headed out of the door.

The veterinarian took a quick look at her. "You're right: she doesn't look well. Let me do some tests and keep her overnight. Has she eaten anything unusual?"

"We just feed her off of our plates."

"But no chocolate or fruit?"

"We haven't had any chocolate for a while, to be honest. And I didn't know a dog would eat fruit."

He laughed. "Dogs will try to eat just about anything." His wife brought over a padded kennel box, and he gently placed Bessie into it. She lay there, eyes shut. "This is easier to clean should she be sick again."

Mrs. Jackson smoothed little Bessie's hair. "I'll be back to see you tomorrow."

Bessie opened an eye, and her ears went up a moment, but then she rested again.

Mrs. Jackson went to the lobby and out front, feeling discouraged. Would Bessie be okay?

And what were they going to do about Mr. Jackson's valet? How long might they keep avoiding him before he felt something was wrong? She felt no closer to understanding how the man was involved with this than when she discovered the gem the day before.

Perhaps she should have told Sergeant Nestor about the gemstone.

Mrs. Jackson lit a cigarette. The day was pleasant at any rate, the air crisp. The holidays were coming soon. What might she get for her Mr. Jackson?

"Waiting for a taxi, ma'am?"

A blond valet she'd seen earlier but not met before stood nearby. She shook her head. "Busy today?"

His name-tag said: Charlie. "Not yet."

Something had been bothering her this whole time. "May I ask you something?"

The man seemed surprised. "Why, certainly."

"My husband and I are helping Mr. Carlo about the matter with Mr. Vincenzo."

He nodded gravely.

"Were you here that day?"

"Yes, ma'am, I was. I already told the police about it, though."

"Told them what?"

He glanced over towards the alley. "One minute he was there, the next he's gone."

"Just like that?"

"Yeah."

"Why do you think he went in the alley?"

Charlie blinked several times, mouth open. "Wait."

"What is it?"

"I forgot. Right before that, one of the maids came out and talked to him. She went right back in, so I guess it slipped my mind."

This interested her at once. "Which maid was it?"

He squinted, eyes unfocused. "I'm kinda new here ... not sure if I heard the name right. Essie?"

"Effie?"

"Yeah, that's it. Effie. Pretty girl, that one. But Mr. Earl'd get mad if you so much as looked at her."

Mrs. Jackson dropped her cigarette and stepped on it. "And did he say or do anything after that?"

Charlie shrugged. "Kind of seemed annoyed, tell you the truth. He headed over there," he pointed at the alley, "but then a car came up, so I quit looking."

"I see."

"Do you think it means anything?"

"I think you've been very helpful."

Mrs. Jackson rushed to the front desk, where the young man who'd greeted them at their first arrival back here stood. "Might I use your telephone?"

"Certainly!" He placed it upon the counter.

She dialed the police station. "Sergeant Nestor, please."

It took a while for him to answer. "What can I help with, Mrs. Jackson?"

She spoke quietly. "I know who killed Mr. Vincenzo, and I'm almost certain why. But we must hurry if this is to be done without a scene. Come to our suite after tea. But quietly, and bring a few men with you. No uniforms, and not a word to Mr. Carlo."

Sergeant Nestor sounded amused. "Be right over."

When she next caught the eye of the desk clerk, she said, "Might I speak with Maria, please?"

"She should be in her office. I'll call her out here."

He took the phone, speaking quietly into it while Mrs. Jackson watched the grand fountain. A few minutes later, footsteps approached her.

It was Maria, the Head Maid.

"Ah, there you are," Mrs. Jackson said. "Would you send Effie to my room after tea? I'm going to need her help for a few hours."

"Certainly," Maria said, making a notation upon a pad. "I'll let the front desk know where she'll be."

"Perfect! Thank you so much. And tell her not to bring her cart — it won't be necessary."

Mrs. Jackson hurried to her suite, finding Mr. Jackson in the parlor reading a book.

When he saw her, he closed the book and set it aside. "How's Bessie?"

This distracted her, just a bit. "What? Oh, yes. They're going to watch her overnight." She had to focus. "This is important. Is Mr. Raymond coming to dress you this evening?"

Mr. Jackson put down his paper. "I haven't called to tell him not to." He hesitated, then his mouth fell open, his face horrified. "No."

She nodded. "Yes, sorry to say. Sergeant Nestor will be here after tea."

Mr. Jackson put his face in his hands.

She sat beside him, moved. He'd trusted the man, and to get confirmation of his crime must feel like a blow. "I'm sorry. That new blond valet saw his sister speak with Mr. Vincenzo right before he went to the alley. But I just can't see her knowingly sending the man to his death."

"So someone sent her there to speak with him."

"And drove that truck. And killed him."

His eyes widened, but he quickly recovered. "You called the sergeant ... so I presume you have a plan?"

She sat beside him. "We have a few hours before he arrives. Here's what I think we should do ..."

18

When the knock came at Mr. Jackson's door, Mrs. Jackson answered. "Oh, hello, come in. Mr. Jackson is delayed." She turned round, heart pounding, relieved when the man followed. "Would you care for some tea?"

"No thank you, ma'am," Mr. Raymond said. He closed the door behind him.

She continued on into the parlor. "Feel free to sit here until he arrives."

"That's very kind of you." Yet although he came into the room, he continued to stand, glancing about.

Mrs. Jackson said, "Oh, that reminds me! I found something of yours." She went to her handbag and fished out the red gem.

When she showed it to him, he looked astonished. "Wherever did you find it?"

Mrs. Jackson smiled. "You see, that's the problem. If you consider all the places you've been, that is."

The man paled. "What do you want?"

"Nothing. But I'm curious as to why you did it."

His face grew guarded. "I don't know what you're talking about."

Mrs. Jackson slipped the gem into her pocket, then rested a hand upon the back of an armchair. "Let me see if I can figure it out. You break the lock in the key rack when no one's looking and steal the truck. You lure Mr. Vincenzo to the alley with your sister's help. Then you drive up in the truck and bring out the shovels and crowbars. Once there, he helps you dig out the manhole leading to the sewers and hoist it up. You have him look down into there, and while he's doing that, you give him a good whack on the head."

A gasp came from her room.

Mr. Raymond jerked towards the sound, face alarmed. "Who's there?"

The doors opened from all three sides and policemen came in, dressed for the street. Mr. Jackson came in from his room.

Sergeant Nestor entered from Mrs. Jackson's room. Along with the sergeant was Effie Raymond. "Stanley," Effie said, "what have you done?"

"You can't prove a thing," said he.

Sergeant Nestor appeared entirely relaxed. "Oh, but we can. You see, from talking to your coworkers at the Howell-Green Procurement Agency, I learned something interesting: you never wear gloves. From the truck drivers' coworkers I learned another interesting thing: those men were meticulous about their truck. They did a thorough clean-down before leaving for their vacation, inside and out. All the men did their clean-outs at the end of the day, so I have several witnesses to it.

"And what do we find on the truck now? Fingerprints, upon the steering wheel, the door-handles, two crowbars, a large stick ..." he seemed to be at a loss.

Mr. Jackson exclaimed, "So **that's** what you used to mark the manhole!"

Sergeant Nestor nodded, his face suggesting he'd not considered that. "And upon one of the shovels, which although you tried wiping it down, also had Mr. Vincenzo's blood type upon it. I'll be willing to wager that when we go to the station, those fingerprints will be yours. His fingerprints lie upon the other. Mrs. Jackson has given an excellent rundown of the crime. The question we all have is: why?"

Mr. Raymond crossed his arms.

Effie looked heartbroken. "He told me why. When we argued. When I spilled the soap, right before you two arrived. He said, 'Effie, I can never forgive what he did.'"

Mr. Raymond took a step forward. "Don't tell them about that! After all you've been through?"

Mrs. Jackson had a theory as to what this might be about. "Effie, dear, tell us what happened. No one else need know."

Effie glanced around at the men filling the room, then hung her head. "I thought Earl loved me. He said he'd leave his wife. But then when I came with child, he told me he'd talked to Mr. Carlo about it. He never could leave: his wife would cause a scandal." She let out a sigh. "So I went up north and had my girl there."

Ah, Mrs. Jackson thought. "Mary Bluff?"

Effie stared at her, mouth open. "How did you know? I named her after my mother!"

"Your Mr. Vincenzo left her three thousand dollars in his will."

Effie's eyes filled with tears. " I knew he cared about her." She fished in a pocket for a handkerchief. "She's with good folk. I send money every month." Effie began to cry. "I thought it'd be too hard to come back. But the work's better here. And I still loved him, even after all he's done." Then her face twisted in anguish. "He was her father." She turned on her brother. "I'll **never** forgive you for this!"

Mrs. Jackson felt a great sadness. The man wanted to be with his only child.

Mr. Jackson said, "I agree it's a difficult situation. But enough to kill a man over?"

Mr. Raymond flinched, then his face reddened, fists balling up.

Mr. Jackson glanced at Effie. "Would he not help?"

Effie sniffled, wiped her nose. "No, Earl's paid for everything." She raised her eyes to her brother. "Stanley, what's this really about? What did he do to you?"

Mr. Raymond's hands began to shake, and he stumbled backwards, face white.

412

Alarmed, Effie lunged forward. "Stanley!"

She and one of the policemen rushed to the valet's side, helping him to a chair.

"I feel ill." Mr. Raymond put his face into his hands, looking very young somehow. "I don't even know where to begin. It all seems too horrible to relate."

Sergeant Nestor pulled up a chair and sat across from him, then drew out a pad and pencil. "Just start where you feel best, son."

Mr. Raymond nodded, hands still covering his face. "I was seven. Effie was only four, so she probably don't recall it. But my parents had a terrible fight. I remember Papa saying, 'You betrayed me with **him**?'. At the time, I didn't understand, but when Papa stormed out, I followed. I wanted to be with him. I don't think he knew I was behind." His hands dropped to his lap, and he began panting as if he'd just run a mile.

Sergeant Nestor nodded. "Go on."

"Papa went to this building and up two flights. They were long flights. Straight, made of white stone. I didn't go up the second one. I stayed on the landing. It was dark, but I felt scared to let Papa see me there. At the top there was a light and a door. Papa banged on the door. The man answered. They argued, fought." He squeezed his eyes shut. "He pushed my Papa down the stairs!"

Effie gasped.

His hands began to shake. "I saw that man's face up there lit by the lamps as clear as day."

413

Mr. Jackson looked horrified. "Earl Vincenzo."

Mr. Raymond glanced back at him, then nodded. "It was. I didn't know he'd been seeing Effie until she brought him by, before she came with child." His jaw tightened. "My Papa dying like that killed Mama. But at her grave I promised I'd make Vincenzo pay for what he'd done. Come to find out he'd hurt dozens of women. And then, when he cast my sister aside too, I couldn't stand by no longer."

Effie blurted out, "He thought you were his friend!"

"Then my plan worked."

Sergeant Nestor said, "How did you get him to go to the alley?"

Mr. Raymond smiled to himself. "While Effie was up north, I learned where he worked and went by once in a while. Then I sent letters telling him I knew he'd killed a man. Eventually he let his distress show, and I offered my help. When the two truck-men said they were going on vacation, I made my plan. Told him I'd caught the man who'd been sending the letters and stashed him. I'd bring him close by to meet up and have words. I'd have Effie tell him where and when."

"So that was the message," Mr. Jackson said.

Effie turned pale. "I told him Stanley said he'd meet him in the alley."

Mrs. Jackson nodded. "That new valet Charlie said he seemed annoyed."

Effie's head drooped. "He was. Earl said, 'Now?' And I said, 'Yes, Stanley's waiting for you!'" Tears ran down her face. "I persuaded him to go!"

Mrs. Jackson said to Mr. Raymond, "But how could you have possibly known the manhole cover was there?"

He laughed. "We grew up right behind the Hotel. Used to play in that alley with my friends. I'd seen the manhole many a time, back when there were cobbles. Didn't take but a few minutes with a stick to find it again and mark the spot."

Sergeant Nestor turned to Effie, face stern. "You knew your brother asked you to send Mr. Vincenzo to the alley. And then he turned up dead there. Why didn't you come forward?"

"And doom my brother?" She put her face in her hands. Then she raised her tear-streaked face. "I suspected. When we argued it was because I asked if he had anything to do with Earl gone missing. But when I knew he'd killed him, I didn't know what to do!"

Mr. Jackson said, "Is Mr. Vienna really delayed?"

Mr. Raymond shook his head. "I doubt he knows you're back. I'd been hanging round the operators and happened to catch the call when the one on duty took her break. It seemed miraculous. I figured after the other murders a few months back, you'd be called in. And being your valet I'd know if you got suspicious." His tone turned ironic. "Guess you fooled me."

Sergeant Nestor put his pad and pencil away. "Come along now, lad, it's time to go. Let's not make a scene."

"What'll happen to Effie?"

"She had good reason to suspect you and didn't come forward. I'll have to charge her, but who knows? The judge might be lenient in this case."

Mrs. Jackson said, "May I speak with Effie for a moment?"

Sergeant Nestor took Mr. Raymond's arm and led him to the door. The other men nodded, moving away.

Effie turned to Mrs. Jackson. "I'm so sorry for everything."

She looked so young, so forlorn. Mrs. Jackson put her hands upon Effie's upper arms and spoke quietly. "Look at me. You have nothing to be sorry for. I know what it's like to try your best to do what's right and still lose everything. I just wanted to say something a friend told me recently: don't let what happened then destroy your life now. Whatever happens, someday this will be over. And when it is, go somewhere no one's ever heard of you and live your life. You still deserve it."

Effie hugged her, weeping. "I will, ma'am. I will."

Mrs. Jackson hugged the girl back, feeling maybe the whole ordeal she'd been through had given her something after all.

Once everyone left, Mr. Jackson put his arm around her waist. "Was this the secret of Effie's that you couldn't tell me?"

She smiled, yet she didn't feel it. "It was." Then she turned to him. "I have no secrets from you." Then she sighed. "I know you want to know what happened to me that night we left, because you care. It's just ..."

"It's too soon to speak of it."

And, as Mr. Raymond had said, it seemed too horrible to relate. She nodded.

He gave her a warm smile and kissed her forehead. "Let's go out for dinner."

So they did.

Epilogue

Mr. Stanley Raymond was convicted of the premeditated murder of Mr. Earl Vincenzo and sent to prison.

Miss Effie Raymond was charged with withholding evidence in a homicide investigation and put on probation. She was also dismissed from the Hotel. Under the circumstances, though, the court allowed her to move up north to be with her daughter. The Headwaiter, Mr. Clifton Strait, moved there as well.

Mr. Hector Jackson decided that the couple wouldn't travel any further until George Neuberg had saved up enough to comfortably accompany them, which pleased George no end. In turn, George applied for and was granted the Headwaiter's position, which came with a substantial raise.

Miss Ophelia Denton decided she'd keep her present dancing job, but with reduced hours. She and Mrs. Jackson spent many a pleasant afternoon holiday shopping together.

The dowager Duchess Cordelia Stayman was ever so pleased to receive a box of dominoes from the couple as a gift for her hospitality.

After some negotiation, Harry took the post as Head Valet. He'd known all along what'd been going on there!

Mr. Norman Vienna resumed work as Mr. Jackson's valet, and was Mr. Jackson glad to see him!

When the couple retrieved Bessie, the veterinarian had a surprise for them. The little dog's escape from her leash on the steamer before the couple arrived at the Hotel had its consequences.

Bessie was expecting puppies!

Acknowledgements

Thanks so much to Tina Crist for her beta reading, and to Patricia Loofbourrow for the cover design.

About the Author

I've loved reading since I can remember! I love puzzles and mysteries and intrigue, and of all the cities I've been to, Chicago is my favorite. My four years living in Chicago during grad school were wonderful. Plus I love history. And wasn't the 1920's wild? I've always wanted to write a fun mystery series set in Chicago and now here's my chance.

Claire Logan is a pen name.

A New Year's Shot!

The Myriad Mysteries #3
Claire Logan

To those of you who are facing your fears.

1

It was well past dinner. Dressed for bed, Mr. Hector Jackson and his wife Pamela sat on the floor of his spacious bathroom in the Myriad Hotel beside their black toy poodle Bessie and her five puppies.

The little dogs nestled in a soft thick blanket under the sink, the edges tucked under so the blanket made a raised ring around the new family. A second, matching blanket, had been threaded through the pipes below the sink to make a canopy of sorts for the new little family's bed. The puppies hadn't opened their eyes yet, and wobbled towards the scent of their mother.

Their sire must have been a deep golden brown: one puppy was black, one golden, one black and golden spotted, and two were shades of brown in between. They'd be beautiful animals when grown.

"They're still so little," his wife said.

This made him smile. He petted Bessie's curly black hair. "So they are."

Mr. Jackson leaned back, laying his hand upon the black and white tile. He'd been in Chicago months already and never noticed that his bathroom floor was heated! He wondered how they did it. "A perfect place for such small animals on a chilly night."

His wife giggled, snuggling up beside him. "Indeed it is. Although we need a blanket of our own. This floor's quite hard."

He clambered to a standing position, then held his hand out to hoist his wife up beside him. Looking down at the puppies, he sighed. "They won't stay so small for long. And we can't keep them here." Small and well-mannered as Bessie was, in a hotel suite one dog was quite enough.

"I know. I know." She cleared her throat. "A pity. I wish one day we might have land, and a place we could keep puppies like these ones."

He shrugged. "I have a few places like that. But not here in Chicago."

At that, she laughed. "I suppose we could buy one. But I'm not quite ready to become a farmer's wife in the snow just yet."

He thought the idea of being a farmer rather amusing. He'd never once considered such a thing. A mansion, perhaps, or some villa overlooking the sea. "And here I thought you liked Chicago."

"I do!" She took a deep breath, let it out. "I love being here, with my friends, the gardens, the nightlife." She beamed down at the dogs. "I love my little Bessie." Then she twitched a bit, and looked up at him. "And you, too, of course."

He laughed. "I suppose I should be glad I rate! Even if it's at the end of the list."

She poked his side, grinning. "But I was referring to here. I can be with you anywhere."

A great fondness for her came over him, and he put his arm around her. "That you can. Anywhere in the world you desire, dear girl, I'll gladly go with you."

She beamed at him, fitting herself into his side. The couple moved from the bathroom turned puppy-house, towards his bedroom, everything neatly arranged by his valet and their floor's maid.

This was the kind of life he loved. He loved the feel of thick black carpeting on his bare feet, the fresh smell of the newly cleaned rooms. He loved the golden flame-shaped radiators, the telephone in their rooms, how everything was kept in such order.

And he loved not having to do any of it himself.

They went through his bedroom into their suite's parlor, where a fire crackled still. His wife ventured to the French doors, peering out through the glass, past the balcony, into the darkened streets. "They say it's supposed to be warmer tomorrow." She glanced at him over her shoulder. "For the holiday."

He laughed. "Warmer in winter here means not too terribly icy." He sat at the large wooden table. "Let's see. Who might want a puppy?"

Mr. Lee Francis, the Myriad Hotel's Head Clerk, had already chosen the black-and-gold spotted one — when the pup was weaned, of course — for his wife and baby son. But that left four to give away.

They'd already asked around a bit. His pal George Neuberg — the Myriad's new Headwaiter — was gone from his little apartment most of the day. His wife's friend Ophelia Denton — a showgirl at the Club Patruni — lived in a boarding house, no pets allowed.

His wife's voice broke his reverie. "Did you ask any of the maids?"

"Anyone here all day would be here all day," he said. "Not the ideal situation."

Bessie came trotting out, went to him and put her feet on his leg, whining.

"I'll call for one of the boys to come walk her," his wife said, going to the telephone. Bessie followed her.

They'd bought a wrap for Bessie's midsection to keep her teats warm in the chilly weather, so he fetched it from his closet and put it on her. By this time, the boy had arrived: the eldest one, perhaps seventeen. He tipped his cap to them, then looked down, arms wide. "Bessie!"

From the way she danced, the little dog seemed just as happy to see him.

Mr. Jackson smiled fondly at the pair going off down the hall. "What a wonderful place we live in!"

He felt his wife's arm going round his waist. "Indeed we do."

The couple sat on the sofa in front of the fire while they awaited Bessie's return.

Mr. Jackson felt more than a bit anxious about the coming holiday, most particularly, the thought of their friends out on the town. But he didn't know how to broach the matter to his wife.

Finally, he decided the best course of action was to speak of it directly. "We have to tell them the truth. As much of it as we can."

"Oh?"

He sighed. "It's dangerous for them to be kept in the dark much longer."

Her eyes were huge in the firelight. "Because of the Feds."

When he'd brought her to this place, she'd been running from a life that had fallen into shambles in a truly horrible way. He'd sworn to protect her, a vow he could never break — even if he didn't love her in a way he'd never loved any woman before. "It's the safest course of action."

His wife said, "It's none of their business."

"It is, and you know it. What if —"

She cried out, "I don't want either of them to know!"

"It's not fair for them not to. What if one of these places gets raided? What if they're taken in? Questioned?"

Fear touched her eyes, and he hated it that he should be the one to put that there, when finally she'd found a place to be happy. "My darling, please. Listen to me. They're both fine people. They care about us. But they wouldn't know what to say, or more importantly, what not to. It would grieve them if they were to harm us by some innocent comment." He leaned forward to peer into her eyes. "They'd be furious that we didn't warn them. And the longer we keep this from them, the more likely they'll learn the truth from someone else. They'd be hurt, feeling that we didn't trust them. Wonder what else we've hidden."

Her eyes fell.

"I love you." He reached over, lifted her chin, and tears stood in her eyes. "I love you more than anything in this world. I left everything for you: my home, my titles, my family. I would die, right now —"

She flinched.

" — before I let anything happen to you. I would take you right this minute and leave everything and everyone I have here before I allowed anyone to bring you back there. I'm on your side. Do you understand?"

She flung herself upon his chest sobbing, and he held her close, stroking her black curly hair.

"Shh," he said finally, as her sobbing turned to coughing, then to quiet tears. "All will be well, dear girl. All will be quite well."

2

The next morning, Mrs. Jackson felt better. And as she crept out of her Mr. Jackson's room, across the parlor, and into her own bedroom, she decided that he was right. She was thirty years old now, a woman full-grown, not some pampered child.

Secrets had been what got her into this mess. And she'd hidden from her friends long enough. Everyone involved needed to be told, before this all got out of hand.

But what would they think of her? Would they assume her to be a fiend, some deranged murderess who fled rather than face her crimes?

Most of what had happened was all too public. But the worst of it happened in private, betrayals by people she trusted and loved.

Her Mr. Jackson was right: George and Ophelia were good people. But in their shock and dismay over the news, would they go to the Feds themselves?

As the sky began to lighten, a knock came at her bedroom door. "Mrs. Knight! How lovely to see you."

Mrs. Octavia Knight, a professional lady's maid, came in and took off her hat and coat. "As you, ma'am. I hope you slept well?"

"I did."

Mrs. Knight began drawing a bath at once.

Instead of arriving at nine, Mrs. Knight now would examine the Almanac and arrive an hour before sunrise each day. In this way, Mrs. Jackson might be ready to help Monsieur — the Myriad Hotel's young Head Chef — with his rooftop kitchen gardens at dawn.

When Mrs. Jackson first arrived, she'd truly needed Mrs. Knight's help. But now, it was just nice to see the woman, chat about nothing for a bit, and be able to provide a bit of help to her in return. Mrs. Knight had an ill husband and a daughter almost out on her own, and Mrs. Jackson felt sure the extra money came in handy.

As Mrs. Jackson soaked in the tub, she said, "What might you think if a friend told you something terrible? About themselves."

Mrs. Knight hung a long-sleeved woolen forest green day dress upon the bathroom's clothes stand. "I'd feel grateful for her trust in me."

Mrs. Jackson hadn't considered that. And she recalled what Mr. Jackson had said. Would Ophelia be hurt that she hadn't told her sooner? Feel she didn't trust her?

"If she'd been a friend," Mrs. Knight said, "a real friend, and she regretted what she'd done, and was trying to be a better person, to truly change, then I'd have nothing to fear, now, would I?"

"True." Mrs. Jackson washed out her hair, got up from the warm water. The towels here were so beautifully thick and soft. "You've been very helpful."

It was lovely to have Mrs. Knight dry her hair for her before she went out into the cold. The Hotel had an electric hair dryer in the room, but it was rather heavy.

Mrs. Knight moved a stray bit of hair into place. "There! All ready for the day."

Mrs. Jackson smiled at her. "Thank you. We'll be staying in tonight, so enjoy your evening."

"Will you be needing me in the morning?"

"No, you take tomorrow morning off. My treat. Spend some time with your family."

"You're very kind, ma'am. Tomorrow at seven, then?"

Mrs. Knight also took care of her clothing and dressed her for dinner. "Right you are," Mrs. Jackson said. "I'll call if anything changes."

Mrs. Knight smiled fondly at her. "You have a wonderful day."

**

When the elevator reached the roof, Mrs. Jackson stepped onto the roof and unclipped Bessie's leash. The little dog immediately went to the paneled wall beside the elevator shaft to relieve herself. As the elevator

431

closed, Mrs. Jackson took in the glorious sunrise, the crisp cold air, the beautiful blue sky.

And she coughed.

Taking one last drag from her cigarette, she stepped upon it, coiled up Bessie's leash into the pocket of her overcoat, and moved forward. As usual, Bessie began sniffing the entire rooftop.

The rooftop of the Myriad Hotel was as grand and spacious as its inside: fine stone tile paved the way. Large boxes spread across this end of the rooftop, in this area raised to knee high, all carved with intricate patterns. The boxes held dirt and many plants covered in oiled canvas to protect them from the bitter cold.

The young Monsieur already worked there, cutting off a row of cabbages one by one with quick strokes of his knife, then gently placing them, leaves and all, into the low wheeled cart beside him. A young man of average height with black hair and pale blue eyes, Monsieur was a culinary prodigy, his name and portrait gracing more than one of the many magazines here. Since coming here as Head Chef, the Myriad Hotel's restaurant had never fared better, and reservations for those not staying in the Hotel were at a premium.

She felt a great fondness for the young man, waving at him cheerfully when he glanced up. He merely nodded as she passed by.

Mrs. Jackson knelt beside the cart to select a knife on the rack at its end similar to the one he bore. "How many more of these do we need?"

He sliced through the stem of one. "This should be enough." He returned the knife to its holder. "Let's dig the parsnips next."

Fetching long thin trowels, they went down long rows to an area where the boxes stood waist high and found a box entirely full of parsnips. After breaking through the frosty earth on top, they began to wiggle free one fat pale carrot-shaped root at a time. These went in a basket on top of the cabbages.

"If I might ask, sir: what's Paris like? I've never been."

Monsieur's face broke into a rare smile. "Lovely, especially in the spring. I particularly enjoyed walking near the river."

"Do you think you might ever wish to return?"

He shrugged. "It's a crowded place, even more so than here. Perhaps one day, if only to visit friends. I have many there from my days in the Cordon Bleu." He smiled to himself, perhaps recalling some fond memory. "But we write often." He took a foot-long parsnip from the dirt. "It's been terribly busy of late, but once I get some men properly trained, I might be able to plan a holiday. During the Hotel's slow season, of course."

She coughed, and it rattled her chest a bit.

Monsieur peered at her gravely. "I hope all is well?"

"Why yes," she said. "Oh, you mean this cough? It's nothing; merely a tickle."

"Good," he said. "For some, cold air is good for the constitution. For others, it causes illness. My younger sister was one such, and it gave her no end of trouble when she was small." A few of his men had emerged upon the rooftop, and he gestured for them to take the cart. "Let's get the young greens together for today."

In the far area behind the elevator shaft stood a extensive greenhouse. Inside were rows of various plants under glass, including an assortment of young lettuces. Monsieur took up a basket large as a tire under one arm, resting it upon a cart. Then he began clipping whole handfuls of the small leaves, tossing them in the basket.

"I remember your sister," Mrs. Jackson said. "Have you heard from her?"

"Not in some time," Monsieur said gravely. "They sent her out West, if you recall."

Mrs. Jackson remembered her, a pretty little girl with dark hair. The dry air out West was said to be good for the health. "Well, if you do, please give her my regards!"

Monsieur smiled at her. "I most certainly will."

***

Mr. Jackson woke at the knock on his bedroom door. Putting on a robe, he went to answer.

His manservant (here they called the man a "valet") Mr. Norman Vienna stood there. A lovely young man with light skin and brown hair.

434

Rather a bit like George, if he was to say. He hadn't considered it before. "Come in. How was your honeymoon?"

"We had a marvelous time, sir, thank you for asking."

"I appreciate you coming in on the holiday."

"Not at all, sir." He gave a sheepish smile. "To be honest, I've been away long enough." He began going through Mr. Jackson's closet. "Rather enjoyed myself, but the bills come in soon."

Mr. Jackson laughed. "Quite so."

Mr. Vienna went into the bathroom, and the sound of water came forth. When he emerged, he said, "Congratulations on the puppies!"

Mr. Jackson felt amused. "Thank you, sir. If you're interested in one, we have four to give away."

Mr. Vienna laughed. "Oh, I don't think the wife would be pleased at that. Not at all. She's not fond of animals." He went to the dresser, retrieving and laying out a clean shirt atop it.

"Pity. But not everyone is. They're a lot of work!"

Mr. Vienna glanced over at him, then moved to the closet. "Going out today, or just the Hotel?"

The Myriad Hotel had any number of amusements — one might never leave it! "I hadn't planned! Perhaps something suitable for both."

Mr. Vienna nodded, his eyes upon the clothing. Then he selected a dark brown tweed suit. "Just the thing! Not too much for breakfast downstairs, yet warm enough for going out. If the weather turns bad, just pop upstairs and fetch your overcoat."

"Splendid!"

Mr. Vienna straightened the bed a bit then laid the suit atop it. "I'll see to your bath, then, sir."

After a nice warm bath and a shave, Mr. Jackson felt much improved. By the time he'd dressed, the door to his wife's bedroom opened, and he heard the sound of little Bessie rushing across the parlor. The little dog hurried past them and to her pups.

"A conscientious mother, that one." Mr. Vienna helped Mr. Jackson into his coat and began to brush it.

"She really is. Couldn't have asked for a better dog."

His wife came to the doorway to the parlor and leaned upon the door-frame. Her light brown cheeks were slightly ruddy from the cold outside, her black curls a bit tossed under the forest green cloche she wore.

She looked gorgeous.

Mr. Vienna grinned, giving her a short nod. "I'll leave you to your day, then." He turned to Mr. Jackson. "Tonight, then?"

Mrs. Jackson said, "I told Mrs. Knight we'd be staying in tonight, and tomorrow morning as well."

"Well there you have it," said Mr. Jackson. "Take a bit of a holiday with the wife. Just put it on our bill."

Mr. Vienna's eyes widened. "Thank you, sir!" He bowed. "Tomorrow night, then. Sir. Ma'am."

"Have a lovely day," his wife called out. Then she went to him and straightened his cravat, which he felt sure didn't need it. "That was very generous of you."

He shrugged, amused. "Remember? Mr. Carlo's been picking up the tab."

3

The upper halls of the Myriad Hotel were the very peak of luxury: marble floors, rosewood paneled walls. Fine brass fixtures high on the walls cast warm soothing light upon the way.

A magnificent painting of the lake tossed by a storm hung above a long narrow brass table across from the elevator, with two seats fashioned in rosewood and upholstered in deep blue velvet beside it.

The elevator door was exquisite Art Deco work carved in brass: a valiant man sounding a horn.

Inside, a man in Hotel livery operated the elevator, bringing them to the lobby.

The same marble floors, but in this elevator area, the marble extended also to the walls. Brilliant electric bulbs overhead lit the scene. In the wide grand lobby itself, little shops lay around to the left, surrounded by rosewood paneling and brass trimmings, with Art Deco murals high upon the walls.

People were everywhere: visiting the shops, gazing at the huge fountain the in the center of the room, going in and out of the brass-edged front double doors, ascending

438

and descending the wide staircase to the right. The couple went past the staircase and to the beveled glass dining room doors. Attendants stood by to open the doors for them, and they ventured inside.

Mr. Jackson seldom saw Mr. Montgomery Carlo, the Hotel's owner. But when he and his wife went down for breakfast, the big swarthy man stood near the Headwaiter's station, beside the Myriad's new Headwaiter, George Neuberg.

A slender, fit, tanned young man, George seemed focused on a paper Mr. Carlo held up for him. George glanced up as the couple approached. "Good morning, sir! Your usual table?"

Mr. Jackson nodded, barely holding back a smile. "If it's available." He held out his hand to Mr. Carlo. "A pleasure to see you."

Mr. Carlo hesitated, just a tad, then shook. "Busy here, getting ready for tonight."

"Ah." Now it became clear: New Year's Eve. "A special party, then."

Mr. Carlo was already back to the paper. "Indeed."

George came round. "This way."

Mr. Jackson found the whole dance amusing. He and his wife knew exactly where the table was: they'd been going to it for months now. Yet for them to go on their own would have set everyone aflutter.

As they moved towards the table, Mr. Jackson said, "Hope your family's well." They had been hosted by George's parents numerous times on their yacht.

"Just dandy," George said. "My Pa's just ordered a new car."

Mr. Jackson let out a surprised laugh. "Really."

"A brand new Pierce Arrow Coupe!" He sounded impressed. "Didn't know the old man was making that kind of money."

"Well, people around here do like boats," Mr. Jackson said. "And your father makes some magnificent ones."

When they got to the beautifully set table, and George had seated them, Mr. Jackson said to him, "When would be a good time for a chat?"

"Heh," George said. "After Carlo leaves, to be sure."

"I'll stop by later then."

As George returned to his post, Mr. Jackson looked over at his wife, who was perusing the menu. "Roasted parsnip soup." She turned to him, eyes wide. "We dug those this morning!"

She took such delight in seeing what she'd helped gather appear in the menu for that day. "I'm sure it'll be delicious." The young man who took on the role of Head Chef for this place certainly earned his keep!

One of the new waiters approached, a young fellow almost as dark-skinned as he, taking out a notepad. The man's name-tag read: Floyd. "Care for some drinks?"

"Coffee, heavy cream, if you please," Mr. Jackson said. "The more the better. And no sugar." He turned to his wife. "And you?"

"Tea," she said, as always.

"Right away," Floyd said.

Just then, the Myriad Hotel's most illustrious personage, the dowager Duchess Cordelia Stayman, came through the glass-paneled doors. Going to the Headwaiter's station, she ignored George entirely, and seemed to be mildly lecturing Mr. Carlo on some matter.

But then she followed after George, her lined face lighting up when she saw them. "Oh, Mr. Jackson! And my dear Mrs. Jackson! How lovely to see you!"

After George seated her across the small square table from him and returned to Mr. Carlo, Duchess Cordelia said, "The happiest of New Years to you both."

"That's very kind of you," Mr. Jackson said. "And to you as well."

His wife leaned forward. "I hope you're well."

Duchess Cordelia leaned back with a satisfied smile. "I am. What a perfectly lovely day it is out!"

"Oh," he said. "You've been out and about already?"

"I have," the dowager said. "I take a turn around the park every morning, rain or shine. It's good to get outside once in a while."

Mr. Jackson was reminded of his fitness club membership. Other than the few times he and George had gone to play tennis, he'd quite forgotten it. "I shall keep that in mind."

"Any plans?"

His wife said, "We plan to stay in tonight."

"As do I," the dowager said. "I'm much too old for late nights and parties these days. Besides, the premiere of 'The Love For Three Oranges' broadcasts tonight!

Mr. Jackson wasn't sure what she meant. "Oh?"

"Oh, yes. Haven't you heard? It's the opera broadcasts on KWY."

His wife said, "What's that?"

"Radio, my dear. It sends music right through the air, to this contraption Albert made! Whenever we would travel, we listened to broadcasts all over the world. We finally have a proper station here in Chicago." She beamed, clasping her lined hands together just under her chin. "And they've been playing opera!"

"Oh," Mr. Jackson said, impressed. He very much liked the opera, but hadn't gone in years. Perhaps he'd have to get one of these contraptions made for him.

"Right down at the Civic Auditorium. But I don't have to go there past all the wildness tonight — I can just listen in my room!" She gave him a satisfied grin. "So I am quite settled. A cup of hot cocoa beside the fire with opera and a new book is all the entertainment I need."

Mr. Jackson said, "Would you like to visit the library after breakfast?"

The dowager beamed. "That would be wonderful."

4

Once Mr. Jackson had escorted his wife and the dowager Duchess to the library, he went up to his rooms to check on Bessie. As it turned out, Bessie and her puppies were asleep. So he returned downstairs to the front desk. "I'd like to access my safe, if you please."

The flier he'd secured there lay folded underneath a bound stack of cash — just in case — and his wife's pistol. Mr. Jackson gazed at the pistol for a long moment, then put the flier into his jacket pocket and returned to where George had been. By this time, Mr. Carlo had left, and George appeared to be taking notes.

George glanced up as he approached. "Ah! There you are." The two shook hands. "I hope all's well?"

"Might I have a word? If you're not too busy."

George gave him a fond smile. "Never too busy for you, old chap."

Mr. Jackson followed George to his office, a smallish affair with lots of cabinets and a bit of a desk. George gestured for him to sit, so he did.

George threw himself into his chair. "What's the news?"

How might he begin ...

He pulled out the flier, heart pounding, and opened it. Upon it sat the words "Wanted For Questioning." It also had a portrait of his wife.

George grew very still. "Wait." He glanced up at him. "Is this ... Pamela?" He took the flier, read through it. "Oh," he said. "So this is her." He handed it back. "Quite an old photograph, I'd say."

Mr. Jackson realized just then he'd not been breathing. Perhaps others might not recognize her either. He refolded the flier and put it into his pocket.

"So why are you showing me this?"

A wave of relieved fatigue swept over him, and he leaned one elbow on the desk, resting his forehead upon his hand. "Because I'm sorry it took so long for me to tell you. You of all people deserve to know."

George nodded slowly. "Thank you. Really." He seemed to be at a loss for words. Then a laugh burst from him. "It sounds funny, but I feel honored."

Mr. Jackson felt surprised. "Really?"

"I do." He laughed once more. "A lot of shady stuff goes on here, Hector. Quite a lot." He leaned back, putting an ankle over his knee. "It's more than a bit refreshing to see someone in this town who actually tells the truth."

Mr. Jackson let out a weary breath. "I try, George. I always have." Then he felt amused. "Makes keeping your stories straight much easier."

A laugh burst from George. "I daresay! Hey, want another round of tennis? I should be able to find a few hours next week sometime."

Mr. Jackson rose, extending his hand. "I would very much enjoy it."

***

Later, the couple relaxed in the parlor of their suite, along with their dear friend, Miss Ophelia Denton.

Mr. Jackson put more cream into his coffee. The small sounds new puppies make came from his bathroom. It was early yet, and although most of the buildings lay in shadow, the sky outside was still blue. Fireworks echoed through the closed doors to the balcony around the buildings along Lake Shore Drive.

His wife sat quietly, sipping hot lemonade. She'd been particularly quiet since he'd related his discussion with George, which worried him. Mr. Jackson said to Miss Denton, "Where will you ring in the New Year?"

Miss Denton said, "The Green Mill, of course! If we can get a table. If not, we might go to the South Side."

Mr. Jackson said, "So you like jazz, I take it."

Miss Denton beamed. "Ever so much."

Mr. Jackson drank his coffee, which had gone cold. "Too bad George had to work tonight."

Miss Denton laughed, her reddish-blonde curls wagging around her chin. "Goes with the job."

Although being promoted to Headwaiter gave George a much improved income, it also meant he had

445

to work most every holiday night. "Still," Mr. Jackson said, "it's a pity he'll miss the fun."

Miss Denton had been drinking hot tea, but her hand stopped mid-air. "I forgot to tell you!" She put down her teacup. "The girls and I are having dinner downstairs, so we'll see him then. And Georgie said he'd meet up with us after work. We just need to phone with where we are around one or so."

Mrs. Jackson nodded. "I'm glad to hear it, Pet," she said. "You should get out and have some fun."

Miss Denton reached over to take her hand. "My dear Pam. I know how horrible a time this is for you."

Mr. Jackson hoped his wife would reveal more of why this time was so difficult for her. But she merely gave Miss Denton a smile, which never reached her eyes.

He expected the melancholy. She'd lost her husband and son under terrible circumstances, fleeing with him to Chicago that same day.

And it hadn't yet been a year since. Every little thing must remind her of her family. Hoping to change the subject, he said, "However did you get the evening off?"

"Oh!" Miss Denton became more animated. "We got a bunch of new girls in, enough to let one of us have the evening. So the boss had a secret ballot! You had to put in two names you thought deserved it. Of course everyone put in their own. But I got the most votes for the other." She put her hand to her heart. "I can hardly believe I won."

446

His wife took the younger woman's hand. "Oh, Pet — I can! You're always filling in for the others, and staying late to help clean up. You most certainly deserve it."

Miss Denton blushed, and the look on his wife's face moved him. She loved the girl ever so much.

His wife turned to him with a real smile. "I'll be happy to stay in tonight. Maybe I've grown old." With that, she let out a chuckle. "But the late nights don't appeal to me as much as they once did."

Mr. Jackson smiled at her. "I quite understand the feeling." He leaned forward. "Before you go, Miss Denton, I need to speak with you."

Miss Denton's fine auburn eyebrows rose. "Oh?"

He gave his wife a quick glance. "There's something you should know, tonight of all nights."

Miss Denton giggled. "Okay, Father Time — I'm no innocent!"

That amused him. "It's that the Feds are always around tonight. Just keep out of trouble, if you can."

The young woman shrugged. "As much as anyone. What's this about?"

He sighed, taking the flier once more from his pocket, making sure to cover his wife's real name with his finger as he did.

Miss Denton gasped, glancing from his wife's portrait to him to his wife. "They want you ... for this?"

His wife put her face in her hands.

"But why? What do they think you've done?"

"She didn't kill anyone," Mr. Jackson said confidently. "But the Feds think she might have." He glanced at the flier. "I suppose." He looked back at her. "In any case, try not to attract too much attention?"

The young woman felt the paper of the flier. "And this is real. This isn't some sort of joke."

Mrs. Jackson's hands fell from her face. "I wish it were. Why do you think we came here?"

Miss Denton let go of the flier and sat quietly for a moment. "Who else knows?"

"Mr. Carlo," Mr. Jackson said. "The fellow who owns this hotel here. Some of his men, I suppose." The man was a minor ruffian in a city full of them. But he was wealthy, which helped a great deal. "I told George about it earlier."

"Well, I don't believe it." Miss Denton took Mrs. Jackson's hand. "That old rag means nothing to me. I'm not going anywhere." Then she laughed. "Except tonight, of course." Miss Denton rose, so they did as well. "I'm off, then!"

Mrs. Jackson said, "So soon?"

"Me and the girls are having a party of our own." She beamed. "Martinis and Maybellinis." A laugh burst from her, and he wondered how much she'd already had to drink today. "We'll be spiffy tonight!"

"Do be careful," Mrs. Jackson said anxiously. "Call us if you need anything."

Miss Denton gave her a fond bemused smile, then leaned over to kiss her cheek. "I will."

Hugs all round, then she was out the door and gone.

The couple moved towards the sofa, but there came a knock on the parlor door. "I'll see who this is," he said. "You go on and relax."

At the door was their new floor maid, Lela, a woman in her later forties with her long brown hair up in a bun. "Good evening, Mr. Jackson! Care to have me set a fire for you?"

"Why, that would be splendid!" He moved aside to let her pass.

"Something told me you'd be staying in tonight," Lela said. She bent over the unlit fire. In a moment, a lovely warm light spread over the logs. "If you need more wood than that there," she pointed to the basket of small logs beside the fireplace, "just give us a ring."

"Will do, thanks."

Once the woman was gone, he sat beside his wife. She rested her head on his shoulder, and he put his arm round her with a contented sigh.

"At least that's over with," his wife said. "I feared so much that Ophelia would ... I don't know. Look differently at me."

"Now why would she do that?"

She sounded a bit dejected. "I don't know."

"Cheer up," he said. "She didn't."

For a while they sat watching the fire. "Another year past." He kissed her forehead. "And look where we are!"

He loved the way she relaxed into him. Just a few months ago, things were very different. This time last year, she'd wanted nothing to do with him. "Yes," she said. "I do love it here. No schedules, no obligations, no one to manage."

"And no one managing you." He laughed to himself at a distant memory. He'd not had anyone managing him for some time.

She sat up, facing him. "Yes! That was the worst of it. Not being able to go anywhere without telling someone and getting permission."

He nodded.

She resumed her snuggling into his shoulder. "I must have made everyone mad with frustration over me." She chuckled then. "I would never do what they insisted."

He kissed her curly black hair. "I can imagine." In that, they'd been much the same. Free spirits, they were.

He'd been one of the few who guessed she'd bolt for the station after the horror of that night was said and done. How fortunate that he'd gotten to her before she disappeared forever.

He'd done everything he knew to keep her safe here. And safe they were.

No one was going to harm her, not if he had anything to say about it.

5

The very minute Ophelia Denton left the couple's suite, she went to the elevator.

She wasn't born yesterday. Clearly, Pam was hiding something. And if Mr. Hector told George about it, he probably let more slip than what he'd just said.

She wanted all the details.

But as she waited for the elevator, she couldn't help but look around. This was the most amazing hotel ever! The picture glass alone must have cost a fortune.

Her Mama had been a simple woman, but she'd known what her daughter wanted without Ophelia ever having to say. Use your connections to move up in the world, baby girl, she'd said. *This city's hard on a woman alone.*

And as the elevator doors opened, Ophelia sighed. *I wish Mama would have lived to see it.*

Here she was, in this grand hotel, with a gorgeous, rich woman who loved her.

Now, Ophelia knew she could have left the boarding house and got herself into an adjoining suite. The couple had the money.

Pam had bought her a new coat and shoes. Mr. Hector had paid for her taxis every night since he learned she got off work at two.

But it didn't feel right. Besides, she liked the girls in her boarding house. And she liked going out with them on her nights off.

Her life felt just about perfect.

She emerged into the lobby. Even though she'd been there a hundred times, the fountain in the middle of that giant room made her stop and stare. Holding her handbag with one hand and her cloche hat with the other, she gazed at the water going up past the balcony on the second floor.

But now was not the time for gawking. "First things first," she murmured.

Ophelia went to the dining room. When she got to the Headwaiter's station, one of the maids stood there. "Welcome to the Myriad, Ma'am! What name is your table under?"

"Oh, we're not eating here 'til later. Is George Neuberg available?"

"One moment," the woman said.

After a few minutes, George showed up. "Ophie! Come on back. Want some coffee?"

"No, thanks." She followed him past men assembling meals on fine china, more men cooking, past racks of bread and rows of clean pots, back to a small office.

A real nice wooden desk full of papers, several cabinets, and a clock on the wall. George gestured to a chair in front of the desk. "Have a seat!" He sat behind the desk, leaving the door open.

"Looks like you've moving up in the world!" She took the chair he'd indicated. "You sure this is all right? Me being here?"

George laughed. "If anyone asks, I'll tell them you're interviewing." He leaned his elbows on the desk. "What can I do for you?"

Ophelia leaned back, crossing one leg over the other. "Mr. Hector showed me the flier."

George suddenly sobered. "Well, what'd you think?"

"There's something they're not telling me." And suddenly, she wondered if maybe they didn't trust her? "What did they tell you?"

George shrugged, glancing away. "That she was mixed up in some kind of Mob thing."

Ophelia felt surprised. "Oh."

"They both were. They tried to leave, but some others got involved? I don't know the details. It went bad and men were killed. So they had to get out of town," he shrugged. "I guess."

She nodded. Things like that happened here, too.

Their eyes met. "He swears she didn't kill anyone —"

"Of course she didn't. I can't see her hurting anyone!"

George turned somber. "And I guess her husband and son were killed too."

"They told me she'd lost them when we first met." But she hadn't realized it was right before they came here. "What a terrible thing to happen!"

George nodded. "And then to come to a new city? Starting fresh, I suppose. He'd been here before, just for a short time on business. But she'd never been."

"The poor dears." Ophelia felt truly sorry for them. "I wish I knew how to help."

George got real quiet. "My Pa said once that the best gauge of a man is whether he stands by his friends in trouble." Then he nodded, like he was talking to himself, really. "Seems to me that's the best way to help them."

She went over what they'd said in her mind. "They said the Feds were after them."

George's eyes widened. "Really." He stopped then, pondering a bit. "Yeah. It said that on the flier, now that I think of it."

"Well, they think she had something to do with those men dying! Anyway, they were worried we might get into trouble tonight."

George snorted. "With all the hundreds of speakeasies packed in like sardines tonight, the chance of any we go to being raided is nil." He gave her a wry smile and a wink. "But I'll keep you girls close and my eyes open."

Ophelia giggled. "I'll see you tonight, then."

"You bet."

She went back out and on down the street to her home, feeling real pleased and happy. George was the cat's pajamas, he really was.

He'd never once been anything but a perfect gentleman, and he never missed a chance to go out with her and her friends. The girls all liked him too. And were they envious! They couldn't get over how good-looking he was. And him going out with them seemed to make her landlady Mrs. Kilpatrick happy.

Letting the old lady and the girls think she and George were sweet on each other was a bit of a lie, but as her Mama once said, a little white lie never hurt anyone.

6

Upstairs in the parlor, the couple were having a cozy evening by the fire, listening to the sounds of the party outside.

After a while, the fire burned low, and Mr. Jackson got up to check on the dogs. There Bessie lay, raising her head when they entered. Her puppies lay sleeping around her.

Mr. Jackson said, "Ready for a walk, girl?"

Bessie delicately stepped around her new babies and trotted over, so he put her wrap and her leash on her.

"I'll keep an eye on them until you're back," Mrs. Jackson said.

Mr. Jackson and Bessie went to the elevator doors. The elevator-man smiled and waved at Bessie. "How's our little Mama tonight?"

Bessie's ears went up, and she wagged her tail.

Mr. Jackson said, "She seems well."

"And her pups?"

"They're well also." Mr. Jackson got an idea. "Would you like one?"

"Me? Naw. I've got no place to keep one. Not fair to have a dog stuck in a tenement all day."

Mr. Jackson nodded. He wouldn't have kept Bessie when they found her starving right here outside the hotel, if his wife didn't love the little dog so. But the black toy poodle had certainly grown on him.

The elevator opened, and Bessie's little claws tapped on the marble floor as they went through the magnificent lobby. They passed the enormous fountain and headed towards the front doors.

The men there opened the doors for him, one on each door. "Good evening, sir!" One said.

"Good evening," he replied absentmindedly.

Hundreds of little bulbs high above the circle drive gave the place a warm inviting glow. He and Bessie moved right, towards the street, and into the crowds moving past the Myriad Hotel along Lake Shore Drive.

Warmth from the heat of the sun still radiated from the pavement, but a chill in the air spoke of a cold front coming in. Automobiles went to and fro. People clogged the darkened streets, dressed to the nines. Fireworks rose from Lake Michigan to boom high overhead. Horns, both from cars and from the hands of the passers-by, and cries of "Happy New Year!" came forth.

He looked down at little Bessie. What must she think of all this commotion?

At his gaze, her ears perked up, her tail wagging.

They walked along to the light, and went across Lake Shore Drive to the boardwalk along the rocky beach. Bessie stopped here and there to sniff, and Mr. Jackson let her. She hadn't gotten out much since her pups were born, and it seemed rude to hurry her.

"Oh, what a cute doggie!" A woman in a white fur coat and dark bobbed hair hung off the arm of her rather handsome beau, peering down at Bessie.

Mr. Jackson tipped his fedora at the pair. "Happy New Year!"

"Happy New Year!" the man said, and the two made their way along past.

The night was clear, the moon not yet up. "My dear Queen Bess," he said to the little dog, "I think this is going to be a good year."

***

Hector Jackson awoke from a sound sleep.

Bam-bam-bam

"What in the world?"

Bam-bam-bam

He got up, pulled on trousers and a robe, and made his way to the parlor door.

His wife called out from his bed, "What's wrong?"

"I'll find out."

When he opened the door, Mr. Carlo stood there in the hallway.

"Good grief, Carlo," Mr. Jackson said. "It's the middle of the night."

"Sorry to wake you at this hour," Mr. Carlo said, "but I need your help."

Mr. Jackson turned on the parlor light. "Come in."

"No need for that; I'll wait."

"Wait for what? What's going on?"

"Get dressed; I'll tell you on the way."

At first, he was going to protest. But then his curiosity got the better of him. It was one in the morning. What could possibly have happened?

Rubbing sleep from his eyes, Mr. Jackson turned off the light and returned to his room, leaving the door open. His wife lay sleeping. So he got dressed, put some water out for Bessie, then got his hat. He left a note in case his wife might wake before he returned, then moved to the open door.

Mr. Carlo still stood in the hallway.

Mr. Jackson locked the parlor door behind them. "Now what's this about?"

"Hurry," Mr. Carlo said quietly, leading him along the hall to the elevator. "A man's been murdered."

The elevator stood open and ready. As they descended, Mr. Carlo said not a word. Rather, he put a key into the wall and pressed a gold button there.

"Thank you, sir," the elevator-man said. The man was elderly, yet his back was straight, his bearing proud.

The elevator descended past the lobby, past what felt like two more floors. Then the doors opened onto a well-lit hall carpeted in rich burgundy. Mr. Carlo told the elevator-man, "Stay here." Then he grabbed Mr. Jackson's left sleeve for a second. "This way."

He let go, walking off; Mr. Jackson followed him down the hall.

"The crush at the bar must have been terrific," Mr. Carlo said. "The man just fell off his barstool about five after midnight, stone dead."

Mr. Jackson still felt foggy. "You're sure it's murder?"

Mr. Carlo chuckled. "The man's got blood all over his shirt and a bullet-hole in him. I doubt that's natural."

"Oh," Mr. Jackson said, suddenly chagrined. "And no one saw anything?"

Mr. Carlo scoffed. "The minute he hit the floor, the place emptied out." He came to a door and opened it. A thick red velvet curtain hung there, blocking the entryway. "That's why I need your help." He pushed the curtain aside and stepped through, head turned back towards Mr. Jackson as he spoke. Rather loudly. "We have to learn who did this before the cops show up!"

Utter chaos lay beyond: overturned tables and chairs atop liquor bottles and shot glasses atop streamers and confetti. Bits of dropped clothing lay here and there: a masquerade mask, a black stiletto, a feathered and bejeweled headband.

In the midst of it all stood a stern-looking man. "Well, sirs," Sergeant Benjamin Nestor said, "I'm afraid you're just a bit too late."

7

Apparently, the rush of people fleeing the speakeasy was so frightened and tumultuous that it attracted the notice of a passing patrolman. He ran to a telephone and called the matter in at once, fearing some ghastly scene awaited them below.

On the floor, it was just as Mr. Carlo had said: a dead man, evidently done in by just the wrong sort of shot.

Mr. Jackson said, "Do we know this fellow's name?"

Mr. Carlo shook his head.

Sergeant Nestor gestured to one of the uniformed men behind him, and they began to search the body.

"Surely someone stayed behind," Mr. Jackson said. "Not even the bartender?"

A waiter came out from the back. "He's in here," the young man said. "Says he don't feel good."

One of the uniformed police stood. "A pack of cigarettes, a memo book, seventeen bucks and a business card." He scrutinized the card. "A.B. Nelson: Small Repair Our Specialty." He shrugged. "The address is on the East Side."

"Hand over the card and the book," Sergeant Nestor said. "The rest in his belongings file."

The memo book looked brand-new. "A phone number." Sergeant Nestor flipped the page. "And another number." He showed that to Mr. Carlo.

Mr. Carlo turned red. "Tonight's code to enter here."

Sergeant Nestor snorted. "What you serve people is between you and the Feds. What I care about is who killed this man and why." He looked wearily around the room. "We're going to be here all night." For the first time, he seemed to notice Mr. Jackson. "What are you doing here?"

"Dragged out of bed by Mr. Carlo," Mr. Jackson grumbled. "I'd much rather be upstairs." He put his hat back on. "So if you don't mind ..."

Mr. Carlo planted his fists on his hips. "Now you wait just a minute —"

Sergeant Nestor held up a hand. "Before you go, I'd like to know two things. First, where you were at midnight —"

"That's easy," Mr. Jackson said. "In bed asleep next to my wife."

" — and second, what you see here."

That last bit threw Mr. Jackson for a loop. "What?"

"I've come to realize that you see things in a different way." Sergeant Nestor grinned. "So, sir, if you wouldn't mind?"

Mr. Jackson had helped the sergeant in a couple of cases before, but that didn't mean he was some sort of expert! He rubbed his eyes and let out a yawn. "Where's the lighter?"

Mr. Carlo said, "Huh?"

"My wife's a smoker. The man had cigarettes in his pocket. Where's his lighter?"

Sergeant Nestor called over to his men. "You find a cigarette lighter anywhere?"

They shook their heads.

Sergeant Nestor said, "That's a start."

Mr. Jackson felt out of sorts. "You're going to have a hard time learning much without any witnesses."

"Okay, wise guy," Sergeant Nestor grumbled. "See anything else?"

At that, Mr. Jackson really looked at the room. The man on the floor, where the shot must have happened. "Whoever did it was right next to him. They had to have gotten blood on themselves, or at least powder. And a gunshot's far from quiet." He yawned, feeling weary. "Yet no one even noticed until the dead man fell on the floor?" His voice echoed in the room. "How many people were **in** here?"

Sergeant Nestor nodded. "Well, sir, we have at least one witness. Let's go talk to him."

***

The bartender, Mr. Ralph D'Angelo, was a young man, not yet thirty. He sat in the back room pale and sweaty,

463

like he was about to be sick. "It was people everywhere. The man just had his head on his arms, leaned over like he was tired. I woulda asked him to go take a table so others could order but there was too many asking all at once. Then all of a sudden he wasn't there. First I knew anything was wrong was they started screaming." He bent over, elbows on his knees. "Never saw a dead person before, not like that."

Sergeant Nestor put his hand on the man's shoulder. "It's okay, son, just tell us what you can."

"I've been here six years and never saw so many in here. They couldn't dance, could barely pass by. There was a band on stage, and some of the flappers got up to sittin' on the stage 'cause there was no seats."

"So what happened at midnight?"

"Just like I said. Right before, everyone wanted a drink all at once. I was the only one there." He put his head in his hands. "I started just handing out bottles —"

Mr. Carlo said, "What?"

"I kept note for their tabs. Most of 'em was regulars."

"Well, that'll help," Sergeant Nestor said.

Mr. Carlo's eyes narrowed. "If you think I'm giving out my customer list, you —"

Sergeant Nestor held up a thick hand. "You can cooperate, or I can close this hotel down."

The two men scowled at each other for a moment, then Mr. Carlo's face fell. "Very well. But I'll not have anyone dragged in for questioning. You hear?"

"We'll be discreet." The sergeant turned to Mr. D'Angelo. "So you're handing out bottles. What then?"

The man let out a short laugh. "Midnight was all corks at once, and the band, and the singing, and the horns. A cannon could have gone off and no one would've hardly noticed!" He stopped then, pensive. "That man should never have died there." He sat quietly for a moment, then looked up at the sergeant. "I didn't even know it'd happened til the screaming."

Sergeant Nestor pulled up a chair beside the man. "Then what happened?"

"Everyone's looking down with their hands on their faces. Then people started pushing to get out. I'm surprised no one else is dead: it was a stampede. Women got shoved down crying, men were climbing over each other —" He stopped then, eyes far away. "That was the worst of it."

"That explains the blood on the floor on the way in," Sergeant Nestor said.

Mr. Jackson stared at him, appalled. "What?"

Sergeant Nestor nodded, then turned to one of his men who stood in the doorway. "Check with the hospitals around here. Someone's bound to have turned up. But don't scare them. They're more likely to be a witness than the killer."

He turned to Mr. Jackson. "What do you think?"

The answer came to him at once. "My guess is that the killer's a woman. She likely left shortly before midnight."

Mr. Carlo said, "A woman?"

Mr. Jackson felt amused. "Raise your arm and hold it in front of you." When Mr. Carlo did so, Mr. Jackson quickly moved towards him, intending to stand close enough that they were touching.

But before that came close to happening, Mr. Carlo flinched away, offended. "What are you on about?"

Sergeant Nestor was nodding.

"You see?" Mr. Jackson raised a finger. "A man would never let another man get so close as to do this to him, even one he'd known for some time, and presumably trusted with his livelihood."

"Oh," said Mr. Carlo, surprise on his face. "I see."

"It's likely women stood on both sides of him."

"So," Sergeant Nestor said to the bartender, who if anything, looked more unwell. "What woman stood on the man's left side?"

"I swear to you," the man said, shaking his head, "I don't recall."

8

The three others drew aside.

"He's clearly lying," Mr. Carlo whispered. "I'll get it out of him."

"No, no, no," said the sergeant, just as softly. "He's not the one we're after. Besides, if he has some connection with the woman and he's harmed — and she learns of it — she'll only flee." He tapped his chin. "No, I think other forms of persuasion might be better served." He turned to the bartender. "You're free to go. sir." He handed the man a card. "If you recall anything else, be sure to phone me."

"Yes, sir." Mr. D'Angelo stood, somewhat unsteadily, and began collecting his coat and hat.

Sergeant Nestor called to one of his men. "See this fellow home, will you? He doesn't look at all well. Make sure he gets into bed safe. He's had a difficult evening." As the officer and Mr. D'Angelo left, Sergeant Nestor said to Mr. Carlo, "Now we'll learn where he lives, and perhaps even who else lives with him. Now for your tab list, sir."

Mr. Carlo scowled.

Mr. Jackson said, "Anything else?"

Sergeant Nestor snorted. "Can you think of anything else?"

Curse my active brain, Mr. Jackson thought. Somehow, the one waiter who'd stayed around had disappeared. "Where are the other waiters? The bouncers? The band? There are a whole line of people who should be here, if only to get paid." He turned to Mr. Carlo. "Another list for the sergeant."

"Good man," Sergeant Nestor said. "I'd entirely forgotten about the bouncers. You go up to your wife; I'll stop by tomorrow sometime. After lunch, perhaps?"

"Very well," Mr. Jackson said. "Good night."

As Mr. Jackson left, the sergeant shouted, "I want this place dusted for prints. I don't care if it takes all night."

So Mr. Jackson trudged back to his rooms to the groans and grumbles of the other officers and got into bed without his wife even stirring. Though he'd been afraid of the matter keeping him awake all night, he fell asleep at once.

***

When Mrs. Jackson woke, her Mr. Jackson lay in bed with his clothes still on, his jacket, hat, and shoes in a pile beside the bed. "You poor dear," she murmured, smoothing his brow. "What did that Mr. Carlo have you up to this time?" She'd recognized the man's voice before she drifted off, but even that hadn't kept her awake to make sure all was well.

I must be feeling safe here, she thought.

She tried to make him more comfortable, loosening his collar and removing his belt before covering him up with a kiss on the forehead. Then a check on Bessie and the puppies. Bessie was ready to go out, dancing around. "Shh," Mrs. Jackson said as she put Bessie's wrap and leash on.

She brought Bessie into her bathroom to freshen up. A quick change into a long navy blue day dress of fine wool, thick stockings and stout shoes, a long wool jacket, cloche hat, and gloves, and they were out of the door.

The sun was up: it was past time to meet Monsieur.

As she waited for the elevator, she had a tickle in her throat, which turned into a cough.

When she emerged from the elevator, she unhooked Bessie's leash and stood by the elevator door smoking as Bessie made her rounds nearby. The day was cold and overcast, the sun a pale ball in the sky.

She finished the cigarette before moving further. Monsieur didn't like her smoking around the plants; apparently the tobacco was harmful to them.

The young Chef stood, dusting off his hands as she approached. With him were several other young men around large tall carts holding baskets full of long fat carrots. He nodded to her, then dismissed the men, who took the carts and moved past her back the way she came. "Good morning," Monsieur said.

Mrs. Jackson said, "Did your New Year's go well?"

He shrugged. "I don't care for drink, and I was here at the crack of dawn." He chuckled. "I slept soundly enough. Better than your husband, from what I hear."

"Oh?"

Monsieur blinked. "Apparently, a man was killed downstairs. I presumed that Mr. Carlo called in your husband. The staff were all speaking of it when I went to check on the bakery."

"Yes, he went out," Mrs. Jackson said, "late last night. But this is the first I've heard of anyone killed."

"Forgive me," Monsieur said. "I'm sure your husband can tell you more of it."

Monsieur set her to covering the area where the carrots had been with a thick layer of compost. This lay in a wheelbarrow with a large scoop in it.

Yet breakfast-time beckoned: he needed to return to the kitchens.

So she poured the material, which looked and smelled of rich earth, to cover the entire bare space, with Bessie running around at every movement. Then she smoothed it with the back of the large metal scoop. "This will teach me not to be late," she told Bessie, only half grumbling.

By the time Mrs. Jackson and Bessie returned to their rooms, Mr. Jackson had a full breakfast set upon the parlor table! "I thought you might feel hungry."

When Mrs. Jackson undid the wrap, Bessie ran to her puppies, her little claws clacking on the tile of Mr. Jackson's bathroom.

Mrs. Jackson washed her hands, then put her coat, hat, and gloves on the sofa, sitting in an armchair beside him. "That was quite thoughtful of you," she said. "And how are our little guests?"

He smiled warmly at her, passing her a dish of scrambled eggs. "They seem well. One opened his eyes!"

She chuckled at the news and laid her napkin on her lap. "How our babies have grown."

Mr. Jackson nodded, mouth full.

She loved the sight of his dark, dark skin upon the fine white china. "Monsieur spoke of a commotion downstairs. A murder?"

Mr. Jackson chewed, swallowed. "Yes, unfortunately. In the speakeasy."

She felt intrigued. "So there is one down there!"

He chuckled. "It's rather grand, actually. Although not nearly as large as the one Miss Denton performs in."

"She'll be glad to hear it."

"Mr. Carlo wasn't too pleased that the sergeant was there already," Mr. Jackson said, "but I suppose it couldn't be helped. He said he might stop by this afternoon."

"Mr. Carlo?"

"No, forgive me. The sergeant." Mr. Jackson frowned slightly. "I wonder why?"

Mrs. Jackson shrugged. "I'd be surprised if he thought we might help."

"Well, he might need the help, to be honest. The place was an utter disaster! Even the tables were overturned. It sounded as though it was much too crowded, then in the fright of discovering the body, the entire lot rushed out at once." Mr. Jackson shook his head. "It must have been a madhouse."

"Hmm." Mrs. Jackson took a sip of her tea. "More likely the fright was at the prospect of being found by the police, not only at a speakeasy, but with a dead body to boot."

Mr. Jackson chuckled.

She picked up a half-slice of toast. "I'm just glad he called you down, not me."

"For shame! Wishing your poor husband dragged from his bed to gaze upon a murder scene?" He poked her side.

She let out a yelp, and began giggling.

Bessie padded out, giving them a disapproving eye.

"Oh, dear. We'll mind our manners," Mrs. Jackson said to Bessie. Then she said to Mr. Jackson, "I suppose we should be quieter, if only for the sake of the puppies." But then a giggle came from her once more.

Bessie let out a "ruff" and returned to her pups.

Mr. Jackson said, "You know you've misbehaved when your dog comes out to reprove you!"

She put the remains of their breakfast on a saucer beside Bessie and refilled the little dog's water bowl.

Outside the French doors lay dreary and gray, and Mrs. Jackson felt glad to stay in their rooms. Who would want to go out on New Year's Day if they didn't have to?

They lit the fire and sat on the sofa, he reading the news, she a copy of The Great Impersonation. Duchess Cordelia had recommended the book, describing it as a most exciting tale. And once Mrs. Jackson got past the horrible vile fellow at the start of it, the tale was proving to be quite interesting thus far.

From time to time, Bessie came out to snuggle on the floor beside one of them. Then she'd hear a slight sound from her children, it seemed, because her ears would perk up, and she'd trot back over to them.

Mid-morning, Mrs. Jackson put Bessie's wrap on and called down for someone to come walk her. Soon one of the veterinarian's many sons knocked on the parlor door.

Bessie immediately ran to him. A bright-eyed boy of ten, he smiled shyly at them, clipped Bessie's leash on, and went right off down the hall as Bessie danced about alongside him.

Mrs. Jackson smiled after them, feeling warmed. "They do love our little dog so."

Mr. Jackson said from the sofa, "How about we have luncheon downstairs?"

Mrs. Jackson closed the door. "That would be splendid!" Then she laughed, going to him. "Pet says I'm terribly old-fashioned when I say that."

"What?"

She sat on the sofa beside him. "Splendid."

He chuckled. "It's a perfectly respectable word."

She suddenly felt somber. The sofa's velvet felt soft yet a touch bristly. "But they don't say it here. It marks me as an outsider."

She felt his hand in her hair, his kiss on her forehead. He spoke softly. "Chicago is full of outsiders, dear girl. No one will care about one or two more."

She buried her face in his chest, listening to the slow beat of his heart. He wasn't afraid in the slightest. But when would the fear of being found, captured, brought back ... when would it ever leave her?

9

Mr. Jackson held his wife in his arms. The prospect of being discovered still terrified her. "Do you want to stay somewhere else?"

He knew before she laughed he'd said the right thing.

"And leave our friends? Of course not. I like it here! Besides, the puppies are much too young to travel."

He shrugged. "Then stop this worry." He kissed her curly black hair, her light brown forehead, lifted her chin to gaze into those beautiful blue eyes. He kept his voice light. "You hear me? I forbid it. Worry when it's time to. But before then, it does nothing but upset the digestion."

She gave him a broad smile in return. "You are ever so sensible, as always." Then she turned round, leaned her back upon him. "Now tell me about this murder."

Mr. Jackson burst out laughing. "Is it the gory detail which intrigues you, or the puzzle of it all?"

"The puzzle, of course," she said, as if this were obvious. "Tell me everything."

So he related what he'd seen: the empty underground speakeasy in shambles, the man lying dead with a gunshot in his side.

"You say there were no witnesses?"

"Well, the bartender stayed at his post," Mr. Jackson wondered why, when most everyone else had not. "And one waiter, but he slipped out soon after. I think his concern was the state the other man was in."

"Not everyone has seen sudden death," his wife said soberly. "It changes you."

From what he'd gathered, she'd seen her fair share. But then she'd been an actual investigator, long before they were ever married. "I suppose it does."

"Well, this is a situation," she said somberly. "One dead man and no witnesses. I suppose old Nestor had his men up all night dusting for prints."

Mr. Jackson laughed in surprise. "Exactly right!"

She shrugged. "It's what I'd do in his place."

"You'd make a fair cop," he said. "Ever consider it?"

She turned to face him, and he immediately realized his error. Her people didn't exactly have a good relationship with the police, and he should have recalled it. But her face was amused, not angry. "Now why in the world would I ever want to do that?" She turned around to snuggle her back into his side once more. "Particularly with such a nice warm spot here."

"You silly girl," he said fondly. Then he recalled the date. "I forgot to say it: Happy New Year."

She took his arms in turn, wrapping each one of them round her. "Happy New Year to you too, my love."

***

476

After Bessie returned from her walk, it was time for luncheon. So the couple tidied the area around Bessie and her pups (so as not to cause the maids too much trouble), put the "Please clean room now" sign on, and left for their meal.

Lee Francis, the head clerk, now stood at the front desk. "Good to see you!"

Mr. Jackson said, "Happy New Year, sir." He extended a hand for the fellow to shake. "I feared you might not be here today."

"Just filling in: my clerk had to leave just now." He rubbed the back of his neck. "Afternoon shift starts soon, then I'll be on my way." His tone turned bright. "And how's our little puppy doing?"

Mr. Francis and his wife had already chosen out one of Bessie's puppies for their new son. Mr. Jackson smiled. "He opened his eyes today!"

"Already? That sounds like a good sign."

"Indeed it is."

"Well, I won't keep you. Enjoy your luncheon."

George beamed when he saw them. "Happy New Year to you both!"

Mrs. Jackson took George's hand. "Dear George. I hope those young ladies didn't keep you up too late."

He chuckled. "No later than I've kept myself in the past. No, I saw them safe in their house by three."

Mr. Jackson thought it amusing how his wife's eyebrows raised. "Three?"

George gave her a bemused smile. "I didn't need to be here until noon. So plenty of time for napping."

As Headwaiter, most of George's work seemed to be greeting important guests (of which there were many) and making sure the front room was properly staffed. He'd made some improvements to the seating flow and to the decor. He'd also moved to an apartment around the corner.

George escorted the couple to a table. "Have any plans for today?"

"Not really," Mrs. Jackson said. "We'll probably stay in for dinner. But you're welcome to stop by, if you like."

"I may just. One of my waiters is running late, but he should be here shortly." He glanced back at the door, where a well-dressed pair stood waiting, then winked at them. "Toodle-ooo!"

The couple laughed softly as he left.

Maria, the Myriad's Head Maid, a stout woman with dark curls, approached, holding a notepad and pencil. "The usual?"

Mr. Jackson said. "The Chef's Special for us both." They'd gotten the Chef's Special menu ever since Monsieur arrived here, and the young man had yet to disappoint. "Coffee for me, lots of heavy cream, but no sugar, and —"

"Tea for the missus. Yes, sir, right away." She headed off to the next table.

His wife laughed. "She's got us pegged."

The meal was — in a word — delicious. A thick potato soup, dotted with bits of bacon and rosemary. Hot sugar-cured ham with a cider sauce topped by preserved figs. Small wedges of mild cheddar, made by Monsieur here in the Hotel. Dill-pickled cucumbers, thinly sliced. A salad of new greens with a lemony sauce.

They lingered over their meal. The warm glow of the room, the music from the piano ... it soothed him.

"I wonder where Duchess Cordelia is," said his wife. "Do you see her?"

"I don't," he said. "Perhaps she took her luncheon in her rooms."

"That must be it."

He patted her hand. "I'm sure she's fine. Not everyone cares to stir from their rooms on the holiday."

"True." His wife returned to her tea.

Just then, Mr. Carlo entered the dining room. George and all the waiters came subtly to attention, their faces taking carefully neutral smiles. Mr. Jackson laughed.

His wife peered at him. "What is it?"

He gestured with his chin. "Carlo's here."

"Heh," said his wife.

George gestured their way, and Mr. Carlo made a beeline for their table.

His wife said, "I wonder what he wants."

As usual, Mr. Carlo had an impatient air. "Well?"

"Good day to you too," his wife said.

Mr. Jackson chuckled. "Well, what?"

"The sergeant's here to see you. He said he told you he'd be by after luncheon."

Mr. Jackson checked his watch: 1:40. "I didn't think he'd brown-bag it and sit at our doorstep."

That even made Mr. Carlo laugh. "Yeah, he's sure keen about this one. Probably because it's in my hotel."

The sergeant never seemed to get along with those of money, and particularly seemed to have it in for Mr. Carlo. "Oh, very well," Mr. Jackson said. He glanced at his wife, who seemed bemused by the whole affair. "I think we're done here, don't you?"

She beamed at him, and for an instant he thought he might never breathe.

But then she rose. "Come on then," she said. "Can't keep the old guy waiting."

10

B ut Sergeant Nestor wasn't at the desk. The clerk solved that mystery. "He's gone up to wait for you," the young man said.

"Thank you." Taking Mr. Jackson's offered arm, she followed Mr. Carlo to the elevator, watching amused as the burly older man fidgeted, tapping his foot. She felt a bit sorry for the elevator's young operator, who certainly couldn't make the contraption go any faster!

She ventured, "I hope your family's well?"

She'd had chance to meet his wife and daughter in the spring, when they first arrived here at the Myriad. She hoped the mention of loved ones might settle the man.

But he gave her a sharp glance. "Margaret's taken ill. Her husband's out of town, so Maisy's home with her."

"Nothing serious, I hope?" The terrible flu that had ravaged the country recently seemed to have subsided somewhat. And Chicago had fared better than most.

He shrugged, suddenly downcast. "The doctor doesn't think so. But I'll not take any chances."

Margaret was his only child; Mrs. Jackson understood his sentiments. "I'll light a candle for her healing, sir."

Relief and gratitude crossed the man's face. "That's very kind of you."

The elevator door opened, and they went along the hallways to the couple's rooms. But the sergeant wasn't in the hall.

Mr. Jackson took out the key, but the door opened on its own. "What's this?"

"Perhaps the maid's here," said Mr. Carlo. "Why she's here without her cart, I have no idea." Then he called, "Lela?"

Hearing no answer, the three moved into the parlor, closing the door behind them.

A voice came from Mr. Jackson's bathroom. "Oh, my — aren't you a handsome set."

They found the sergeant in a squat position, admiring Bessie's puppies. He glanced up at them. "Your little stray's done quite well for herself here."

Mr. Carlo looked horrified. "You have a litter of **puppies**? In **my** hotel?"

Mrs. Jackson felt quite amused.

Her Mr. Jackson, on the other hand, sounded positively exasperated. "What are you doing in my bathroom? How did you get in here?"

Sergeant Nestor shrugged, bouncing up to a standing position. "I had the maid let me in."

She seldom saw her Mr. Jackson at a loss for words. But then he recovered himself, glancing at Mr. Carlo and the sergeant. "Would either of you like one?"

To Mrs. Jackson's surprise, Sergeant Nestor seemed to seriously consider the offer. "My oldest son might like that dark brown one. I'll ask him!" He gestured to the door. "In the meantime, let's discuss the case at hand."

At that, Mr. Carlo seemed to recover from his sudden shock. So they all went to the parlor, sitting around the rosewood table.

Mrs. Jackson thought it best to be polite. "Care for some tea?" But her offers were declined, so she sat with the rest. "How might we possibly help you?"

Sergeant Nestor hesitated.

"I don't want this in the press," Mr. Carlo said.

At the exact same time, Sergeant Nestor said, "No one will talk to my men."

They looked at each other.

Mr. Jackson put his arm around her shoulders. "I won't have my wife down there."

She felt amused at this. "But if you need our help, whatever we can do," she looked up at her Mr. Jackson, "we'd be happy to."

Sergeant Nestor put his elbows firmly on the table. "We found lipstick upon the man's collar and cheeks —"

Mr. and Mrs. Jackson nodded, then glanced at each other in surprise.

"— this confirms that a woman might be involved."

Mr. Carlo exclaimed. "The place was packed with women. But a murderess?"

Mrs. Jackson scoffed. "I assure you, sir, a woman can have as black a heart as any man."

All three men gaped at her. Then Mr. Jackson drew back, hand to his chin, gazing at the table.

"Well," Sergeant Nestor said, "three shades of lip color were found on the body —"

"That makes things more interesting," said Mrs. Jackson.

"Yes, " Sergeant Nestor said, perhaps irritated by her interruptions. "So at least three possible suspects."

Mr. Jackson stirred. "Did your fingerprint dusting bear any fruit?"

Sergeant Nestor let out an ironic, amused chuckle. "Too much fruit. Hundreds of partial prints. It's going to take a whole team to sort this one out."

"Hmm," said Mrs. Jackson. "So that might not be so helpful."

"It'll help narrow things down," said the sergeant, "particularly those prints near the dead man." He leaned back. "Who we've not yet identified, by the way."

Mr. Carlo said, "So no one knew the man's name?"

The sergeant shrugged. "If they do, no one's saying. No one's answering the number on the business card, but I don't expect a shop would have anyone in on a holiday. My men have questioned everyone scheduled to work that night, including the band members, but they all claim they never saw a thing."

Mr. Carlo stood. "I'll get it out of them."

Sergeant Nestor held up a hand. "Now, now, sir: you simply can't proceed like this! Just leave it to me. I don't want anyone giving a name out of fear — in my experience, that only makes this take all the longer." He stood, facing the man. "Encourage them to cooperate with us. But no strong-arm tactics, or I'll bar you from the investigation. Is that clear?"

Mr. Carlo scowled, then nodded.

Sergeant Nestor sat. "I'll take some of that tea, if you've got it handy."

They didn't actually have it handy, but Mrs. Jackson called to have some sent up. When she returned to the room, Mr. Carlo was seated again.

Sergeant Nestor was saying, " — remembers a man buying one the other day, and —"

So she said, "Buying what?"

The sergeant glanced up. "The memo book. In his pocket. It was new." He looked over at Mr. Jackson. "What all did you tell her?"

Mr. Jackson shrugged. "We really haven't discussed it that much."

Mrs. Jackson didn't want to contradict him. Besides, she was interested in what the sergeant had to say. So she made her way back to her chair.

Sergeant Nestor sighed. "Very well." And with that, he went into a story of panicked drunken people pouring out onto the streets around the hotel just after midnight, with an equally panicked young officer phoning him at home. Coming upon the room, and Mr. Carlo and Mr. Jackson entering. The scene, the position of the body. "I suppose that brings you up to speed on this one."

She considered the matter. "So he only had the notebook in his pocket? No wallet?"

"Nope. A pack of cigarettes, seventeen bucks and a business card to a repair shop."

"And he was shot in his side. Just the once?"

"Right," said the sergeant. "Small caliber."

She'd figured that, since they never mentioned an exit wound, nor anyone else being injured by it. "So it's still in there. I suppose that could help."

"It will," Sergeant Nestor said. "The gun was pressed to his left side, fired through the man's vest. The bullet appears to have gone straight through his heart."

Mrs. Jackson remembered the night her husband died. His face. The bullet-hole over his heart. His last words to her.

"Heh," Mr. Jackson said. "Personal indeed."

Mr. Carlo nodded.

Mrs. Jackson took a deep breath, trying to make her voice bright. "And the perfect timing! Right when the noise was so great you could have probably screamed and not been heard."

Sergeant Nestor said, "From the reports so far and the man's face, I don't think he even knew what hit him." He seemed to consider this for a moment. "Strange, to one moment be alive, the next dead." Then he shrugged. "Not the worst way to go, I suppose."

Mrs. Jackson didn't know what to say, and neither did anyone else, it seemed, for the next sound was the parlor door-bell. "Tea's here." She went to the door.

The maid poured tea all round, a bit awed to have Mr. Carlo there, it seemed, but soon she was out and the parlor door shut.

Something still bothered Mrs. Jackson, though. "So no one knew the man was dead until he fell?"

"Apparently not," Mr. Jackson said.

"A dead man doesn't sit on a barstool without help," Mrs. Jackson said. "So the murderer was had to have positioned him afterwards. Perhaps folding the man's arms on the bar, resting his head upon them." She demonstrated. "Like so. Otherwise, the dead man would just slump over. Right?"

Sergeant Nestor nodded. "The bartender said he saw the man positioned that way."

Mr. Jackson said, "Someone had to have seen who did that for him."

Mrs. Jackson said, "Right. But it's something anyone might do for a friend who's passed out, or very drunk, or feeling unwell. So —"

"So no one thought anything of it," Mr. Jackson said.

Mrs. Jackson nodded. "Exactly."

Mr. Jackson peered at her, face filled with concern. "Wait. Didn't the bartender say he saw the man hunched over the bar **before** twelve?"

Mr. Carlo's face froze in surprise. "He did!"

"Heh," Sergeant Nestor said to Mr. Jackson. "Good call. I'll have the autopsy-man look for sedatives."

Sedate a man, then shoot him?

Sergeant Nestor and Mr. Carlo exchanged a glance. Mr. Carlo said, "Now you see why I keep them here."

The sergeant raised his eyebrows.

Mrs. Jackson thought it an odd choice of words. But so far the man had refused any payment for their lodgings. "In any case, he — or she, most likely — drugs the man, gets him settled," she tried to picture the scene, "then at the stroke of twelve, shoots the man and makes for the door. Did your doormen see any women leave right before the commotion?"

"The doormen won't be in until tonight," Mr. Carlo said. "But it's likely there were dozens of women going in and out: to the toilets, to smoke, both alone and with their men."

She persisted. "But any acting strangely, or someone who didn't come back in."

"We could ask, of course," Sergeant Nestor said. "But I think someone calm enough to not only plan but actually do this might have the presence of mind to act casually on the way out." His eyes narrowed. "That is, if they even left before the panic."

488

Mr. Carlo put down his tea. "Why would anyone knowing a stampede was about to occur stay around?"

Mr. Jackson had a strange look upon his face. "Are there any other ways out of the room? Other than the one hallway and the way we came in?"

This gave Mrs. Jackson a shock. "There were two ways out?"

"Of course," said Mr. Carlo. "But you can't take the elevator without a key."

Sergeant Nestor said, "Who else had the key?"

11

It turned out a great many people had the key, including the bartender. "The first to 'discover' a body is the most likely suspect," Sergeant Nestor said, "so I made a call. Our friend has a prison record."

"Well," Mr. Carlo said, annoyed perhaps at the play for suspense, "what did the man do?"

"Robbed a grocery at gunpoint," the sergeant said, "eight years ago. The man said it was to feed his family, so they gave him a light sentence. But I have the fellow in for questioning right now." He tapped his chin. "I think he knows more than he's saying."

Mr. Jackson said, "It's interesting that the man had his own way out, yet never took it."

"Which is one of several reasons I don't think he did it," Sergeant Nestor said. "But I think he may know who did. Or at the very least, know who this dead fellow really is."

Mrs. Jackson nodded. It made sense. "Have you located any of the other customers?"

Before Sergeant Nestor might speak, Mr. Jackson said, "No. It's not the customers we need now. Who we need to talk with at once was that old elevator-man."

"Already done," Sergeant Nestor said. "He doesn't recall anyone coming up that elevator most of the evening, well," he gestured at Mr. Jackson and Mr. Carlo, "except you two."

Strange, Mrs. Jackson thought. "Most of the evening?"

The sergeant turned to Mr. Carlo. "Later that night, one of your cleaning women came on, a pretty brown-haired girl. He says it was perhaps three. He didn't recognize her, and it surprised him as they're supposed to take the service elevator —"

"So there's yet a third way out," said Mr. Jackson.

Mr. Carlo nodded.

Mrs. Jackson said, "He didn't recognize her?"

Sergeant Nestor gave her a quick glance. "She claimed she was new, and had been given the wrong key. You need one for the service elevator, you see. But she had the key, and wore the uniform, and had a name-tag, even, just like the rest."

Mr. Jackson said, "What name was on the tag?"

"Maria."

Mrs. Jackson said, "I know Maria! She's Head Maid, works days. That can't have been her: the woman's at least forty."

Sergeant Nestor raised an eyebrow. "I suppose we'd best talk to this elevator-man again."

While Sergeant Nestor was on the telephone with the elevator-man (who was at home), Mr. Carlo called Maria upstairs to the couple's rooms.

"My name-tag went missing three days back," Maria said. "They're making a new one for me. Not that I much need it: I've been here over twenty years."

"So you have," said Mr. Carlo. "Now, keep it to yourself that I called you up here, will you?"

She gave the room a quick glance. "It's about that fellow downstairs dead, isn't it."

"It is," Mr. Carlo said. "And the fewer who know of it, the better."

"Right," she said firmly. "No one will hear of this from me!"

"Very good," Mr. Carlo said. "You may go."

Once Maria had left, Sergeant Nestor turned to them. "I got a fair description of her from the elevator-man on duty last night: dark brown hair, blue eyes. He said she came to his shoulder, and the man's —"

"Almost as tall as me," Mr. Jackson said.

Mrs. Jackson nodded. "Did you find that bullet yet?"

Sergeant Nestor shrugged. "Autopsy won't be until tomorrow at the earliest. The holiday?"

She'd forgotten. "Right." For a moment, she felt foolish. Then she moved around to sit on the other side of Mr. Jackson. "In any case, sitting on barstools, her arm round him, he probably put his arm round her," she demonstrated with her hand, as if holding a gun at the

492

level of her lower chest, right below her breasts. "She'd have to hold the gun left-handed. So she's either left-handed, or —"

"Fairly well-practiced shooting with either hand," her Mr. Jackson said.

"Yes," she said. "And there's something else: I'm too short to be the killer. I'd have to angle up to be sure to kill him." She shuddered, recalling the heat of a muzzle flash and the skimpy little dresses young women wore to nightclubs here. "I wouldn't want to try doing that with bare arms! In any case, for that to go straight into his heart, she'd have to be taller than me, by a good bit."

Sergeant Nestor gazed at her. "You'd make a fair cop."

She scoffed at the very suggestion. "Not me. I'm only helping you because you helped me in the past." She smiled to herself. "And I do love a good puzzle."

The parlor door-bell rang, and Mr. Jackson went to get it.

"Hello," George said, and he sounded surprised. "We having a party?"

12

"You gotta be kidding me," George said. The police officer and Mr. Carlo had gone, and he sat in the parlor with Hector and Pam.

"I assure you, we're not," Hector said. "We've helped with this sort of thing before. Remember when you had the bad lemon-cake?"

George grimaced, his stomach clenching at the memory. "How could I forget?" He'd come close to dying that time.

"And the trouble with the Head Valet?"

He felt astonished. "You helped with that, too?"

Pam gave him a smile that made him feel very young, and more than a bit foolish. "We most certainly did."

How could they possibly have been involved with all this without him knowing? George peered at them, bewildered. "And that officer wants you to help once more. With a murder?" He had a sudden fear for them. "Isn't that dangerous?"

Hector sighed. "I suppose it could be. But we owe them both a debt of gratitude: they're the ones helping to keep our secret. And if they need our help, small as it might be, then we're glad to be of service." He leaned forward, his face suddenly serious. "But you mustn't tell anyone. I don't think Mr. Carlo was very happy for you to see the four of us here together."

George nodded. "My job depends on good publicity. And I wouldn't like our young Chef being linked to something like this."

Hector nodded.

Pam looked absolutely appalled at the notion. "Certainly not!"

Which was odd. He wasn't aware she even knew the little fellow. "What can I do to help?"

"Nothing at present," Hector said. "Today, as I've been reminded, is a holiday." He stretched. "And I plan to enjoy it."

***

Mr. Jackson meant what he said, but of course life got in the way.

George got bored sitting and left. Then his wife said, "There's something troubling me."

This sparked his attention at once. "Oh?"

"Mr. Carlo." She hesitated. "I don't like how he speaks of us."

He tried to recall what Mr. Carlo might have said to offend, but failed to. "I don't understand."

"Remember when he and the sergeant were here? He said, 'you see why I keep them here'?" She stopped, took a deep breath. "And you said 'Mr. Carlo has been picking up the tab'. Do you see? My concern is —"

He'd been staring at her, mouth open. "You have a remarkable memory for detail."

She scoffed. "So they tell me. What I'm saying is —"

"You think he thinks he's bought us."

A small laugh burst from her. "Yeah, and he's in the process of making his own little empire." She shook her head bitterly. "I just got out of one Mob family — I won't be dragged into another!"

Mr. Jackson felt floored. "Forgive me." She was absolutely right. What could he say? "Letting him cover the tab was easy, and ... convenient, and ... I'm sorry to have caused you this worry." They were in a dilemma, but one he thought would be easy to remedy. "I'll take care of this at once."

She shrugged, her manner relaxed. "There's really nothing to forgive."

"His demeanor when he woke me last night — well, I suppose it was this morning, really — it now makes sense. If I hadn't been half asleep when I answered the door, I would've told him to buzz off"

"Well, it may be a good thing you didn't," his wife said. "The evening might not have gone nearly so well."

"True." If Carlo had thought his generosity meant he might call on their service at any hour of the day or night, then balking at what he considered a reasonable request could have meant the end of their stay here. And he had nowhere in particular planned for them to go.

He'd been lax, lulled into a state of complacency. "I've just let myself become too comfortable." He leaned forward. "It won't happen again."

She gave him a warm smile. "This place is altogether too lovely." She laughed softly. "It's meant for relaxation and comfort, not mysteries and intrigue." She leaned over to kiss his cheek, then winked at him. "I'm going on the balcony for a smoke."

Bessie came out to put her little paws on his leg, so on went the little dog's wrap and leash, and off they went.

When they got down to the lobby, they met the veterinarian coming out from his offices down the hall. "Afternoon," the man said. "Off for a stroll?"

The three continued towards the lobby. "We are," Mr. Jackson said. "Looks like a fine day."

The veterinarian stopped. "Oh. No, don't take her out there: it's well below freezing! We've been walking them in the gardens." He gestured to Bessie's feet. "Much too cold for their little paws when they're inside all day."

"I didn't consider that." Mr. Jackson felt somewhat embarrassed.

The veterinarian smiled at him. "Don't mention it. Glad I caught you." He hurried out the front door, turning his collar up as he went.

"Well, Miss Bessie," Mr. Jackson said quietly, "I suppose we'll just have to take a tour of the gardens."

The beveled glass door to the gardens lay underneath the wide staircase, down a wide hallway. Once inside, a lush, grand garden stretched before them. Bessie pulled off the walkway towards the dirt, where she made the most of the opportunity beside a small tree.

That done, they began their stroll along the pathway of grayish-brown brick. The trees, the bushes, the flowers. A moist smell of dirt, a sound of running water. All was quiet, serene, as they strolled along the winding path. The vaulted, glassed-in roof reminded him of his childhood home, and he wondered how his sister fared.

She'd received his letters, sending a long reply to a P.O. Box address in an entirely different part of the country. As always, she wrote of home, family, and children — particularly her newest son — and the funny little things they did.

"Mama was quite pleasantly surprised to hear of your marriage! But I've told no one else, and I've said nothing at all about your wife. Everyone believes you're off on one of your adventures. And from the sound of it, they're not too far from the truth."

He imagined her amused smile.

To the left, a pond appeared, a small waterfall feeding it. But he hardly saw either. His sister was one of the smartest people he knew. What she wasn't writing stood out like a lantern at midnight.

Back home, their city must be in a terrible mess for her to not once mention the doings in it. Several notable men lay dead. The only witness to what happened was missing. And those hunting her hadn't found a clue.

His sister would surely have told him if they had.

He chuckled as Bessie's little feet padded along beside him. It was very much like the situation they now faced.

Should he have involved his wife with this murder in a speakeasy? Or had George been right? Was this too dangerous for them?

He shrugged to himself, knowing no one might see. They were in it, and once his wife got her mind set on something, wild horses couldn't drag her away.

They crossed a small bridge over a narrow, gently rushing creek, the windows of the hallway beside this place peeking through the shrubbery. Far ahead, Duchess Cordelia Stayman sat on a bench where the path turned back towards the door.

She was normally optimistic, lively, upbeat. But today, she sat quietly, face downcast, even the beaded strands on her day gown drooping.

Perhaps feeling the somber mood, Bessie stopped, gazing up at him, and he took the little dog into his arms, kissing her curly black hair.

Duchess Cordelia looked over, voice full of emotion. "My dear Mr. Jackson. Come, you won't be a bother."

Mr. Jackson put Bessie down and walked over to her. "I hope you're well?"

She sighed. "Not really. Sit beside me, if you will."

He sat, Bessie beside his feet, her head upon his black leather shoe. "What troubles you, my Lady?"

Duchess Cordelia shrugged. "Today would be our fourth anniversary."

And now her Albert, his friend, would never return. A tinge of melancholy struck. "I'm sorry."

"Sitting here, in the place he loved ... well, it makes me feel closer to him somehow."

Mr. Jackson nodded.

She placed a lined hand on his. "Enough of this. How is my favorite little family?"

He chuckled at that. Bessie had become like a child to them. "Everyone is quite well."

She patted his hand. "Good." She set her hands in her lap. "I suppose they have you wrapped up in this thing downstairs."

He laughed. "Nothing escapes you, does it?"

"Well, this is my place just as much as it is Monty's," she said firmly. "I live here, and it's my duty to keep up with the goings-on."

"You are a delight!"

The old woman blushed. "Why, thank you, sir."

"If you don't mind me asking: what have you learned?" With any luck, she'd know something useful. "It could be ever so helpful."

"Not much," she admitted. "But when I went out for my morning constitutional — and today, it was quite cold! — the new Head Valet, Harry — you know Harry, right? The redhead?"

"Of course," Mr. Jackson said.

"Yes. Well, Harry was talking to the other valet. Charlie, I think it is. In any case, I happened to hear Harry say that his neighbor was there! In that bar! Last night! And he saw a cute little platinum blonde slap the man who died!" She stopped, evidently considering this. Then she looked up at him. "Do you think she could have done it? Killed the man?"

Mr. Jackson chuckled. "A woman? Why would you think that?"

"Well, it's all over the place. One of the patrolmen that was here last night is married to the maid for tenth floor's second cousin, and the maid of course called to find out what'd happened as soon as she heard."

He laughed. "I see."

"And of course she told all the other maids at luncheon that a woman did it, and Lela told me when she was dressing me just now."

"That makes sense. Did Harry's neighbor happen to know this woman's name?"

"Well, I don't know!" She blushed, embarrassed. "I was listening when I shouldn't have. Should I ask?"

"Not at all," Mr. Jackson said. "It'd be best if I asked him myself."

"Perfectly right," Duchess Cordelia said. "It'd be much more proper if you were to, rather than me."

"I'm glad you think so." Mr. Jackson wondered how he might bring the matter up with their new Head Valet.

Bessie yawned, and Mr. Jackson wondered how much sleep a new mother of puppies might get, even these many days out. His sister hadn't gotten much sleep with hers, and she'd had them one at a time. He rose, offering his hand. "Care to accompany us back to the lobby?"

She rose, with her mood seemingly improved. "I daresay I will!"

When he returned Bessie to their rooms, his wife was bundled up on the parlor sofa in a thick robe, with a freshly lit fire going. "My word, it's gotten cold out! Even colder than this morning!"

He freed Bessie to return to her puppies. "At the suggestion of the veterinarian, we took our walk in the gardens. And guess who we saw there?"

"Cordelia," his wife said warmly. "How is she?"

He sat beside her, going over the entire conversation in his mind. "Ah. Missing dear Albert, of course."

"Pity that."

"But ... she did have news about our little to-do downstairs."

"Really."

"Apparently it's all over the Hotel staff that a woman did it, and a 'cute little platinum blonde' was seen slapping our poor fellow before he died."

She coughed, raspy and deep. "That's interesting."

"Guess the man wasn't too popular with the ladies."

She laughed, and it turned into a coughing fit. Which concerned him. "Sounds more like he was a little **too** popular with the ladies."

"A woman scorned, perhaps?"

"Yet one who from the description couldn't have killed him."

"Because of her height?"

"Well, yes. But with that hair, she would've definitely made an impression on our bartender, particularly if she were sitting beside a man who's now dead."

"True." He hadn't noticed, really, before now. But dark hair was surely more in fashion these days for women. The colorists had signs out everywhere. "Are you well?"

She shrugged. "It's just a cough, that's all. Smoking seems to help."

"Well, I don't like it." He got up, went to the phone. When he returned, she hadn't moved, still gazing at the fire. "The doctor will be along shortly."

She laughed. "Shame on you! That poor man. To force him to go out on a holiday. And in this weather?" She fished in her robe pocket, handed over a folded paper. "This came for you while you were out."

He opened a full piece of notepad paper with a long list of names on it.

"Of course, they all deny to the police they were in a speakeasy last night. But they visited the hospital for various things related to being shoved down in a stampede: a broken nose, a twisted ankle. Or else, they were mentioned as being seen in the club by one of the staff. Regulars, if you will." His wife drew her robe more tightly around her. "He's marked those with a star."

Regulars might know who this dead fellow was. He folded the paper, put it in his pocket. "Excellent."

***

The doctor, who was on retainer with the Hotel, came shortly after. "Bronchitis," he said. "I've seen a dozen of these this week, what with the weather." He left a medicine for the cough. "If she runs a fever, get some Aspirin from the pharmacy. But do call if she's not well in a week."

So he phoned Mr. Vienna and Mrs. Knight, telling them that his wife was ill; they were staying in for dinner and most likely breakfast as well. Then he called to make sure they were paid anyway.

Later that evening, he telephoned Club Patruni to ask for Miss Denton. "My wife is sick, and tomorrow I must go out. Would you stop by to check on her?"

"Is it serious?"

"The doctor doesn't think so."

"Okay." Band music roared in the background. "I gotta go."

"Thanks for your help."

The line clicked. He laughed.

The next morning, he let his wife sleep late, and although she was a bit put out at missing her appointment with the young Head Chef, she did seem better. So after telling her not to expect him until after dinner, Mr. Jackson went to the manager.

Mr. Flannery Davis appeared to be hard at work, far too much so to get up when Mr. Jackson entered. But he did offer a chair. "Please, sit down." He put down his pen. "What can I do for you?"

"I'd like a reckoning of our bill, if you please. I recall you offered us a week's stay when we first arrived, but it's gone well past that."

Mr. Davis blinked. "Is there a problem?"

"Not at all, but I prefer to keep up with my accounts. We've been at the Myriad twice, this last time for several months. I presume at some point, you'd like to be paid?"

The man seemed at a loss for words. "Well ... yes! But Mr. Carlo said —"

"Mr. Carlo is not my concern." Although it was a slight lie, it wouldn't do to show his hand just yet. "I'd like to pay my bill. See to it at once. And I'd like a bill once a month from here on out." Now what would be the best way to do this? "Would you give me your bank information, so I might have the sum transferred?"

"Uh ..." Mr. Davis stared at him blankly, mouth open. "I suppose." He fished around in his desk, then copied some numbers onto a paper. "This is the routing number, and this is the number for the account."

"Very good. Please have the bill sent to my room."

To Mr. Jackson's surprise, Mr. Davis stood, holding out his hand. "Very good, sir! I'll speak to Mr. Carlo about it at once."

Out in the hallway, Mr. Jackson chuckled, shaking his head. He wondered what Mr. Carlo was going to think of all this.

13

M r. Jackson went to the front desk, where a young man with brown hair stood ready. "Do you have a pay phone handy?"

"There's one over there," the clerk said. He pointed to a small door embedded into the wall, between the gift shop and the front of the building.

He gaped at it. "How have I never seen that before?"

"Heh," the clerk said. His tag read: Leo. "Probably because you never needed it 'til now."

"True. By the way, do you have change for a dollar?"

***

As Mr. Jackson had said he'd be gone the day, Mrs. Jackson decided to have a relaxing day of her own. She soaked in the tub (without wetting her hair, so she didn't have to use that awful heavy dryer).

She ordered breakfast in her rooms. She took Bessie for a walk in the gardens. A young man she didn't recognize strolled far on the other path towards the exit with his child, a brown-haired boy of four or so, skipping beside him.

And she was reminded of her son.

Bessie stopped, peering at her.

She picked the little dog up, holding her there in the middle of the walkway as the tears flowed. *My baby!*

How could she bear to never see him again?

The tears turned to deep, raspy coughing. Bessie began to squirm, so Mrs. Jackson put her down, walking to the little bridge over the even smaller creek. A railing made of stout branches stood there, and she held onto it for a while, watching the rushing water.

She had to accept it. She could never see him again.

If only he could have grown up like that little boy, living happily with his father! No matter what her Mr. Jackson said, she couldn't help thinking her husband's death had been her fault.

She walked along past small trees, flowers, shrubbery, and gradually, she felt calmer. The garden wasn't nearly so well cared-for now that Albert Stayman was gone.

Another loss.

She sat at Duchess Cordelia's favorite bench, near where the tree her husband Albert planted used to be, now also gone.

The ancients said time healed you. But she wished time would get busy. She felt tired of crying all the time.

I'll visit Cordelia, she thought. *Maybe that'll help.*

She found the dowager in her favorite place, the library, reading a novel. The old woman beamed when she saw her. "Oh, my dear Mrs. Jackson!"

Everyone else in the room turned to frown at them.

"Oh," Cordelia said in a whisper, "I always forget."

Mrs. Jackson smiled warmly at her. "Let's go outside." She and Bessie led Cordelia out to the lobby. "Care for a soda?"

"I suppose."

This was not like Cordelia at all! Taking the old woman's arm, she brought her to the soda shop. "Have you been here before?"

"With my Albert once. He's not fond of sweets, so we never came back."

"But did you like it?"

"I suppose I did." She gave a slight smile, then sighed. "Let's see what they have."

Hundreds of bottles holding various colors of liquid sat in a vast array along the walls, clear to the ceiling. In the corner high at the right-hand ceiling behind the counter, a large stuffed owl held residence over the door.

Apparently the owl would blink when a shipment came for the speakeasy. At least, that's what her Mr. Jackson had told her.

The young man behind the counter said, "What can I get for you ladies?"

Mrs. Jackson turned to Cordelia.

"Oh!" Cordelia looked surprised. "I don't know."

"A root beer float for me," said Mrs. Jackson.

"I've never had that," Cordelia said. "Make that two."

"Put the charge to my room," Mrs. Jackson said, "3205. And take a tip for yourself, if you please."

The young man beamed. "Right away!"

They went to one of the small tables and sat. Two couples also sat in the room, but one left a moment after. Cordelia sighed. "They remind me so much of Albert and I." But then she smiled. "Thank you for reminding me there is life without him."

Every little thing must make her recall their time together, Mrs. Jackson thought. Particularly still living here, where they'd been happy. She took the older woman's hand. "It all happened so suddenly. The whole thing's terribly difficult to take in."

Cordelia nodded, reaching for her handkerchief to brush at her cheek.

The young man came up with two tall glasses, each with a straw and a spoon. Setting them down, he brought out the receipt for her to sign, then returned to his post.

Mrs. Jackson and Cordelia sipped their drinks in silence, Bessie nestled beside them. The dowager's situation was such an echo of hers. Yet the poor woman had only empty rooms for company. "My Lady, do you like animals?"

Cordelia smiled warmly at Bessie. "I do, very much!"

"Once we're finished, I have something to show you."

14

The three returned to Mrs. Jackson's parlor. Upon being freed from the leash, little Bessie rushed into Mr. Jackson's bathroom. The two women followed.

Cordelia gasped in delight when she saw what lay there. "Puppies!" She turned to Mrs. Jackson, hands to her mouth. "Why did you never tell me?"

Mrs. Jackson felt amused. "We weren't sure what Mr. Carlo might think. Besides, it's perfectly natural, don't you agree?"

But the dowager Duchess Cordelia Stayman was on her knees in her heavily beaded day dress cooing at the little creatures. "Oh, my stars, they're adorable!"

Mrs. Jackson chuckled. "The spotted one's already spoken for. But you may have whichever of the rest you wish. As soon as they're old enough, of course!"

Cordelia sat upon the tile floor, leaning upon one hand. "That golden one reminds me so much of Albert's hair when we were young." She sighed, but it was wistful now, not sad. "I'll name him Bertie." Tears came to her eyes. "To remember my Albert by."

Mrs. Jackson squatted beside her and took her other hand. "I think that's admirable."

The golden pup wobbled, staring up at them with unfocused eyes. Bessie lay upon her side, eyes closed, as her children made their way to her.

"Well," Mrs. Jackson said, "It'll be a few months before he's ready to leave his mother. But you may visit every day if you wish."

Cordelia sat up, clasping her hands under her chin. "I would so enjoy that."

Mrs. Jackson helped the dowager to her feet.

"They look so well-cared for," Cordelia said. "And so well-fed, too."

Mrs. Jackson smiled fondly at the little family. "They have a good mother."

A knock on the parlor door surprised her. "Please, have a seat in the parlor," said Mrs. Jackson. "I'll see who this is."

She was surprised to see Miss Ophelia Denton at the door. "Oh, my dear Pet!" She gave the young woman a hug, then drew back. "Please, come in!"

The two walked into the parlor; the dowager still stood in the middle of the room.

Mrs. Jackson said, "I'm sure you remember Duchess Cordelia Stayman —"

Ophelia curtsied. "Of course!"

This made Duchess Cordelia laugh. "Now, now, none of that bother." She reached out her hand. "It's so good to see you again."

Mrs. Jackson said, "Come, both of you, sit down." Once they'd sat, she said, "What brings you here?"

"Mr. Hector said you were sick, and I should come check on you." She glanced at the dowager, then back. "But you look okay to me."

As if on cue, a rasping cough burst from deep within. "I feel fine."

"Goodness!" Cordelia looked appalled. "That cough sounds terrible."

This made Mrs. Jackson laugh, which turned once more into coughing. "I feel perfectly well, I swear to you! The doctor said bronchitis, and he left a medicine."

Ophelia's pretty face turned severe. "And are you taking it?"

"Silly girl," Mrs. Jackson said. "Of course I am!" She patted the younger woman's hand. "The cough is quite improved, really."

Tears came to Ophelia's eyes; she threw herself into Mrs. Jackson's arms. "My whole family died of a cough just like that," Ophelia sobbed. "I won't lose you too."

Mrs. Jackson patted Ophelia on the back, looking to Duchess Cordelia.

"I'm afraid I'll have to side with Miss Ophelia on this one," the dowager said. "You should not be out roaming about if you're ill, not even in the Hotel. You're still

513

young! And you have your husband and friends to think about, not to mention those dear little dogs." She rose. "I'll order you some tea. Lemon and honey are good for the lungs —"

"Not too much honey," Mrs. Jackson said, "I can't abide the taste of it in tea."

"Well, you can have some on a spoon then. But we must get you well!"

After a flurry of activity — including another hot bath — Mrs. Jackson found herself bundled into her robe and slippers (both courtesy of the Hotel) and seated in front of the parlor fireplace.

Wisely, Bessie stayed out of the commotion, only emerging from time to time to ensure all was well.

Ophelia turned off the hair dryer and fluffed Mrs. Jackson's hair. Duchess Cordelia handed her a cup of lemon tea and a spoon (full of honey). "Now," Duchess Cordelia said, "we shall restore you to health."

***

The pay phone cubicle was barely large enough to sit in. Consulting the telephone book, Mr. Jackson had been contacting the people on the list.

But he wasn't having much more luck than Sergeant Nestor did.

"Why would I tell you anything?"

"Are you with the police? I don't have nothing to do with police."

"Oh, no, mister — I'm staying well out of this one."

But then this last man said something strange. "You should become an announcer! You've got a great voice for it."

This he found quite amusing.

Finally, after meeting with the few who would meet with him, and eating at a little diner along the way, he returned to the speakeasy, well after dark. He found one of the bandsmen setting up for the night's show.

"Sure, I saw the little blonde slap him. Don't blame her, the way he carried on! Been here three nights running, with a different gal on his arm every night."

Interesting, Mr. Jackson thought. The bartender acted like he'd never seen the dead man before. "You know the man's name?"

He pulled a chair into place. "Nope."

"What did the other women look like?"

"All the same, really — light skin, brown hair. On the tall side."

"Would you know the last one if you saw her again?"

"Mister, you ever been up on stage? These lights make it hard to see anybody out there clear like."

Mr. Jackson sighed internally. "Would you happen to know the blonde's name?"

"No, but my girl might."

His "girl" was one of the waitresses, a saucy overpainted woman half the bandsman's age. "Why would I give a man information about her?"

"To be honest," Mr. Jackson said wearily, "I don't care much about her."

The young woman's eyebrows raised, looking quite the skeptic.

"I'm just trying to figure out who this dead guy is."

She seemed surprised at that, and after a moment's thought, said, "I won't have some man going round asking for her. She's a good girl: I won't be the one to give her a reputation."

"Not even to get word to her that her man's dead?"

The woman put her hands on her hips. "You really want her to find out that way?"

At that, he felt foolish. "You're absolutely right. Forgive me." What was he to do now? "May my wife call on you, then? Somewhere not here."

She shrugged. "Sure." But she didn't move to write anything down. "Why can't she just come down here?"

He hesitated. "She ... well, she came to grief over alcohol several years back, and —"

The young woman gave a sharp nod. "Gotcha." She went over to the bar and wrote a number on a paper napkin. "Who's gonna be calling? So I know it's her."

For an instant, he forgot what his wife's name here was. Then it came to him. "Pamela Jackson."

She handed over the napkin. On it said, "Calliope," and a number.

He took Calliope's hand. "Thank you. Very much."

She looked into his eyes. "You seem like a good guy. Don't make me out to be wrong."

He smiled at her. "You have my word, miss, I'll not make a move to contact either of you."

She turned away. "Have your missus call before six. But not before noon." She grinned at him over her shoulder. "That is, if she wants me to answer."

***

Duchess Cordelia and Ophelia Denton refused to leave until Mr. Jackson returned. So they had luncheon, tea, and dinner together, interspersed with calls downstairs for one thing or another.

When her Mr. Jackson finally appeared, Mrs. Jackson was stretched out on the sofa with a poultice on her chest and a hot rag on her forehead, feeling quite fussed over.

Mr. Jackson, on the other hand, looked more than a little surprised. "Whatever is going on here?"

Duchess Cordelia frowned at him. Frowned! "You should be ashamed of yourself, sir, for leaving your wife in such a state. She was out and about! Sick as she was!"

Ophelia nodded.

Mrs. Jackson laughed. "They've made me a project! I happened to cough, and got pounced upon."

Ophelia said, "You were in the worst coughing fit I've heard in some time!" Angry tears came to her eyes once more. "It's no laughing matter!"

Mrs. Jackson felt chagrined. "Come, Pet."

The young woman came and knelt before her.

Mrs. Jackson took her into her arms, laying her head upon her shoulder. "I'm sorry to make light of this, I really am. Look at me." Taking the girl's tear-streaked face in her hands, she said, "I don't plan to die any time soon. The doctor's been here, and he said if I got worse, to call. Many people this week have this thing I have, and it's because of the weather, not flu." She peered into Ophelia's eyes. "You hear me? I'm still right here."

Ophelia smiled at that. "I'm sorry to fret so."

"You fret because you care about her," said Duchess Cordelia. "As do I."

Mr. Jackson stood there, mouth open. Finally, he said, "Forgive me; I never meant to burden you ladies with this." He came over to stand beside her. "I'll not leave until she's well."

That set them both to mumblings:

"Oh, it's been no burden —"

"It's no bother, really —"

"Thank you," Mrs. Jackson said, clasping Ophelia's hand with one hand and Duchess Cordelia's with the other. "I feel much better." And she did. Maybe this tending-to was what she needed. "It really has been lovely to spend the day together." A wave of tiredness came over her. "But I think I'll be off to bed now."

Once they left, she discarded the poultice and the rag (both of which had gone cold), and let her Mr. Jackson put her to bed. There he sat, telling her the story of his day. "Let me see if Sergeant Nestor might come by, this time without breaking into our bedrooms."

That made her laugh.

***

When Mr. Jackson called that night to let Mrs. Knight know his wife was still sick, the woman offered to come care for his wife the next day. "I've been a nursemaid before," she said, "and my other appointment for today has cancelled."

So he called Monsieur to apprise him of the situation.

The sound of pots and pans lay far in the background. "When I heard her cough, I knew it was serious."

"The doctor said it was just bronchitis."

"Many died of the flu when I was in Paris," Monsieur said. "I wouldn't take any such cough lightly."

And Mr. Carlo's daughter was ill as well.

Mr. Jackson began to feel concerned. "I have a nursemaid coming in the morning," he said, "if she's not improved I may call the doctor back."

"Good idea," Monsieur said. "Let me know how I might help."

"I will." He never considered that coming here might expose his wife to contagion! Of all the things to have to worry about, he thought. Going to his wife's room, he found her sleeping, so he lay down beside her.

She had no fever, nor did she act unwell. He wrapped his arm around her, laying his head close to hers. He didn't know if he could bear to lose her, now that they were finally happy.

15

When Mrs. Jackson woke, Mr. Jackson sat dressed for the street, drinking coffee and reading the news. "Good morning," he said cheerfully.

The sound of water running in the sink came from her bathroom. "What's going on?"

"Mrs. Knight has informed me that she's an experienced nursemaid. So I've asked her to give us an opinion on the matter and care for you today."

"I don't feel sick," she said, then began coughing. It did rather rattle in her chest a bit.

Mrs. Knight came in from the bathroom. "I don't like the sound of that at all."

"Smoking helps the most. And that medicine of the doctor's helps calm it as well."

Mrs. Knight glanced at Mr. Jackson. "Any fever?"

"No," Mrs. Jackson said, before he might reply. "Nor any other symptom."

"My pardons, ma'am," said Mrs. Knight. "But sometimes you can have a fever when you're asleep, and never know it."

Mrs. Jackson felt reproved.

"Not that I've seen," Mr. Jackson said, and he sounded concerned. "Is that important?"

Mrs. Knight let out a breath. "Flu is unlikely without fever, usually one that's quite high."

Mr. Jackson said, "That's a relief."

"Have you coughed blood?"

Mrs. Jackson stared at Mrs. Knight, suddenly frightened. "No, never!"

"Then the doctor is likely correct: you have bronchitis." Mrs. Knight smiled warmly. "A few days' rest and you should be good as new."

"All this fuss over nothing," Mrs. Jackson grumbled.

"You still must rest," said Mrs. Knight. "You won't recover otherwise." She went to the bathroom.

A laugh burst from Mr. Jackson.

"What is it?"

"Just remembering how hard it was to get you to rest when you had your surgery," he said.

Must he bring that up now? "I promise to, if only for Ophelia's sake. The poor dear — I regret worrying her."

Mrs. Knight returned with a towel; two poultices lay upon it.

"Duchess Cordelia put one of those on me," Mrs. Jackson said.

"Did she now?"

"Just last night."

"Huh," Mrs. Knight said, sounding impressed. "I'd like to hear the story of where a Duchess learned nursecraft." She lifted one of the cloths. "Come now, let's put this one on your back."

***

Mr. Jackson called the sergeant to let him know of the delay. It took twenty minutes to get the man on the line. And when he did, it sounded like an entire crowd was in the background.

"It's just as well," Sergeant Nestor said. "We're terribly busy. Because of the holiday, you see." He scoffed. "The autopsy-man has a whole list of them to do. He took the man's fingerprints, but won't get to a proper study until tomorrow at the earliest. Never mind us — you take care of your wife."

The man hung up before Mr. Jackson could tell him about the blonde. It didn't seem really enough to go through all that waiting again, so he returned to sit beside his wife. She was sittiing up in bed in her nightgown, legs straight out, bent over so her face nearly touched her knees, having her back pounded upon.

"Brings up the phlegm," Mrs. Knight said as she pounded. "That's the trouble with these medicines the doctors give. They calm the cough. But the cough's purpose is to bring out the infection inside, so it doesn't fester into pneumonia."

"Oh." Mr. Jackson felt chagrined. "So ... did he advise us wrongly?"

"Not at all," said Mrs. Knight. "The medicine is wonderful for helping the patient sleep. But more is sometimes needed in cases like hers."

His wife coughed, and it did sound better. "I'm grateful you're here for her."

Mrs. Knight looked quite pleased. "Thank you, sir." To his wife, she said, "Now let's roll onto your left side."

"I feel like a side of beef," his wife said. She grinned. "I shall be quite tenderized."

Mr. Jackson laughed, kneeling beside her. He kissed her forehead. "You really are a silly old girl." He smoothed her hair, feeling a great fondness for her.

"What did the sergeant say?"

"He sounded up to his ears in work!"

"Ah," his wife said. "The holiday."

"Right you are. So nothing will be done, or come back, or whatever, until tomorrow at the earliest."

She chuckled. "This place is ever so modern. But it seems some things never change."

***

Once the pounding finished, Mrs. Jackson did feel better. The couple called up for luncheon, ordering some for Mrs. Knight as well.

It being after noon, Mrs. Jackson gave this Miss Calliope a call. The woman agreed to meet at a local bistro two days hence for a late luncheon, on the condition that Mrs. Jackson pay.

That seemed most amusing.

With the pounding and poultices and steam heat, and Mr. Jackson hardly leaving her side, soon Mrs. Jackson was her old self again. Everyone agreed she was fit to go out, she thought none too soon.

On the way to meet with Miss Calliope, she went to a chapel, lighting a candle for Mr. Carlo's daughter Margaret's healing as well.

16

Calliope Washington was past the large salad — with everything on it — and into an equally large sandwich. "Didn't think you were real."

And she'd ordered dessert!

Mrs. Jackson sampled her chowder, wondering how the woman kept her figure. "I most certainly am. What can you tell me about the man who died?"

Calliope grinned at her around a mouthful of food, then swallowed, wiping her lips. "Straight to the point, are we?"

Mrs. Jackson dropped an oyster cracker to Bessie, who snapped it up. "I tend to be." She chuckled to herself. "You know his young lady well, I take it."

Calliope shrugged. "She used to waitress at the Myriad. In the restaurant, until the old guy took a fancy to her and told her she'd get better tips downstairs." She took a long drink of her soda. "She didn't want to at first — her ma's a teetotaler — but I told her what her ma don't know won't hurt her."

Mrs. Jackson laughed. "Her ma never comes to visit?"

"Oh, no — they don't have that kind of money. It's hard to even get a reservation for breakfast these days."

"I see."

"So anyway, about a year later, she took a job at this other place that paid better. I guess that's where she met the guy."

"Any idea what his name is?"

"Aaron something." She shook her head, frowning. "Can't remember. She can tell you all that."

"So you didn't socialize?"

She pushed the sandwich plate aside and gestured for dessert. "Sure, we went out on the town, the days we all weren't working."

The waiter brought a huge slice of chocolate cake and set it before her.

"Coffee, if you please," Calliope said.

The waiter turned to Mrs. Jackson. "And anything else for you, ma'am?"

She'd finished her soup. "Tea would be lovely." She turned to Calliope. "Did you see what happened?"

She shook her head. "I didn't even see him, or the gal he was with, that's how busy we were." She took a bite of cake, swallowed. "I've been there three years and never seen the place so full."

"That's what they tell me."

Calliope had already eaten a third of the cake. Once the waiter had gone, she gestured with her fork. "We don't tend to give out names like you lot do. And you're never sure if someone's giving you the right name anyway. He said call him Aaron, so that's what we called him." She shook her head. "They're saying that that last gal was the one who shot him."

Mrs. Jackson didn't think it would hurt to admit it, so she nodded.

"Hell of a way to go, even if he did break her heart."

Mrs. Jackson understood that feeling all too well. She leaned forward. "I don't mean your friend any harm. The police don't even have to know her name if she doesn't want it. But I don't feel right not finding out anything that might help them learn who did this."

Calliope set down her fork, eyes on her plate. After a moment, she nodded. "Her name's Trixie. Quinlan. And she lives right down the street, by the El train."

***

Trixie Quinlan was maybe twenty and at three in the afternoon, still in her bathrobe. She beamed when she saw Bessie. She cried when told the news. "I wish I'd never left him that way," she sobbed. "I told him he was rotten, good for nothing. That was the last he heard me say. I'd take it back if I could."

They were sitting at a wobbly wooden table in the center of a dismal little one-room: a bed up against a wall and a pot-bellied stove in the corner. The window beside the dresser looked out onto a window from the other building and the brick around it. Mrs. Jackson took her hand. "I'm sorry."

Trixie nodded, her eyes upon the large doily covering most of the table. Something an older woman might make, if given the time. "I loved him. I truly loved him. Why did he do that?"

"Men do strange things sometimes."

Trixie bit her lip, eyes wide, staring. Then tears filled them again, began to drop upon her lap.

"What happened?"

"What do you mean?"

"On New Year's Eve. I heard you slapped him."

"I did. One of the other waitresses where I work said she'd just done a shift at the Myriad and saw him there with another girl. So I left. I went there and used her code to get in. There he was!" She started to cry again. "He never even said he was sorry."

"What was she like?"

"Thin, brown hair. And she was old! At least thirty. Not even pretty, either."

The poor girl must feel humiliated. "Would you know her if you saw her again?"

"Oh, yes," Trixie said. "I've seen her hanging round work before this. But I better not see her again, or I'll give her a piece of my mind!"

Mrs. Jackson said, "Is there someone who can come stay with you? Or a place you can go?"

She was quiet for some time "My mother lives in Pilsen." She nodded, wiped her nose. "Ma'll say I told you so. But I'll go home."

"It'd be good to have someone with you right now."

"Will there be a funeral?"

Mrs. Jackson shrugged. "So far they don't even know his name. I came here to find out who he was."

Trixie gasped, hands to her mouth. "All this time, and they didn't even know his name? It's Aaron Lucas! I'm pretty sure he lives on the East Side."

"You've never been to his house?"

"What kind of girl do you take me for? Of course not! And before you ask, he's never been in here, either." She gave a satisfied nod.

Interesting. "How long were you together?"

"Almost a year," she said. "We met at the Mulder. That's where I work."

Mrs. Jackson nodded. Sergeant Nestor would know where that was. "I have to ask. Or else the police will want to. Where were you on New Year's Eve?"

"When I got home my landlady gave me a message."

"What message?"

"I got fired for leaving like I did." Trixie's face grew somber. "Never been fired from anything before." She stared towards the table. "I bought a bottle. I was here. Drinking. Until daybreak. I never felt so low in my life."

"Did anyone see you?"

She let out a laugh, gesturing to the window across the way. "Half the city was in that party over there. Every so often a different one of them would lean out and tell me to come over. But I never did."

All easily verifiable. She didn't think this girl could have killed the man anyway. "So what did your Mr. Lucas do? For a living?"

"Oh, he was an accountant."

"Really? Where did he work?"

Trixie's face became evasive. "On his own. He had his own business, out of his home, doing books for people. He was really busy." She pointed to a framed, half page magazine clipping with a photo of the man and a headline: Aaron Lucas: Rising Star. "He said business was good! Really good. He always showed me a real good time."

Mrs. Jackson smiled to herself. "That sounds lovely. Can you give me your mother's number in case we need to get hold of you? Like if the police need you to identify the body."

Her hands went to her mouth. "Oh. Does he look really awful?"

"I haven't seen him, but he's surely been cleaned up by this time. No blood or anything like that." She tried to make her voice reassuring. "It's only if they can't find any next of kin. To make sure it's really your Aaron, and not someone else that only looks like him."

She nodded. "I see." She rose, went to the dresser, wrote on a piece of paper, handed it over. "Yes, please call me. I want to be at his funeral."

17

Mrs. Jackson went back to the Hotel. She'd have an easier time with what came next if Mr. Jackson accompanied her.

After returning Bessie to her puppies, she found Mr. Jackson in his room reading the afternoon paper. He glanced up. "There you are! Have any luck?"

"I have. Let's call to see if the sergeant is in."

Luckily for them, Sergeant Nestor was indeed in. When they arrived at the station, the couple were shown back at once.

The place was utilitarian, yet busy. Sergeant Nestor's office was no different.

The sergeant was occupied with papers when they were shown in. "There you are! Good to see you looking well. Have a seat." He finished writing, then set down his pen. "What have you learned?"

Mrs. Jackson opened her mouth to speak.

Mr. Jackson said, "One of the men in the band saw a short blonde woman slap the dead fellow a few days before he died."

"And?"

Mrs. Jackson, amused, waited for Mr. Jackson to turn to her expectantly. Then waited just a bit more. "Our young lady's name," she said calmly, "is Trixie Quinlan. She says the dead man is an independent accountant named Aaron Lucas. She even has a magazine clipping using that name with the man's portrait. They've been together almost a year, and she's never been to his home. She thinks he lives on the East Side. At least a dozen people saw her at home on New Year's Eve, well until dawn." At that, she felt sad. "She's on her way to her mother's house in Pilsen," she fished out the slip of paper, "and she's willing to come identify the body if there's no next of kin."

The sergeant took the slip of paper. "Interesting."

Mr. Jackson leaned forward. "How so?"

"Because the dead man's fingerprints came back. His name is actually Mark Boyle, and he's done time for embezzling."

***

Mr. Jackson felt astonished. "He's done time, too?"

The sergeant nodded, pulling out a file from his drawer and opening it; the dead man's portrait lay inside. "Same place as our bartender, but in different lockups. It's doubtful that they ever met. No, embezzling carries a much higher charge: Mr. Boyle here got fifteen years, out in ten for good behavior." He squinted at the page. "Says here he got out a little over a year ago."

Mrs. Jackson said, "Right before he met Trixie."

Mr. Jackson said, "The bandsman saw Mr. Boyle there three nights running, with a different girl on his arm each night."

Sergeant Nestor let out a laugh. "That explains all the lipstick." He leaned forward. "Where'd she know him?"

"I knew I forgot something," his wife said. "At the Mulder. She works there. That's where they met."

The sergeant nodded. "I know the place."

"The girl she found him with goes there as well," his wife said. "A thin unattractive woman at least my age with brown hair."

"Shouldn't be too hard to find her at the Mulder, if she's there a lot," Sergeant Nestor said. "Did she give you a name for this woman?"

His wife shook her head.

"Well," the sergeant said, "I better go have a talk with the Mulder, and see if they can tell me more about this woman. Or our 'Mr. Lucas' here."

"I'm curious," Mr. Jackson said. "What else did you find? About the card? The phone number?"

"No one's answering the phone number," Sergeant Nestor said. "I'm having the phone company track down the address. The repair shop recognized Mr. Boyle; he'd come in asking about getting his lighter fixed."

Ah, he thought. "So he might have left it there?"

"Nope," the sergeant said. "He said he'd think about it and took the card."

His wife let out a laugh.

But Mr. Jackson felt curious about another matter. "Did his autopsy show anything?"

The sergeant shrugged. "As we thought, he'd been drugged. Your usual sleeping powder — you can find it at any pharmacy. But it needs a prescription, so that'll help narrow down any suspects we find."

That sounded helpful. Mr. Jackson said, "Anything else you'd like us to do?"

"Not at present," said the sergeant.

"Oh," his wife said. "Miss Quinlan would like to be notified about the funeral."

"We gotta find the man's next of kin first," the sergeant said. "We're having trouble tracking anyone down. But I'll let you know."

So with that, the couple went back to the Hotel.

"It's odd," Mr. Jackson said, once they were back in their parlor. "Your Miss Trixie was with the man almost a year and didn't know his real name."

He regretted saying so almost immediately. From the look on his wife's face, this case was coming much too close to home for her liking.

Feeling a surge of compassion, he took her in his arms. "Forgive me; I'd forgotten all that happened." Yet he didn't know what really went on that night they fled the city.

He felt rather than saw her nod. "She's escaped with her life, her health, and a mother she's willing and able to return to. It's more than many who meet up with such a man can hope for."

This surprised him. But she sounded so forlorn that he didn't want to press her further. "Would you like to go down for an ice cream soda?"

She smiled up at him. "I think that would be lovely."

***

Fetching Bessie, the couple went down for their soda.

Mrs. Jackson did indeed feel that this case came much too close to her own story.

But she'd vowed not to let her past ruin her. She had much to think of today.

Like what magazine would run an article praising a convicted felon? Surely a reputable organization would have checked the man's credentials before running the story. So this could only be some tabloid.

Even so, this whole thing seemed strange.

Once they finished their sodas, she said, "Let's bring our Queen Bess up to her young subjects and have a go at the park, shall we?"

"Very well," Mr. Jackson said. "It might be nice to get outdoors. You go ahead; I have some business with the front desk."

So she brought Bessie to her puppies and returned to the front desk where Mr. Jackson was waiting for her. The park was close by, tree-lined paths and cold air and an overcast sky. And after they'd gone round and were on their way back, coming the other way was none other than Trixie Quinlan!

"They said you'd be out here," Trixie said.

"My goodness," Mrs. Jackson said. "However did you find us?"

She looked embarassed. "Figured you had something to do with the place. So I went to the front and told them we were supposed to meet." She shrugged. "They said you'd just left."

Oh, dear, thought Mrs. Jackson. If she could be found so easily by this slip of a girl, others could find her too. "Was there something we might help you with?"

Trixie peered up at Mr. Jackson. "This must be the man Calliope told me about."

Mr. Jackson tipped his hat. "Hector Jackson, at your service."

Trixie took a deep breath. "There's something I didn't tell you. Back at the house."

The couple waited.

"Um," she said. "I think Aaron was mixed up in something bad."

18

Mr. Jackson, his wife, and little Miss Trixie walked along the park paths as the young woman told her story. They'd met at the Mulder, it was true. And they'd go out every weekend, and most nights she had off. But when he'd take her out on the town, he'd spend a lot of money. Too much money.

"At first it was fun," Miss Trixie said. "Then it started to scare me, especially when we started meeting up with these men." She fell silent.

His wife spoke up. "What kind of men?"

"They were really rich," Miss Trixie said. "They'd talk about jobs, and the men with them had guns. I may be dumb, but I'm not stupid. They had to be hit men. You know, gangsters." She stared down at the path. "I loved him. I didn't want to believe it. When I'd say something about it all, he'd never really lie. They were clients. He was doing work for them. Sure they were rich. He was good at his job, and they paid him well for it." She sighed. "But now he's dead."

Mr. Jackson shook his head. She had to know the truth. "His real name's Mark Boyle —"

Miss Trixie stared up at him, startled. "What?"

"— and when you met him, he'd just gotten out of prison." He felt sorry for the girl. "Ten years for embezzling."

She stopped in the path. "So was everything he told me a lie?"

His wife said gently, "I don't suppose we'll ever know."

The girl — she was very young, nineteen or twenty at most — began to cry, and his wife consoled her, taking Miss Trixie into her arms.

Such a sad story, he thought.

His wife handed the girl a handkerchief (courtesy of the Hotel). "Now, now," she said. "This man isn't worth spoiling your makeup over. Wipe your eyes. We need to get our overcoats, but then we'll take you home."

***

Mrs. Jackson thought that the sight of two-week-old puppies snuggled up next to Bessie might make Trixie feel better.

"Oh, they're so little! And that one looks just her!" She looked up at her. "I wish I could have that little black one. But I don't think my Ma would like that."

Mrs. Jackson stood. "They're not old enough in any case." She adjusted her overcoat. "But let's get everything settled first. In a few months, when they're ready to leave their mother, we can talk about it then."

Trixie stood, gazing down at them. "They remind me of my cousins when they was born."

Mrs. Jackson rested her hand on Trixie's back. "Babies are much the same, wherever you go."

"I want a baby someday." Trixie's tears began to flow once more. "I wanted to marry Aaron," she sobbed, "He said we could have a house together, and a family. And now he's dead."

19

In the taxi on the way to her mother's home, Mr. Jackson watched the girl. Miss Trixie sat stunned, as if everything in her life had gone horribly wrong.

Mr. Jackson said, "We found cigarettes in his pocket."

Miss Trixie nodded.

"Did he have a lighter? Or did he use —"

"Oh, yes," Miss Trixie said. "He had one of those old Pist-o-liters. You know, the kind that looks like a gun?"

They both shook their heads. "It wasn't on him," Mr. Jackson said. "Do you recall anything else about it?"

"It wasn't on him? He used it all the time! Let me see — it's cast iron, kind of heavy. It sort of pulled his pocket down. And it had a piece chipped off the corner of the handle. But loved that thing — he never went anywhere without it. He told me one of his friends gave it to him, way back when."

"Did you ever recall anything about his friends? Like their names?"

She shrugged, downcast. "We met with a lot of guys. And their flappers. None of the girls knew him, though, not until we were introduced. That's what surprised me so much, made me so angry there at the end. He had other girls with him, and I never knew!" She stopped then, staring at her knees. "The one I remember most was a big guy. He never sat down with us. And he kept staring at me. Made me glad Aaron was there. It gave me the heebie-jeebies!" She shuddered. "They called that guy Simon once. But mostly Jasper. I don't know which was his real name." She stared at them, mouth open. "Do you think they were all lying?"

"Hard to say." Mr. Jackson thought it likely, though. "Anything else?"

She gave a one-arm shrug. "I mostly just talked with the girls. But there was this one other man that really scared me, even more than the rest. They met up together right before Aaron died. They called him Mr. Russell, and they sent all us girls to get them drinks when they talked."

"Hmm," Mr. Jackson said, recalling something similar when he was a boy.

"Then when we got the drinks," Miss Trixie said, "They wouldn't let us sit with them! We had to take our own table." She sniffled, just a bit. "I don't mind waitressing. But I didn't like sitting like that by ourselves in some bar, with all those men looking at us like we were the buffet. I told him so later."

"Wait," his wife said. "Wasn't this at the Mulder?"

"No, he didn't like drinking there, 'specially right before he died."

"So where was it?"

She glanced at the cabbie, who seemed a bit too particularly interested. "I'll write it for you."

She opened her bag, taking out a notepad and pencil, then passed a slip to his wife.

They weren't in too bad an area. "We'll get out here." He handed over a bill to the man.

After the cab left, Mr. Jackson flagged down another.

Miss Trixie said, "Why'd you do that?"

After they got in, Mr. Jackson said, "I'm not sure it's a good idea to talk about this right now."

They rode to Pilsen in silence.

That first cabbie knows where we were going, he thought. And it worried him.

Mrs. Quinlan was an older version of the girl, but her hair was long, brown, and up in a bun. Mr. Jackson made introductions. "Might I use your telephone?"

"Certainly."

Mr. Jackson called the Myriad. "Is Mr. Carlo in?"

After a few minutes, Mr. Carlo answered the phone. "What's all this about?"

"You know a fellow named Russell? Has a man called Simon Jasper."

Mr. Carlo gasped.

"I'm taking it that you do. There's a girl with information you'd find interesting. But she's not safe here. One moment." He covered the receiver with his hand. "Mrs. Quinlan, is there somewhere you can go?"

"My sister's in Cicero. What's this all about?"

"Your daughter's in trouble," his wife said, "and it'd be best if you two weren't here for a while."

Mr. Jackson spoke into the telephone. "Would you take her and her mother to Cicero?" He gave the address where they were right now. "And keep an eye on them."

"I'll come for them myself." The line went dead.

That was rather rude, he thought. Then he turned to Mrs. Quinlan. "There's a friend of mine named Mr. Carlo. He's going to take you and your daughter to your sister's and leave men to watch over you."

Mrs. Quinlan nodded. "So it's that kind of trouble. I've heard of Carlo and Russell both." She held out her hands, and Miss Trixie went over to hug her. Arm around her daughter, she looked up at him. "Thank you for helping us."

"My pleasure."

The couple waited at Mrs. Quinlan's kitchen table over tea as the two women packed some clothing, every so often stopping to cry and hug each other.

Mr. Jackson whispered to his wife, "It must be wrenching to have to flee your home at a moments' notice like this, not knowing if the place you go to will be entirely safe either."

She nodded. "It was." But then she smiled. "You've been quite the champion, both times."

He laughed softly, not wanting the ladies to hear. "Thank you. But I'd honestly like to keep everyone safe, if possible."

Finally, Mr. Carlo arrived. Mrs. Quinlan seemed more than a bit awed to meet him, yet also a bit afraid. "Let's sit down a moment," he said, "and my men'll take you and your mother's luggage out to the car."

***

So everyone sat around the kitchen table.

Mrs. Jackson watched as Trixie told her story. Something had happened during that telephone conversation between Mr. Jackson and Mr. Carlo, and she was curious to know what.

Mr. Carlo seemed only to care about this Mr. Russell: where they met, who he had with him, what the dead man was doing for him. "And you say he didn't want to go to the Mulder anymore?"

Trixie shook her head. "No, he didn't even want to step inside that last month. Oh," she said, "I got the name of that other woman: Mabel Franklin."

Mr. Carlo flinched. "What other woman?"

Tears came to her eyes. "The one Aaron was with."

Her mother put an arm around her daughter, handing her a handkerchief.

The girl still used his fake name. "Did he ever say why he worked for those men?"

Trixie sighed. "I asked him the same thing, that night we saw Mr. Russell. He said they hired him when no one else would."

From the corner of her eye, she saw Mr. Jackson nodding. That's how these mobsters got people. Promise them a job, money, status. Safety. Then they were trapped. "It sounds like your Aaron was loyal to them."

"He was," Trixie said. "He said he'd do just about anything for them."

Hmm. "Do you want to stop by and see Aaron before you go? I'm not sure how much longer they'll be able to keep the body."

Trixie took her mother's hand. "My ma and my auntie and my little cousins have got dragged into this, all because of me." She sighed. "I knew what sort he was. But I just didn't want to see it. If anything should happen to them —"

Her mother said, "Oh, honey —"

Mrs. Jackson took Trixie's other hand. "You can't blame yourself. You didn't know this would happen."

It was if the girl didn't hear a word. "Now I've lost everything: my job, my place, everything I had there. And my ma's gotta move, and who knows if my aunt and cousins will have to move? And it's all because of me." She shook her head. "I don't want to see Aaron like that anyway. Dead." She turned away. "I'd rather remember him how he was."

20

When Mr. Carlo had learned all he wanted, he led Mr. Jackson and his wife out front.

Several men and three cars stood at the curb. A burly brown-skinned fellow seemed to lead them; Mr. Carlo gestured for the man to come closer.

This man had a stillness to him, both at rest and in motion, which gave Mr. Jackson the feeling that he stood before some giant ship sailing upon calm water. "This is Mr. James Gray," Mr. Carlo said. "He's been watching for news of you."

Mr. Gray tipped his fedora in one smooth motion. "You'll have plenty of warning should someone discover you're in the city."

Mr. Jackson liked the fellow at once. "We're most grateful, sir."

Miss Trixie and her mother had followed behind. His wife put an arm around Miss Trixie's shoulder. "Keep them safe as can be."

"We will." Mr. Gray smiled warmly at the young woman and her mother. "Now, if you'll point out which items you want moved into storage and which sold —"

Mrs. Quinlan paled, but she nodded, and the three returned inside.

"I'll go with them," Mrs. Jackson said. "This must be a terrible ordeal."

So Mr. Jackson and Mr. Carlo stood on the front porch, taking in the view.

It was a pleasant neighborhood, of brick homes and curious little old ladies pretending to trim front gardens.

Mr. Jackson wondered what was going on with the Mulder. Mark Boyle had obviously been doing the accounts for whoever owned it. Why would he suddenly refuse to drink at his own speakeasy?

Mr. Carlo's voice startled him. "What's happened?"

Mr. Jackson smiled to himself. He'd expected this conversation. "Whatever could you possibly mean?"

"Your bill."

Mr. Jackson chuckled. "I should ask the same question. When I went to the front desk today, your manager — who earlier seemed quite eager to help — now says my bill isn't ready. Is there a problem?"

"Well, no ..." Mr. Carlo seemed at a loss for words. "I thought we had an arrangement."

Mr. Jackson wanted very much to laugh, but thought it best not to. "When we arrived, you quite generously offered us a week's stay. It's been many months past that." He folded his arms. "I'd just like to keep current, if that's all right with you."

Mr. Carlo's eyes narrowed. "I've offended you."

"Not at all, sir. We're here, willing to help in any way we can. But ..." Should he say it? "We don't share the same goals." He gestured out into the neighborhood. "My father had the back room deals, the men on the street corners. Some very much like your Mr. Gray in there. Yet my father's life was ever one of looking over his shoulder, in case some underling wanted to seize power." It'd been something much more mundane that had killed his father. But he wondered at times if the life his father had chosen might have caused it. "I wish you whatever success you desire. But I have no wish to be part of it. My only goal is for my wife to live free — safe, happy, and in peace."

The women came out front and this time, he did laugh. "Besides, we too might need to disappear one day, and I'd not like your Mr. Gray after us."

Mr. Carlo laughed. "Fair enough." He clapped Mr. Jackson a bit too hard on the shoulder. "I'll have the bill to your room before dinner."

"Thank you, sir."

"Well, to be honest, I could use the money." He glanced aside. "Find out who did this. Every day the speakeasy is closed, with police everywhere ... it's beginning to cost me."

Mr. Jackson nodded. "Sorry we didn't tell you about the dogs. It never occurred to me you might object."

Mr. Carlo shrugged. "I don't think Margaret wants one. But Maisy might. She's home alone all day, and —"

Mr. Jackson smiled to himself. "It'll be months before they're old enough to travel. But she can come by any time she likes and pick one out."

Mr. Gray and the women emerged. Mr. Jackson gestured at the man with his chin, and he came over. "How may I help?"

Mr. Jackson described the taxi ride, and the cabbie who seemed rather too interested in their conversation.

Mr. Gray nodded. "I'll have my guys watch the place. If Russell's men show up, we'll take care of it."

His wife stood off to one side, speaking with the women too quietly to hear. They hugged her, and smiled over at him.

Miss Quinlan and her mother went into one car, the rest of the men into the second. Once they were off, Mr. Carlo rode with Mr. and Mrs. Jackson in the third car, back to the Myriad.

Mrs. Jackson said, "Mr. Boyle would do just about anything, huh?"

Mr. Jackson nodded. "I thought the same thing."

Mr. Carlo stared at them. "You think Russell had the man killed."

Mr. Jackson took a deep breath. "It's quite the possibility. If our Mr. Boyle had balked at doing something for them there at the Mulder —"

"Or somewhere else," his wife said.

"Yes, exactly." Mr. Jackson brushed a bit of lint off his fedora, which sat upon his knee. "Tell me more about this man Russell."

Mr. Carlo said, "He's a small man, ex-boxer. The sort who shoots first and asks questions later. The man's got something in his eyes that scares me."

Mr. Jackson thought it touching for a man in Mr. Carlo's position to admit that to them.

"Runs small-time loan sharking and bookie operations on the East Side. But his big thing is liquor. He has speakeasies all up and down the waterfront. Gets in trouble with the other gangs once in a while. But they generally leave him alone."

His wife said, "Why?"

Mr. Carlo seemed surprised. "Why?" He leaned back, hand to chin. "Hmm. That's a good question. I think the man's more interested in money than territory. He's never really bothered me." He seemed to have decided something. "I think the big operations don't consider him a threat."

Mrs. Jackson said, "Are you on good enough terms with," she gestured around with her hand, "that lot to find out whether one of them did it?"

"I can try," Mr. Carlo said. Then he relaxed, just a bit. "But I know Mabel Franklin. She's a hitter for hire."

21

All Mr. Jackson could do was to stare at he man. "Really."

Mr. Carlo nodded, with a look on his face that suggested he'd had her do some work for him in the past. "If she'd been hanging around the Mulder, I'd expect she had a target there."

Mr. Jackson expected his wife to be surprised, or perhaps even alarmed.

But instead, she said, "If you can set up a meeting, I'd like to talk with her."

"Heh," said Mr. Carlo. "This'll be interesting."

They arrived at the Myriad Hotel, and Harry came round to open Mr. Carlo's door. But Mr. Carlo waved him away. "Just dropping off."

"Yes, sir." Harry opened the door for Mr. Jackson and his wife.

Once they got out of the car, Mr. Jackson remembered the conversation he'd had with Duchess Cordelia. He took his wife's arm. "Let's wait here a bit."

His wife nodded, taking out a cigarette.

"Why do you want to speak with Mabel Franklin?"

His wife snorted softly. "She sounds like a professional. There's no way she'd be seen out in public, in front of over a hundred people, with the man she was hired to hit, on the night she planned to kill him. So if she was there —"

"She likely saw the killer."

His wife nodded.

The couple stood looking out past Lake Shore Drive, past the waterfront, out over the icy lake. Cars came and went, the valets and bellhops moving to and fro.

Once the rush passed and Harry returned to his post, Mr. Jackson said to his wife, "Over here."

Harry, the Myriad's new Head Valet, was a young man with red hair, who grinned when the couple approached. "What can I do for you?"

Mr. Jackson said, "The to-do downstairs the other night. I hear your neighbor was there."

Harry chuckled. "I thought Duchess Cordelia was listening in." He crossed his arms. "Well, what do you want to know?"

Mr. Jackson shrugged. "What all did he tell you? About the murder, I mean."

Harry looked completely surprised, his arms dropping to his side. "I think he would have said if he saw that. But there were way too many people in there for him to have seen much."

"Well, he saw the young lady slap him," Mrs. Jackson said. "Did he see the man with anyone else?"

Harry shrugged. "You'd have to ask him." He peered at Mr. Jackson. "I doubt he'd talk to you on his own." He gestured with his chin. "Let me see if he'll meet up with the both of us about it."

Mr. Jackson felt quite pleased. "Splendid idea."

***

The couple went to their rooms, and without even taking their shoes off, cast themselves upon Mrs. Jackson's bed. Bessie came jumping up on the bed to lie between them.

"What a day," Mrs. Jackson said. "Do you think they'll be able to protect little Trixie?"

"Carlo? I imagine so."

Recalling the conversation in the first cab, she felt a certain anxiety for the young woman and her family. If this Mr. Russell learned that Trixie had been speaking to Mr. Carlo ...

"There's nothing more we can do for her," Mr. Jackson said. "Sooner or later, we have to trust him."

She sighed, relaxing. "You're entirely right, as usual."

He chuckled. "But I've decided to pay him what we owe in its entirety. That way, if we need to leave —"

How thoughtful! She rolled to face him. "We won't be bogged down by detail."

He laughed. "Or worse, have Carlo's men after us for the bill." He gazed up towards the ceiling. "But it's been quite the adventure getting this all together. I'll have the money transferred tomorrow."

The room was quite warm. She slid her hand under her pillow, savoring its coolness. "But we won't leave just yet, will we?"

He rolled towards her, getting up to lean upon his elbow. "Certainly not! We have such a lovely hideaway here. And I shouldn't like to leave our friends."

This amused her. "How is George getting on?"

"Busy. Nowhere near saving enough to travel with us." He laughed softly, lying back upon his pillows. "He's young. Likes to enjoy himself. I was the same at his age."

Mrs. Jackson hadn't known him at all when he was George's age, other than unsavory rumor. "I'm glad he's doing well."

"I'm going to suggest he buy property," Mr. Jackson said. "Something he can rent out. That'll help matters."

This seemed a good idea.

"He'd certainly be able to get a loan for it, either from the bank or his father."

Mr. Jackson went on like this for a while, as she lay watching him make plans for their next trip.

But that sounded a long way off.

Of course — as usual — her Mr. Jackson was right: Mr. Carlo knew the dangers here much better than either of them ever could.

"And I have something in mind," he said, which made her listen, "just in case." He turned just his head to face her. "Ever fancied a trip out West?"

She shrugged. "Never considered it."

He rolled towards her, going up on one elbow again, his face animated. "What if we bought property out that way? No one would ever imagine us going there!"

She considered it. "What sort of property?"

"What sort of property would you like?"

She gazed at the ceiling. "A big place. Somewhere we could grow a garden. With room for puppies to run. But something useful, that made the place we go to better." She looked over at him. "I wouldn't want to become a burden on anyone."

He nodded soberly. "That's a good idea." He lay upon his pillow, still facing her, his beautiful dark eyes wide. "A nice quiet place for us to retire."

She laughed softly. "Retire? What nonsense is this? You're only four and thirty!"

"We've no need to leave just yet." A wry smile lay upon his lips. "Which is fortunate, as I've just conceived the plan. It'd be many years before such a grand and lovely place might even be found, much less fashioned into what we wanted."

She snuggled into her pillow. "Good. Because for now, I'm quite fond of my life here."

22

As promised, Mr. Carlo's bill came sliding under the door shortly before dinner. After Mr. Jackson retrieved it, the couple peered at it together.

It seemed quite reasonable, with notation of "50% off for services rendered" above the total. A fair compromise, all things considered.

"Good grief," his wife exclaimed. "Have we spent that much? How will we pay for all this?"

He smiled at her. "Prices are overly high here, but the money here is much better than back home." He rested his arm upon her shoulders and kissed her forehead. "This is but a drop in one of many accounts."

She let out a breath. "I never imagined. However did you get all this money?"

"Sound investments, since I was little more than a boy. Never risking more than I could bear to lose, and making a great many friends of those who might help."

She stared at him in astonishment. "But —"

"But nothing. I've never taken a dime from anything criminal, except perhaps the inheritance I begged from my father. Back then, I had no idea what he was really up to. I was indeed the prodigal son, yet on returning home rich, I hardly received so much as a kind word." He sighed. "I suppose the circumstances made it difficult. But I wish we could have parted on better terms before he died."

His wife nodded.

"Have no fears about money, dear girl. We'd have to go through a lifetime of spending to match what I have now, even if not a penny more was added to it."

Her head rested upon his shoulder, and he felt her arm go round him. And he felt so grateful for his wife beside him, his friends, even for the little dog scratching at his leg to be walked. His life was very good.

***

Mr. Vienna and Mrs. Knight came that evening to dress the couple for dinner, and after checking on Bessie and her pups (who were all sleeping), the couple took the elevator down to the lobby.

As the couple approached the dining room, the Head Clerk, Mr. Francis. moved towards them. "Mr. Carlo asks if he might meet with you."

Mr. Jackson wasn't sure what to say. "Right now?"

"Yes, sir. He has dinner set up in the conference room."

"Oh," Mr. Jackson felt surprised. "Then of course."

Taking his wife's hand, he followed Mr. Francis to the door beside the front desk to the room they'd been questioned in the first morning they'd arrived here. But this time the table had dinner set upon it, with platters on the sideboard and the young waiter he'd met a few days before standing by. "What an unexpected surprise!"

"It smells wonderful," his wife said.

After they'd eaten and Floyd had cleared everything away, Mr. Carlo came in.

Which Mr. Jackson thought odd. But he rose to shake the man's hand. "A pleasure to see you!"

"And you." Everyone seated, Mr. Carlo waved Floyd away. Once the young man left, he said, "So about our mutual little friend and her family: all is well."

Mr. Jackson said, "That's a relief."

"And about your question, Mrs. Jackson, I've asked around a bit. Russell wouldn't see me, but everyone else I've asked denies anything to do with it." He scoffed. "It's a silly thing to do, in front of a crowd like that."

True, Mr. Jackson thought. A back alley or poorly lit street corner seemed much more likely. "But something went on between Russell and Boyle, wouldn't you say?"

His wife nodded. "I forgot to tell you: I made some calls while you and Bessie were out on your walk. Apparently, Mr. Russell has started paying the tabloids for news articles about his men, to help his operation gain respectability."

Mr. Jackson stretched. "Seems strange to go to all that work if you're planning to kill a man."

"Well, sir," said Mr. Carlo, "with your permission, your wife and I will learn the truth of all this." He turned to her. "Miss Franklin has agreed to meet tomorrow afternoon."

"That's fine," Mr. Jackson said. "I have some things to take care of tomorrow in any case."

"Very good," said Mr. Carlo. "Meet in front at two."

The couple returned to their parlor. To their surprise, Sergeant Nestor sat perfectly comfortably at their table.

"Good grief, Nestor," Mr. Jackson said. "What are you doing in here?"

"Well, I needed to speak with you. The front desk said you and Carlo were in a meeting. Since apparently I don't have the clout to get a desk clerk to interrupt said meeting, I found a maid to let me in. I figured you'd show up here sooner or later."

"And here we are," said Mr. Jackson, more than a little perturbed. "What do you want?"

"Don't be cross," he said cheerfully. "You've got to admit this is much nicer than the station. And I couldn't resist taking another peek at your puppies. I think we will take the dark brown one, when it's old enough." He gestured for them to move closer. "Please, sit down."

Glancing at his wife — who seemed merely amused at the situation rather than disturbed by it — they sat. Mr. Jackson said, "I presume you have some news?"

"If the one person who seems to know our dead man disappearing along with her mother is news."

Oh, dear, he thought. They'd completely forgotten to tell him.

Sergeant Nestor peered at them. "But I get the feeling this isn't news to you."

"Forgive us," Mrs. Jackson said. "We have news of our own. Miss Quinlan told us about Mr. Russell's involvement, and we feared for their safety."

The sergeant shrugged. "Everyone knows Russell owns the Mulder. The tough part is pinning anything on him."

Mr. Jackson leaned forward. "Miss Quinlan knows of meetings that went on with her Mr. Boyle and Mr. Russell, along with the names of some of Russell's men. Not sure if that'll help, but —"

"We know who they are," the sergeant said. "We know where they meet. I doubt she knows anything worth mentioning, and even if she did, I'd not like to put a speakeasy barmaid in front of a jury."

"Well," Mr. Jackson said, feeling a bit at sea, "the only other news is that a woman named Mabel Franklin could be involved."

Sergeant Nestor groaned, hand on his forehead.

Mrs. Jackson said, "So you know her."

"Yeah, we've met." The prospect of dealing with her seemed to daunt him. "The woman's got a whole cast of characters ready to give her an alibi at any moment. I'd have the phone in my hand with her dead on the slab in front of me and twenty gals would swear she was right there at their house." He shook his head. "Even if she didn't have half the mobsters in the city owing her, there's no way to convict." He looked at him. "Please don't tell me she did this."

"We don't think so," Mr. Jackson said. "But Mr. Carlo and my wife are going to meet with her tomorrow."

Sergeant Nestor raised his eyebrows. "Oh?" A laugh burst from him. "To be a fly on the wall at that meeting!"

Mr. Jackson felt quite amused.

His wife said, "Miss Quinlan saw Miss Franklin with Mr. Boyle earlier that evening. It's why Trixie slapped him. So it's very possible Miss Franklin saw the woman that killed him."

"Hmm," said the sergeant. "And you think she'll tell you if she did?"

Mr. Jackson wondered that as well.

His wife hesitated, just a bit. "If I were to work as a ... what might one call it? Woman assassin? Then I'd want my pay. The very fact she was there with him in public meant she didn't plan to do the deed that night, but at some later date. So whoever did kill him just cost her a lot of money." Her face grew thoughtful. "As a matter of fact, she might be after our murderess too."

23

Sergeant Nestor leaned forward. "Then we have to find this woman before Mabel Franklin does. I want her arrested, not dead in the street!"

"We'll do our best," Mr. Jackson said. "But if Miss Franklin gets the idea we're working with you, she won't tell my wife a thing."

"You have a point," the sergeant said. "I'll stay away from now on."

Good, Mr. Jackson thought, still annoyed at the man's intrusion. "Anything else we should know?"

"I learned more about the man Boyle embezzled from," Sergeant Nestor said. "But I'm afraid that turned out to be a dead end."

"What do you mean?"

"Victor Hoffmann had put his — and his family's — life savings into the company. The theft ruined them all. The company had to liquidate. The man went into bankruptcy. The cost of the trial threw his family into poverty. I tracked down his assistant, who now works at a local jeweler. He told me Mr. Hoffmann was despondent, particularly as the trial dragged on and the bills began to pile up. Mr. Hoffmann's no suspect: he took his own life before Boyle ever saw a day of prison."

Mrs. Jackson gasped.

Sergeant Nestor nodded. "His parents are alive, but have alibis for the evening. He has a younger sister named Pauline, but she married and moved away some time ago. There seems to be bad blood between them: I don't think the parents approved of her husband."

Mr. Jackson said, "Did you happen to ask as to the sister's married name? Or where she moved to?"

"She lives in Oak Lawn now. She wasn't home when I called on them, but I spoke with her husband, a Mr. Milton Shapiro." The sergeant shrugged. "Perfectly respectable businessman. He swears she was at home with him on New Years' Eve."

Mr. Jackson felt close to the answer. "That phone number on the notepad — who was Boyle going to call?"

"No one's answering the number, and the address is an abandoned building. But we found some cigarette butts which looked recent."

Another mystery.

His wife said, "What about the bullet? I presume you found the shell casing."

"Yep," Sergeant Nestor said. "A twenty-five caliber automatic Colt pistol cartridge. You can buy them anywhere. The particular gun it was used in hasn't been involved in any other crimes."

Mr. Jackson said, "What about Mr. D'Angelo? He claimed he'd never seen Mr. Boyle before then. But I've found two people already who saw him there each of the two nights earlier."

"Who?"

Mr. Jackson said, "A waitress, as well as one of the band members."

His wife leaned forward. "That bartender has to know something. What else did you learn about him?"

Sergeant Nestor said, "My man that brought the bartender home said Mr. D'Angelo lived by himself in a one-room apartment."

"That sounds very much like poor Trixie," his wife said quietly.

"He pays his rent, keeps to himself, doesn't cause trouble." Sergeant Nestor looked uncertain. "I've had him in for questioning once already. I'm concerned we might lose our killer if he starts thinking we suspect him and calls her."

"But —"

"I've got men on him," the sergeant said. "He's not going anywhere."

They were missing something, of that Mr. Jackson felt certain. But what? "There had to be a reason Mr. Boyle suddenly stopped going to his speakeasy." He turned to his wife. "Perhaps your meeting with Miss Franklin tomorrow will bring us at the very least, that answer."

24

They met her outside a stylish bistro in the Loop. Tall, willowy, brown-haired, with an angular face. Her high-fashion red woolen dress hung from her slender body in just the right way, this year's wide-brimmed hat angled perfectly on her head.

Miss Mabel Franklin wasn't exactly unattractive, Mrs. Jackson thought. It was just that she didn't care if anyone in the world thought so.

A certain kind of man found that tremendously appealing.

Mr. Carlo was clearly that kind of man. He seemed changed in her presence: tongue-tied, almost shy.

Mabel Franklin came close to ignoring him.

"So it is really you," she said to Mrs. Jackson. "The queen of the South here, in the flesh!" She grasped Mrs. Jackson's hand with black silken gloves which went to her elbow (presumably better when shooting someone), her eyes positively aglow. "And you're really here!"

Mrs. Jackson found this amusing. "In the flesh."

They moved inside, to a table apparently kept open just for her. "Please," Miss Franklin said, "sit down." After they sat, she said, "What can I do for you?"

"Mark Boyle. Why were you going to kill him?"

"Oh, I don't know. I never ask, and they never tell." A wistful look came over the woman's face. "The one who got away." She let out a small, bitter laugh. "I could've used the money. A thousand dollars gone," she snapped the fingers of her right hand, "just like that."

"So you don't know why he was there instead of at the Mulder."

She shrugged, shaking her head.

Mr. Carlo sounded upset. "This woman's ruining my business! I'll pay you that much right now if you let me take care of this myself."

Without so much as looking his way, Miss Franklin held out a gloved hand. After fumbling a bit, Mr. Carlo deposited a thick wad into it.

Did they have to worry about him now, too?

Mrs. Jackson leaned forward. "You haven't made a name for yourself by being stupid. So I know you weren't planning on killing him that night." She leaned back. "Tell me what happened."

Miss Franklin rolled her eyes, giving an impatient sigh. "He asked me to dinner. We'd just been there two nights before, so I knew the place. We get seated at a table, order. We'd been there a while, had a couple of drinks. Suddenly, he gets up, goes over to this ... child, really. A pretty little thing, but much too young to be there. They argue, she slaps him. When I ask what's going on, he won't answer. So I go freshen up. The place was crowded already: there was quite a line. When I get back, this brown-haired tart was all over him! I told him you can't be doing this: you gotta pick. He told me if I didn't like it to leave." She shrugged. "So I did. Me and my girls went to a movie."

"Tell me about the girl," Mrs. Jackson said.

"Hmm ... about my height. Brown eyes ..."

"Left-handed?"

Miss Franklin considered this for a moment. "Yes, I do believe so."

That had to be his killer. "What was she wearing?"

"A black sequined dress." She sighed. "A pity you're going to kill her. She has style."

25

While Mrs. Jackson was otherwise occupied, Mr. Jackson and several of the maids carefully transported the puppies in their blanket — supported by a large tray — down the elevator to the veterinary's. Bessie followed closely behind.

That accomplished, he and George Neuberg went to the fitness club. They played several rousing games of tennis, then sat in the sauna.

Few men were there at this time of day. So they reclined in a sunny corner, completely to themselves other than the occasional waiter, sipping iced tea.

George said, "Might I ask something?"

"Of course," Mr. Jackson said.

"You tell me that you're involved with not only finding a murderess, but keeping an assassin from finding her first."

Mr. Jackson laughed. "Yes, well said."

"But why? Why are you doing this?"

He considered this for a moment. "When I was a boy, someone I very much cared about was murdered."

George gaped at him.

"I tried for years to learn why he was killed, but never did." At this, he felt more than a bit melancholy. "Perhaps in this case, I can." He shrugged. "Or perhaps not. But what I really mean to say is ... if I were killed, I'd want someone to care enough to find out why."

George grasped his hand tightly for a moment, then gave it a couple of short pats. "I know you'll succeed: I can feel it."

Mr. Jackson felt his spirits quite renewed, "I'm grateful to hear it. Right now, I feel at a loss."

"If there's any way I can help —"

"Certainly I'll let you know." He sipped at his iced tea. "Do you think you'd ever like to go out West?"

George shrugged. "Never even considered it."

"Well, my wife and I love it here, every bit. But sooner or later —"

"You'll have to move on. I get it." He fell silent for a while. "And you want me to go with you."

"Sure. Why not?"

"Where, out West?"

"Oh, I don't know." He chuckled to himself. "I haven't even talked to my men about it yet." He put the tall glass on the little table between them. "I was just thinking of the future."

George smiled to himself. "That's very kind of you. And in theory, of course I'd want to tag along. But I couldn't possibly say one way or the other until I knew the details."

"Fair enough." For now, it was only a thought, an idea of a definite place that was all their own. "What kind of place would you like?"

George put his hands behind his head, gazing at the ceiling. "Some place busy, full of people and things to do. Cosmopolitan, if you will."

There was one such place that came to mind. But would they be able to have land in that big city where puppies could run? What if he couldn't find a place with what everyone wanted in one spot?

George laughed, turning his head towards him. "Don't mind me. If you gotta choose, go with what your wife wants. From what my Pa tells me, that makes everyone happier."

***

On the way back to the Hotel, Mrs. Jackson stopped by Ophelia's boarding house. Mrs. Kilpatrick, a dumpy old lady of perhaps seventy, opened the door. "Oh, yeah, she's here. Come on in and I'll fetch her."

Leaving Mrs. Jackson in the front hall, she yelled up, "Ophelia! There's some lady to see you!"

Ophelia Denton came running down the narrow wooden stair in a day dress and stockinged feet, then stopped when she saw her. "Oh!"

Mrs. Jackson almost laughed. "May I come up, or would you like to go for a walk?"

By this time, every door was open, as girls peeked out to see the commotion.

Ophelia blushed. "You can come up if you like."

So Mrs. Jackson went up the creaking staircase to Ophelia's room. One room, with posters, dried flowers, bits of dance card, portraits, ticket stubs, and other memorabilia covering the walls. A narrow closet hung open, holding various dresses, with three pairs of shoes at the bottom. The bed was unmade and stockings lay upon the floor.

"Oh!" The girl rushed to move aside the mess and cover the bed. "Want to sit down?"

A narrow bit of table was pushed up against one wall with two chairs. Mrs. Jackson selected one. "Here is perfectly fine."

Ophelia plopped herself upon the other. "If I knew you were coming, I would've cleaned up."

"Don't fret yourself," Mrs. Jackson said. "How are you? I thought I'd stop by."

Ophelia gave a one-shoulder shrug. "I have to work tonight."

"A pity."

The girl let out a short laugh. "Not really; it pays the rent." That seemed to spark some memory, because her face changed, became bold. "No, I like my job just fine."

Mrs. Jackson smiled to herself. "It's good to be doing what you love."

"Are you feeling all right?"

Mrs. Jackson nodded. "I still have a bit of a cough, but it's not nearly so bad as it was."

Ophelia lowered her voice. "Did you really go see that awful woman?"

"I did! She was actually very nice." Mrs. Jackson related the conversation they'd had. "I thought it was funny, seeing Mr. Carlo like that."

"But ..." Ophelia leaned forward to speak at a whisper. "Aren't you scared she's gonna tell someone who you are?"

"Her? Not at all. I mean, I don't know for sure! But just think of it. Any of the mobsters she tells either won't care or be glad I got out. Less competition for them."

Ophelia's face grew thoughtful. "Oh ..."

"And if she went to the Feds, well, that'd be the end of her career!"

"But shouldn't you tell the police you met her?"

"I already did. Before I even went. They know her, but they can't put her in jail. They don't have any proof."

"That's not right," Ophelia said. "For her to just get away with doing stuff like that."

Mrs. Jackson let out a sigh. "I know. But sooner or later, she'll make a mistake. And then she'll get caught. Criminals always do."

26

When Mrs. Jackson returned to the Myriad Hotel, Bessie came running out to greet her.

Mr. Jackson had tea and sandwiches set up for them in the parlor. He sat at the small tea-table near the window reading the news. "Ah, there you are!"

She kissed his cheek and sat across from him at the tea-table. "Did you and George have fun?"

"We most certainly did." He closed the paper, set it down. "Learn anything interesting?"

"Well, as a matter of fact, yes. Mark Boyle had invited Mabel Franklin to dinner. And guess what? They'd been there two nights earlier."

Mr. Jackson nodded. "The three women were actually just two."

"Yes! And like Trixie said, Miss Franklin saw the girl slap Mr. Boyle. But then a tall, left-handed, brown-haired woman wearing a black sequined dress forced herself into the scene while Miss Franklin was in the powder room. When Miss Franklin returned, there was an argument —"

"Naturally."

"And Miss Franklin left." She leaned forward. "Mr. Carlo has paid her the money she lost in order to, and I quote, 'take care of this myself'."

"So now we have Carlo to worry about."

"Yes." She got up, went to the food, got some of the small sandwiches and some tea, and returned to her chair. "Other than that, well, she didn't know why they wanted the man dead, or why he'd prefer to meet at Carlo's place rather than Russell's." She shrugged. "Apparently they just tell her who and she does the job."

Mr. Jackson nodded. "And since she didn't do it, she hasn't told you anything to implicate herself in anything else." He sipped at his cup, which from the smell of it, was coffee. "Smart."

"She is, very much so. I wonder how she got into such a life."

"Well," Mr. Jackson said, "I don't suppose that's something we'll ever know."

"Did you ever get a chance to meet with Harry's neighbor?"

"As a matter of fact, I did: they were out front when I arrived from the fitness club." He hesitated. "I don't know if it's even worth mentioning."

She could tell by his face the encounter hadn't been a pleasant one. "Oh, dear. What happened?"

He let out a breath. "Unpleasant young European fellow with a terrible thick accent." An ironic laugh burst from him. "If he would've been the remotest bit polite, we could've just conversed in German."

This amused her: he knew more languages than anyone she'd ever met. "Oh, you scoundrel: you let the poor man struggle!"

"Hmph," he said, sounding more than a bit annoyed. "He deserved it." He shook his head. "He wouldn't even look at me, and only would speak to Harry. As if I weren't even there!"

She sighed, taking his hand. "I'm sorry."

"He told us much the same as you did. But then he said something interesting. Right before midnight, the young woman took something from the man's pocket."

"His wallet?" Could this have been a robbery? But only the wallet was gone: his money hadn't been taken.

"I thought perhaps instead she might have taken the lighter. We never found it. But then the man had very little on him, so who knows?" He held his cup midair, face thoughtful. "There is one way to perhaps learn what's going on at the Mulder, though."

"Surely you don't mean —"

"Yes, dear girl. George doesn't work tonight." He set his cup down, giving her a broad smile. "I think I'll take him out on the town."

27

It took a bit of doing for Mr. Jackson to get the codes for entrance into the Mulder. Fortunately, the place only changed the codes once a month, and Trixie Quinlan was able to provide them.

The girl's aunt's home was smallish on the inside, but with plenty of room out back. She had four sons, and the sounds of them tumbling around outside in the twilight echoed through the hallway as Miss Trixie told them the information.

As Mr. Jackson and Mr. Carlo returned to the Hotel, Mr. Carlo said, "Now, you're just there to look. There could be any number of reasons Boyle didn't want to drink there. So try to stay out of trouble."

Mr. Jackson thought this quite amusing. "Trouble? Me? I am the very soul of discretion." It was likely he wouldn't discover anything at all. But if something was wrong, he felt sure he could sniff it out.

"Well, good luck," Mr. Carlo said. "You're not going alone, are you?"

"No, not at all — I'm bringing a friend along."

Mr. Carlo nodded. "Good."

Mr. Jackson felt relieved that Carlo hadn't asked who would accompany him. Strictly speaking, George wasn't supposed to fraternize with the guests like this. But what Mr. Carlo didn't know wouldn't hurt him.

The Mulder was, on the face of it, a little hole-in-the-wall restaurant on the South Side, with "the best pizza in town". But when Mr. Jackson asked for a double burger with Worcestershire sauce and a ginger ale float, the man led them to a door and down a winding stair.

Mr. Jackson turned to George. "Pretty fun, eh?"

The man at the door below was lit by a single bulb overhead. "Need anything else?"

Miss Trixie had said they'd say this to you if they thought you might be a cop. Mr. Jackson grinned at the man. "A million bucks would help."

The men tensed up.

"But a blue garter works just fine."

Both the men laughed. The man who'd led them downstairs said, "You're all right, Mister." Opening the door, the second man gestured for them to enter.

Between the Myriad Hotel's speakeasy and Club Patruni (where Miss Ophelia Denton danced), this lay in-between in size and capacity. A band played up front, and a woman sang. It was only half-full this early on a Friday night, and they were led past the bar to a smallish table off to one side.

Mr. Jackson tried not to stare at the waitresses: their skirts went up past their knees!

"Heh," George said. "A leg man, are you?"

"I never considered it." He felt his cheeks burn. "I suppose I am." He'd never had a second glance at any woman other than his wife before.

Then he smiled to himself. His wife was lovely, at home, and waiting for his return. Hopefully they'd find out what they needed to know here quickly, so he might get back to her.

A waiter wearing a full apron came by. "What'll you have, sirs?"

"Whiskey sour for me," said George.

Mr. Jackson said, "Whatever you've got on tap."

"Coming right up."

A companionable silence fell. Mr. Jackson surveyed the room. The staff seemed happy. The customers conversed in a relaxed manner, and drank without ill effect. What could possibly be going on? "Do you see anything at all odd here?"

"Nope."

Mr. Jackson felt pleased with the evening so far. With the promotion to Headwaiter, he and George didn't get to spend nearly as much time with each other as they used to. But once George had some men trained up, he'd have more time off.

George said, "I thought you didn't drink."

"I'm not sure if my grandfather was that religious, or if he just thought it unsafe, but he forbade any kind of alcohol on his property. So I never got the taste for it. But

I didn't think it wise to stand out by not ordering." Mr. Jackson shrugged. "No one says I have to drink it."

George laughed. "Right you are."

The bartender didn't seem to be making anything. Rather, he stood there talking to the waiter.

George sighed. "I wish they'd hurry up; I'm thirsty."

"Don't be in such a rush," said Mr. Jackson, but privately, he agreed. What could they possibly be discussing?

Just then, every door in the place — some he hadn't even noticed — opened up, and dozens of men wearing suits streamed in, holding guns. One called out, "This is a Federal raid!"

Mr. Jackson sat there, for the first time in a while struck silent with terror. This was a scene from his worst nightmares.

The Feds had caught him.

28

The Agents began grabbing customers, barmaids, waiters, dragging them out.

Mr. Jackson's mind raced.

Had they actually done anything illegal? He didn't know. If they pressed charges, though, started to dig deeper, then they might learn about his wife.

He couldn't have that happen.

What could he do? What should he say?

Then an answer came to him.

It wasn't ideal by any means. But if they got the right sort of men questioning them, it might work. "George, say nothing. Not even a word. If they insist, tell them you won't answer without me present."

"But —"

"Do you trust me?"

The men moved from table to table, getting closer.

George nodded.

"Even if I might say or do something that harms your reputation?"

Their eyes met. "I trust you with my life," George said. "Do what you must."

Mr. Jackson and George were frisked, put into a truck, then taken to a Federal holding area with everyone else in the bar, including the women. They all sat in a large, grimy cell for some time.

And he worried.

If my idea doesn't work, what then?

Calm yourself, he thought. You have lawyers. Better yet, you're married. You can't be forced to testify against her. You can't even be forced to give her real name.

Unless they saw the flier, they might not even realize who she was.

But if he did get out of this mess tonight, though, home and safe ... what should he do?

Should he take his wife and leave?

No, he decided. She'd be heartbroken, terrified, yet again wrenched from what had become home and family. To do this to her twice in one year ... it seemed inconceivable.

I'll wait, he thought. See how this plays out. She doesn't need to know.

Eventually, Hector Jackson and George Neuberg were put across a table from two stern-looking men. The men sat far from each other, yet kept glancing at each other, and at George.

My lovely George, Mr. Jackson thought, feeling a bit more hope with each glance the two men made. This just might work.

A third man stood at the door behind them, presumably to intimidate them, to block the door in case they might run, or perhaps both. Mr. Jackson had seen these tactics before, but he hoped George wasn't too unnerved by it all.

So far, no one had spoken.

Perhaps these Feds thought the two would become daunted by the silence and tell everything. Now he felt glad he'd warned George to say nothing.

Finally, the man Mr. Jackson had pegged as the leader spoke. "I'm Special Agent Andrew Chapman," he gestured to the man beside him. "This is Special Agent Claude Haley," he gestured at the man at the door, "and that is Special Agent Fred Scott. Do you know why you're here?"

Mr. Jackson shrugged, heart pounding. "I presume it's illegal to sit in a speakeasy."

Agent Chapman frowned. "Not exactly." He glanced at George.

"Well, since we'd only just arrived," Mr. Jackson said, "then I can't imagine why we're here."

"You know," Agent Chapman said, recovering his composure, "I can't imagine why you were there. A rich businessman staying at one of the premier hotels in Chicago along with the same hotel's Headwaiter, in some dingy speakeasy on the South Side?"

"I'm impressed," said Mr. Jackson. "So I'll tell you why we were there." With that, he told them about the murder in the Myriad Hotel, the current facts of the matter, and how curiosity about what could possibly be going on at the Mulder brought them there to see for themselves. "Sergeant Benjamin Nestor of the Chicago Police Department can corroborate all this."

Agent Chapman nodded to Agent Scott, who left, locking the door behind him. Then he leaned his elbows on the table. "So you're assisting in a murder investigation? Why?"

"Well, the owner of the hotel asked me to. I've assisted him before."

"I see." It was fairly obvious that the man did not. "Mr. Carlo." He scoffed. "We've heard of him."

Mr. Jackson nodded.

"Well, we'll talk with this Sergeant Nestor, then we'll decide what to do with you." Then he glanced over at George. "You need anything?"

Mr. Jackson put his hand on George's. "We'd appreciate it if we might be kept in the same room. We're such very good pals, you see."

"Ugh!" The Agents looked appalled, drawing back.

Agent Chapman stood, obviously annoyed. "All right; we're done here. Both of you clowns, out!"

On the sidewalk outside, Mr. Jackson and George looked at each other for a moment, then broke down laughing. "The look on his face," George said. "That was inspired."

Mr. Jackson couldn't stop laughing until they'd flagged down a taxi, collapsing into it. "Oh, goodness." He wiped a tear from his eye. "This has been the most fun I've had in a very long time."

29

When Mr. Jackson arrived back at the Hotel to a cheerful, sleepy wife and her happy little dogs, he didn't mention anything to her about the Feds. "It seemed like a perfectly ordinary bar. I'm not sure at all why Mr. Boyle feared to go there."

Satisfied, his wife went peacefully back to bed. He didn't fall asleep for some time.

The next morning, as the sky was just beginning to pale, Mr. Jackson sat up in bed, brooding. This wasn't over yet.

The Feds knew where he and George were. If they should inquire further ....

Just wait, he told himself. Making any sudden moves now would only make them suspicious.

He took a deep breath, let it out. No sense worrying over something that might not even happen.

His wife opened her eyes, turning to him with a smile. "You're up early."

He smiled at her. "I suppose I am. Did you rest well?"

"I did." She got up on an elbow. "You look worried. Is anything wrong?"

He shook his head, leaned over to kiss her forehead. He hated lying to her. But what might he say of the truth? "I wish now that we hadn't gone to the Mulder. If we should have to do more investigation, well, now they know our faces."

She nodded, lips pursed, then sat up, hugging her knees. "Well if so, we can ask the sergeant to send his own men there next time."

Mr. Jackson let out an amused laugh. "I can just imagine his budget officer's face on that regard. From the sound of it, the Chicago Police Department barely has enough men to respond to the crime scenes, much less do much about them."

After his wife had left and before Mr. Vienna was to arrive, Sergeant Nestor knocked at their parlor door. The man looked none too pleased. "What possessed you to go to the Mulder, of all places, alone?"

"George Neuberg was with me," Mr. Jackson said.

Sergeant Nestor scowled. "Ugh." He stormed into the room. "You're lucky the both of you are still alive."

That seemed odd. "Here, sit down." Once the sergeant had seated himself at the rosewood table, Mr. Jackson said, "Why do you say that? What's wrong?"

"You know why the Feds are interested in the Mulder? Because it's been the center of a bad liquor operation. Dozens of people have died so far."

"Oh." Mr. Jackson felt chagrined. "Good thing neither of us had a chance to drink."

The sergeant let out a short laugh. "They'd not stay around long if they began poisoning their own customers. But they've sold bad liquor to smaller operations to try to drive them out of business. If they'd learned you were with Carlo, they might have killed you both, thinking you to be his spies."

"Whew." They'd been very lucky. "I had no idea."

Sergeant Nestor scoffed. "The Agent I spoke with last night quizzed me for almost an hour about what I might know about it." He laughed then. "Whatever you did to get them to throw you out must have really angered him. He ranted about 'those upstart young men' for a full twenty minutes."

"Heh," Mr. Jackson said. "Fortunately, I found myself in front of two gentlemen who had yet to admit to their true hearts' desires. Naturally, I took advantage."

The sergeant raised an eyebrow. "I have no idea what you're talking about."

"Never you mind." Since the Agents thought he and George were together, they evidently never even considered that he might also have a wife. And suddenly, in a flash, Mr. Jackson realized something. "The phone number. Boyle had gone to the Feds!"

"Yes!" The sergeant sounded impressed. "And when he disappeared, they felt forced to raid the Mulder before Russell destroyed the evidence."

"Did he? I mean, did they find anything?"

The sergeant shrugged. "If so, they didn't tell me."

"Please don't say anything to my wife about the Feds. She's under enough strain as it is."

Sergeant Nestor nodded soberly.

Mr. Jackson let out a relieved breath. "So what are we going to do about Ralph D'Angelo, the bartender? Mr. Carlo has said some things that make my wife and I think he's going to take matters into his own hands."

"Well, that's more than a little concerning," the sergeant said. He sat quietly for a moment. "I'll have my men put Mr. D'Angelo into protective custody. Come down to the station too if you like. Maybe this guy needs a different approach, and I think you can help."

30

When his wife returned from helping Monsieur with his rooftop gardens, when they'd been dressed for breakfast and their retainers had left, Mr. Jackson told her about Sergeant Nestor's visit. Of course, he left out the part about the Feds.

She seemed both surprised and confused. "So why was he here in the first place?"

"He heard that we went to the Mulder and was worried for us. This Mr. Russell sounds like the worst sort of man."

"I suppose." She had a slight frown. "I also called on Miss Trixie Quinlan at her aunt's house. That is to say, I telephoned. It must have been just after you left there. The missing wallet bothered me. What I learned was that he never carried one."

"Strange, although not all men do."

"Something's going on that I don't understand. If the killer did take the lighter, why?" Her frown grew deeper. "And the sergeant wants us to go to the police station right now ... why?"

He put a hand on her shoulder. "Trust me: it's nothing bad. He's worried about Carlo going after the bartender, and thinks that together, we might be able to persuade Mr. D'Angelo to talk."

His wife shook her head. "Something's not right."

"You're welcome to stay here if you prefer."

"No. It's not that." She took a deep breath, peering at him. "Are you lying to me?"

For some reason, he felt moved. "Come sit closer."

So they sat beside each other on the sofa, and he wrapped his arms around her.

"Everything I've told you is true." How could he possibly say this? "But I left something out." He remembered how she reacted when they first arrived to even a hint of this, and he pulled her close. "You must promise not to be afraid. I would not lie to you in this: we are safe, and all is entirely well."

She looked up at him, eyes huge. "I trust you. But only if you tell me everything."

That made him smile. "When George and I went to the Mulder, we'd not been there ten minutes before the Feds arrived."

She gasped. "No."

"Oh, goodness, yes. Dozens of them. I felt terrified." With that, he told her the entire story: being dragged away, the long, frightening hours in the holding cell.

But then he told her about meeting the three Agents, and the way he and George tricked them. By the end, they were both laughing, with tears in their eyes.

He took her face in his hands. "I never wanted to lie to you. But you looked so happy when I came home. You slept so peacefully. I ... I didn't want to cause you more grief and fear." He took her hands. "You've gone through too much already."

She nodded slowly, her eyes upon his. "Thank you for telling me." She sighed, head downcast. "I understand so many things now, things I wish I would have before." Then she smiled. "If the sergeant thinks we can help in some way, then I'll be happy to."

***

So after breakfast, Mr. and Mrs. Jackson went down to the police station.

Mr. Ralph D'Angelo sat quietly in the holding room, clearly curious as to what had happened. "Do I need a lawyer?"

"Eventually, yes, you might," Sergeant Nestor said. "But right now, I'm more concerned about your safety." He leaned forward. "I think you know who killed that man. You were right there. I don't care how busy you were; you had to have seen at least some of what went on." Sergeant Nestor sat across the table from him. "Now, I don't know if you are trying to protect this woman because you care about her, or you're trying to protect her because you're in on it." He held up a hand at the man's protest. "But there's something you might not know: there's an assassin after her —"

The bartender seemed to notice the couple at that point. When he glanced at them, they both nodded.

Mr. D'Angelo's face turned a remarkable shade of greenish pale.

" — and we have to find her before they do. Or before Mr. Carlo or his men find you and decide to beat her name out of you." Sergeant Nestor leaned back. "That's why you're here: to keep you alive." He took a deep breath. "If you help us find her, you won't be charged with anything at all. You have my word."

The man hunched over the table, hands clasped together in front of him, and was silent for some time. "Okay," he finally said. "Yeah, I know her." He shut his eyes tightly. "She used to be my wife."

31

Mr. Jackson stared at the man. He found himself sitting beside the sergeant. "What happened?"

Mr. D'Angelo sighed, running his hands through his hair. "We married at sixteen, for love. Her parents didn't like it, but they let us live with them. Her parents became like parents to me. And I persuaded them to risk everything we had on an investment." He took a deep breath. "We lost it all. Then things got even worse." His eyes shut, and his lashes grew moist.

After a moment, he opened his eyes. "We had barely a thing to eat. The utilities turned off our lights, then our heat. We'd go out, me and my wife, to find sticks for the fireplace so we didn't freeze." His face twisted in anguish. "But then I learned her parents had sold their wedding rings to pay the mortgage." He let his hands drop to the table. "It was more than I could take! So I pretended I had a gun, and —"

"Robbed the grocery," Sergeant Nestor said.

Mr. Jackson felt his wife's hand on his shoulder, and he grasped it, feeling bleak.

Mr. D'Angelo shook his head, still staring at the table. "It only ended with me in prison. She divorced me, her family disowned me." He shrugged. "I'm not sure which hurts more."

They fell quiet for a moment.

"Mr. D'Angelo," the sergeant said. "What's your wife's name? We're very concerned for her safety. We have to find her before these people do."

He glanced at all of them. "She got remarried. Her name's Pauline Shapiro."

Sergeant Nestor rose. "Her husband lied to me! I'm going to go drag both of them in, right now."

"Wait." Mr. Jackson sat gazing at the bartender for a moment. If someone was watching the station. If someone knew Mr. D'Angelo was here. If anyone had followed him and his wife there ... this could turn ugly, fast. "I think I know a safer way for us all."

32

With each day's passing, Milton Shapiro felt more and more uneasy.

The police had come to their door asking where his wife had been on New Year's Eve. Of course, he'd said she was with him: it was his duty to protect her.

But she hadn't been there. She hadn't been home until close to dawn

She'd said she was going out with her friends. She was young, and pretty, and of course he let her go. It wasn't fair to keep a young woman from enjoying herself. When he asked her about it after the police left, she swore she'd been with her friends.

But now he wasn't so sure.

His mother had told him it was a mistake to marry a so much younger woman. "She'll find a young man and you'll be paying alimony, just you wait and see."

But this wasn't about where she'd been or who she'd been with anymore. They said a man was murdered.

Pauline refused to speak of it. But with each day that passed, she became more relaxed, almost happy. She wasn't even using the sleeping powder the doctor prescribed for her anymore.

And for some reason, it worried him.

So when the phone rang, he almost jumped from his chair, thinking it was the police come at last.

Instead, a deep, rich, soothing voice spoke: "This is Mr. Hector Jackson from KWY Radio in Chicago. Is this the home of Mrs. Pauline Shapiro?"

"It is. May I ask what this is about?"

"Certainly, sir. Do I have the pleasure of speaking with her husband?"

The man's voice was so impressive, well, he just had to answer. "Why, yes! I'm her husband."

Pauline poked her head around the corner. "What's going on?"

Milton gestured frantically for her to come close by, so she might hear, too. "My wife's on the line."

"Congratulations," Mr. Jackson said, "from KWY Radio in Chicago. You've won a brand new automobile!"

Milton felt stunned. "We have?"

He and his wife stared at each other. She said, "How did I win a car?"

"Well, ma'am," Mr. Jackson said, "if you didn't enter into the drawing, then someone must have put your name in."

Pauline looked flabbergasted. "I suppose so!"

"Congratulations, my dear. You've won a brand new Pierce Arrow Coupe, tax and license paid, with fuel for a year. A magnificent luxury vehicle, indeed! Now, all that's needed is for you and your husband to come to the Chicago Civic Auditorium at 3 P.M. tomorrow to pick it up. Make sure to bring your identification!"

Milton thought this sounded too good to be true. "When did this contest happen?"

"Oh, we've been having the drawing for weeks now," Mr. Jackson said. "To celebrate the inaugural season of KWY Radio in Chicago. You're the envy of the city!"

Milton got out a notepad and a pen. "You say your name is Jackson?"

"Yes, sir, Mr. Hector Jackson from KWY Radio, Chicago. I will tell you, sir, that the station is quite pleased a winner is coming all the way from Oak Lawn! A nice expansion of their audience, I must say."

"Yes, yes," Milton said distractedly, "of course. And 3 P.M. at the Chicago Civic Auditorium."

"Yes, sir. Would you like directions?"

"No, no," Milton said. "I know where it is."

"Splendid. It'll be a lovely day: a buffet, a few speeches from our director, and of course, the Pierce Arrow Coupe! You do drive, I take it?"

"Well, yes." They had a Model T. Perfectly respectable, to be sure, but nothing at all like what this man had described.

"Wonderful. Mr. and Mrs. Shapiro, we are really looking forward to meeting you."

Milton hung up the phone. He and his wife stared at each other.

Her face burst into smiles, and she flung her hands into the air. "Woo hoo!"

"Don't get too excited," Milton said. "This sounds like some kind of swindle." He picked up the receiver. "Connect me to KWY Radio, Chicago."

He called KWY Radio, he even called the Chicago Civic Auditorium. They agreed: didn't Mr. Hector Jackson have a marvelous voice? And yes, they were indeed giving away a car tomorrow.

So the next afternoon, Milton and his wife, excited and nervous both, got into their Sunday best and made the trip into downtown Chicago.

When they reached the Civic Auditorium, balloons and streamers festooned the front. A valet took their car. A beautiful woman with light brown skin, blue eyes, and bobbed black hair put a enormous bouquet into his wife's arms. "Congratulations!"

Milton could only gape at the spectacle. Attendants opened the doors.

Cheers erupted. Smiling faces were all around. Music poured forth. Mr. Jackson's voice came from overhead. A host of dressed-up couples mingled inside holding champagne glasses.

In the lobby stood a sparkling new auto!

Milton was surprised speechless. This was real!

Just then, an older man in street clothes stood beside him. "Mrs. Pauline Shapiro?"

Milton turned to his wife, who had a dazed look on her face. She focused on the older man. "Why, yes!"

The man, for some reason, looked sad. "I'm Sergeant Benjamin Nestor. You're under arrest for the murder of Mark Boyle."

33

Mr. Jackson switched off the microphone and turned to George Neuberg. "Tell your father thanks for loaning us the car."

George laughed. "He's gonna love this story."

In Mrs. Shapiro's purse lay a pearl-handled gun and a cast iron Pist-o-liter with a piece chipped off of the handle, both of which were taken from her by forensics men before the police proceeded further.

The couple rode with Sergeant Nestor down to the police station, and were allowed to watch — safely behind glass — as Milton and Pauline Shapiro were questioned. Or rather, as the two of them argued — both with each other and the lawyer Milton Shapiro had immediately called in.

Mr. D'Angelo sat in the corner, having been cautioned by the Sergeant not to say a word, no matter how his former wife might provoke him.

Pauline blurted out, "I don't deny any of it!"

"Mrs. Shapiro," the lawyer said, "I must urge you —"

"Oh, can it," she snapped. "He killed my brother. So I killed him."

"But sweetheart," Mr. Shapiro said. "He wasn't responsible for your brother's death!"

"Wait," Sergeant Nestor said, notebook open. "Please, all of you. Start from the beginning. We know your brother lost his business after Mr. Boyle stole his entire receipts from him. We know that during the trial, he took his life."

Pauline began to cry.

"But what we don't know is how you ended up here. Can you tell us anything more?" The sergeant turned to Pauline's lawyer. "She's already confessed. It'd help later on if she cooperates."

"I don't care what you do to me," she sobbed. "Victor was my brother! He'd been saving to start his business ever since I was a little girl. We gave him whatever his business needed. My husband and I, our parents, that man ruined us all. Ralph wouldn't have gone to jail if not for him."

"But you left him when he did," the sergeant said.

"Yeah, I left him," Pauline said. "My parents wanted me to. They had set me up with Milton here." She glanced at him. "No offense, darling, but you had money and they were dead broke." She sighed, giving Mr. D'Angelo a quick glance. "I don't think Ralph ever forgave me for it, though."

On the other side of the glass, Mr. Jackson murmured, "On the contrary: I think Mr. D'Angelo still loves her."

Mr. Shapiro looked devastated; Mr. Jackson felt sorry for the man.

She continued, "I saw an article about Boyle in some tabloid. And it made me so angry! Here he was getting praised, with a new name and reputation, while my brother lay dead. And it also scared me."

"Scared you?" Sergeant Nestor sounded confused. "Why?"

"That guy threatened to kill all of us — my parents, everyone — if my brother pressed charges. Seeing him there out free like that made me scared he'd come kill us." She clasped her hands together so tightly her fingers went bright pink, her knuckles white. "That was when I decided to do it. Kill him. Before he got to us."

Sergeant Nestor sounded tired, like he'd heard this story too many times before. "So what happened then?"

"I called the tabloid, said I was calling for my boss who wanted to do an interview and did they have his information? They gave me his address and everything. After that I started checking up on him. He was with some mobster, running around with booze, women ... that made me even more sure I was doing the right thing. My Ma and Pa, Ralph ... they might hate me now, but I couldn't let Boyle kill them. And to see him out happy ... it was unfair."

Mr. Shapiro said, "Didn't he do his time, though? In prison? Wasn't that enough?"

She rounded on him in a rage. "No! Not for stealing from my husband, my father, my brother. Not for driving Victor to suicide. Not for any of it! And he wasn't even sorry, not once."

"Hmm," Mr. Jackson murmured. "That's what got her."

His wife, standing beside him, nodded.

Sergeant Nestor said, "So what happened next?"

"I made his acquaintance at the grocery he always went to. Just flirted a little."

Mr. Shapiro's jaw dropped.

Mr. D'Angelo shook his head.

"Then I suggested he bring me to the speakeasy where Ralph worked. Ralph wasn't happy to see me there, but he didn't say anything, just pretended he didn't know me. Then the guy brings out the lighter my brother gave him, cool as a cucumber."

"But you didn't kill him then," said the sergeant.

"No, but that very next day I got a gun. It was so loud in there already you could hardly talk, and I figured on New Year's it'd be even worse."

Sergeant Nestor said, "Is that why you picked that night? The noise?"

She laughed, but it was bitter. "I thought it justice. That was the night my brother shot himself. Now I was gonna shoot him back." She shook her head. "What a night that was! Between some old hag trying to get his attention —"

Mrs. Jackson flinched, and he recalled that she and Mabel Franklin were about the same age.

"— and my first husband glaring at me the whole night," she scoffed, "it was a wonder I could get my sleeping powder into his drink without anyone seeing."

Mr. Jackson nodded.

"I suppose you know the rest. He went nighty-night. I shot him and took back my brother's lighter."

"So why didn't you leave?" Sergeant Nestor seemed genuinely curious. "Why'd you stick around?"

"I don't know, to be honest," Pauline said. "I think I wanted to see if he really was dead. So I went to the side there by the curtains and watched. But then he fell on the floor, and everyone started screaming and running! Men were pushing, acting crazy to get out. The whole thing scared me. So I hid behind the curtains and there was a door. But I couldn't make any of the elevators work without a key."

Sergeant Nestor smiled, turning to Mr. D'Angelo. "And you had a key."

The bartender hung his head.

Pauline scowled. "The idiot gave me the wrong one."

"A man was dead!" Mr. D'Angelo held his hand up. "I know, I wasn't to say nothing. But I never seen a man dead before. I dropped the key, my hands shook so. And ... I couldn't think straight. I just wanted her out of there before anyone saw her! I just gave her what I had. Then the police showed up, and that waiter, and —"

"You had to deal with what was happening in front of you." Sergeant Nestor sounded sympathetic. "My forensics man found a key under the bench by the wall the night of the shooting. We were wondering what lock it went to. And I recall you saying the man shouldn't have died there."

Mr. D'Angelo shook his head. "If I'd have known she was going to do that, I'd have called for the bouncers."

Sergeant Nestor turned to Pauline. "So how'd you manage to escape?"

"I found the main laundry. There was a name-tag on the floor beside one of the hampers. I put a fresh uniform on. The elevator guy let me out, and I went home."

"We got a warrant and searched your home when you left for the Auditorium," Sergeant Nestor said, "where we found a black sequined dress with powder burns on it and what I assume is Mr. Boyle's blood."

Mr. Shapiro put his face in his hands. "She didn't come home 'til almost dawn, then rushed to the bathroom and wouldn't tell me where she'd been." He turned to her. "Why wouldn't you tell me?"

"You didn't need to get mixed up in this," she said. "Why'd you have to go all noble and tell them I was at home with you? My friends were ready to say I was with them." She sighed. "I could've handled it."

Mr. Shapiro sat stunned. "Why would I protect you? Because I love you!" He sounded torn, desperate. "I wanted to make them leave us alone!"

The lawyer put his hand on his forehead. "Didn't I tell you not to say anything, sir?"

"I know," Mr. Shapiro said glumly. "But I'm not very good at it."

Epilogue

Mrs. Pauline Shapiro was convicted of the premeditated murder of Mr. Mark Boyle and sentenced to twenty years in prison.

Mr. Ralph D'Angelo visited her every week.

Mr. Milton Shapiro was charged with obstructing a murder investigation. Due to his lack of criminal record (and fine standing in the community), Mr. Shapiro was given probation. Eventually, he divorced Pauline and married a sensible woman closer to his age.

Mr. Montgomery Carlo was charged with violating fire marshal's rulings on safe occupancy, then fined. True to his word, Sergeant Nestor failed to mention the use the room had been put to.

Agents Chapman, Scott, and Haley found the bad liquor. Mr. Russell was sent to Federal prison, which was in an entirely different city. Getting Mr. Russell out of Chicago made several mobsters that were in Chicago breathe a definite sigh of relief.

Mr. Carlo wasn't happy that Sergeant Nestor got to Pauline Shapiro first. Mabel Franklin, on the other hand, visited Pauline Shapiro in prison, and after a bit of sparring, the two became fast friends.

Both KWY Radio and the Chicago Civic Auditorium received generous donations from a Mr. Hector Jackson. It's unclear which of the three was more pleased.

Mr. Jackson began the search for places out West that met everyone's specifications — just in case.

After a few months, Bessie's puppies were old enough to venture out on their own.

The Myriad's Head Clerk Mr. Lee Francis and his wife took home the gold and black spotted puppy for their little son.

Sergeant Nestor's oldest son chose the dark brown puppy for his children.

Duchess Cordelia brought the golden-haired puppy to her suite as her new companion. She purchased specially-made dog boots so that little Bertie might venture out with the dowager on her morning constitutionals, no matter what the weather.

Mrs. Maisy Carlo chose the light brown puppy, who followed her around the Carlo's spacious home and played happily in their equally spacious backyard all the day long.

Miss Trixie Quinlan and her mother decided to stay in Cicero with Trixie's aunt. She and her young cousins were delighted to receive the black female puppy.

When she saw the little dog, Trixie beamed. "I'm going to name her Bessie!"

Acknowledgements

Thanks so much to Patricia Loofbourrow for the cover design. Also, to my newsletter readers for their help with names for this series.

About the Author

I've loved reading since I can remember! I love puzzles and mysteries and intrigue, and of all the cities I've been to, Chicago is my favorite. My four years living in Chicago during grad school were wonderful. Plus I love history. And wasn't the 1920's wild? I've always wanted to write a fun mystery series set in Chicago and now here's my chance.

Claire Logan is a pen name.

The Greenhouse Pane!

The Myriad Mysteries #4
Claire Logan

To those of you who have survived the worst.

1

The Chicago sunshine was bright, crisp and still a bit cool. Mrs. Pamela Jackson stepped out onto the rooftop of the Myriad Hotel, two toy poodles beside her. As the elevator closed behind her, she unhooked the dogs from their leashes, allowing them to roam about and do their business.

Ahead lay the vast and impressive Hotel gardens, dozens of raised boxes tended by Chef Monsieur and his crew. Most days, Mrs. Jackson would come up to help. But she'd risen late that day, and Monsieur had already left for the kitchens to prepare the days' meals. But a few of the men still worked there, smiling and tipping their caps as they passed.

She lit a cigarette, strolling to the right and around the elevator shaft after the dogs. She passed a door marked "Stair", then took a few steps towards what she thought of as the "back" of the rooftop.

The right side of the rooftop held a swimming pool, surrounded on two sides by covered lounge chairs with small drink tables between them. A stand lay behind the row of chairs facing her, which later in the day would serve drinks. Tea tables and chairs sat nearby. Beside that was a covered cart which contained towel, swimming caps, and other items — in case guests had forgotten them.

Closer to the far banister lay a concierge stand with telephone. At this hour, no one manned it, but you could call down — or out — for anything you might need. A modest hut roofed in white tile lay just before the far banister, with doors for gentlemen and ladies to refresh themselves, change clothes, and shower.

A stunning huge greenhouse took up much of the left side of the rooftop. The greenhouse itself was made up in clear glass, separated by silver which had faded by old patina into gray. It was a masterful work, soaring well above the rest of the structures here.

Straight ahead, far beyond the greenhouse and pool area, lay the service elevators, only accessible by key. The men who passed her earlier waited there with their carts. Large double doors opened; the men disappeared inside.

Mrs. Jackson strolled up to the little dogs, who were sniffing the area beside the greenhouse doors. She smiled down at them. "Find anything?"

The little dogs, one black, the other a much smaller black-and-gold spotted pup, looked up at her, ears raised, wagging their fluffy tails.

Mrs. Jackson laughed. "I've no food for you, sillies. You just ate!"

The day was lovely, quiet, still. Mrs. Jackson strolled to her left, along the length of the greenhouse, to lean on the waist-high stone banister.

She gazed out over the Chicago skyline. The automobiles were specks, the trucks ants in the distance.

It was a beautiful day. Yet she felt melancholy.

Bessie had given birth just before the New Year. The Myriad's Head Clerk, Mr. Lee Francis, had picked out her black-and-gold spotted pup as a companion for his baby son. Spot, as they called her, would be going to her new home today.

The last of Bessie's puppies to leave them.

She ran her fingers over the two empty black leather leashes in her hand. When she'd found the toy poodle starving outside the front door to the Myriad, she'd had no idea how old the little dog was. How long would it be before Bessie left her, too?

A deep voice called out, "There you are!"

Mr. Hector Jackson walked up to her. A tall, very dark, and quite handsome man, he'd dressed for the day, wearing one of his gray tweeds.

She turned to her Mr. Jackson, glad to see him. "Here I am!"

He chuckled at that, taking her arm. Then he sobered. "I don't like you standing so close. Isn't it dangerous?"

"I asked about this when we first arrived. You can't see it unless you look up while out on our balcony, but Monsieur told me there's a landing just ten feet down.

For safety to those below, in case one might accidentally drop something over the side. There's a ladder somewhere to fetch things. If one fell over, they'd get bruises. But serious injury would be unlikely."

"That's a relief." Mr. Jackson did sound relieved.

The couple strolled back the way she'd come, the little dogs following, then trotting ahead. As they walked, he asked, "And how fares the city? Has it behaved?"

She laughed. "As it ever does, I suppose." He always did know how to make her smile. "What brings you up here today?"

He stopped. "Two things. First, I wished to see you. The morning sun frames you in a most glorious light."

She felt herself blush.

"The other is this. It just arrived." He handed her an opened envelope containing an embossed card:

YOU ARE INVITED
TO A ROOFTOP GALA
To Honor the Esteemed Horace Rothmore
On the Thirtieth Anniversary
Of His Grand Green-House Creation
Please Join Us
Myriad Hotel Rooftops
The Thirteenth of May
At Half Past Seven
RSVP

Mrs. Jackson handed it back to him. "How exciting!" She'd never heard of the man before, but the idea of a party on the rooftops felt intriguing. "What does one wear to such a thing?"

He grinned. "Oh, I'm sure we can find you something suitable." He glanced over at their dogs, who were sniffing round the pool. "Come away from there. Bessie! Spot!" As the dogs returned, he said to Mrs. Jackson, "Breakfast should be set up by now."

"Oh! That sounds wonderful." Clipping the dogs onto their leashes, the four set off for the elevator.

While she waited in front of the carved Art Deco doors for their elevator to arrive, Mrs. Jackson listened to Mr. Jackson's plans for the day. They sounded quite extensive! Breakfast in their suite, then shopping, out for lunch with their friends Ophelia Denton and George Neuberg, then a visit to the gardens at Grant Park. They'd come back to the Hotel to leave Spot with her new family, then dress for dinner and dancing.

At the end of all this, he said, "We shall keep you well-entertained."

"My word. And what's the occasion?"

He gave her a warm, fond smile. "Well, dear girl, if **you** can't think of it, I'll not spoil it by telling."

That seemed fair enough.

When the lovely doors opened, the couple and their dogs entered the rosewood-paneled elevator. The uniformed elevator man, a different one than had brought her up there, tipped his hat. "All the way, or just to your floor?"

"Just our floor, thank you," Mr. Jackson said. "We'd have gone down the stair, but that door at the top's been jammed a week now."

"They should have fixed the lock by now," the man said. "If I see Eugene, I'll send him up to look at it."

Eugene did all the "dirty work" around the place. But to be perfectly honest, there was no "they" — other than a few temporary hired hands for big jobs, he was one man in his early thirties caring for an enormous hotel. It wasn't surprising that he hadn't gotten to it.

Although to Mrs. Jackson, it sounded as if they hadn't yet told him of the problem.

The elevator doors opened. The hallways at the Myriad were splendid: tan marble floors, rosewood paneled walls, with brass fixtures casting lovely golden light. The suite doors had been painted to match the flooring and trimmed in brass. Lovely scenes of the city and lake guided them to their suite: 3205.

The couple entered through the door to Mr. Jackson's room. As they did, the smell of ham, eggs, and fried potatoes wafted out.

Will and Floyd glanced up when they came inside. Will was a pale fellow with light brown hair; Floyd was a slender young man almost as dark-skinned as her Mr. Jackson, though not nearly so tall.

Will was just setting their plates. "There you are!" He placed a plate with two small meaty bones on the table.

Floyd brought out a teapot and a small coffeepot, and began pouring their drinks.

Mrs. Jackson knelt to unhook her dogs' leashes. "You're up early!"

Mr. Jackson said, "Will, I almost forgot. Congratulations on your new position!"

Will had just been promoted to Assistant Head Waiter, and would be helping the Myriad's Head Waiter — their friend George Neuberg — oversee the waitstaff.

Freed from their leashes, the dogs ran to sniff out every corner of the suite.

Will beamed. "Thank you, sir."

Mr. Jackson held her jacket, and Mrs. Jackson slipped out of it and her shoes with a sigh. She so loved the feeling of the thick soft carpet.

"I'm just filling in," Will said. "I have the evening off. My family and I are driving to Oak Park for dinner."

Mr. Jackson said, "Oh? What's the occasion?"

"It's my grandmother's birthday."

Mrs. Jackson said, "How wonderful!"

Mr. Jackson handed each them a tip."Please give your grandmother our regards."

"Thanks! Glad to," said Will.

Floyd said, "Enjoy your breakfast." He pushed his cart out, and after looking round for the dogs, Will carefully closed the door behind them.

The couple sat side by side around the small round table, perhaps a foot apart. She sat to his right, as she'd always done, even with her first husband. Mrs. Jackson felt comfortable, safe. It was pleasant, eating beside the dear companion she'd grown to care for.

The food was delicious: the ham, faintly sweet and spicy, the potatoes fried with herbs, the eggs fixed just how she liked them. "Dear Monsieur," she said fondly. "He knows exactly my tastes." Then she chuckled to herself as she cut the ham's rind into small pieces. "I suppose he must, with as long as I've known him."

Mr. Jackson swallowed a bite. "Very true."

Bessie and Spot had stationed themselves by her chair, tails wagging, their faces upturned and expectant. She chuckled at them, setting the treat between them.

As they all ate, Mrs. Jackson puzzled over the mystery of their special day. Mr. Jackson had planned out everything!

But why? What was the occasion? Was it a holiday? "Let me see the newspaper, if you please."

He handed it over; she opened it.

The headlines were the usual scandals of the day. Inside the first page was much the same.

On the second page, the advertisements began. These were her favorite part — she liked to see what the women here were wearing, so she might best blend in.

It would certainly help when out shopping for this rooftop affair.

So many styles! And most of the newest sported skirts which showed much too much of the lower leg, and without a hint of a sleeve!

The styles seemed daring in the extreme, so different than what she was used to back home.

But she needed to fit in if she were to live here.

Finally she found a velvety dress with long sleeves, with a skirt draping almost to the ankle. She showed it to Mr. Jackson. "I think I'd like this, but in green."

"Oh," he said, "That'd be lovely." He peered at the paper. "We'll go there first."

She turned the page and found what looked like a society section.

A library tour. An astronomy meeting. A charity luncheon. Some heiress named Lydia Rothmore Von Bilten was starting a garden club.

Mrs. Jackson had wanted one day to find a place where she could have a garden of her own. Where puppies could run freely.

The thought made her smile.

Maybe she'd join this garden club. She'd learned about gardening from her mother, and learned much more from working with Monsieur here at the Hotel, growing food for the Myriad's tables. But it would be nice to meet other ladies with similar interests.

The rooftop gala wasn't even mentioned. Strange, that. But perhaps it was a private affair.

She folded the paper, began to eat. But the mystery of what her Mr. Jackson's plans might be about tickled at her mind.

Today seemed an ordinary spring day. Rather like —

She set her fork down. Instead of images of their first day in town, the shopping and ride to the hotel they now stayed in, she recalled the face of her first husband the night before that, as he lay dying.

"I'm sorry," Mr. Jackson said. "I'd hoped we might at least make it through breakfast."

Mrs. Jackson leaned her elbow on the table, her forehead upon her hand, just trying to breathe. Her beloved lying there, his last words echoing in her mind ... time had dulled the pain, but it was fierce still.

Bessie trotted over beside her, laying her soft little head upon Mrs. Jackson's foot.

She felt Mr. Jackson's hand, warm on hers. "You don't have to face it alone. We can get through this."

She nodded, the pain still too much to answer. Then she squeezed his hand, just a little. Took a deep breath. "Thank you."

He smiled at that, taking up her left hand to kiss it. The ring he'd given her glinted in the morning's light: a raised silver band with a clear stone set smoothly into it. "He did the right thing. Were I in his place, I might have done the same."

She turned her face to look at him, forehead still leaning on her hand. "And yet he died for it."

Mr. Jackson let out a breath. "That's the way of it sometimes. But it's worse to live with regret." He glanced aside. "Much worse."

She straightened, curiosity overcoming her pain. "What is it you regret?"

He shrugged. "Most of my decisions have been poorly done." Then he smiled, kissing her hand. "But not this one."

Then the reason behind his planning came to her. "Happy anniversary, my dear."

He gave her a fond smile. "Happy anniversary to you as well."

2

The couple went shopping for clothes, and Mrs. Jackson found the exact dress she wanted. Once they'd found a bright green bow for Bessie to wear on her collar at the gala, they met for lunch with their friends George Neuberg and Ophelia Denton at an outdoor café near Grant Park.

The couple had arrived at the cafe early, but for some reason their two friends showed up late. Even so, Mrs. Jackson was well-pleased to see them.

George was a tanned, dark-haired fellow, the Headwaiter at the Myriad Hotel. Ophelia was about Mrs. Jackson's height, with strawberry-blonde curls, and worked as a dance girl at Club Patruni. Ophelia wore the new dark mustard-colored hat and coat Mrs. Jackson had bought her for the holidays, and she looked gorgeous.

Blushing, Ophelia gave her a hug; George and Mr. Jackson warmly shook hands.

George and Ophelia both smiled, yet their smiles seemed strained.

"Let's go in," Mr. Jackson said. "We have a big day ahead of us."

"Sounds good," George said.

As they followed the waiter to their seats, Mrs. Jackson said, "We saw Will this morning. How's the training been?"

George chuckled. "It'll be nice to take an actual vacation once in a while."

"That does sound good," Mr. Jackson said.

The waiter stopped. "Your table." It was a lovely white wire table with four matching chairs and a large blue-and-white striped umbrella covering it.

The four of them sat. The waiter handed over their menus and left. George gestured to the dogs. "How's our little family?"

Mrs. Jackson chuckled. "I think we're all well. Giving Spot an outing before she ventures to her new home."

Ophelia beamed at the little gold and brown dog, leaning down to ruffle the pup's fur. "You'll get to run in a real yard!"

Mrs. Jackson sighed. It seemed unfair to be parted from the last of the little dogs she'd grown to love. But equally unfair to have growing pups cooped up in a hotel suite. They barely had room for Bessie.

Would she ever see Spot again?

I'm being silly, she decided. She got to see Bessie's golden-haired puppy almost every day.

Mr. Jackson took her hand. "I hope the both of you are well."

Ophelia gave a little half-shrug. "My friend Ethel's just been turned out of our boarding house." Ophelia turned to George. "That's why I was late meeting you."

Mrs. Jackson said, "Whatever for?"

"She was caught with a man behind the theater," Ophelia said. "Mrs. Kilpatrick was furious! She said she'd not run a house for loose women." Ophelia's shoulders drooped. "Her mother took her home."

"I'm sorry," Mrs. Jackson said. "What will she do?"

Ophelia shrugged. "Find a new job, unless she can get a place to stay here in town."

They sat for a moment, silent.

The waiter approached. "Are you ready to order?"

Ophelia chose a chicken salad, George ordered a club sandwich, Mrs. Jackson chose grilled fish, and Mr. Jackson ordered a plate of spaghetti with meat sauce. They also ordered tea, except for Mr. Jackson, who asked for coffee with heavy cream. Mrs. Jackson also ordered a glass of water.

"I've not been here before," said Mr. Jackson. "But Mr. Carlo recommended the place to me."

Mrs. Jackson thought that sounded good. But neither Ophelia nor George seemed cheered by this.

Ophelia was barely one and twenty, and she'd been close with Ethel. But what might be going on with George? She said to him, "Are your parents well?"

He shrugged, glancing away.

The waiter returned, setting out their drinks. After pulling their little dogs out of the way of the waiter, Mrs. Jackson said to Mr. Jackson, "This place has remarkably good service!"

The waiter smiled to himself and left.

She poured her water into a saucer and placed it on the ground for the dogs. Once they were done drinking, she fastened their leashes so they might not move too far from her chair. "I'll have something for you to eat soon."

The little dogs wagged their tails, ears up.

The day was beautiful, without wind, or even a cloud in the sky. People passed, and birds fluttered by.

But Mr. Jackson seemed lost in thought, George and Ophelia, glum.

Finally, the food arrived. "Oh!" Mrs. Jackson said. "This smells delicious."

The others perked up, nodding their agreement.

After checking carefully for any bones in her filet, she chopped a third of the large filet onto the dogs' saucer. When she placed the saucer back on the ground, Spot and Bessie set to eating at once.

Her grilled fish was cooked perfectly, with a savory lemon and herb sauce and a lovely crisp skin.

While they ate, Mrs. Jackson watched George. He spoke little, picking at his food.

About half-way through their meal, Ophelia said, "Off to powder my nose!"

Mrs. Jackson smiled at her. "And such a lovely nose it is, Pet."

Ophelia giggled, blushing.

Mr. Jackson rose. "I'll be right back."

The day was bright, with not a cloud in the sky. Mrs. Jackson gazed over at George as she sipped her tea. "You seem positively morose."

George sighed. "My father wanted to have 'a talk' over breakfast."

"Oh, dear."

George snorted. "Yeah. Apparently, it's 'high time you settled down'. By which he means married, preferably chained to his business somehow." George's father built yachts, and here on the shores of Lake Michigan had a thriving business among the well-to-do of Chicagoland.

"Can he **force** you to?"

This seemed to calm him. "Well, no. But I overheard my mother crying. She asked my dad what's going to become of me. She said things like, 'am I never getting grandchildren?' and 'what did we do wrong?'. I think they feel a failure because of me."

"I'm sorry."

"I can't fit myself into the life they want. Don't get me wrong: I love boats. Even making them, the sanding and building. But sitting at a desk all day, running a business ... it would drive me mad."

This sparked a memory of something her Mr. Jackson said once, long ago. She felt quite amused. "We shall have no madness here!"

He chuckled. Then his face sober. "And then last week it was Mr. Davis."

She had to stop a moment to recall who the man was, and it must have showed, because George said, "The Myriad Hotel's manager?"

"Oh," Mrs. Jackson said. "Yes."

"He's getting on, and he wants to split the duties so he doesn't have to see the customers. He wants to focus on the finances, let someone else take care of the front of house business." George shrugged. "I thought it ideal, and I even applied. But Mr. Carlo wouldn't hear of it. He said he needed a 'family man' for the job. How did he put it? 'We won't be able to hire women and half the ones we've got will leave if they must worry about their superior making advances'."

Good grief. "That seems so unfair."

George shook his head, running his right thumb up and down along the top of one of his red and black striped suspenders. "But it would be wrong for me to marry." He hesitated for some time. "I'm not a regular man, and I don't think I ever shall be."

She nodded, giving him a fond smile. "I've known that since the day we visited you in the hospital."

George had barely survived poisoning. When she saw the way her Mr. Jackson had reacted to the scene, and the look George had given him in the hospital ... it had been quite touching.

He sighed. "I wish I were different. Or much older. It would make life easier. No one questions a 'confirmed bachelor'." At that, he laughed softly. "Or a spinster."

"But alas, my dear, you are **you**. You alone must decide what's best for your life."

George sat staring at the table.

Right then, Mr. Jackson and Ophelia came up. Ophelia looked at his half-eaten sandwich. "You didn't have to wait for us!"

He chuckled. "I suppose I better dig in."

Yet now, it was Ophelia's turn to fall silent, staring at her salad. What might be going on?

Mrs. Jackson turned to her Mr. Jackson sitting beside her, and took his hand under the table. "I'm so glad to be here." Not only glad to be here with him, but also with George and Ophelia, where she might be of help with their problems.

He kissed her cheek. "I'm glad you're glad, dear girl." Then he turned to the others. "After we're done here, why don't we visit the gardens?"

***

At the Grant Park gardens, Ophelia strolled arm in arm with George. "What were you talking to Pam about?"

George smiled to himself. "Oh, nothing."

"Now you got me curious."

He laughed softly to himself. "Didn't pick **you** to be the jealous type!"

"Not that." They kept strolling along, while she got her thoughts together. "It's just that ... she'll never tell me anything."

"Really?"

It was her turn to laugh. "Well, not really. I mean, if she likes or doesn't like something, then sure. But I can tell she's awful sad, and she'll never say a bit about it."

George shrugged. "She lost her first husband and her boy. Blow like that, she might never be happy."

Ophelia thought about this for a while, the gorgeous flowers around them fading from her view. "When we were come out of the bathrooms, Mr. Hector asked me if he and Pam were go away forever, if I'd follow. And I didn't know what to say!"

"Why wouldn't you?"

She had to think for a bit on that. "Well, it'd depend on where they were going. I like it here."

"They said they were going out West somewhere."

"I don't think they ever said, not to me anyway."

He was quiet for a bit. "Is that all?"

"Well, to be honest, no. This thing with the Feds after her ... it worries me." She'd never told anyone this, certainly not a man. "I love her," she whispered. "With my whole heart." She felt shaky inside, hardly able to breathe. But when she glanced at George, he simply walked along, peering at her as if truly interested in what she said. "Like a man loves a woman."

He nodded.

This made her feel better. Safe somehow. "I'd do anything for her. But ..."

"You don't know what exactly happened."

A surge of relief: he understood. "Yeah!"

Ophelia didn't know what she'd been so scared of. Georgie wasn't the kind of guy who'd laugh at you anyways, not over something serious.

They walked along a bit, then George said, "We already know most of it. She got mixed up in the Mob. When she tried to get out, they killed her husband and little boy over it." He looked out over the gardens. "It sounds like Hector and her husband were friends — he told me he made a solemn vow to keep her safe, no matter what. Even if he had to die himself." His voice shook. "The only time I've **ever** seen him scared, ever, was when he thought the Feds might find her."

He got real quiet as they walked along, then he took a deep breath. "Whatever happened, it's been over a year now. Does it really matter that much? I mean, is there anything that could've happened to her, or that she could've done, that'd make you not love her anymore?"

Ophelia didn't know. Mr. Hector said she didn't kill anyone. She just felt unsteady about it. "No. But I still want to know! I've told her everything. About my brother being killed in the war and the rest of my family dying from the flu." She had to stop then. "All that, and I don't even know her real name."

George nodded. They started walking again, but slower, falling behind.

She had to breathe for the rush of emotion come over her. "I grew up with a girl named Blanche. She died from the flu. But when we were together I told her everything, because I loved her. And she told me everything, too. I want that with Pam." Ophelia got out her handkerchief. "When I first met her, I promised I'd never ask what happened. Before. It was a foolish promise. And now —"

"You regret making it."

She let out a breath. "Yeah."

George gave her arm a squeeze. "Well, it's not like they're packing their bags!"

That made Ophelia laugh, in spite of how awful she felt right then.

"Let me talk to Hector, get a sense of what their plans are and where they're thinking about."

Ophelia nodded. "That sounds good."

George patted her hand. "Never you fret." He chuckled softly. "Who knows? I might be able to get some information out of the old boy."

***

As Bessie and Spot trotted beside them, Mrs. Jackson thought the roses were just as pretty this time of year as any, even though many were half in the bud. The green of the leaves was so vibrant in the afternoon sun.

She glanced back. "I wonder what those two are whispering about."

Mr. Jackson said, "How is our dear George?"

"His parents are pressuring him to marry."

He turned towards her, surprise and alarm upon his face. "Anyone in particular?"

"I don't think so. At least, he didn't say. But it's weighing on him. As much as he wants to be his own man, he very much wants to please his parents." A laugh burst from her unbidden. "And I doubt they ever wanted him to just be a Headwaiter, even at such a fine establishment as that one."

This made her think of her first husband. His hopes and dreams for their future were so at odds with what his parents had wanted for him. He'd found himself trapped, feeling obligated to continue in the family business, struggling against the burden of it all until the day he was murdered in it.

For the past year, the question had run through her mind every day: what could I have done to save him?

She rubbed the scar on the bend of her right arm. Even if she could forget that night, this reminder of it would never leave her.

"Does it still pain you?"

She shook her head. Not like that.

Mr. Jackson said, "George has some decisions to make, that's all. I just hope he can be honest about it."

Up ahead, a cluster of brightly colored parasols approached, coming the other way. With them, an old friend, some much younger couples, two small children, and one of Bessie's puppies!

Mrs. Jackson waved. "Sergeant Nestor!"

Irritation went through the older man's eyes, then he let out a laugh and tipped his cap. "Can't seem to get away from you two."

Mr. Jackson smiled to himself. The sergeant had helped hide them from their pursuers this past year. Yet they did seem to run into each other more often than either of them liked.

Sergeant Nestor turned to the men. "This is Mr. and Mrs. Jackson. Oh," he said to the children, "and Bessie, Brownie's mom."

Brownie was so big now! And well-cared for. And happy. Mrs. Jackson's eyes stung. It seemed silly to put it in that way, but her "baby" was truly in a good home.

There was a round of "nice to meet you."

The children's little eyes got wide. "Can we pet her?"

The man holding Brownie's leash said, "Let's let them greet each other, then I'll show you how to introduce yourselves."

He brought Brownie over for a bit of a family reunion. Bessie, Spot, and Brownie danced around, quite glad to see each other!

Mr. Jackson said to the rest, "This is Mr. George Neuberg and Miss Ophelia Denton."

Another round of "how do you do?"

Mrs. Jackson felt quite amused. "What brings you out here today?"

"Heh," said the sergeant. "My day off."

One of the women in the back pushed a covered carriage. One of the men held a large basket. "Ah," she said. "A lovely day for a picnic."

Sergeant Nestor grinned. "So it is."

"Well, we won't keep you from your outing," said Mr. Jackson. He tipped his fedora. "A pleasure."

After some untangling of leashes, and a host of "goodbye" and "nice to meet you," the two groups parted, each going their separate ways.

Ophelia said, "Sergeant Nestor seems a nice man."

Mr. Jackson laughed, rolling his eyes. "He's nice, all right!" Then his manner sobered. "But he's been sincerely helpful to us, and I'll not forget it."

***

The couple and their friends returned to the Hotel to dress for dinner. As they entered the Myriad Hotel's expansive lobby, Mrs. Jackson saw the Myriad's Head Clerk Lee Francis and his wife Laura off to the left across the crowded lobby, waiting at the front desk.

Spot began pulling, jumping, wagging her tail ears up as they went.

"She's eager to see them," Mrs. Jackson said, but she didn't feel it. She'd grown to love little Spot, and on top of losing so much this felt like yet another loss.

Laura handed their little boy to her husband and knelt down. "Hi, Lulu!"

Mrs. Jackson said, "Lulu?"

The woman grinned. "Yep! Lee and I thought if we ever had a girl, that's what we'd call her. But we have a pretty little girl right here!" She beamed at the little dog, hugging her.

Hmm, Mrs. Jackson thought. She didn't much care for the name, but the dog was theirs now.

"Hey," Mr. Francis said. "That reminds me. Did you happen to see anything when you were up there on the roof today?"

Mrs. Jackson glanced at her Mr. Jackson; they both shook their heads, shrugging.

"Well, some of the greenhouse panes were broken. We're not sure what happened, but a couple of boys got on the elevator at the ground floor right after the man brought you," he pointed at Mr. Jackson, "claiming you'd asked them to meet you up there."

Mr. Jackson looked perplexed. "I did no such thing!"

"We saw no one," Mrs. Jackson said.

"Well," said Mr. Francis. "It was right before the man's rest break. The man who spelled him said he saw the boys go back down after you two did, but that they were well-dressed and seemed well-behaved. He never thought to ask what they were doing there."

Mrs. Jackson said, "We're most sorry that happened."

Mr. Jackson said, "We'd be happy to pay for the breakage, if you —"

"No need," Mr. Francis said. "It's been turned over to the police." He turned to his wife. "Ready to go?"

Mrs. Jackson said, "Off so soon?"

"Oh, yes," Laura said. "We're going right back home. We should let this little one get used to her new yard!"

Mrs. Jackson knelt to run her hand over the little dog's black and gold spots, feeling a pang of grief. "I'll miss you."

"Aww," Laura said warmly. "We'll have to bring her by to visit sometime."

Mrs. Jackson rose, smiling at her. "We'd like that."

But as "Lulu" left for her new home, Mrs. Jackson felt disturbed. Boys breaking the Myriad greenhouse's windows? Then blaming **them** for it?

Why would anyone do that?

3

Leaving the little family behind, George followed Hector, Pam, Bessie, and Ophie up to the suite to dress for dinner. Waiting for them were their dinner clothes, Mr. Jackson's valet Norman Vienna, and Mrs. Jackson's lady's maid, Mrs. Octavia Knight.

George considered how to approach the many things he wanted to speak with Hector about.

But after the valet brushed their dinner jackets and left, Hector turned to **him**. "My wife told me of your difficulty."

George had actually forgotten about that for the moment. "That's one way of putting it."

"I suppose you could just tell your parents you haven't found the right girl yet."

He considered it. "Now that feels like a lie. I know they'd never understand the truth. But to give them hope ...? No. It wouldn't be right."

"Well," Hector sounded surprised. "It just might take some time. I didn't think I'd be interested in **any** woman, not until my wife came along."

George laughed. "You said you liked her legs."

Hector blushed. "Yes, very much so."

"They're fine legs, I saw them on the boat last summer. That swimming outfit she wore. But ... I don't know. I just don't care for women. Not like that. They don't interest me in that way."

Hector nodded slowly. "I understand. I do. It still astonishes me that after all the years of consorting with men that I found a woman like her." He chuckled softly. "And that she's consented to have me trail behind."

George chuckled. "That one does tend to be a force of nature."

Hector grinned. "Well put."

George slumped down on the bed, dejected. "What am I going to do?"

Hector sat beside him, put his arm round his waist. "Would you like me to talk with Mr. Carlo?"

"Goodness sakes, no. I'm not even supposed to be friends with the guests, not to mention —" He felt his ears burn.

The telephone rang.

Hector stood, clapped him on the shoulder. "My apologies. It was a foolish idea." When he got to the phone, he turned back. "Perhaps try a different establishment. I'm sure someone needs a man with your ability!"

George hadn't considered it. "Yes, I think that might be a good plan."

***

While George and Mr. Jackson were being dressed by the valet, Mrs. Jackson and Ophelia were being dressed as well.

After Mrs. Knight painted their nails, Mrs. Jackson said to Ophelia, "You seem very quiet today, Pet."

She nodded. "I've got a lot on my mind."

"Anything you want to talk about?"

Ophelia glanced at Mrs. Knight.

Mrs. Knight rose. "I'll do your rinsing now, ma'am, while your nails dry." She left for the bathroom.

"Come now, Pet," said Mrs. Jackson softly, "what's troubling you?"

Ophelia hesitated for some time. Then she sighed. "Last night. I get men waiting outside the club sometimes. They want to say hello, or that they liked the show, or give me flowers. Usually, it's fun. But this one wouldn't let me pass! I had to call for the bouncers to get to the taxi."

"That sounds disturbing."

"Don't get me wrong, I wasn't hurt. But it was. Disturbing. It scared me. But the worst part was he looked plainly at my hand," she lifted up her left hand, "before he came up to me."

"I'm sorry."

"I can't help thinking: what if that's what happened to Ethel, and no one was around to help?"

"Is that what she told you?"

Ophelia hung her head. "No. But how is anyone to know? Mrs. Kilpatrick didn't even ask her side of it." She crossed her arms. "It's unfair."

"Most of what happens to women is unfair."

Ophelia snorted softly. "If I were married, I'd not be able to work there. So I suppose there's a balance."

"No one there is married? I don't understand."

Ophelia shrugged. "The ladies who do the costumes. They're married." Her head drooped, and she fell silent.

"Is that all that troubles you?"

Ophelia raised her head, her lip trembling. "Tell me who you really are."

4

How Mrs. Jackson wished she might have a peaceful, quiet life, with nothing she had to hide! But she never could. "If I do, one day someone else could ask. They might not let you pass, in a place where no one was around to help. And they could ask much less nicely."

"I don't care," said Ophelia. "I love you, that's why I want to know."

Was she sentencing Ophelia to death? "And I love **you**," she said quietly, and meant it. "That's why I don't want to put this burden upon you."

"It's not a burden," Ophelia whispered. "How can I ... how can you truly love me, yet not tell me who you really are?"

Mrs. Jackson sat there, heart heavy. Maybe if she just told her this one thing, that might be enough. She leaned forward, mindful of her still-damp nails, and whispered into Ophelia's ear.

Ophelia just sat there for a moment. "Why didn't you just **say** so?" Then she got a confused look on her face. "What do I call you?"

"Pam is fine." She took a deep breath, then let it out, feeling both contentment and loss. "If all goes well, I shall be Mrs. Pamela Jackson 'til the day I die." She smiled to herself. "There are certainly much worse things to be."

She thought that would make Ophelia laugh, but instead she peered at her with those beautiful hazel eyes, waiting for more of an answer.

"The longer I stay hidden out here," Mrs. Jackson finally said, "the longer the people who hunt me will look out here, instead of hunting the ones I love."

Ophelia grabbed her hand, instantly spoiling both their nails. "Oh, Pam. I'm sorry. I didn't mean to hurt you. Or your people. I just don't want any secrets between us."

Mrs. Jackson sighed, feeling grieved. "I don't mean to hurt you. But there are some things you don't want to know." How could she possibly put the horrors she'd been through into words, so soon? "It's better for us all if you don't know."

***

After they got their nails redone, Ophelia went with the rest to leave little Bessie with her minders over at the vet's place. A bunch of little boys, but they all seemed to be having fun.

Then Ophelia went with George, Pam and Mr. Hector to dinner at a really nice place, with candles on the tables and everything.

Pam said Mr. Hector would pay for everything, so she planned to get herself a good dinner.

But she felt unhappy.

Pam's people knew who she was. They knew everything. Why couldn't Pam just give her the truth?

Mr. Hector said to George, "Is this party going to make you very busy?"

George shrugged. "We're hiring some new waiters for the event. I'll miss it entirely." He gave an amused snort. "Busy enough downstairs with dinner service. But Mr. Carlo'll be up there to keep an eye on them."

Ophelia said, "Is that the owner?"

"Yeah," George said.

She could tell by the way he said it that George didn't like him much.

The waiter set down their drinks, took their order.

The whole while the waiter was there, Ophelia felt fidgety inside. The minute he left, she blurted out, "Where are you going?"

5

Mr. Hector's eyebrows rose. "Well," he said, "we haven't decided yet."

Ophelia glanced at George.

George said, "That's not what you told me. After whoever phoned your room."

Mr. Hector sighed. "I wanted to talk with my wife about this before I said anything."

Oops, Ophelia thought.

Mr. Hector leaned back in his chair, looked away. "My men found a place. An abandoned casino."

Pam let out a laugh.

Mr. Hector smiled at her. "I thought you'd like that. But my cousin tells me it looks a wreck. Been abandoned ten years now. It needs a proper inspection before I'd even consider it." He shrugged. "So we really **haven't** decided yet."

Ophelia sighed. "You asked if I'd go with you —"

A brief look of alarm flashed through Mr. Hector's eyes, and Ophelia realized this was something else he'd wanted to talk with Pam about. Before. "I'm sorry,"

Ophelia said. "I just can't answer until I know what's going on."

Pam nodded slowly, eyes going watery.

Ophelia grabbed Pam's hand. "I want to **want** to go. I really do. But —"

Pam sighed. "I understand." She looked over at Mr. Hector. "It was hardly fair to ask. So soon, before we knew we'd have to go."

Mr. Hector shook his head. "That's just it. We've been very lucky. But when we do have to go, it might be at a moment's notice. It could be tonight. Or it could be ten years from now. I have no idea." He leaned his elbows on the table. "That's what I suppose I was asking: if we did have to leave tonight, would you come with us?"

"Gosh." Ophelia felt fluttery inside, almost scared. "I don't know."

Pam squeezed her hand. "It's okay." But her voice sounded so very sad. "You have a life here —"

George twitched, and he got that thinking look.

" — and," Pam's eyes went to Mr. Hector, "it wasn't fair for him to ask you to make that big a move without knowing more."

Ophelia felt alarmed. "I don't want to cause a fight," she said quickly. "I'm sure he only wants what's best."

Pam gave her a warm smile. "Our fighting days are over." Then she chuckled. "Although it was ever only arguing, as much as I sometimes wanted to fight him."

George let out a surprised laugh.

"Oh, dear," Ophelia said, surprised too. "You didn't always get along!"

Mr. Hector chuckled. "No. That we didn't."

***

After dinner, the four went dancing at the Trianon. As Mr. Jackson danced with his wife, he thought about what had gone on. "You were entirely correct with what you said at dinner."

She chuckled. "And what did I get right this time?"

That made him laugh. "It wasn't fair to ask Miss Ophelia to leave with us without giving her more information."

"I wish now that you hadn't," she said sadly. "Talked to her. At least I could maintain the illusion that she'd actually come along."

This was why he hadn't wanted to bring up the matter, today of all days. "Now, you don't know one way or the other —"

"And that's the problem." Her manner became fierce. "I know what you're thinking: we can't tell them exactly where we're going! Not if there's any chance they'd not come, too. Someone might pick them up and want to know." She shook her head, then stopped in her tracks, shoulders drooping. "This is no good. They're doomed, whether they stay or go."

He took her hand. "Don't think like that."

"I can't help it. It'd be easy to learn they were close to us." Her beautiful eyes filled with tears. "I can't bear the thought of them coming to harm on my account."

He took her face in his hands and kissed her forehead as the other couples swirled round them. "They'll be well-protected, day and night. You have my word."

She smiled up at him, looking relieved. "Thank you."

He took her arm. "Let's sit for a moment."

George glanced over, but Mr. Jackson shook his head, gesturing for them to continue dancing.

The couple took seats facing the dancers around a small round table. His wife took out a cigarette, which he lit.

He needed to task some of his men to protect those two. As much as he hated to admit it, his wife was right: anyone making it this far wouldn't hesitate to get rough in order to learn what they wanted to know. And he couldn't put all his trust in the sergeant, or even Carlo.

After a few minutes, he said, "Feel better?"

"I do."

"I'm sorry I didn't speak to you about this first. But George overheard the call, and asked, and I felt excited about the prospect, and —"

She gave him a warm smile. "You didn't want to lie to him. I understand."

"Not sure I could. He's good at picking it up."

The song ended. George brought Miss Ophelia over. "Thought we'd take a breather. Mind if we join you?"

"By all means," Mr. Jackson said.

So the two pulled up chairs and sat.

"I'm going to need your help," Mr. Jackson said to no one in particular. "If this place my cousin told me about turns out to be sound, I'll need advice on what to do with it. Once I get the blueprints, that is."

George nodded, a solemn look on his face.

"Then you'll know all about it." Mr. Jackson looked at Miss Ophelia. "Fair enough?"

She nodded, not meeting his eye.

Which bothered him. She wasn't letting this go.

He hoped she wouldn't do something foolish.

After a while, George took Miss Ophelia dancing once more, and Mr. Jackson sat with his wife as she finished her cigarette.

But his mind was entirely on plans for the future.

"I've not seen you like this before," his wife said. "What's got you so intent?"

"I feel like this property could be the one. I hope so. Just think of it!"

She chuckled. "Running a casino's a lot of work. I thought you didn't much like it."

This surprised him. "What, **working**?" He shifted to lean on an elbow towards her. "I'll have you know that I built a cabin with my own hands, and helped build a cottage with my men when I was a boy. Good solid things, too." He leaned back. "I don't dislike work, but I see no reason for effort if it's not needed."

He considered it, then laughed softly to himself. "If **you** think this, I'm sure others do too!"

She laughed "As you once said, the perfect disguise! Certainly no one would expect us to be in the middle of nowhere renovating an abandoned casino."

He thought this amusing. His entire plans had been on collecting a team to do what surely needed doing.

Perhaps he didn't much like work after all! "Well, if things turn out the way I'd like, it'll be renovated long before we arrive."

***

As he danced, George caught a glimpse of Hector past the crowd.

Ophie said, "They doing okay?"

George smiled down at her. "Yeah. Talking." He craned his neck to see. "I think she's smoking."

Ophie nodded.

They continued to dance.

George liked dancing. He didn't get to do it much anymore. And Ophie was a great dancer. So this was kinda fun.

George kept thinking about what Pamela said, about already having a life here. And in the excitement of maybe going on some adventure with Hector, he'd never even thought of that.

What would his parents think, him running off? Would he be able to come home, see them again?

He'd never asked.

And somehow, he got this feeling: when Hector and Pamela Jackson left Chicago, they weren't coming back.

It made sense. If they really were running from someone — he couldn't quite believe it to be the Feds — then they couldn't come back. None of them could.

But the situation scared him. Could he do that to his parents? Just disappear?

He was their only child. They had such hopes for him. Besides, he loved them. The thought of never seeing them again hurt.

"What's wrong?"

Ophie's voice startled him. Heart pounding, he said, "Just thinking too much."

She giggled.

Hector had been right. If they needed to go, they might not have any notice.

George knew he had to figure this out, and soon.

6

If George couldn't move ahead at the Hotel, he needed a better plan. And one thing George knew he could do was sport. So the next day before work, he went to the fitness club Hector had introduced him to.

George had gotten his own membership, and now went there more often than Hector did. So he'd gotten to know the people there, particularly the owner.

Fortunately for him, Mr. Abney was at the desk, taking towels out of a crate, fluffing and refolding them. He glanced up. "Well, hello there, Neuberg! Don't often see you here this early! What'll it be today?"

"I was wondering if you needed a front manager," George said.

The man's face turned guarded. "Really?"

"Yes, sir."

He seemed even more uneasy. "What made you want to change your position? I thought you just started as Headwaiter last summer."

George shrugged. "I like it there fine. But it looks as if I'm not going anywhere with the company."

He glanced away. "I'm not hiring."

"Are you certain? I mean, look at you. You're the owner, and your business does exceptionally well." A laugh burst from him. "Surely you could hire someone to fluff the towels!"

Mr. Abney set the towel on the counter. "How old are you, son?"

"Twenty-seven."

"Spend time in the war?"

"No, sir. I mean, I never saw combat. My family builds boats, so my father got an exemption so I might work the shipyards. I have design experience, but it was mostly machinery work."

"So you served beside many women, I take it."

George nodded.

"So why haven't you settled down, then, hmm?"

George hated lying to the man. "Just haven't found the right girl, that's all."

Mr. Abney scoffed. "This is a men's club, son. Quality gentlemen come here —"

George began to feel desperate. "Wait —"

The older man held up his hand. "I'm not casting any aspersions on your character. I myself didn't marry until I was almost thirty!"

He reached over to put a hand on George's shoulder. "I don't think there's a thing wrong with you." He took a deep breath. "But as someone who's been in your shoes, I have to tell you straight: these folks will. And the older you get, the more they'll talk. You're a good-looking, fit man, with steady finances, surrounded by a sea of unmarried women. They'll wonder why you won't marry. Are you shell-shocked? Immoral? A bootlegger? Or," his voice went to a whisper, "of an unsuitable temperament to be round unclothed men."

George was so stunned he couldn't speak.

He took his hand off of George's shoulder. "I'm sorry to have shocked you with such language, sir, truly I am. I don't believe this of you for one minute. Why, if I did, I'd tell you to find work in Towertown."

"What's that?"

"Heh," Mr. Abney said. "You don't want to know." He sighed, glancing away. "I like you. You have a good job and a fine reputation. I want you to succeed. If you were married, you're right: I **could** use a hand here." He peered at him. "You want to move ahead. I understand. We all do. But you have your whole life ahead of you." He gave a nod, with a look that made George think of an owl. "Slow down, son. First things first."

George stumbled down the steps, hurt, deeply embarrassed, angry.

Now he understood his father's concern at him refusing to marry. His mother's worry, her tears.

Was he destined to forever be in a dead-end job? Even if he took over his father's business, would there be people refusing to buy his yachts, looking at him with suspicion — merely because he hadn't **married**?

Things couldn't go on like this.

7

A week later, Mr. and Mrs. Jackson (and Bessie) stepped out of the elevator onto the Myriad Hotel's rooftop. Jazz music hung in the air. Before them stood a thin black metal railing with electric lights strung atop, and a sign in a black holder with a large arrow pointing to the right: GALA.

The railing guided them to the right, around the elevator shaft and past the exit door to the stair. Brass stanchions stood on either side, and a fat velvety-black rope with brass on both ends blocked their path.

The metal railing had been placed all the way to the concrete banisters on both ends of the rooftop, separating Monsieur's kitchen gardens from the party before them.

And what a scene it was!

To the left, torches, candles, and electric lights lit the area almost as well as day might. A huge buffet had been spread along the rail, and a dozen people mingled in front of the grand greenhouse. Someone had moved an upright piano to the roof, and a jazz quintet in the far left corner closest to the gardens explained the music.

To the right, the pool was dark, only lit slightly by the far reaches of the dazzling display and the fat votives placed on the pavement around its edge.

The night was clear and warm with no moon. Stars twinkled overhead.

Mrs. Jackson said, "A perfect night for a party."

Mr. Jackson chuckled softly.

She felt weary. They'd been awakened by a telephone call in the midst of night. And even though her Mr. Jackson had gotten up to answer, she felt as though she'd missed some sleep.

Mr. Jackson hadn't mentioned the call the next morning, and she'd forgotten about it until now. What might it have been about?

Mr. Montgomery Carlo came hurrying up to unhook the rope. "Welcome! Right this way." A big, swarthy man with hooded dark eyes, Mr. Carlo was the owner of the Myriad Hotel.

Mrs. Jackson felt touched that he would personally show them such kindness. Although they **were** in the Myriad's best suite. And Mr. Jackson was known to be a fabulous tipper.

Mr. Carlo led them over to a woman wearing a fine mink stole, a beautiful set of large pearls, silver-rimmed spectacles, and a blue silk dress overlaid in lace. She was at least seventy, with silver-gold hair and bright blue eyes. She'd been speaking with a dark-haired man barely out of his teens until Mr. Carlo tapped her shoulder.

"Mrs. Lydia Von Bilten, Mr. Charles De Rege, may I present Hector and Pamela Jackson."

The young man rolled his eyes.

"Oh!" Mrs. Jackson said, taking the old woman's lace-gloved hand. "I'm so glad to meet you! I read about your garden club in the paper."

Mrs. Von Bilten smiled at her, but the smile didn't reach her eyes. "A pleasure."

Mr. Jackson had reached out his hand as well, but apparently the woman didn't take notice.

Mr. Carlo gave them a glance. "This is Mr. Hector Jackson, one of our hosts."

The woman nodded to him. "Good to meet you."

Still she didn't take his hand, so Mr. Jackson tipped his fedora. "A pleasure."

Mr. Carlo seemed put out. "We'll let you return to your —"

Mrs. Von Bilten turned away.

A tall, brown-haired waiter who was perhaps twenty passed by. The tag on the man's chest read: Hugh.

Young Charles snapped his fingers at the man. "You there! Another drink."

Mr. Carlo said to Mr. Jackson, "I'm dreadfully sorry. Come, let's see what Monsieur has prepared for us."

Monsieur, of course, was the Hotel's Chef. He wasn't at the affair, being over thirty flights below running dinner service with George. But one of the waiters he'd

658

hired, a short blond fellow with spectacles, stood ready to replenish the table. His name-tag read: Russell.

And the table was well-stocked. Canapés of all sorts, cubed meats, sliced cheeses, diced fruit speared upon toothpicks. An array of cut vegetables alongside sauces galore. Olives, nuts, bacon-wrapped figs.

Mrs. Jackson looked back: instead of surveying the table, Mr. Jackson stood watching the brown-haired waiter as he moved about the room. She went on tiptoe to speak in his ear. "He **is** nice, isn't he?"

Mr. Jackson let out an embarrassed laugh, blushing. "I suppose."

She took his hand. She knew he fancied men, but it wasn't like him to be so obvious about it. "Let's get you some dinner, shall we?"

Russell had been slicing cheese into cubes with a rather large knife. He dipped the knife in water and wiped it perfectly clean.

Mr. Carlo had been sampling several of the bacon-wrapped figs.

Neither had noticed a thing.

A very pale red-haired waiter who wore his hair short in the back with long bangs parted in the middle stood at the end of the buffet, carefully pouring flutes of champagne. His name-tag read: Victor.

Young Victor's hand shook slightly as he poured. Cases of bottles rose to his waist beside him.

Mr. Jackson chuckled. "I see now why the sergeant isn't here."

Mr. Carlo laughed. "What the police don't know won't hurt them."

Mr. Jackson glanced in the direction of the brown-haired waiter and sighed. "I suppose I **should** eat something." He picked up a porcelain saucer and began filling it.

Not wanting to look at the champagne, Mrs. Jackson gazed out across the rooftop. Two black wire tables large enough for six and matching chairs had been placed on either side of the greenhouse entryway.

Past the greenhouse, a thin man in his middle forties with straight black hair parted in the center and a waxed mustache leaned against the banister smoking a cigarette from a long thin holder as he flirted with a blonde half his age.

The man wore black gloves and a black coat, embroidered in purples and reds, which reached to the floor around his forest green shirt and trousers.

The blonde's sleeveless dress was sequined in red, dipped low in front, and to Mrs. Jackson's surprise, showed the woman's legs almost up to her knee! A matching headband across her forehead and bright Cupid's bow lips.

Perhaps sensing Mrs. Jackson's gaze, the woman turned her head, giving a bright smile and a wave.

"Ah." A young woman's wry voice came from behind. "You've seen our Bohemian."

Mrs. Jackson turned to face her.

About the same age as the waiters, this woman held a half-full champagne flute in her left hand. She wore a fine, richly beaded dark brown dress reaching to her mid-calf with lacy quarter length sleeves and a matching headband over curly brown hair. The young woman held out her right hand as Bessie sniffed at her shoes. "Ruby Carlisle."

Mrs. Jackson took Ruby's hand. The woman had a dark brown mole on her left lower cheek, just above the level of her mouth. Real, not painted. Quite fashionable. "A pleasure." She let go, looked around. "What brings you here?"

"I could say the same. We're a family of sorts. My father was a greenhouse architect for many years."

"I see."

Ruby gestured with her chin at the Bohemian. "He builds greenhouses too. Although I wonder why he bothered to show up. He hates Horace."

"Really."

Ruby laughed. "They all hate each other. But it's best to be seen. You never know when some event will bring your next client."

Mrs. Jackson said, "You're so knowledgeable. Are you a designer as well?"

"Here? I'm a woman. I might be able to find work in Paris, or perhaps Milan. But this is an old boy's club, always has been." She shrugged, then downed her drink. "I have no interest in it. My sister, perhaps."

The brown-haired waiter passed with an empty tray. Ruby set the glass upon it. "Get me another."

His answer was too low for Mrs. Jackson to hear, but from their body language, the young man had said something rude and insulting.

Ruby rolled her eyes and let out a sigh.

Definitely not the usual for waiters at the Myriad Hotel. "Is your sister here?"

Ruby gave a one-shoulder shrug, glancing away. "You'll meet her soon enough."

At that, Ruby drifted off without saying goodbye.

Mr. Jackson came up with a saucer full of hors d'oeuvres. He handed Mrs. Jackson a glass of water. "Who was that?"

"Her father used to build greenhouses. I guess most all of them do."

"Interesting," Mr. Jackson said, then popped a grape into his mouth.

Mrs. Jackson took a drink of her water. It was tepid, but she was thirsty.

"There's a reporter here," Mr. Jackson said. "And a photographer. Apparently some actress is expected."

A gruff male voice broke in. "There's always one of them at these sorts of things."

Mrs. Jackson turned to face the man.

At least sixty. Short, wide, graying, holding a well-worn brown leather briefcase, smelling of pipe tobacco. With a tweed overcoat and brass spectacles, he seemed somewhat underdressed for the affair.

She held out her hand. "Pamela Jackson. And this is my husband, Hector."

The man tipped his cap. "A pleasure."

Mrs. Jackson said, "Are you a greenhouse designer?"

"Heh," the man said dismissively. "Wouldn't catch me dead in one of those things, not in this city."

Mr. Jackson laughed. "So what brings you here?"

"I'm supposed to meet someone." He sighed, taking out a pocketwatch on its chain and peering at it. "Late, as usual." Replacing the watch, he retrieved a well-worn pipe from his overcoat's pocket, set the briefcase between his feet, and lit the pipe.

Mr. Carlo, a man holding a notepad, and a man holding a camera all rushed past.

Mrs. Jackson turned towards the commotion.

A willowy woman in her late thirties with straight brown hair cut in a bob and bright red lipstick stood at the velvety rope, accompanied by a tall, muscular man. Both wore black; the woman's sleeveless dress was beaded down to the fringe covering her mid-calf. Her beaded headband had several raven's feathers at the back arrayed as a fan.

"The actress," the old man said, as if it were obvious.

663

The reactions of the rest were interesting. The Bohemian didn't stir, although the blonde pulled at him, urging him to. Finally, the young woman abandoned him to dash across the rooftop towards the pair, heels clattering. The old woman gave a glance over her shoulder, then returned to her conversation. Ruby looked bored, the waiters awestruck.

Mr. Carlo waved off the onlookers, escorting the actress and her companion — the man looked like a bodyguard more than anything else — to the buffet.

And as yet, there'd been no sign of the architect. Where was he?

8

Right then, George Neuberg was in the dining room of the Myriad, overseeing the dinner service. Directing the waiters, taking reservations, escorting the more important guests to their tables. It was all routine by now, even to the matrons who inevitably complained about something.

Will was doing quite well — going table to table promoting the evening's special, shaking the hands of the more important guests, checking on the waiters.

A silver-haired woman in a tan beaded dinner gown came up to his podium, a small golden poodle in her arms. "Oh, Mr. Neuberg! I'm so happy to see you!"

"Why, Duchess Cordelia! It's always a pleasure." He offered his arm, which she took. "Right this way."

He escorted the woman to her table and held the chair for her. As she sat, Floyd came up with a small porcelain bowl of chopped meat, setting it on the floor beside her — for her dog.

"Simply marvelous," said the Duchess to them both, setting little Bertie on the floor. "Thank you ever so much."

George smiled at her. "You're **most** welcome." Duchess Cordelia Stayman was one of the good ones. She never made a fuss, even though she was related to Mr. Carlo somehow. The woman really seemed to care about people's welfare. And she invited the staff to her rooms for dominoes every Tuesday.

Pity about her husband.

Thinking about Albert Stayman reminded George of his father, and as he returned to the host station, he wondered what he possibly could do to solve the dilemma he found himself in.

He liked this job. It suited him. But if he were to travel with Hector and Pamela, he needed to earn more. And every interview he'd had brought up his unmarried status.

It felt so frustrating!

Another couple came up, and he checked their reservation. Not guests of the Hotel, so he waved Floyd up, passing the couple off to him.

And then there was the issue of Hector and Pam leaving. He didn't know if he could bear never seeing Hector again. But abandoning his parents without even saying goodbye seemed unthinkable.

What should he do?

The telephone rang. "Yes, sir. I have a spot open for 8:45." He made a note in the schedule. "You're quite welcome, sir."

A hand fell on his shoulder. Replacing the receiver, he turned towards whoever this might be.

Will stood there. "Is all well?"

George blinked. "I suppose. Why?"

"You don't seem yourself tonight."

George shrugged. "Got a lot on my mind."

Will chuckled. "Don't we all. Listen, 24 wants to pay his tab tomorrow. I told him we don't do that unless they're Hotel guests."

"Heh." George felt amused. "I'll handle it. Come on, you'll learn something."

As they went to table 24, George thought: *is this what being a father feels like?* He wasn't sure, but as he privately informed the gentleman that he could either pay his bill or the police would be notified, he felt pride at the awe in the younger man's eyes.

The older gentleman hemmed and hawed, and red-faced, got the money from his table. "Thank you kindly, sir," George said. "Come again."

Dad's just trying to steer me the right way, George thought. *He loves me.*

But in his situation, George didn't know what the right way was.

***

The rooftop was warm, the day's heat radiating from below. Mrs. Jackson enjoyed the chance to sit, listen to the musicians.

Normally at an event like this, her Mr. Jackson would be chatting with everyone. Instead, he'd spent the entire evening either on the phone or jotting on a notepad he'd hidden away in his tuxedo.

She looked over at him as they sat together. "You're awfully quiet."

He smiled warmly. "Just pondering my next move."

"Wait. Did you hear back already?"

He beamed. "I did."

"So **that** was the mysterious midnight call!"

He chuckled. "My cousin had spent three days going over the place. It's two hours to the nearest telephone, and he was in such a hurry to report back that he forgot the time. But the news is good. The foundation and weight-bearing beams are perfectly sound. It'll need a new roof, and plumbing, and updated electrical —"

"But we're putting in an offer."

He nodded.

Mrs. Jackson threw her arms round him, right there in front of everyone. "Oh, I'm so pleased." Tears of relief sprung to her eyes: they had someplace to go.

Mr. Jackson patted her back, then hugged her, kissing her hair. "You see? It'll all work out."

She pulled back, fetching her handkerchief so as not to ruin her makeup. "But what if they don't accept the offer? What if —?"

"Now hush. Flan is **very** good at negotiation." He laughed softly to himself. "Even better than I. Now stop fretting and try to enjoy the party!"

The door to the stairs opened. A man perhaps her age entered the rooftop and called out, "He's coming!"

A few moments later, a pale, dark-haired, overweight man in his late fifties staggered onto the scene through the door to the stairs, accompanied by two men wearing the livery of the Hotel. He mopped his brow with a handkerchief, panting.

Mr. Carlo strolled over, holding out his hand. The man shook it, then fanned out his tuxedo, which even from here seemed damp with sweat. The two bellhops tipped their hats to Mr. Carlo then disappeared around the corner with the other man, presumably to take the elevator down.

Mr. Jackson sounded incredulous. "He climbed thirty-three **floors**?"

Mrs. Von Bilten, her insolent young companion, and the rest began moving towards the man. "Thirty-four, actually," Charles said dryly as he passed.

The old man moved fastest, pushing past the others to get to the architect.

Mrs. Jackson said, "Perhaps the man's afraid of elevators. Many are."

"Good grief," Mr. Jackson said. "That's dedication!"

This made Mrs. Jackson take pause. Why would a man climb thirty-three flights just to attend a party? The party **was** in his honor, but ... "It's not like you to hold back on such good news."

The old man seemed angry, gesturing at him. The architect said something to the older man which seemed to mollify him.

Mr. Jackson chuckled. "Just an oversight, my dear. It was rather late, and I'd given the matter over to Flan. So by the morning, it'd gone completely from my mind." He gave her a fond smile. "I promised never to lie to you, and I try always to keep my promises."

She felt abashed. "Well, yes, of course." Taking a deep breath, she rose. He rose also, and she took his arm. "Why don't we meet our guest of honor?"

For such it had to be: even the Bohemian had deigned to saunter over to the architect, wearing a wry, derisive smile as he offered his hand.

Mr. Horace Rothmore had dark blue eyes. His face was pale, and he had a nervous way about him. Even so, she liked him. He reminded her of someone.

Mr. Jackson offered his hand. "Hector Jackson at your service, sir."

Mr. Carlo, who'd hovered nearby, said, "This is one of our hosts for this evening."

Mr. Rothmore had already grasped Mr. Jackson's hand. "Good to meet you, sir."

Mr. Jackson turned to her and said, "May I present my wife Pamela."

The architect beamed. "And what a lovely woman she is, too!" He grasped her hand in both of his.

A bit sweaty, but she appreciated the gesture. "Thank you, sir."

Mr. Carlo said, "Would you care to sample the buffet? We also have a fine array of refreshments, if you wish to indulge."

He perked up. "I would indeed!"

Mr. Carlo and the architect moved off.

Mrs. Jackson said to Mr. Jackson, "What's this about being the host?"

A short, wry laugh burst from him. "Since I've done service for Mr. Carlo, he's refusing to take the entirety of our bills. Since I refused to stay unless he did, he's put a portion towards the hosting of these affairs." He shrugged. "A perfectly reasonable arrangement."

The man's appearance, his smile, his manner, the way he moved ... "He reminds me a bit of —"

Mr. Jackson nodded. "Yes. I see it now."

Grief pinched her face, her chest. "If he would've lived." Her eyes stung. "He of all people deserved to live." *If only I'd died instead*, she thought. Her beloved could've lived out his days with their son. "Maybe I should go back. Let them kill me too."

Mr. Jackson's embrace was quick, warm and gentle. "My dear girl. This is all nonsense. What good would dying do? You did the best you possibly could!" He gently grasped her upper arms, drew her away, his dark eyes peering into hers. "Why torture yourself so?"

He'd never said this before, and it surprised her. "I don't know. It's so unfair for you to be chased out into the wilderness, when you've done nothing wrong."

He smiled to himself. "I chose to follow you." He took her chin, gazed into her eyes. "They could chase us over the entire world, and it wouldn't matter. I'll keep you safe and well, to the end of our days." He stroked the side of her cheek. "I promise."

Mr. Carlo called out, "Mr. Horace Rothmore will give us a tour of his greenhouse in twenty minutes!"

Pleased murmurings all round.

"This should be interesting," said Mr. Jackson. "I've not yet been inside."

9

Mr. Rothmore looked chagrined when the strange old man refused to enter with them.

Mr. Jackson thought that the greenhouse was everything one might expect: vaulted glass ceiling, lush foliage, spongy earthen paths. The place reminded him of his wife's request for a garden at their new home.

The sound of water came from the other side of the greenhouse. Out West was often dry, and in places, barren. How might he have a garden like this created for her there?

Mr. Rothmore had been speaking as they walked. "The upper panels are on a mechanical timer set to the sun's passage during the spring through the fall, to open in the afternoon for proper ventilation. Also, there are controls to adjust for temperature and humidity, as well as shade covers which deploy automatically. This is all to ensure the plants are kept at their finest."

This seemed a remarkable plan. He made a mental note to approach the architect at some later date about a custom design for their property — whichever one they ended up acquiring.

But he hoped the owners accepted his offer. The place intrigued him. Why spend so much time and money to set up a casino — which sounded like a sure bet out there with the cowboys and gamblers — then abandon it?

He laughed softly to himself. It didn't matter. All that mattered was that the building was sound, and barring any unforeseen circumstances, would soon be theirs.

The young woman his wife had been speaking with earlier stood nearby, seemingly put off by his laughter. "What's so funny?"

He shrugged. "Just thought of something amusing."

An older man with an impressive moustache and a floor-length embroidered jacket turned to the young woman. "My dear Oyster, not everything is about you."

She flushed red, scowling.

This made him laugh. "Oyster?"

The man gave him a strange look. "A personal joke, I suppose." Then he seemed amused. "The way she clams up when you ask her anything."

The young woman shook herself, rolling her eyes.

The group had made their way to the fountain, a mini-waterfall reaching almost to the roof. Beside it, a large stack of wide bags labeled, "Decorative Stone" reached almost head-high. Some crates of tools, two ladders, and the unassembled bits of much smaller black wire tables and chairs lay neatly stacked beyond that.

Pointing to the area in front of the waterfall, Mr. Carlo said, "We're putting in a small patio for our guests to enjoy."

The burly man beside Mr. Carlo said, "That pile looks a bit high. Isn't that dangerous?"

Mr. Carlo shrugged, patting a bag of stone. The stack didn't budge. "It'd take a strong man to topple that."

The rest laughed.

They moved on, around the greenhouse. The views were lovely, and the air was pleasantly warm. Even so, it seemed a bit close in there, and Mr. Jackson felt glad to exit into the fresh night breeze.

***

An hour later, Mrs. Jackson looked around and let out a weary sigh. There had been toasts, and dancing, but she didn't feel much like either.

The younger folks — including the waiters —were drinking heavily, chasing after and teasing each other. The older ones alternated between ignoring and sniping at each other. The actress and her bodyguard were nowhere to be seen.

The jazz quintet played dutifully. Even though she applauded them at their breaks, to the rest they seemed in a different world, completely unnoticed by the crowd.

All this time, Mr. Jackson had been scribbling on his notepad, as intent on his work as if he'd been downstairs in their suite, rather than at an event.

The old man paced about, unlit pipe in one hand and briefcase in another. Finally he went to the architect, shaking his pipe angrily. The architect spoke sharply, then pointed towards the greenhouse and went inside.

The exchange seemed to mollify the old man. He approached their table. "Mind if I join you?"

Her Mr. Jackson glanced up with a startled expression. "Of course! Please do."

The old man pulled up a chair, looking disgruntled.

Mrs. Jackson said, "I hope all is well?"

The old man said, "I told my driver it'd take ten minutes. It's been two hours!" He crossed his arms, a scowl on his face.

Bessie went to the man and put her paws on his leg.

The man's scowl faded. He patted Bessie's head. "Pretty little thing you've got there."

"This is Bessie," Mrs. Jackson said.

"Well, hello, Bessie."

Bessie wagged her fluffy black tail, ears up.

"Come on, girl," Mrs. Jackson said. "Let's get you something to eat." They went to the buffet, where she picked out two saucers of food, one for her, the other for Bessie, and returned to the table.

From over by the pool came an outraged shriek and a huge splash.

Mrs. Jackson sat, putting Bessie's saucer on the ground beside her. "I wonder what that's all about."

Several minutes later, Ruby came storming across the rooftop towards Mr. Carlo, hair and clothing drenched, makeup streaming down. "Your waiter pushed me into the pool!"

Gasps came from all sides.

Mr. Carlo scowled, pointing towards the brown-haired waiter. "You there! Get over here this minute!"

Hugh came past their table, yelling, "It's a lie! She —"

Ruby yelled, "You ruined my dress!"

"That's not true!" He pointed back at the pool. "She ran past me and jumped in! I —"

"You're fired," said Mr. Carlo. "And you'll be getting no reference from me."

"This is unfair!" Throwing up his hands, Hugh rushed towards the pool.

Mr. Carlo watched him go, then seeing no further upset, turned to Ruby. "I'll have your dress replaced, miss, no charge."

Ruby didn't look mollified. "It's one of a kind, custom-made."

Mr. Carlo handed over a card. "Just contact my manager with the details. We'll have another one made up for you right away." He snapped his fingers at Victor. "Get this young lady a towel."

Victor turned even paler than he already was. "R-right away, sir." The young red-haired waiter returned with a rather large golden towel edged in cobalt. Hands shaking, he draped the towel over the shivering girl's shoulders, covering her to her knees.

"Heh," the old man said. "Most interesting thing that's happened all night."

Mrs. Jackson glanced around. The food, after having sat on the buffet all this time, was nothing special. She finished her glass of water. "I wonder where our guest of honor's gone to?"

The old man snorted. "Probably saw some plant that needed tending." He heaved himself up, then grabbed his briefcase. "I'll go fetch him."

Mrs. Jackson rose. "Might I join you?"

Mr. Jackson scrambled to his feet. "My apologies! I completely —"

"Pay it no mind," Mrs. Jackson said, feeling amused. "This gentleman and I are going in search of our architect."

But her Mr. Jackson' eyes were back on his notepad. "Very well, dear. I'll await your return."

Mrs. Jackson chuckled as she and the older man went along. "This is so unlike him! He's usually the life of the party." She peered down at her little dog trotting beside them. "Isn't that right, Bessie?"

The old man laughed, then held the greenhouse door open for her. "A man who does business at a party is my kind of guy."

The inside of the greenhouse was humid, well-lit, and utterly silent. Mrs. Jackson called out, "Mr. Rothmore? Are you in here?"

Bessie whined, pulling on her leash.

Mrs. Jackson followed. "It seems like she smells something."

Bessie led them past lush plants, towards the waterfall. The water no longer flowed.

Near the ground, beside the drying stone structure, a panel lay open. Next to that, a pair of men's shoes pointed down, attached to two legs covered by two large bags of decorative rock.

They'd found the architect.

10

As it was somewhat hidden by a large plant, Mrs. Jackson hadn't noticed the stained glass door on the other side of the waterfall until then.

She might not have noticed it at all, but it opened.

The old man's eyes were searching the ground. "Do you see a briefcase anywhere? It'd be just like mine."

Mrs. Jackson shook her head. "No."

The brown-haired waiter stuck his head in. "I went round to see where she'd come from and I found the door ajar." His eyes went to the architect and he gasped.

"Call for the police," the old man said. "There's been an accident."

The young man disappeared, his running footsteps heading towards the phone stand by the pool.

A gurgling sound came from underneath the bag.

The old man said, "Good gravy! Could he possibly have survived?"

"Help!" Mrs. Jackson cried out.

The old man retreated, eyes wide. "I have a bad back. I'm not allowed to lift anything heavier than my briefcase, by doctor's orders. Certainly not something like that!"

She tried pulling on the bag. It shifted, just a little. But a moan came from the man.

Was she hurting him? This bag needed to be lifted, and she knew she wasn't strong enough to do it alone. "Go, then. Hurry. Get help!"

***

George was just getting the 8:45 crowd seated when the front desk clerk came rushing up. "A Mrs. Kilpatrick is here to see you."

George felt confused. "Did she say what it's about?"

"No, sir, she just said it was urgent."

Will stood off to one side, at a table full of guests. George got Will's attention. "I need you to take the reins for a minute."

"Sure, boss," Will said cheerfully.

"I'll be right back." George followed the clerk through the frosted glass double doors to the lobby.

Mrs. Kilpatrick stood at the front desk, her apron still on, holding a handkerchief. When she saw him, she visibly relaxed. "Oh, dear goodness, they found you! I tried calling but they said you were busy, so I —"

George held up a hand. "What happened?"

"It's Miss Ophelia. The Patruni club called. She never arrived —"

Terror hit. Something happened to Ophie? All sorts of horrible scenarios began going through his mind.

"— but I don't understand it. She left **early**! She told the other girls she was going to the library first. Why would she go **there**? Do you know what's going on?"

George took a deep breath, heart racing. He had to think. "We'll need a taxi —"

The night clerk nodded. "Right away, sir."

He put his hand on the older woman's shoulder, feeling shaky. "You did the right thing." He felt like he couldn't breathe right. "I'll take you home in case she calls there." He took a deep breath, trying to calm down. This lady was counting on him. "Then I'll go look for her myself."

11

Mrs. Jackson crouched, tears streaming down her face, as the gurgling noises from the architect slowed. She'd liked the man, and now he was gravely hurt, maybe even dying.

Settle yourself, she thought. It'd simply been an accident, nothing more.

Soon the greenhouse was filled with people running towards her, Bessie barking, women sobbing, men shouting. The old lady had her hands to her face, wailing, "Noooo! Noooo!" at the top of her lungs.

Mr. Jackson rushed to Mrs. Jackson. "Are you hurt?"

"No," said Mrs. Jackson. "But he was making a noise. He might still be alive! Help me get these off him."

At once, Mr. Jackson went round to grasp a corner of the bag.

Mrs. Von Bilten, whose mink stole was now nowhere to be seen, clasped her hands in front of herself, as if she might be praying. "Oh, please let him be alive!" Then she shouted at the rest, "Well? Do something!"

Mr. Jackson and the Bohemian lifted the bags off Mr. Rothmore and placed them to the side.

But Mr. Rothmore lay unmoving.

Mrs. Jackson felt for a pulse and could find none. She looked up at the rest and shook her head.

The old lady began sobbing. Charles comforted her.

Mr. Carlo was aghast. "How could this possibly have happened?"

The Bohemian said, "I don't see how this was natural. The stack hasn't toppled. It's like ... like the bags were **dropped** upon him."

Mr. Jackson pointed. The two ladders that had been stacked together by the disassembled chairs and tables were now leaned upon the steel supports on each side of the stack. "Two people did this. Or one exceedingly strong man."

All eyes went to the burly man and the actress standing to his left.

The man took a step back, eyes wide, hands to his chest. "Surely you can't think **I** would do this? Why would I want this guy dead? We'd only just met!"

The woman placed her left hand on his, and a glittering large ring lay there. "He can't have done it," she said to them all. "He was with me until we heard the shouting."

The little blonde next to the Bohemian giggled. "I was coming from the toilet and saw them kissing!"

The actress blushed. "He just proposed."

"Oooh," the blonde said. "I love your ring."

"Enough!" The old man sounded outraged. "A man is **dead**! And my **property** has been stolen!"

Mr. Jackson said, "What property?"

"That's none of your concern." He looked around, scowling. "Where's that waiter gotten to?" He pointed towards the back door. "I told him to phone the police!"

Mr. Carlo's face turned horrified. "He was **in** here?"

"After we found the body," said Mrs. Jackson. "He seemed as surprised as we were." But she felt curious. "Do you know what that panel here is for?"

"Electrical," the old man said gruffly. "The water turns off when the panel's opened."

Mrs. Jackson moved gingerly around the dead man to peer into the panel. The space was just large enough to fit a briefcase similar to the one the old man held.

She glanced back at the old man. "What was it he came for?"

The old man ignored her, still searching the ground around him.

Ruby peered at the scene from behind the rest. Her hair was wet, and she still wore the towel. But her makeup was perfect.

Bessie pulled at her leash, away from the quieted waterfall, past the dead man, and past the piles of unassembled table and chair.

"Look here," the Bohemian said. "At the marks on the ground." He stared back at them, face astonished. "It looks like he was dragged!"

At any other time, George would've found Mrs. Kilpatrick incredibly annoying. But she'd evidently thought about the events of the day.

"Miss Ethel called, asking for Miss Ophelia." The woman's hand went to her mouth. "Oh. I shouldn't be telling you this."

"No," George said. "It's fine. She already told me what happened."

"Well," Mrs. Kilpatrick said, embarrassed, "The girl called, after I told her not to. I almost didn't want to let her take the call, but that dear little Ophelia's been downcast ever since Ethel left."

George glanced outside the cab: no sign of Ophelia anywhere. "Do you know what the call was about?"

"No ... they whispered for some time." She puffed up, suddenly offended. "I don't have two lines, sir, for me to listen in on private conversations. They may be young. But these are grown women, and will I treat them as such."

"No offense, meant, ma'am: I only wondered if maybe they were to meet somewhere."

The woman looked rattled. "I never considered it!" She bit her lower lip. "I don't think so. Miss Ophelia just happened to mention to Zinnie that she'd go to the library before work, or I'd never have known."

After George dropped Mrs. Kilpatrick at her home — with strict instructions to keep the girls off the line in case Ophie might call — he had the taxi take the route someone might walk to the library.

The whole time, he peered out of the window, heart in his throat.

If she wasn't at the library, he didn't know what he was going to do. Where could Ophie have gone? Had someting happened to her? He couldn't think of any other reason for her not to arrive at work.

"What's she look like?"

George turned to the man, startled. "I —"

The taxi driver chuckled. "Never seen a man get so worked up about anything other than his gal."

His gal? He and Ophie were friends, sure. If he had his way, they'd go dancing together every night. But she'd never wanted anything else, which suited him just fine. "Short, reddish blonde curls, dark mustard-colored hat and coat."

"Sounds sweet," the man said. "Sure hope you find her. You getting married?"

George felt just a little annoyed. "No ..."

"No offense. Just ... you might want to grab this one before she gets away. If you take my meaning."

George flopped back in the seat, mind reeling. His heart thudded in his chest. He'd never conceived of such a thing. "Just get us there, will you?" He had to find her. He couldn't bear the thought of never seeing her again.

***

Meanwhile, the group in the greenhouse peered at the ground. Definite drag marks, scratched into the soft mossy walkway, with dribbles of what looked like water along the way. Following these led to the front corner of the glass structure.

Mrs. Jackson smelled an acrid, metallic odor. Much of the ground was dark. Water had been splashed upon the area, but spatters of blood lay upon the foliage. "Where did this blood come from?"

Those assembled there looked at the dead man, still face-down on the ground, then rushed to his side.

"We should take pictures of how we found him," the Bohemian said, "for the police."

The photographer, who'd not moved from staring at the dead man, jerked as if startled.

Charles De Rege said, "Isn't it a bit late for that?"

Mr. Jackson said, "It's a fine idea." He turned to the photographer. "Go on, sir."

The photographer looked as if he might be sick. But he took several photos of the area.

"I don't see much blood here beside him," said Mrs. Jackson. "I wonder where it came from?"

The old man growled. "Let's have a look."

Amidst protests of "No!" and "We should wait for the police!" and "We shouldn't move the body!" he pushed past and turned the architect over.

Mr. Horace Rothmore's throat had been cut.

12

The actress fainted, her gentleman only barely catching her. Mrs. Von Bilten screamed, sobbing, and dashed out. The little blonde said, "I better make sure she's okay." and followed her.

The burly man moved his fiancée to the side, leaned her onto a small tree and fanned her with his fedora. The old man surveyed the scene, scoffed, and left through the back door. Young Miss "Oyster" hurried to follow him.

Astonished, Mr. Jackson murmured to himself, "This is a murder!"

The camera flashed as the photographer took a picture of the dead man.

Charles De Rege drawled, "You **really** think so. And what **other** brilliant ideas do you have?"

Mr. Jackson, to his credit, ignored the young man. He took his wife's hand. "Let's find that waiter."

The two went out of the back door into relative darkness, lit only by the inner glow of the greenhouse. When they reached the telephone cabana, the older man and Miss "Oyster" stared at the pieces of wrapped electrical cord in their hands.

The young woman looked up at him, fear in her eyes, and spoke too loudly. "The phone wires were cut!"

Startled murmurs as the others heard. Several came over to investigate.

Who would cut the phone wires, when they had a dead man —?

He felt horrified. "The murderer's here with us!"

Only the killer wouldn't want the police notified. Only the killer wouldn't want the architect to get help.

And the young brown-haired waiter was nowhere to be seen.

He'd fancied the man earlier, but now he felt decidedly alarmed.

Did they have a madman on their hands?

13

When George got to the library, he gave the driver a dollar tip and ran inside. Then he stood in the lobby, unsure which way to go. Where could Ophie have gone? Why would she even **be** here?

A middle-aged woman came up to him. "Might I help you, sir?"

How to find her? "Um, did you see a young woman?" He measured her height with his hand. "This tall, strawberry blonde, wearing a dark mustard-colored coat and hat."

"I did," the woman said. "She wanted the periodicals." Then she paused, scrutinizing his face. "I hope nothing's amiss?"

She made it here. He took a deep breath, let it out, heart pounding. "Can you show me that section?"

She smiled at him. "I most certainly can."

When he saw Ophie sitting in front of stacks of newspapers, he felt so relieved he thought he might cry. "You're okay!"

"Of course I'm okay," Ophie said. Then she shook herself, glancing around. "Why are you here?" Then she gasped. "Gosh. What time is it?"

George looked round: there were no clocks in this room. "It's well after nine. Mrs. Kilpatrick was frantic. The club called —"

Ophie's hands went to her mouth. "I completely lost track of the time."

He plopped himself down and threw his arms around her, head on her shoulder. *She's okay.* "I thought some horrible thing had happened to you."

Ophie put her arms around him. "Oh, my dear Georgie." She sounded touched, and pleased as well. "I'm so sorry to scare you." Then she drew back, turned to the papers. "I couldn't get wanting to know what happened to Pam out of my mind! So I thought that if I came here, I'd find something about it in the papers."

George sat up. "And did you?"

"I found the city news. Lots of tabloids, too." She shook her head. "She was in the middle of a huge scandal! No wonder she doesn't want to go home."

Ophie turned pensive. "It looks like it was more than she just got mixed up with the Mob. She went after the Mayor, who it sounds like was **in** the Mob! But this goes **way** back before just a year ago." She surveyed the papers strewn about her. "I can't find the most recent copies."

"I'll help," George said. "What am I looking for?"

She pointed to a large collection of racks, each containing hanging folders stuffed full of old newspapers. "That's the section. Ugh, it took me forever just to find which city, even with the librarian's help."

George felt uneasy. "How much did you tell her?"

Ophie giggled. "I told her I had a project for school."

Whew, George thought. "First let's see what you've got. It might give us some clues."

She began laying out both legitimate newspapers and cheap tabloids, the most recent first, so only the headlines showed:

CITY WATCHES, WRESTLES WITH TRUTH
HOW COULD SHE?
IS MAYOR A VILLAIN?
LIAR, LIAR
MAYOR DENIES EVERY ALLEGATION
THIS MANY LIES?
"MAYOR GAVE ME ENGAGEMENT RING"
HOW OLD <u>WAS</u> SHE?
DOZENS DEAD: MAYOR ACCUSED
AN INDECENT MAN?
ACCUSATIONS GALORE
COMPELLING TESTIMONY

George stared, speechless. "And she was ...?"

"The main one accusing him. But so many came forward that I'd be surprised if he wasn't impeached."

"I hadn't heard any of this." A chuckle burst out. "But then, I'm not much for reading the news." And it seemed there were enough scandals right here in Chicago to make up for it. He stood peering at the papers. "It sounds like she was winning! You're right: something had to have gone terribly wrong for her to have run, much less here."

"Well, didn't you read that flier? The one Mr. Hector showed us? It said, 'Wanted for questioning.' I can't imagine the Feds would want to question her unless something absolutely huge happened."

"Yeah," George said absentmindedly. But he couldn't imagine what that might be.

***

Mrs. Jackson stood looking at the cut wires, but she was thinking of what her Mr. Jackson had said: *the murderer is with us.*

But why murder someone at a party in their honor?

A shriek, in the direction of the elevator shaft. One of the twins stood facing the door to the stair, hands to her face. In front of her, his back to the door, stood the young brown-haired waiter Hugh, holding a shiny clean carving knife. "Not gonna let you do it!"

Everyone rushed over.

Mr. Carlo shouted, "Put down that knife, this instant!"

The young man's words were slurred. "You fired me, sir. I'm not yours to command, no more."

"Son," the old man said, hand out. "Come on. You don't want to hurt anyone. Gimme the knife, son."

Hugh's hands went to his sides, his fists balled up. He screamed, "I'm not your son!"

Mr. Carlo and the old man rushed him. Instead of fighting, Hugh ran for the pool. A chase began, everyone seemingly wanting to catch him.

But instead of going in the water, he ran past it, past the toilets and the towels, and heaved something small over the edge, which made a jingling noise as it went. Then he dropped the knife, speaking in the group's general direction. "You'll never get away. I won't let you get away with it!"

Mr. Carlo and the old man grabbed Hugh then, marching him over to a table. Mr. Carlo said, "Stay there, you, or we'll tie you to the chair!"

"They can't get away with it," the young man sobbed. "I won't let them do it. No, sir. Not like before."

Mrs. Jackson had followed. "Who?"

Hugh's eyes were red. He made a wild gesture in the direction of the group. "Them."

She peered into the young man's eyes. "Did you call the police? Or did you cut the telephone wire?"

He focused on her. "Both. They're not gonna get away with this."

"Bah," said Mr. Carlo. "Surely we have the murderer right here. He's only trying to pin it on someone else."

Mrs. Jackson straightened. "No. He couldn't have done it. Just look! His shirt is spotless, and he's got not a drop on him. And that knife had no blood on it either."

Mr. Carlo twitched. "You there," he said to Victor. "Get me that knife."

Victor fetched the knife by the very tip of its handle, hand shaking. And sure enough, the blade was as clean as the day was long.

Mrs. Jackson crouched beside Hugh again. "What did you throw over the side?"

"The key to the stair," he said. "They'll not sneak down that way!"

Mrs. Jackson stared at him. Why would he lock the stair? Why did he think the killer was still here? "You said, 'them.' Did you see them do it?

Right at that moment, the lights went out.

14

Ophelia had just found the paper she wanted! Now she couldn't see a thing.

Far off, people shrieked, called out. "Ophie," George said, a quaver in his voice. "Are you okay?"

"I'm okay." She felt a bit scared. "But I can't see."

His words were kind. "Come to my voice."

The table was in the way. Papers rustled to the floor. She felt round until she found him, and sat beside him.

He grabbed her hand. "How are we going to get out of here?"

She shrugged, then realized he couldn't see her. "I don't know. But I wonder why the lights failed." She pondered that for a moment. "If were windows, so we could see if we're the only ones without power."

"That's a good question," George said. "Do they have a generator? Even candles would do. Although I can't see wanting flame around a building full of paper."

Ophelia giggled at the idea.

George said, "Maybe we should wait for someone to come get us. Or for the light to go back on. I don't remember the way here."

"Okay." She liked holding George's hand.

After a while, he said, "Did you get what you needed?"

"I suppose. But the most recent news from that city is gone. I wonder why?"

George got quiet for a while. "I know you just want to help. But what if Hector and Pamela are keeping things quiet to protect us?"

"What do you mean?"

She could hear him take a deep, shaky breath, let it out. "Someone's **after** them! What if those guys took the papers to see who comes looking?"

Ophelia tried to figure what he meant. "You mean, like a signal?"

"Yeah. Why would someone go looking for that specific person, about something that happened all that way away, more than a year ago? They'd have to have a reason." He fell silent again, just for a bit. "It'd be easy to set a man in every big city, have him frequent the libraries, the records hall, and wait for some palooka to take the bait."

Ophelia felt scared. "So what do I do?"

George let out another breath. "Let it alone. You found what you wanted. You know there was a scandal. You know people are after her, people mean enough to kill her husband and son. They either think she knows something and want to shut her up, or they think she did something and want revenge for it." A rustling sound, as

698

if he moved. "I don't know which, and neither does Hector. But he's spending way too much on a place for them to run to at the very **thought** of these people finding her." He got quiet for a minute. "I don't think it's the Feds."

"Who else would it be?"

"Well, somebody in the Mob's after them too, right? Back where they come from."

"Ohhh." She wasn't scared of the Feds, not really. They were government guys. But ... "You're scared they're going to come after us."

"Yeah."

So she and George either had to go with Pam and Mr. Hector, or stay here and hope the men didn't find them. "What do you want to do?"

He took a deep breath. "I'm staying. I can't leave my parents like that, just disappear. Besides, if these guys figure out I knew them, they'd go after my parents. I can't leave them here to face that alone. They have no idea what's going on."

She never even thought of that. If they couldn't find her, would these men go after Mrs. Kilpatrick, the girls at the boarding house, the girls at Club Patruni?

It scared her. She didn't know what to do. She still didn't have an answer to Mr. Hector's question. And she felt like she should. "Sometimes I don't think Pam really cares about me."

George got quiet for a while. "I think she cares about you a whole lot."

"But —"

"The problem's not that she doesn't love you. The problem's that she's scared to."

This felt like someone punched her in the chest, and for a minute, she couldn't breathe. After her mom died, she felt like that for a long while. She felt cold inside, empty. And then a woman followed her into an alley.

Pam. She'd never met anyone like her.

"At least, that's what Hector thinks," George said, "and I agree. He doesn't know any more than you do, and he married her anyway, because he loves her." He got quiet, then chuckled softly.

"What's funny?"

"Oh, just the goofy smile he gets when he talks about her. But you know what he said? That he was never, ever gonna say he loved her, because that's when he'd wake up to find her gone."

She felt dismayed. "Gosh. I wish I would've known that earlier!" Is that why Pam hadn't come by this whole week, or telephoned her?

Had she made a huge mistake?

George's voice startled her. "What happened with Ethel?"

"What do you mean?"

"Mrs. Kilpatrick said you got a call from her. Before you left for work."

The "Yeah. Her mother's making her get married to the man that she went behind the theater with."

"Does she want to marry him?"

Ethel had been crying. "She doesn't know. She thinks he might be trifling with her."

"That doesn't sound good."

"She doesn't know what to do. She's twenty-four and still not married. And now this. Her mother's worried for her safety if news of it should get out."

"Oh." George sounded surprised. Then he snorted. "Sounds a bit too much like me."

"What do you mean?"

"Heh," he said. "My parents are trying to make me get married, too."

"To who?"

"It's not like **that**. They just want me to settle down." He laughed. "I suppose to them, anyone would do."

"I'm sorry." Then something came to her. "You were at work!"

"Yeah."

"Won't you get in trouble?"

He let out a laugh. "Probably."

"So why'd you come after me?"

He got real quiet then. "I thought something happened to you."

Oh, boy, she thought. Was **that** what this was all about? "Please, Georgie. Don't get stuck on me." She felt sad. "I told you. Back at the park. I'm not the kind of girl who can give you what you want."

He chuckled. "It's not like that. I like you. We have fun together." He rustled around, then said, "I don't **need** anything from you! All I want is to be around you. I want to take **care** of you, make sure you're okay!" He got quiet for a minute, and when he spoke next he sounded excited. "It'll be swell! Between the two of us, we'll have plenty of dough. Go dancing every night we can, and maybe travel with Pam and Hector someday!" His voice turned like he thought of something funny. "They'll probably be here a while yet. And when they go, maybe we can find someone new."

The thought of Pam leaving gave her a lump in her throat. She would marry Pam herself, if such a thing were ever possible. She squeezed his hand. "I hope they never go. But ... you really want me? Like I am?"

He had a smile in his voice. "You're perfect, Ophie. Exactly the way you are."

15

The sky held waves of green. Mrs. Jackson had never seen such a thing in her life.

On the rooftop of the Myriad Hotel, the group sat in a circle under the light of the torches, seemingly above the chaos that must be going on below.

"My grandmother told me of this," the old woman said. "Hasn't happened here in a hundred years."

The reporter took out his notepad and began scribbling, while the photographer twisted around trying to take pictures of the sky.

"They're called auroras," the old man said. "Caused by the sun, they think. Although I don't know why we're seeing them here. They're supposed to only be up North."

No one had an answer.

Bessie seemed not to mind their new sky one bit. She lay curled beside Mrs. Jackson's right foot, eyes closed.

Ruby pulled her towel around her, sounding afraid. "Why don't the elevators work?"

Russell took off his spectacles and wiped them on his apron. Then he gestured at the electric lights, which were cold and quiet. "They run on power."

Mr. Jackson leaned over to whisper in her ear. "The door to the stair is locked, and the only key available's on the street. How are we going to get down?"

"Well," she whispered back. "If this fellow did call the police, they'll figure out a way to us. I can't imagine old Nestor taking this as anything but a challenge."

He laughed.

Mrs. Von Bilten snapped, "What could you possibly find funny?"

Bessie twitched, letting out a yelp, and looked around before settling back in.

Mrs. Jackson felt contrite. "Nothing. We were just saying that if young Hugh here did call the police, well, we happen to know the man who'd arrive. He'd take getting up here as a challenge."

Cornelius Ober laughed, as did young Charles.

The musicians looked at each other. "Police?"

Bessie's ears went up.

"A man's been killed," said Mr. Carlo. "He's in the greenhouse there. Nothing to be alarmed at. We'll have to make do until the police arrive."

The saxophonist said, "What do you want us to do?"

Everyone looked to Mr. Carlo, who shrugged.

Mrs. Jackson pointed to Hugh. "He threw the key to the stairs over the side. We might just have to wait."

The rest looked various forms of disgruntled.

Mrs. Jackson said, "Forgive me, but I don't actually know many of your names."

"Ah." The Bohemian rose and bowed. "Cornelius Ober at your service." He sat then gesturing to the blonde beside him. "And this magnificent gem is Miss Millicent Book."

"Call me Millie." She beamed. "I'm a singer."

Mrs. Jackson pointed to the actress sitting beside the young woman. "And you are?"

She raised an eyebrow. "Rather chagrined that you don't know!"

"I'm so sorry," Mrs. Jackson said. "We're not from around here."

Mr. Jackson said, "I suppose I've been remiss. I should've taken you to more cinema."

The actress smiled to herself. "Well, in any case, I'm Ada Leb."

Millie gushed, "Only the bee's knees!" She turned to Ada, face aglow. "I never thought I'd get to shake your hand! And here you are, Miss Ada Leb, actually sitting beside me!"

Mrs. Von Bilten sneered. "Alvira Lebensohl, you mean. Born to a back-alley butcher and his cheap dance-hall whore."

Ada raised her chin, unruffled. "Every actress has a stage name. My real name is public record. Say what you like about my parents, but they taught me manners, which is more than I can say for you."

Charles snorted.

Mrs. Jackson admired Ada's courage. "And who is your lucky young man?"

Ada's fiance tipped his fedora, then took Ada's hand. "Ernest Lock, ma'am."

"A pleasure," Mrs. Jackson said. She turned to the old man. "And you are?"

"Lewis McKenney." Mr. McKenney seemed both impatient and disgruntled by the whole affair.

The musicians were Sidney Nanton (the pianist), Otis Zachery on the saxophone, and Maurice Foots on the trumpet. Perry Young played the string bass, and Dennis Edmond the drums. The reporter was Bence Gereben, a strange little thin man. The photographer was named Walter Margin.

"Thank you," Mrs. Jackson said. "We're Pamela and Hector Jackson." She picked up her little dog, snuggling her close. "And this sweet girl is Bessie."

A round of "how do you do", and most smiled at little Bessie before Mrs. Jackson returned her to the floor.

Except for Mrs. Von Bilten. She snapped, "How is this nonsense going to find his killer?"

Mrs. Jackson shrugged. "I've no idea. But I like to know who I'm speaking with." Then Mrs. Jackson raised her voice. "Young lady, you can come out now."

Silence, for an uncomfortable amount of time — Mrs. Jackson hoped she hadn't been wrong — then a woman who looked precisely like Ruby emerged into the torches' glow from the direction of the elevator shaft, still clutching her golden towel.

Mr. Jackson gasped. "I never suspected!"

Millie said matter-of-factly, "They're famous. Always getting into some sort of trouble."

Chin held high, the young woman approached the group as if her double wasn't sitting right there. Victor got her a chair, the others scooted over, and she sat, not looking at anyone.

Mr. Jackson said, "However did you guess?"

"Just look at them," said Mrs. Jackson. She pointed at the newcomer. "I knew the minute I saw her, back in the greenhouse after the murder. A woman having been pushed into a pool would have her hair and makeup ruined. Yet this one's hair only wetted, not soaked. And her makeup is perfect."

The twins glared at each other.

Mr. Jackson chuckled. "And it seems the 'one-of-a-kind' dress has its pair."

Mr. Carlo scowled.

"**I'm** Ruby," Perfect Makeup said. "Not her."

Mrs. Jackson turned to the other girl, who, while dried off, still looked somewhat like a drowned rat. "Then who are **you**?"

The girl snorted. "You really **aren't** from around here, are you? Pearl Carlisle, at your service."

Mr. Jackson laughed. "Ah. Oyster."

Cornelius Ober chuckled.

"Hmm," said Mrs. Jackson. "So why pretend?"

"I was doing an interview downstairs," said the real Ruby. "I was the one invited, and I didn't want to cause a scene by arriving late. So I sent Pearl in my place."

"I don't think so," Mrs. Jackson and Mr. Carlo said.

They looked at each other.

"You were both invited," said Mr. Carlo. "Mr. Rothmore insisted."

Pearl laughed. "Why would we lie about **that**?"

"I don't know," Mrs. Jackson said. "But Ruby has your real mole drawn on." She turned to Ruby. "So Ruby, you were pretending to be **her**, not the other way round." She leaned back. "Which makes me wonder: why would Miss Pearl want to be up here so badly?"

Pearl glanced away, drawing her towel around her. "I despise interviews."

Cornelius Ober said dryly, "Yet you give so many of them."

Pearl rolled her eyes.

"And in each one," Mr. Ober said, "you talk about your father's work. Touching."

"He was a great man," Pearl said.

"My condolences," said Mr. Ober. He looked around. "I think we all feel the same."

"Wait," Mr. Jackson said. "Your father died?"

"Several weeks ago," Mr. Gereben said. "It was in the papers." He preened, just a bit. "I did the story myself. The result of injuries sustained in the War."

Mr. Ober scoffed.

Both the twins looked away.

"Oh, I'm so sorry," Mrs. Jackson said quickly.

Hugh let out a soft snore.

Mrs. Jackson pointed to the sleeping young waiter. "Does anyone know what he was going on about?"

Russell said, "Not exactly. But he's been acting nervous ever since," he gestured with his chin at Pearl, "that one arrived."

Mr. Jackson leaned forward. "Nervous?"

Mr. McKenney snorted. "Sure acting strangely for a man in love."

"No," Russell said. "Not nervous like that. Like he was scared of her. Or angry, and didn't know what to do about it."

Mrs. Jackson said, "Pearl, he said something to you when he got you your drink. What was it?"

Pearl shrugged. "Must not have been anything worth remembering, because I can't recall." She laughed. "That **was** several drinks ago." She went quiet. "I knew him back in school. He's always been twitchy." She looked around at everyone. "I got nothing against him. I even bought him a drink."

Victor nodded, his long bangs falling across his face. "I remember: she did."

Mrs. Jackson thought through what she'd seen, heard. "Whoever killed this man did so with a knife. Yet not only is our very drunk waiter's shirt flawless, the knife he brandished is clean. So —"

"I suppose he might've changed his shirt and washed up," Mr. Ober said.

The old man said, "I wonder. What marks might you find on **that** outlandish suit?"

Everyone looked. Every bit Mr. Cornelius Ober wore was dark, down to his calf-high black leather boots. Perfect for hiding blood.

It was then she noticed a large deep red spot staining the embroidery of his floor-length coat, at about the level of his knee.

Pearl had venom in her tone. "Everyone knows you hate the man."

Mr. Ober laughed. "Nonsense. I was by the banister giving an interview with our reporter and photographer here," he gestured at the men, who nodded, "when someone said they heard screaming." He glanced at the others. "I presume that's when you found the body?"

Mr. Jackson said, "It was."

Charles pointed to the man's coat. "What's that stain from, then?"

Cornelius Ober peered down. "This?" He chuckled. "A bit too much fun three parties ago. My wash lady never could remove the stain. But I adore this coat simply too much to get rid of it."

Mrs. Jackson said, "Mr. Ober, why do you hate Mr. Rothmore? What's he done?"

The man crossed his legs at the knee and looked away, taking a drag from his cigarette on its long holder before blowing a smoke-ring. "Nothing I can prove, mind you. But every time one of us would do a showing, a pane or three would be broken." He shrugged. "Happened to me more than once."

Mr. Jackson leaned forward. "And you blamed him."

"Everyone did," Ruby said. "He never had anything broken, ever."

Well, Mrs. Jackson thought. This surely **was** personal. And more than a bit ironic. "It seems we all have alibis for the crime. But if you recall, the man was dragged to where we found him. Bags of stone were then dropped upon him —"

The old woman flinched.

"— and the scene was tidied up. That took time. And some strength. And balancing on a ladder as you push over a fifty-pound bag of stone? It isn't easy. So —"

The trumpet player Mr. Foots looked incredulous. "Wait just a minute. Bags of **stone**?"

Old Mr. McKenney said, "The same."

Mr. Foots put his hand upon his forehead. "Mercy. That poor man."

Mr. Carlo snapped, "You lot go back there and play." With the torches and candles, the lighting was dimmer than before, but good enough. "I'll not have you sit here when I'm paying you."

The five band members looked at each other, got up in a resigned manner, and returned to their posts. After a minute or so, soft music wafted overhead.

Soon one person wanted a drink, another something to eat, and the group dissipated.

Cornelius Ober and Millie began a slow dance. Mr. Lock and Ada Leb moved to a table and began quietly conversing. Mr. McKenney got another drink, then lit his pipe, facing Victor in an apparent discussion.

Russell checked on the buffet. He then went to the photographer, Mr. Margin, and began conversing. Mr. Margin opened a large flat case he had with him and took out one of the many portfolios inside.

Mrs. Von Bilten sat crying. Charles made an attempt to console her, but she said something which seemed to offend him. The young man threw his arms up and went to the banister, standing between the jazz band and the greenhouse.

Mrs. Jackson, Mr. Jackson, and Mr. Carlo stood in the middle of the party area. Bessie lay curled up beside Mrs. Jackson's feet.

The pool was only faintly lit by the guttering votives encircling it. Between those and their better-lit area lay only darkness.

Hugh still slept, his head on his arms upon the table. Mrs. Jackson was reminded of their last case, the man shot dead in the speakeasy.

She said to Mr. Carlo, "I think this young man either knew something, or saw something. I'd very much like to have a talk with him when he awakens."

"I'm sure the police will too," Mr. Carlo said. "Threatening guests with a knife? Public drunkenness?" He shook his head. "And he seemed such a decent sort."

Mr. Jackson said, "What do you mean?"

Mr. Carlo chuckled. "We check the background of our new hires. They're dealing with money and personal items, after all." He gestured at the young man. "College man. He was on the varsity swimming team."

Mrs. Jackson said, "Was?"

Mr. Carlo shook his head. "He's taking a year off. A death of someone close to him. A roommate, I believe. He wouldn't get into detail about it. And then the year before, his father passed away."

"Poor fellow," Mr. Jackson said. "He's evidently gone into paranoia."

Mr. Carlo gazed up at the swirling green overhead. "Maybe I was too hard on the lad." Then he let out a laugh. "Too bad he threw the key over the side."

Mrs. Jackson said, "Might it not have landed on the lower level?"

"Heh," Mr. Carlo said. "I wish. But the heave-to the boy gave that thing? It's probably across the street."

Mr. Jackson shrugged. "Take heart. It's considerably more comfortable here than in the stairwell."

"Well," Mrs. Jackson said, "don't forget our suite is only the one floor below."

"Yes," Mr. Jackson said. "But even if we could get down there, we'd have half this lot — plus Sergeant Nestor — in our suite for the rest of the night."

Mr. Carlo laughed. "True enough." He looked over at them. "So perhaps it turned out for the best. Care for some refreshments?"

Mrs. Jackson got some tea; her Mr. Jackson chose coffee. Interested in the photography, she strolled over to where Mr. Margin sat.

The man glanced up when they approached. "Care to join me?"

Mr. Jackson said, "Certainly."

So they sat.

Mrs. Jackson said, "Do you accompany Mr. Gereben often?"

He laughed. "I work with whoever hires me. Mostly society affairs, such as this one." He took out a business card and handed it over. Then his mood soured. "I've done work involving Mr. Rothmore before."

Mr. Jackson said, "You make it sound unpleasant."

Mr. Margin sighed. "Well, he could be a capricious and yes, unpleasant man."

Mrs. Jackson said, "Whatever do you mean?"

Mr. Margin hesitated, then drew a second portfolio from his large case, opening it onto the table. "I'd done a spread — at his request — to show as part of a photography exhibit. I'd entered the exhibit at my own cost, and was planning to sell some of the prints there." He fell silent.

Mr. Jackson leaned forward, "What happened?"

"I'd sent the spread over for his review the day before the show. I thought he might want to take out one or maybe two. Sometimes in these cases, that happens. But he telephoned that night, saying he was withdrawing his entire exhibit. He insisted on keeping every photo! But of course I'd made copies." His shoulders drooped. "I can't sell them without his permission, but I can show others my work." He crossed his arms in front of him. "I was out fifty dollars for the entry fee. I wouldn't have come to this affair at all, but Bence is a friend. The photographer he'd hired cancelled at the last minute."

Mrs. Jackson felt curious. "Might I see these photos?"

The photographer shrugged, sliding the portfolio towards her.

The pictures were quite ordinary: the greenhouse, the architect standing before it. Most were of lush plants, fountains, the effects of light being cast upon the ground. But there was one of the architect bent over, speaking with two small boys. Or rather, by his stance, scolding them. "Where was this taken?"

"Around back of the greenhouse." He peered at the scene. "This was at a model showing. Dozens of greenhouse designers made small glass houses for the event. I believe this was outside one of the others."

From the look of it, Mr. Rothmore seemed disapproving, perhaps even angry. "I wonder what was going on here."

"He gave those boys a good talking-to. But I never learned what for."

16

Leaving the party behind and Bessie with Mr. Jackson, Mrs. Jackson took one of the tapered candles and made her way into the darkness between the party area and the water. She then threaded past the guttering votives along the pool to the Ladies' Room.

She was at once faced with where to put the candle. Finally, she dripped some of the wax onto the floor and stood the base of the candle up in it.

It was late; she felt weary. As she sat staring at the flame, her mind returned to Mr. Rothmore, still lying dead in the greenhouse.

His death surely felt personal.

Ruby — or rather, Pearl — said they all hated each other. Perhaps enough to murder?

The hulking bodyguard and his actress had an alibi — the young blonde.

And neither had motive to kill the man.

The Bohemian had motive. But he had an alibi — the photographer and reporter.

The old woman seemed devastated at the architect's death; it seemed she'd had some feeling for the man.

Mr. McKenney had been with her and Bessie when they found the body. The musicians had been playing at the time.

Mr. Carlo, of course, had no motive whatsoever. He hated scandal at his hotel, and this was nothing but.

So who did that leave?

A huge amount of splashing, right outside. Were they really playing around the pool again?

After some time, the splashing quieted, stopped.

Then footsteps. Then a shriek!

A woman cried, "Help! Help!"

Mrs. Jackson stood, arranged her clothing, picked up the candle, and made her way outside.

All of the men, including the musicians, were hurrying across the rooftop towards them.

One of the twins stood there, hands to her mouth, staring at the water.

Hugh floated in watery darkness, face down.

17

As the men arrived, Mrs. Jackson pointed to the man in the water. One of the musicians took off his jacket, handed it to another, then dove in.

Her Mr. Jackson rushed to her side, Bessie bounding beside him. "Are you hurt?"

She shook her head and picked up Bessie. "I just came out here."

The musician flipped the man over and began pulling the unmoving figure back to the steps. The other men pulled the limp man out of the water and turned him face down.

The women trailed up more slowly, gasping when they saw the dead man lying there.

"I know resuscitation," Cornelius Ober said. "You there," he pointed to Victor. "This takes two. Keep his arms near to the pavers, then move them above his head." He crouched, demonstrating, and the waiter followed. "Then quickly down." He moved the arm he held down to the man's side. "We must act in unison. Let's do it again. Up, and down. Up, and down."

The pair continued on.

Russell nodded approvingly. "I've seen this before. They do this at the lake for drownings."

Mrs. Jackson had never seen the technique before. "Did it work?"

The blond waiter looked startled. "It seemed to."

"Lift his legs," Mr. McKenney said, "so the water may drain out."

Victor tried to do so, but it seemed Hugh's legs were too heavy. With a growl, the old man took one of the legs, lifting Hugh's hips above his chest. A gush of water came from the young man's mouth.

Mr. Carlo knelt beside Hugh and began pounding his back in various places. "The nurses do this for fluid on the lungs."

Mrs. Jackson nodded. Duchess Cordelia had helped her in just this way when she had a bad case of bronchitis after the New Year.

The rest encouraged them on.

But after some time, fatigue on their faces, they stopped. Mr. Ober felt for a pulse, and shook his head.

Mrs. Jackson hugged Bessie, feeling devastated. Possibly the one man who might tell what he'd seen, and now he was dead!

Mr. Carlo said to the girl who'd found him, "Why didn't you get him out?"

Drops glittered on the young woman's cheeks under flawless makeup. "I tried. I went in. But he was too far out, and I don't know how to swim!"

Good thing **she** wasn't pushed into the pool, Mrs. Jackson thought. "Did you see what happened?"

"I was on my way to the Ladies' Room. But I couldn't see anything but the candles," she pointed, "down here." The beaded edge of her dark brown dress dripped. "Then I heard the splashing," she pointed, "and so I came around over here. Then I saw his shirt, and it moved. Good gracious, it startled me!"

Mr. Jackson leaned over to whisper in Mrs. Jackson's ear. "Something's not right."

She nodded. Then she called out, "Let's cover him up and leave him be. The police will be here soon enough."

***

Ophelia still sat in the library, darkness all around, holding hands with George.

What he'd suggested didn't seem real. Him and her, together? She supposed he wanted to marry.

Men just weren't like that: they wanted regular women, not someone like her.

Was George lying about her being all right for him? Did he think he was going to **change** her?

No. She couldn't live like that. She wouldn't.

She let go of George's hand, staring into the darkness.

What should she do?

Somehow, her Mama knew the influenza was taking her. And she worried so much as she lay dying. "Bad times are coming, little girl. I can feel it. Just promise me you'll marry. Promise me you'll find a man that'll keep you safe."

But what could she say? She'd never found a man she wanted ... like that. The thought of a man pawing at her felt repulsive.

Maybe it wouldn't be so bad. George wasn't like most men. He was kind and good-natured and sensible. He wanted to take her dancing, and travel the world. He cared about her, and about what she wanted, too.

Pam wasn't going to stay here, whether she went with her or not. And it seemed like the more she tried to push Pam to talk, the more she pulled away. Even that time Pam said her real name seemed to upset her, make her scared.

If what George said was true, maybe she shouldn't be looking for the truth. Maybe it was going to cause more harm than good.

But there, alone in the dark, the truth crept up to her on its own. She could almost hear her Mama speak: *It's time to grow up, baby girl.*

She was twenty-one and a full adult woman. Pam had been through one of the most awful things a woman could imagine. Being held up to public scandal? Called a liar? Then to see her husband and child dead?

She shuddered.

And looking back on what she'd done of the past week, how she'd acted ...

Ophelia felt ashamed of herself.

Maybe instead of badgering Pam and going behind her back, she should have been looking for ways to make Pam's life better. Like Mr. Hector was doing. Instead, she'd been acting like a spoiled child demanding more than Pam might ever be able to give.

George's voice startled her. "I'll tell you everything, Ophie. Everything. Even about me and Hector." He squeezed her hand tight, but only for a moment. "I promise."

She felt entirely confused. Her heart was pounding so loud she thought sure he could hear it. "Wait. You ... and Mr. Hector?"

He sounded like he was smiling. "Of course, silly. Didn't you know?" She heard him breathe in, and it wobbled. "I'll tell you everything. Everything. And you can tell me everything, too."

She didn't know why, or how, or even when, but she found herself with her arms around him, sobbing into his jacket.

George was like **her**!

She didn't have to hide who she was anymore, be scared anymore. Worry about anyone leaving her anymore. And now, there in the dark with her friend, it seemed like everything was finally going to be all right.

18

The group returned to the chairs. Mrs. Jackson felt grieved and disturbed. Mr. Jackson was right: this didn't happen naturally. And the story Ruby gave made no sense.

Hugh had clearly seen something he shouldn't, something he'd been killed to silence. Why would anyone kill a waiter, otherwise?

He'd been trying to tell them what was going on this entire time. He thought he knew who killed Mr. Rothmore, someone he feared would get away with the crime "like last time." But he'd been so intoxicated nothing **he**'d said made sense.

The exchange she'd seen between Hugh and Pearl, well before the first murder, felt suspicious.

But there seemed to be no connection (at least, that she'd seen) between the young waiter and Ruby. If she did hurt him, why?

No one wanted music anymore, so the musicians (along with Mr. Foots holding his own golden towel) joined the rest at the circle.

Mr. Edmond (Mrs. Jackson thought he was the drummer. Or was he the bassist?) said, "Why aren't the police here already?"

Mr. McKenney got out his pipe. "If that waiter really did call them, they might've gotten stuck in the elevator when the power went out."

Mr. Carlo kept shaking his head. "How did he get into the pool? Why wasn't anyone watching him?"

Mrs. Jackson said, "You really think he wandered over there and fell in on his own?"

Mr. Nanton had been sitting leaned over, staring at a folder of piano music in his hand. "It's certainly possible. It's dark, and the toilets are that way. He was so drunk he might have forgotten about the pool."

A bit of silence, then Mr. Lock said, "I meant to watch over him. But he was asleep. Me and Ada got to talking, and I thought he'd stay asleep, at least for a while." He sighed. "I just don't see how he could've gotten all that way by himself."

Mr. Carlo persisted. "There are twenty of us here at least. No one saw him get up? Walk, what is it, thirty yards to the pool?"

Everyone glanced at each other, shook their heads.

Mr. Jackson looked abashed. "I admit, I've been most distracted this evening." He looked around at the rest. "A business deal."

Ada looked at her Mr. Lock, then back at the group. "We've been talking of the best way to break this to our parents. The engagement." She glanced aside. "They're not fond of the match."

"Corny and I were dancing," Millie said.

The musicians glanced at each other and shrugged. "We was playin', like you told us to," Mr. Zachery said.

Ruby they'd all seen. Mrs. Jackson turned to Pearl, who'd wiped most of the makeup off of her cheeks. "What were you doing all this time?"

"She was with me," Charles said. "Over at the banister. Having a drink. Whatever you might think of the situation, these auroras make one hell of a show."

Mrs. Von Bilten cried out, "Don't you care **anything** about him being **dead**?"

Everyone turned to stare at her.

Mrs. Jackson said, "Him? Which him?"

She clasped her hands to her mouth, appalled.

"Heh," Charles said. "Now you've done it."

Mrs. Jackson peered at the old woman for a moment. Then it came to her. "Lydia **Rothman** Von Bilten —"

The old woman flinched.

"You're a relation, aren't you? But you don't like it that I say so. Why is it?"

Mrs. Von Bilten said, "They should **never** have printed that! I told them to change it, but they said it was too late."

Millie said, "What's wrong with you being related? He's a big name!"

"Yeah," Mr. Zachery said. "I'da thought you'd be proud."

Mr. Gereben was scribbling furiously.

Mrs. Von Bilten turned on him. "Stop that this instant! I'll not have a spectacle made of his death!"

Mrs. Jackson said, "You mean a scandal." She knew very well about scandals. "You've been making a spectacle of yourself this entire time. Do **you** know what's going on here? Who is Mr. Rothmore to you?"

"I'd like to know myself," said Mr. Carlo, his face severe. "It's **my** hotel being dragged through the papers. If you know why this man was killed, speak up now."

The old woman's face turned angry. She pointed at Mrs. Jackson. "You." Then she pointed at Mr. Carlo. "The both of you. You should be ashamed of yourselves!" Then she pointed at Mrs. Jackson, and the hate on her face made Mrs. Jackson quail. "Pamela Jackson, indeed." She scoffed. "Young lady, I know **exactly** who you are."

19

George heard footsteps, then the light of a lantern burst upon the scene. Ophie jerked upright and away from him.

"Oh, ho!" A man's voice, sarcasm dripping. "Look what we have here!" He looked back at the group of younger men and women behind him, most holding lanterns. "Young lovers, taking advantage of the night."

George stood. "It's nothing of the sort." He offered Ophie his hand, and she took it. "Come on, let's go."

A lantern had been set on the floor down the hall, at the corner. Hoots and jeers followed George and Ophelia as they went.

Ophie sounded frantic. "We gotta get out of here before word gets to Mrs. Kilpatrick!"

Once they got out of sight of the group, he stopped, faced her. "Nothing bad'll happen." Although with the lantern on the floor behind her he couldn't see her face, he smiled at her anyway. "I have a plan."

Using the lanterns to guide him, George led Ophie to the exit. Outside, all was chaos: some running in the darkness, others staring at the bright green ribbons in the sky, which George had never seen before. Car horns honked. A man screamed over and over that the world was ending.

Other than a bit of light from the ribbons, it was near pitch out. The headlights of automobiles gave off the only real light, making it even harder to see anything after they passed in the darkness.

George flagged down a taxi. "The Myriad Hotel, on the double."

Once the taxi set off for the Hotel, George said to Ophie, "If the power's out here, it's out there, too. I left Will with over a hundred guests at dinner, and he might need our help."

***

Bessie started barking at the old woman.

The couple looked at each other, fear in their faces. If Mrs. Von Bilten knew who Mrs. Jackson really was, what would she do?

Mrs. Jackson wanted to run, to hide. But there was nowhere to run, and she refused to hide any longer. "What is it you think you know about me?"

The old lady scowled. "You're nothing but a cheap gold-digging guttersnipe playing as an investigator that has latched on to one rich man after another. You killed your first husband when it suited you —"

A knife went through her heart. Her eyes stung.

"— and I wouldn't put it past you to be plotting this one's death as well."

729

Mr. Jackson picked up Bessie, who had been barking and growling the entire time. "That is both decidedly unkind and entirely wrong." He smoothed the little dog's hair. "Hush, dear: all is well."

The old woman pointed at Mrs. Jackson, "**You** were the one to find Horace dead! What is it **you** know about his death, hmm?"

To her surprise, Mrs. Jackson no longer felt afraid. "I'm learning more with every word from your mouth. Why do you not want to tell us about your relationship with 'Horace'? If you care about him, why **wouldn't** you want the truth to come out? Why attack those who want the truth? We've seen you out here all evening making a show of your grief, but you're a rich woman with connections. Of course you wouldn't kill him **yourself**!"

Charles let out an ironic chuckle.

"So ma'am, I have to ask. Did you **have** him killed?"

The woman looked horrified. "**Me?** No! Why would I? I **loved** him!"

Several of the men said, "Ohhh!" Their faces were both amused and more than a bit scandalized.

"You don't understand!" The old woman looked close to tears. "You can't possibly understand."

Charles put his hand on her arm. "Grandma, sooner or later you're going to have to tell them."

Mrs. Von Bilten's head drooped. "Very well." She took a deep breath; her voice shook. "Horace wasn't my lover. He was ..." She hesitated a long time. "My son."

20

The entire group stared at her, and you could have heard a pin drop.

Charles handed her a handkerchief, and she wiped her eyes. "I was young and foolish, and got into an entirely unsuitable affair. My parents covered it up after I gave birth, and they sent Horace away. But he was my baby! I loved him! I secretly helped him any way I might. I put him through school, gave him connections. He was a great man —"

Her grandson scoffed.

Mrs. Jackson held up a hand. "Wait. Mr. De Rege, are you Mr. Rothmore's son?"

"Hardly," Charles said. "I'm the legitimate one." He shook his head. "My mother was never good enough. She was hounded out of the house, and married a man my grandmother hated."

"Now, Charles —"

"It's true. Just like my mother. My father wasn't rich enough, he wasn't good enough. Not like her darling Horace! Now that they're dead, I'm being pressured to become some rich thing." He scoffed. "I hate it all." He gestured at Cornelius Ober. "**He** lives as he pleases, does what he likes —!"

Mr. Jackson laughed. "My guess is he's rich as well."

"By doing what he loves!" He turned to Mr. Ober. "Am I right?"

Cornelius Ober took his cigarette from his mouth. "That you are, sir."

Charles De Rege stood, throwing his arms in the air. "I spit on it all! The lies, the deception, the obligation." He pointed back at his grandmother. "Did you know she hired boys to throw those rocks?"

Everyone gasped. Ruby's eyes filled with tears.

His grandmother turned on him in a fury. "Charles!"

"Well, she did. She's all but bankrupted him, pushing him to do one foolish thing after another."

Pearl stood, pointing at Mrs. Von Bilten with a shaking hand. "You harpy! You ruined my father, drove him to his grave!"

Cornelius Ober shook his head. "I **knew** that story about your father dying of his 'war injuries' was false! For one, he never went."

Mr. McKenney said, "He didn't?"

"No," said Mr. Ober. He chuckled. "Just a bit too old to go marching off to this last one, wouldn't you say?"

"Well," Mrs. Von Bilten said, "I always assumed they meant the one before."

"No," said Pearl. "He killed himself. He tried and tried to make his business work. He was a genius! Yet he never got a chance. After you hounded him, broke his priceless works, then stole his inventions ... it became too much." She pointed to herself. "**My** father was first to put in the mechanical timers for the upper windows — but **you** made sure that story was squashed. And when your darling boy put his in, you made sure it was the talk of the town. We did **everything** to help him ..." her voice broke, and she slumped into her chair, putting her face in her hands.

Mrs. Jackson had the feeling of a revelation, without the words or meaning coming to her. Her heart pounded, her hands shook.

The reporter took out a second notepad.

Mrs. Jackson's voice shook. "So you and your sister **killed** him!"

Ruby gasped. "I never meant him **harm**! But Pearl said go do the interview, then meet her at the back of the greenhouse. When I got there ..." She began to tremble. "Oh, it was horrible! Pearl said we had to make it look an accident. So —"

The thought was right there, but she couldn't find it. Couldn't see it. What was it?

Mr. Jackson seemed to be looking at Bessie's back. "You helped her. Dragged him over, cleaned the plants, pushed over the bags of stone."

"What else could I do? She's my **sister**! Could I just let her go to **jail**?"

Mr. Carlo blurted out, "Did you send those boys to throw rocks at my greenhouse the other week?"

This shocked her. Had Pearl known they'd attend this event even **then**? That proved planning beyond what she'd even imagined.

Pearl said, "Thought it'd be good to give him a taste of his own medicine. But they went much too early."

The connection between the waiter and the architect must be these girls. Mrs. Jackson felt angry. "**That's** why you jumped into the pool!"

Mr. Carlo was astonished. "What? The boy was telling the truth?"

Mrs. Jackson felt shaky. "He was. Am I right?"

Pearl said, "So what if he was?"

Mr. Jackson's head rose. "Ah. Yes. He saw you come out of the back of the greenhouse. Cutting someone's throat is messy, even botching it like you did."

Ruby said, "B-botched? But he **died**!"

"After some time," said Mr. Jackson. "No, if she'd brought in a professional, Mr. Rothmore would've been dead long before we arrived." He faced Pearl. "In any case, you had to have been covered in blood. And the waiter saw you. So you did the only reasonable thing: jumped in to wash it off, then framed him for it."

Mrs. Jackson crossed her arms, grieved. And angry. "And an innocent man is now disgraced and dead." But the question still lingered ...

She turned to Ruby. "What do you say to that?"

Ruby held a drink, but her hands shook. "I had to keep him quiet! He was going to ruin everything."

And Mrs. Jackson thought of her husband that night he died. He had everything a man could want: a beautiful home, a wife who loved him, a son ...

Why confront them, when he knew they had guns?

Mr. Jackson leaned forward and spoke kindly. "Dear girl, what did you do?"

Ruby only stared at her drink.

Pearl said, "I put some of my Veronal powder in his champagne. When I gave it to him. He'd come by me and said, 'I have my eye on you!' Well —"

Mrs. Jackson's confusion distracted her from the insight she felt coming to her. "Wait. Veronal?"

"It's a sleeping powder," Mr. Carlo said.

"Oh," said Mrs. Jackson.

Pearl sneered. "You really **aren't** from around here!"

Mrs. Jackson snorted. The girl had no idea. "Never you mind." She turned to Ruby. "But that was well before your sister killed Mr. Rothman. Why did he suspect you even then?"

Mr. McKenney blurted, "Where's my **money**? He was going into the greenhouse to get my money!"

Pearl laughed. "Where you'll never find it. Then once our rescuers arrive, we'll tell the police we had nothing to do with it. Even if they arrest me, I'll make bail, get your precious bribe money —"

Mr. Ober said, "Bribe?"

"Heh," the old man said. "Why I never go in one of these things if I don't have to. I do safety inspections."

Mr. and Mrs. Jackson glanced at each other, and Mrs. Jackson wondered what "safety issues" the greenhouse they just went into had.

Pearl acted as though she hadn't been interrupted. " — and be out of the country the next day." She clicked her tongue.

The clicking of the guns that cold night under the blazing lights as their hammers were pulled back had warned her.

Pearl laughed. "Plus you have no proof. My lawyers already have enough on each one of you here to discredit you to any jury in the world."

The rest looked at each other, dismayed. But Mrs. Jackson's mind was entirely on that cold moon-lit night, back in the place she'd known so well.

When the gun raised against the man she loved, she'd jumped in front of him. The scar on her arm would be there until the day she died.

I was ready to die, she realized. Nothing had been more important than for him and their little son to be alive, safe and free.

But even putting herself in front of the bullets had failed: he lay dead anyway.

*What else could I have **done**?*

The answer came. Her Mr. Jackson had said it, a few hours before: *You did the best you possibly could!*

Just like these girls, she'd done everything she could have. But she'd never believed it until now.

Mr. Jackson put his arm round her, and she leaned on his shoulder, feeling moved.

She'd done everything she could.

She still loved her first husband desperately. She still grieved his death fiercely. But no matter what happened next, even if the men hunting her caught and killed her tonight, she was free from that terrible guilt.

She was free.

An older man's voice came from behind. "Just like the last time."

Millie let out a yelp.

The group turned towards the man's voice.

Sergeant Nestor stood there.

21

Mrs. Jackson felt annoyed. "Good grief. How long have **you** been standing there?"

"Long enough." The sergeant had a dozen police with him, as well as the Hotel's maintenance man Eugene, who held a key.

Sergeant Nestor pointed at the twins. "Don't let these two fool you."

Then he pointed back, into the darkness around the pool. "It's okay," he called out. "You can get the poor lad now." He pointed at Ruby and Pearl. "These two murdered his roommate, then did the same trick as they're trying now. The unsuspecting innocent gymnastics star —"

Mr. Jackson blurted out, "So **that's** how they had such balance with those ladders!"

Sergeant Nestor seemed not have heard. "— and her horrible twin. Which was which? They even confused the judge! So much so that they never saw a day in jail. I say you're both under arrest." He turned to his officers. "Cuff 'em, boys."

Pearl laughed as the officers forced her to her feet. "You have no proof!"

Sergeant Nestor said, "We have a dozen officers who just heard you confess. I'm sure we can find some evidence this time. For example, the Veronal in the boy's system. How did you manage to get him into the pool?"

All round went murmurs of "Yeah!" and "I'd sure like to know."

Ruby looked abashed. "He was only half awake. We used to swim together after school, and I told him it was time for practice. He never really understood what was happening until the end there."

Victor said, "Shame on you! I hope you both hang!"

Mrs. Jackson said to the twins, "Did killing Mr. Rothman make any of it better?"

Pearl rolled her eyes.

Ruby began to cry. "No."

Like her, these two girls had lost everything, even the man they loved. But instead of finding a new life, they'd turned their grief into a lust for revenge. "There's one thing I don't understand. Why kill Hugh's roommate? What was he to you?"

"Heh," Pearl said. "He was Mrs. Von Bilten's lookout man. He'd find out when the shows were to take place. He got a nice fee for sneaking the boys into the show."

Cornelius Ober's mouth fell open. "So **that's** how she did it."

"You'll never pin that one on us," Pearl said. "Double jeopardy."

Four of the sergeant's young officers led the two young women off. The five musicians began packing up their things.

Mrs. Jackson said, "This explains the splashing."

Sergeant Nestor said, "What's that?"

"One thing has bothered me," Mrs. Jackson said. "A champion swimmer would surely know how to keep himself from drowning, even if deeply intoxicated. And then there was Ruby's story. She said she saw the waiter floating. His white shirt startled her! She then went in to help him, but couldn't reach him. Then she called for aid. That was the story. But I was in the toilet not ten feet away. I heard a great deal of splashing for at least a minute. Then her footsteps, then she shrieked and called for help not a second later. And her dress was dripping! That's what made no sense. From the time of her shriek to calling for help, she should've been in the pool if she really were trying to help him. Or out of it with her dress dry. Not out of it soaking wet!" She shook her head. "That woman had to have murdered the man."

If only she'd gone out when the splashing began ...

But how was she to know?

"Too bad I can't put you on the stand," Sergeant Nestor said. "That'd make for some good testimony."

"I know," Mrs. Jackson said sadly. "And I'm sorry for that. I appreciate your care of us, I truly do."

The sergeant said quietly, "That reporter over there's been filling notebooks, and I'm sure the photographer hasn't been idle either. I think we got enough."

Eugene handed an envelope to Mr. Jackson, "A telegram came for you before the lights went out. The front desk is a madhouse, but since I was coming up, they gave it to me. It says it's urgent."

At that moment, George Neuberg and Ophelia Denton burst through the door to the stairs. Ophelia cried out, "You're safe!"

Mrs. Jackson stood, amused. "We are!"

Ophelia flew into her arms, sobbing. "You're safe. You're safe."

Mrs. Jackson smoothed her hair. "My dear little Pet. All's well."

George panted, "We heard someone was dead up here, and ..."

Mr. Jackson smiled fondly at George. "We're perfectly well. Although two others aren't so."

"I'm sorry," Ophelia said to Mrs. Jackson. "I should never have pushed you to talk."

Sergeant Nestor said, "Make that three. Well, I guess I should say five." He called out, "Lewis McKenney, you're under arrest for accepting bribes."

The old man said, "What?"

"Heard it from your own mouth," the sergeant said. "And the money's around here somewhere."

Mrs. Jackson smiled at Ophelia, put her arm around her shoulders, and kissed her forehead, feeling moved. "I forgive you."

The old man grumbled, "All I wanted was to retire."

"Well, you did it the wrong way," the sergeant said. "Go ahead and take him."

As the old man was taken off in handcuffs, George turned to Ophelia. "Look how lovely it is up here!"

Ophelia looked up, wiping her eyes. "Gosh ... it is! You can see the sky ever so well. And the torches, and candles." Her face glowed. "It's quite romantic."

George grinned. "I thought so too." He took Ophelia's hands, going to one knee in front of everyone. "Ophie, nothing would please me more than to spend the rest of our lives together. Will you marry me?" He looked uncertain. "I don't have a ring for you yet, but you can pick out anything you like."

Ophelia beamed. "I think that would be wonderful."

He threw his arms around her. "Then it's settled!"

Everyone standing around broke into applause.

Mr. and Mrs. Jackson looked at each other in wonder.

Mr. Jackson said, "I ... never thought **this** would happen!"

George said to him, "You're not sore, are you?"

"Astonished is more the word for it." He gave George a quick strong hug, then pulled away. "But I agree, this is perfect." He beamed at Ophelia. "For you both."

Mrs. Jackson said, "I entirely agree."

Cornelius Ober had been watching the scene, looking at George, then at Mr. Jackson. He came up to Mr. Jackson and offered his hand. "Have you ever been to Towertown? I know of a club there that I think you and your friends would very much enjoy."

George seemed surprised.

Mr. Jackson grinned at Mr. Ober, shifting the telegram to his left hand to shake the man's hand. "I've never been, sir, but I'd be glad to visit with you."

Amused, Mr. Ober went to Millie and said, "I do believe you were right!"

"I always know these things," she took his arm, and the two headed for the drink table. "Want to go dancing?"

Mr. Jackson opened the telegram, read it. Then he looked happier than Mrs. Jackson had ever seen him. "I have excellent news."

At once, Mrs. Jackson knew. "They accepted your offer on the property!"

"So they did." Mr. Jackson said. He put his arms over George and Ophelia's shoulder. "We have a lot of planning to do!"

"We sure do," George said. "I've got a wedding to plan!"

Ophelia began to laugh.

Mr. and Mrs. Jackson looked at each other, and he smiled. She said to them, "And we'll tell you where it is. Everything about it."

Ophelia's eyes filled with tears, and both she and George hugged Mrs. Jackson, making a perfect square. "We won't make you regret it," George said.

And Mrs. Jackson felt such tenderness for these two, making their way in a place that didn't understand them, that she kissed each of them on the cheek in turn.

Ophelia looked up at George. "You know, I'll make a terrible wife — I can't clean worth beans."

Mrs. Jackson looked across at her Mr. Jackson, who had a wry smile on his face.

George laughed. "Me either. But don't worry: we'll learn together."

Epilogue

Pearl Carlisle was charged with the premeditated murder of Horace Rothmore. Her sister Ruby Carlisle was charged with being an accomplice after the fact. Ruby was also charged with the premeditated murder of Hugh Portman.

With the testimonies of over a dozen police and the several notable citizens in attendance, the twins were both found guilty and sentenced to prison.

Lewis McKenney was charged with receiving bribes. The money was found — on the landing over the side — and seized by the city. However, Mr. Carlo made a deal with Mr. McKenney: tell me how to fix my greenhouse, and I'll do what I can to help. They came to a suitable arrangement.

Walter Margin turned over the photo of the architect speaking with the boys to the police. The elevator-men at the Myriad Hotel confirmed these boys were the ones who'd been riding the day the Myriad greenhouse panes were broken. The boys were charged with multiple counts of vandalism and sent to delinquency school.

Lydia Von Bilten was charged with inciting vandalism. In light of these crimes indirectly leading to her only son's death, the charges were dropped. The old lady was warned not to approach those children again, nor to incite any further mischief, or she would be jailed.

But Bence Gereben's notes became the story of the hour: Lydia Rothmore Von Bilten, the secret bankroller to her murdered love child! After a storm of scandal, she eventually moved away in disgrace.

Charles De Rege and Cornelius Ober struck up a friendship, and after some time, Charles decided to pursue a theatrical career.

George Neuberg's parents were delighted to hear of his engagement! After much thought during his two-week suspension for leaving his post, George reapplied for the front manager position at the Myriad Hotel and was accepted.

Will immediately stepped into the Headwaiter position he'd been training for, staying at the job for some time.

Club Patruni was not pleased to hear they'd be losing one of their showgirls. But Ophelia decided to apprentice with the costume department, and was soon happily sewing on beads and sequins for the show's next line-up.

Her friend Ethel's mother set her up with a young man who'd admired her from afar for some time. The pair hit it off!

Mrs. Kilpatrick was most relieved to hear that Ophelia and George were to be married. "I knew that young man would propose." She offered to make Ophelia's veil.

Mr. Jackson soon had the blueprints for his new property, and the two couples spent many happy hours talking about what he might do with the place.

Mrs. Jackson made arrangements to have Bessie visit her pups on a regular basis. This was most satisfactory to all parties involved.

Ophelia, George, Mrs. Jackson, Mr. Jackson, and Bessie went to the jewelry shop to pick out Ophelia's engagement ring.

Ophelia gasped when she saw it: a raised band of gold with a beautifully cut topaz gem. "It's perfect."

A Mysterious Plant!

the next book in the Myriad Mysteries
is coming soon!

While you wait,

Read

**A Visit to Towertown!: A Myriad Mysteries
Intermission**

Available exclusively on Amazon
Free with Kindle Unlimited

To learn more about the Myriad Mysteries,
visit AuthorClaireLogan.com,
or follow Claire Logan on BookBub.

Sign up to my newsletter at
news.authorclairelogan.com

Vote on where the next mysteries will occur at
vote.authorclairelogan.com

Acknowledgements

Thanks so much to Patricia Loofbourrow for the cover design. Also, thanks to Rebekah Brown for beta reading, and to my newsletter readers for providing names for this series — as well as picking out the location for the mysteries in this book!

About the Author

I've loved reading since I can remember! I love puzzles and mysteries and intrigue, and of all the cities I've been to, Chicago is my favorite. My four years living in Chicago during grad school were wonderful. Plus I love history. And wasn't the 1920's wild? I've always wanted to write a fun mystery series set in Chicago and now here's my chance.

Claire Logan is a pen name.